When Promises Are Forever

Chrissy Garwood/Chrisolite Books
email: chrissy@chrissygarwood.com

Sorell, Tasmania, Australia, 7172
www.chrissygarwood.com

Direct quotations from Scripture are taken from the World Wide Bible (WEB) and are available in the public domain. Other verses are written from memory and are not direct quotes.

Book Layout ©2017 BookDesignTemplates.com

Cover Design: Belinda Pollard

When Promises Are Forever/ Chrissy Garwood —1st ed.

ISBN: 978-0-6489651-2-1 paperback

ISBN: 978-0-6489651-3-8 eBook

When Promises Are Forever

A River Wild Romantic Suspense Novel

Chrissy Garwood

Chrisolite Books
Sorell, Tasmania, Australia

ഃ ☼ ക

I dedicate this book to
my nephew, Matthew Garwood.
His ability to chase after big dreams
without losing his connection to home
is inspirational.

ഃ ☼ ക

Contents

False Impressions

BWR* (Before *White Rose*)
This story begins seven months before we meet Ria Fontana/Evie Romano in *White Rose of Promise.*)i(

*2 Corinthians 6:9a - It should not matter
if you are unknown or well known.*

Sara Messinger sat at her corner desk, a notepad before her. She rubbed her forehead. In recent years, she had enjoyed good health, but this niggling headache was reminiscent of the migraines that had plagued her student days. She looked up from the desktop computer.

Her lamp created an oasis of light in the darkened room. *Where had the time gone?* She twisted her head for a narrow glimpse of the outside world from the fourteenth-floor window. The sun had set, and the neighbouring office tower blocked her view of the Melbourne city lights. She shifted the notepad and jiggled her pen.

The three lawyers she shared this office with had left together at five pm. The young men had initiated a familiar ritual. They would invite her to join them for "Friday afternoon drinks". She always declined. This afternoon, they had left the door into the corridor open behind them, a tantalising reminder that there was life beyond these walls. The well-lit hallway beckoned to her.

If she stretched sideways, she could see across to the opposite door. That nameplate read: Nero Mariani, Partner. She closed her eyes. Her handsome Italian-Australian graduate supervisor had a spacious office overlooking the river. From his desk, he had a perfect view to the impressive building on the other side of the river – the mirrored tower where Nero's wealthy family had their apartments.

Sara swung on her chair. Her lowly status gave her a corner desk with a perfect interior view. Nothing but crowded desks, filing cabinets and bookcases. One day, her hard work would earn her a better outlook. Nero had laughed when she first confessed her ambition. But recently, he'd said he admired her determination to succeed.

Her idle fingers clicked the new pen. Nero had surprised her with the gift this morning. He offered it as a token to "commemorate the momentous occasion". When she returned after the weekend, she would be a lawyer in her own right. And he would no longer be her mentor.

Sara frowned, replaying the conversation. Did the gift signify a more dramatic change? It was not unusual for Nero to ask her to stay behind after the morning briefing. But this had been the first time he'd closed the door. "Here's a little memento of our time together."

She had accepted the slim box with a smile. After removing the lid, she raised the shiny rainbow-striped pen from its white satin bed. Two sparkling diamonds drew her attention to her engraved name. She had reigned in her emotions and kept her eyes on the pen, waiting until she had her tongue under control. "Thank you. It's lovely."

"I know you love bright colours." He had looked pointedly at her shoes.

Sara had laughed. "I couldn't help myself today."

He laughed with her. "Take my pen to court with you."

The tension in her shoulders had relaxed. There was no rebuke for her youthful rebellion. When she first met him, Nero had ordered her to rein in her colour obsession. He warned her that dressing like a party girl was a serious disadvantage if she wanted the legal fraternity to respect her.

As she remembered that conversation, she stretched out her feet under her desk. In celebration of the occasion, she had accessorised her conservative suit with thirteen-centimetre red heels. While experience had taught her to respect Nero's guidance, now it was time to start testing the boundaries.

She closed her eyes against the pain, and the morning recollection continued without invitation.

Nero had placed his hand on her shoulder. "This pen will remind you that I expect big things from you in the future."

She had considered her careful reply. The previous evening, Sara had spent long hours rehearsing her speech in anticipation of this opportunity. "I'm eternally grateful for all your guidance and support." He gazed into her eyes, and she swallowed before she went on. "I have learned so much in the past two years. I know that, without you, I wouldn't be as confident about the future."

"You have promising talent," Nero said, smoothing a stray strand of hair from her face. "I look forward to seeing where your career takes you. You must have dinner with me next week, and we can discuss the next step."

She had played it cool. "That would be great."

He then looked at his watch. "I'll check my schedule and let you know when."

The conversation should have ended there, but Nero leaned closer. For a moment, she thought the thirty-two-year-old was going to kiss her. Her heart raced, and she dropped her eyes.

He removed his hand and stepped away. "I want you to know my door is always open to you."

Sara had walked out of his office without looking back. But even now, she could not stop thinking about the pressure of his hand on her shoulder. He *had* said "*dinner*"? Not a hurried lunch between court cases, or a snack while they discussed her caseload? She must have misunderstood. Especially since he hadn't said anything about checking his wife's busy schedule.

Sara rubbed her eyes before glancing at the time. It was almost ten o'clock now – another hour lost and not a single point added to her legal argument. She picked up her coffee mug. Finding it empty, she set it down with a sigh. The new coffee machine in the kitchenette down the hall remained a mystery to her. Nero had promised he would teach her, but there never seemed to be enough time. It was too far to walk if instant coffee was the only reward. She checked the open file on her computer screen and scribbled some notes.

Knock, knock.

The silhouette of a man appeared in the doorway, setting her heart racing. Had Nero come to see why she was still at her desk? She threw off that thought immediately – this intruder was too short, and broad at the shoulders. Nero Mariani was tall and pencil-thin. And Nero was attending a family celebration this evening.

"Excuse me, ma'am," the deep, shadowy voice said. "I'm going to switch on your office lights. You're the only one left on this floor, and I have to dim the hall lights."

"Thank you."

The overhead lights flashed on, and her eyes adjusted to the brightness. She had dismissed her initial alarm, but now that she saw him clearly, a deeper fear awoke. She could not read his expression. This stranger was a muscle-bound athlete, not the overweight security guard who usually checked on her.

He watched her from the doorway. "Are you planning to stay much longer?"

"I'm almost done." She must not let him think she was afraid of him. "You're not the usual guard."

"No, ma'am," he said with a lopsided grin. "I'm filling in for the evening. I'm sorry to have disturbed you."

He was gone as suddenly as he had appeared. Sara looked down at her notepad, waiting for her heart to stop racing. Fifteen minutes later, she conceded defeat – her imagination gave her no respite. With a continuous motion, she switched off her computer, reached under her desk to dump the notepad into her bag and rose to her feet. The new pen went into her blazer pocket, over her fluttering heart. After another glance to confirm she had everything she needed, she switched off her lamp.

The familiar walk to the elevator took longer than usual. The click-click of her heels echoed along the darkened parquetry hallway. She hurried past a long line of closed office doors. Sara pressed the elevator call button and shuffled her feet. Occasionally, she looked over her shoulder and then she relaxed when the lights above the elevator signalled its arrival.

The doors swished open, and there stood that new security guard. Solid and confident, smiling as if she were an expected guest. Sara took a step backwards.

"Perfect timing," he said. "Are you heading to the lower basement to collect your car, or will I drop you off in the foyer?"

A band of steel tightened around her chest. Her headache rocketed from misery to blinding torture. Sara closed her eyes for a moment, pressing her hand to her temple, willing herself to breathe. In that moment, her embattled mind flew to her friend's cautionary advice about men. According to Gina, there was only one reason any man would come looking for her – she was single, attractive and had "easy victim" written all over her.

With nowhere to hide, she must take her chances. "The lower basement." Sara feigned bravado, but then ruined the performance by catching her heel on the elevator's edge. She stumbled forward, her cheeks flushed, as she retreated to the furthest corner.

He punched the required buttons, and the elevator lights signalled their slow descent. He said nothing more, but his reflection watched her from the mirrored wall.

Invisible fingers crawled up and down her spine. Had he been waiting for her? Sara remembered the self-defence lessons from her university days. She brought out her car keys, jiggling them in her hand. He would discover she was no easy victim.

Sara knew, from courtroom testimonies, the kind of details she needed to memorise. She wanted him to squirm under her scrutiny, but he didn't alter his position. Definitely male, in his mid-forties. Caucasian, brown hair and green eyes. The first hint of a dark beard as if he hadn't shaved for several days. A crooked nose, to match the lopsided smile, and half his left earlobe was missing. The back and sides of his head were shaven with an untidy mop of brown hair on top.

He was medium height – taller than Sara if she hadn't been wearing these foolish heels. Heavily built – the fabric of his dark jacket strained across his shoulders. Either he was a steroid-taking gym-junkie moonlighting as a guard, or the uniform jacket wasn't his.

"You're wondering how I knew where you left your car," he said. "Before I began my rounds, I matched the remaining vehicles to the security log. That's how I knew where to find you. You used a visitor's space today."

"I don't have a designated space," she said. Did he know she was too unimportant to have one? She seized on a different detail. "I'm reassured to learn that there is a security log."

He reached for his pocket. Sara smacked her head against the wall in a futile attempt to put more distance between them. She hated the way she was falling apart.

"Relax," he said. "I'm not about to make a move on you. If that's what I wanted, I had you cornered in your office."

"That's supposed to make me feel safe?" she snapped.

"You're safer here than in most places. Look up there. See that camera? There's always someone watching the live feed, and there's also a time-stamped recording. Here, I'll show you." He brought out his phone, clicked a few buttons and passed it to her.

Careful not to touch his hand, Sara leaned forward. She studied the image: the two of them in the elevator. He raised his free hand, and she squawked.

He smiled.

She remembered her dignity, resisting the urge to smack the mockery from his face. She refused to look at him, but the man on the phone screen waved at her. He pressed more buttons. The image changed. She recognised her car. *There are cameras in the basement?* Her eyes flew to his face, then back to his phone. The screen flashed again, and scrolling text appeared. She gasped. This man had her home address and her mobile number.

She glared at him. "That's an invasion of my privacy."

"Take that up with your employers," he said. "This legal firm has long-standing protocols about the security of their employees. Someone should have explained that to you when you started working for them."

"What's your name?" Sara asked, taking out her phone. She snapped a quick photo, forwarding it to her friend Gina with a second click.

He reached into his pocket again, bringing out an identification card. He held it up for her camera. His lopsided smile matched the twinkle in his green eyes. "Oliver Johnston. I work for *Maximum Security.* We hold the security contract for this tower, and most of the other buildings in this quadrant of the city." He returned the card to his pocket and tapped his phone screen again. "I'm sending you a link which accesses *Maximum Security*'s twenty-four-hour switchboard. They will verify everything I've told you."

The phone pinged in her hand. A typed notification scrolled across the screen:

Maximum Security has been added to your contacts list.

Sara frowned at the phone. Something about that notification troubled her, but what? He continued to grin. The elevator lurched to a stop, and the doors whooshed open. Oliver stepped out and she pushed past him.

"Would you like me to walk you to your car?" he called after her.

"No!"

"Drive carefully, and enjoy the rest of your evening, Sara Messinger."

Sara strode across the concrete car park. Her heels sounded louder than tap-dancing shoes on stage. The noise echoed around the shadowy underground space. She listened for other sounds, scanning the area around her while refusing to look back towards Oliver.

₨ ☻ ₳

The elevator doors closed, blocking his basement view. Oliver turned to the small screen – he knew she'd be worried if she saw him still standing there. But something about Sara had triggered his curiosity. Would she rip off her heels, hitch up her knee-length skirt and run? He weighed the odds and waited. His guess was wrong. He smiled at her determination to preserve her dignity. The slender twenty-five-year-old did not even glance over her shoulder. He imagined what the lawyer would look like with her brown hair loose around her shoulders. Wearing something more appealing than a cheap business suit.

His phone vibrated, and he accepted the call without terminating the video feed.

"Stop wasting time," a female voice said. "There's no risk of her coming back to catch you snooping. She'll go straight home and lock all her doors."

Oliver grinned towards the elevator camera. He was an expert at downplaying his concern. No way would he reveal to the *Maximum Security* second-in-command that his alert level had redlined with her call. She only phoned when trouble was heading his way and their mutual superior was unable to contact him directly. "Hi, Jenny. What are you doing in the control room?"

"I've phoned to warn you. Piper's on his way."

Uh-oh. Oliver's smile wavered. "I thought he went to that big family event?"

"Something came up, and he left early."

"Anything I should know about?"

"He's bringing you some extra equipment. That girl you've been terrorising has been added to the target list."

Oliver sent the elevator upward. "There's nothing in her file to suggest she's a player."

"Someone told Piper she's going to be the next Mrs Nero Mariani."

Oliver frowned. He checked the video feed. He tracked Sara Messinger's car as she navigated the underground car park maze. For an insane moment, he considered asking Jenny for access to the traffic camera feed. He clicked off the video, refocusing on his mission. "I thought Nero was neutral?" Nero's grandfather Enzo and his great-uncle Valentino controlled the cartel.

"The grandfather has some concerns about the safety of his only male heir."

Arriving on the fourteenth floor, Oliver made his way to Nero Mariani's office. He quickly scanned the room, confirming locations for the listening devices. As he passed the wide desk, he glanced at the framed photographs. He paused to consider the photo of Nero with Zemina, the current Mrs Mariani. Her office was next on his list. She was daughter and niece to the two senior partners. Did the thirty-nine-year-old know she was about to be replaced by a younger model?

Unwise Decisions

ஐ ✿ ஐ

*Isaiah 29:14b WEB - the wisdom of their wise men will perish,
and the understanding
of their prudent men will be hidden.*

ஐ ✿ ஐ

Sara woke, shouting at the darkness. She turned on her bedside lamp and shook herself free from the nightmare. It was only one-thirty, too early to be awake. She settled back under the covers. After tossing and turning, she drifted into an uneasy sleep.

The dream reclaimed her. At three-fifteen, she was screaming when she woke again, a quivering mess. She rarely dreamed, or if she did, she never remembered any details. This nightmare was different. As she trembled in bed, a certainty grew that she had dreamed these things before. If that was true, why did the details elude her?

Determined not to fall asleep again, Sara grabbed her dressing gown and went into the open plan living area. While she waited for the kettle to boil, she set up her laptop at the small table and retrieved her notepad. After a moment's hesitation, she found the rainbow pen. Perhaps her mentor's gift would remind her to stay focused on her project.

By five am, she had finished four cups of coffee and filled two pages with scribble. Her notes were impossible to decipher now. She yawned as she squinted at the laptop. The onscreen text was fuzzy too. The insistent ache behind her eyes issued her a further warning. She yawned again and dragged herself back to bed.

This time, Sara knew for certain. She must be dreaming, but everything seemed so real...

How long had she been running? Perspiration dripped from her forehead, and her sweat-drenched clothing stuck to her body. Thick darkness blanketed her, making it difficult to continue. Why was she running? It was too dark to see where she was going.

Then a flash of memory forewarned her about what was to come. She shouted at herself, "STOP."

Her warning came too late. Now she was falling, tumbling and twisting through empty air. Plummeting down towards a river wild and majestic. She couldn't see it yet, but the roar of distant water was already louder than her desperate scream. The darkness retreated, replaced by a navy-blue sky brightened by iridescent rainbow droplets. The glistening spray was warm on her skin.

She entered the water feet first. Foam-crested waves lifted her high enough to touch the sky. When they reached their apex, the curling breakers threw her into the depths. Her body was tossed and pummelled until she forgot why she was holding her breath. She inhaled water, thick and sweet like honey. Her lungs burned. Hope died.

But this was not the end. Strong arms wrestled with her body, dragging her from the water. Sara gasped for air like a beached whale. Her rescuer tumbled her onto her side and out spewed streams of water. When the spasms ended, she fell onto her back. Where was her saviour?

She could see him clearly against the strange blue sky. The man dropped to one knee beside her. What was the security guard doing in her dream? Oliver Johnston had dispensed with his uniform. He was naked, except for a brief pair of black shorts. She could not avert her eyes from the white scars that crisscrossed his torso. Water trickled down his face, the hank of hair clung to his head. His lopsided smile was missing.

He stared at her with solemn green eyes. "Sara Messinger. This is a warning. Guard your heart."

Oliver did not wait for a response. He moved to the water's edge and dived in. Sara cried out, struggling to her feet. She couldn't see him anywhere. She stood on the emerald-coloured rock. Why had he abandoned her on an exposed island in the middle of the river? The waves surged, trying to sweep her into the water. Desperate, she called out, "Come back! Don't leave me here!"

ಐ ✿ ೞ

When morning came, Sara was in the thrall of a terrible migraine. She had been free of this plague for several years. In the back of the cupboard, she found some prescription medication. Should she phone her friend Gina to cancel their weekly luncheon date?

There would be consequences if she did. The young woman worked in the legal firm's secretarial pool. Since Gina had befriended her, Sara's requests for files no longer languished at the bottom of the in-tray, there were fewer typing errors in her documents, and her messages arrived on time. When she had mentioned this change to her mentor, Nero advised her to keep Gina close. Until Sara earned a personal secretary, an ally in administration was essential.

A greater fear kept her from making the call. If Sara stayed in her small apartment, the lingering dreams would reclaim her. How many times had she screamed herself awake last night? She frowned at her reflection in the bathroom mirror, adjusting her makeup. Gina would take one look at those haunted eyes and demand an explanation. Sara usually shared everything with her friend, but this dream was different. It seemed too intimate to share.

Sara searched for a pair of sunglasses and slipped them on.

Deciding what to wear usually took no time. She owned two dresses that were suitable, and she alternated between them. Gina never appeared in the same outfit twice. Sara could not imagine having so much choice. But, today, she struggled with her accessories. Would she wear blue, red or green heels? They all matched the floral dress perfectly. She tried them all. In the end, the decision was made when she toppled over during a wave of dizziness and twisted her ankle. Low heels it would have to be, and she only had one good pair.

Another ten minutes were lost while she searched for her keys. Flashes of memory from last night's dream haunted her every move. She kept looking over her shoulder, half-expecting to find Oliver Johnston watching her. Why had she dreamed about him? Perhaps the clue lay in the dream rescuer's repeated warning? She left the apartment still puzzling over the answers.

৪০ ☼ ೮੪

The taxi dropped Sara at the curb opposite the *Renaissance* nightclub. This was the closest she could get to her destination. It was only a short walk around the corner to *Raphael Towers*, but today it was an epic journey. The crowded riverside promenade seemed full of pedestrians without a destination. She lost count of how many clusters of tourists bumped into her. She walked around distracted family groups and avoided couples walking hand-in-hand. When she arrived, she rested on a bench beside the river.

She sat gazing up at the mirrored building for several minutes before she had the strength to ascend the broad steps. Gina and her extended family inhabited the upper floors of the residential complex. Her friend still lived with her parents. Sara had only visited their luxury apartment twice. Both times, Gina had hurried her back out the door a few minutes later. Her friend dismissed the spacious luxury with scorn.

Once inside the hushed foyer, she focused on remaining upright and moving forward. Bypassing the reception desk, she went towards the *Masterpiece* restaurant. She only needed to step through the door before a man hurried towards her. He wore a suit that wouldn't be out of place in a board room. The host knew Sara by name and escorted her to Gina's regular table on the mezzanine floor. She trailed behind him as he threaded his way through the crowded dining room. The table he delivered her to was the only empty one in the restaurant.

Despite being twenty minutes late, Sara was first to arrive. She pretended to gaze out the window towards the river, her eyes closed behind the sunglasses. When her nausea settled, she checked the time. How long had she been waiting? Perhaps Gina had sent her a message? She glanced at her phone. Sometimes the notifications failed to appear on this old model.

She flinched as she scrolled through their brief interaction from the previous evening. Sara regretted sending her friend the photo of Oliver Johnston. His lopsided grin mocked her from her phone. Gina had responded with a thumbs-down emoji.

She had followed this with a photo of herself with several attractive dark-haired men.

> more my style

Gina had sent a second photo, with Nero as her companion.

> resist temptation
> save yourself for N

Accustomed to her friend's teasing, Sara had sent no reply.

A shadow fell across the table. She jumped, and the waiter apologised for startling her. Sara blushed, ordering a soft drink. As soon as he left, she deleted last night's conversation. To cover her embarrassment, she studied the menu. She cringed at the prices, despite knowing Gina and her guests always dined for free – another family privilege.

It was another thirty minutes before Gina appeared. The twenty-year-old beauty also wore sunglasses, an oversized designer pair with gold frames. Gina dropped into her chair with a moan, her hand pressed to her brow like a melodramatic Hollywood star.

Sara waited. This behaviour was not unusual.

"What are you drinking?" Gina asked when she finally acknowledged Sara's presence.

"Lemonade – I've taken my migraine meds and I can't drink alcohol with them. I've only made that mistake once, and still remember the outcome in technicolour detail."

"I didn't know you suffered migraines?"

Sara frowned at the hint of disapproval. "I haven't had a migraine since I finished my uni exams. The doctor said stress and anxiety were the triggers."

Gina pursed her lips. "I'll wait until I've had a few drinks before I grill you about what 'stress and anxiety' awakened this one." She waved her hand and the waiter materialised beside her with a colourful cocktail. Gina took several long sips before she refocused on Sara. "*My* headache is self-inflicted – too much champagne, and then tequila shots at dawn. My younger cousins offered me a challenge – of course, I won. The ultimate victory is knowing how wretched they'll feel when they drag themselves out of bed."

"It was a good party, then?" Sara asked.

"Horrendous. I wish you'd been there to see the old witch in all her glory."

"That's no way to talk about your great-grandmother."

"Turning ninety is no excuse for her rudeness. Besides, you've missed a generation. She's *Nero's* great-grandmother and *my* great-*great*-grandmother. Everyone fawns over her as if she's a female version of the Godfather from those classic movies. All that bowing and scraping to the great *Doña* Gabriella Marcella Horatio."

"Remember where you are, cousin," a familiar voice said. Sara's glass slipped from her hand and rolled across the table, as the voice continued behind her. "The 'great *Doña*' has spies everywhere. You don't want her to cut off your allowance."

Gina laughed, rescuing Sara's glass. Only a few shards of ice remained of her drink. Sara chased them across the tablecloth with her napkin. How long had Nero been standing there? And why hadn't Gina warned her?

Sara gestured towards Gina in silent question. Her friend's laughing response was to rise and draw Nero into a close embrace.

"See, cousin," Gina said. "I told you even being in your presence unsettles her. You need to spend time with her away from work, so she can get used to you. Why don't you join us for lunch? You can help convince her I'm not exaggerating about last night's fiasco."

"If you're sure I'm not intruding?" Nero asked, already reaching for a chair.

Sara scanned the restaurant. "Will your wife be joining us?"

"You haven't told her?" Gina cried.

It was Nero's turn to frown. The silence lengthened.

Improper Behaviour

꘎ ☼ ꘎

Proverbs 27:17 - As iron sharpens iron;
so a person is sharpened by their companions.

꘎ ☼ ꘎

"What hasn't he told me?" Sara asked.

Gina poked him with her butter knife. "If you don't tell her, I will, and we both know that I'll spice things up to make it more interesting."

"Enough, Gina – okay, I'll tell her." Nero turned to Sara. "I've been trying to find the right moment to break the news – my wife has filed for divorce."

"Oh, no!" The words escaped before she could stop them. "You must be heartbroken."

"He doesn't look heartbroken to me," Gina sniggered. "But he won't say no if a compassionate young woman offers him comfort."

"Ignore my cousin," Nero muttered. "I've had time to get used to the idea. But Gina is right. I'm not heartbroken. Zemina and I came to an amicable agreement six months ago. The divorce will be final in June."

"But you've both been acting as if everything is fine between you. You see each other every day at work."

"Each of our families has old-fashioned views about marriage. We wanted to avoid any misguided attempts to 'save' our relationship. The plan was to make a formal announcement closer to the decree."

"But the cat's out of the bag, now." Gina laughed. "Zemina declined the invitation to last night's party. And the old witch – sorry, Doña Gabriella Marcella – guessed. She shocked everyone. She said Nero's marriage should have been annulled years ago. My mother couldn't help herself. She said failure to provide an heir isn't a legitimate reason for an annulment."

Sara opened her mouth. But before she asked her question, Nero reached across and smothered her hand with his own. All rational thought flew out the window.

"Don't be concerned about me," Nero said, stroking her hand. "Now the secret is out, a great weight has lifted from my shoulders. I can start planning for the future."

"And that's not the only secret that's out," Gina giggled, draining her drink and setting aside her empty glass. The waiter hurried towards them with a replacement. "If you play your cards right, Sara, you will be the new Mrs Mariani in July."

Leaping to her feet, Sara grabbed hold of the table and swayed. Nero eased her back onto her chair.

"I don't know why you're acting so surprised," Gina said. "Why do you think Nero came into the restaurant today? He was looking for you, sweetheart. He's already told the family he's in love with you."

"What?" The colour drained from Sara's face, and her stomach cramped.

"Shh!" Nero whispered, holding a glass of water to Sara's lips and encouraging her to drink. "Gina's embroidering the truth. They know I have feelings for someone, but not your identity. I've had to wait until your two-year supervision was up before I could let you know."

Sara pushed the glass away. "Let me know what?"

"I should have warned you," Gina said to Nero. "Sara's battling a migraine. Perhaps you should take her upstairs so she can lie down?"

Sara considered kicking her friend under the table. But what if she missed? Kicking her mentor would only make this situation worse. She forced herself to smile. "That won't be necessary," she said to Nero. "I'm fine."

"That's reassuring." Gina laughed. "You look anything but fine. But I'll tell you some more horror stories from last night to give you time to recover. Nero wasn't the only target for Doña Gabriella Marcella's outrage. Each member of the family was summoned for a personal interview. She's not happy that I'm unmarried, and thinks working in a lawyer's office is demeaning. I told her I had my eye on one or two influential lawyers, and that appeased her. I got off lightly, compared to some of the others. She saved her greatest reprimand for *poor* Uncle Valentino."

"I'm sure he timed his arrival for maximum effect," Nero said.

"You're probably right. He brought that fashion model – I can't remember her name. The teenager who headlined the recent fashion shows. She was all over him, moody and demanding attention."

Nero nodded. "Not everyone disapproved of his date. One of the older uncles escorted her home after her temper tantrum."

"Uncle Valentino didn't respond when the girl shrieked about his mother's insults."

"Why should he?" Nero asked. "The esteemed Doña was right in her assessment. That girl wasn't worthy of his attention. She's less than half his age and self-absorbed. She lacked enough talent to keep a man like Valentino satisfied for long. He had plenty of offers from women ready to be her replacement."

Sara watched the interplay between the cousins, toying

with her food when the meals arrived. She had never met the relatives they discussed, and neither of them seemed to remember she was there.

⅓☼Ↄ

Sara came alert with a start. Her dessertspoon paused, midway above her plate. "What did you say?" she asked Nero.

"Gina has forgotten to tell you about her misadventure," Nero said. "She spent all evening chasing after one of the Sydney guests. I think his name was Matthew."

"Matteus," Gina corrected him, spooning a generous serving of pavlova into her mouth. "Mm-hmm. Hasn't the chef outdone himself this week." Gina waved her spoon at Nero. "I sent Sara a photo of Matteus and his brother Quin. Matteus is only twenty-three, but he could pass for thirty. I know he's had *plenty* of experience with older women."

Gina ate the last mouthful before she continued. "I made up my mind to find out what he had to offer. I arranged to meet him in a secluded part of the rooftop garden— Nero, promise me you'll take Sara up there. It's perfect for a romantic rendezvous."

"Stop trying to distract me, and finish your story," Nero said.

Gina paused to take a sip of her third drink. She smiled at him. "What makes you think there's anything more to tell?"

Nero reached over and removed Gina's sunglasses. "You weren't drunk enough to trip down those steps."

Sara gasped at the purple bruise that masked her friend's swollen eye. "He hit you?"

Gina replaced the sunglasses with a shrug. "Not Matteus, but he apologised to me afterwards for not being there to defend me. Our meeting was scheduled while everyone was listening to Valentino play the piano. I'm sure I've told Sara that our uncle is a talented classical pianist. There's a small concert hall on the roof where he performs whenever his mother's in town. I enjoy his music, but I was eager to be alone with Matteus. I got more than I bargained for."

"What happened?" Sara asked.

"Matteus's father intercepted him, and he couldn't get away. The little brother was dispatched to postpone the rendezvous. Quin's only nineteen, but he thought I'd accept him as a replacement. He's not used to having anyone say no. I slapped him, and he hit me back. We wrestled, and then my nose began to bleed. He said he was sorry, and took off. Nobody would have known anything had happened if I hadn't been caught sneaking away to change my dress."

"Oh, Gina," Sara said.

"Oh, Gina, indeed," Nero said. "She did a creditable job convincing everyone she caused the injury herself. It helped that she had an open magnum of champagne in one hand and her heels in the other."

"What are you going to do about Quin?" Sara asked.

Gina grinned at Sara across the table. "You're not going to approve, but I'm having dinner with him this evening."

"You can't!" Sara gasped.

"Why not? Someone has to teach that boy he shouldn't start something he can't finish."

For the second time, the colour drained from Sara's face. Nero reached for Sara's hand. "Are you okay?"

"That's an excellent question," Gina said with a laugh. "Perhaps now is the appropriate time for Sara to tell us what *she* got up to last night?"

Sara stared at her friend in disbelief. "I-I d-didn't get up to *anything* last night. I... it was a m-mis-understanding."

Nero swung his eyes from Gina to Sara. "What *kind* of misunderstanding?"

"I was working late at the office, and a security guard kept checking on me." Sara looked at Gina in desperation. It sounded silly now. Sara twisted her napkin in her hands, not wanting to see Nero's response. "When it was time to leave, he was waiting for me in the elevator. I panicked and sent Gina his photo so he knew I could identify him if he... if he..."

"And did he?" Gina asked, ignoring Sara's distress.

"Of course not," Sara snapped. "I'm not like you. If I'd been assaulted, I'd have gone to the police."

Gina did not attempt to hide her reaction. "Finally – the truth. I knew you disapproved of my promiscuous behaviour, but you're always too polite to say anything." The spiteful girl rose to her feet. "But I'm relieved about last night. It would have been a pity if that security guard stole your virginity. Especially as Nero's been dreaming about being your first love."

Sara closed her eyes, afraid she would disgrace herself by losing her lunch. The waves of nausea took too long to settle. When she looked again, Gina had gone.

Nero still held her hand. "Please forgive Gina. She's obviously more upset about what happened to her than she'll admit. She enjoys shocking people, and I'm sure she makes up most of the drama that's supposed to have happened. I'm not sure I believe the boy deliberately attacked her. He comes from an honourable family. I'll find out if she's really having dinner with him, and warn him to be careful."

Sara blinked and pulled her hand away. She fumbled for her handbag. "I need to call a taxi." Her vision blurred, and she couldn't make the phone unlock.

Nero removed the phone from her hands and slipped it into his pocket. "Let me take care of you..."

Faulty Assumptions

❦ ☼ ❧

*2 Corinthians 6:4 - Show yourself a servant of God
by enduring greatly, through affliction,
hardship and distress.*

❦ ☼ ❧

Oliver was preparing to leave when his apartment intercom buzzed. He checked the screen and grimaced. He was already late. This left him no choice but to take the bunch of flowers with him to meet his unexpected visitor. He grabbed the plastic-wrapped bouquet as he pressed the button. "Good morning, Piper. I'm on my way down."

When he arrived at street-level, his ordered taxi was waiting. Piper Maxwell, his intimidating employer, stood on the footpath beside it.

"I've paid the driver to wait," Piper began. He frowned at the flowers. "Is there something you need to tell me?"

"These flowers are a peace offering for my mother," Oliver said. "I'm having lunch with my parents today. Tell me you're not asking me to cancel again."

"There's no need to cancel," Piper said, his expression neutral. "I have a simple question to ask, and then you may go."

Oliver prepared for trouble. Piper would not come to his door unless he expected some kind of reaction. The agent needed to be careful, because nothing would escape Piper's eagle eye.

"Tell me about the girl."

Oliver took a slow breath before he answered. "There's nothing to tell. Jenny's already grilled me and accepted my explanation. I felt sorry for the kid – I didn't mean to frighten her. I pride myself on being a good judge of character. Yesterday, I reviewed the Friday surveillance footage in case I needed to amend my report. I stand by my initial assessment. There's no evidence that she's an active player."

"How many years have you worked for me?" Piper asked.

Oliver blinked. "Too many for you to be asking these questions."

"This is the first time I've had to ask. Can I still rely on you?"

"When have I ever let you down?" Oliver allowed a hint of his annoyance to shine through. "Look at my service record. I've never failed you. Haven't I always followed your orders?"

"And I want to keep it that way. Start by being honest with yourself. Admit Sara Messinger got under your skin."

Oliver met his commanding officer's glare without blinking. He was confident he could keep his thoughts to himself.

Piper nodded. "Keep me updated."

"That's what this is about?" Oliver asked. "You want me to watch out for this girl?"

Piper prepared to walk away. "What you do in your spare time is your business. But if you should happen to see her, keep me informed. Didn't you say you had somewhere to be? I'm not taking the blame because you're late."

Oliver got into the seat beside the taxi driver. He confirmed the address as he buckled his seatbelt. He frowned at Piper's departing figure. What had his employer hoped to achieve? Oliver shrugged. Why waste time worrying about something in the future? He had more pressing matters to deal with today.

The thirty-minute journey to his parents' suburban home passed in a blur. Oliver studied the unfamiliar car parked at the curb outside the house. It had South Australian number plates. His mother was always adopting strays. He hoped this was not a bad omen.

He paid his fare and walked past the car, checking the interior through the windows. There were two children's booster seats in the back and discarded clothing covered the front passenger seat. Any hope the occupants of the car were visiting another house shattered as he walked up the footpath. There were laughing children in the backyard.

Taking the side path, Oliver went directly there. Two boys were kicking a soccer ball around the large patch of lawn. The taller boy sent the ball flying towards Oliver, who stopped it. He rested his boot on top of it.

"That's my ball," the smaller boy said, running over. "Give it back."

"Peter, remember your manners," a voice called from the shady veranda. A man wearing a grey suit stepped onto the lawn.

His presence surprised Oliver – another prediction wrong. He'd expected a woman to come with these boys – his mother was a perennial matchmaker.

The stranger approached with an outstretched hand.

"You must be Oliver. I'm John Edwards. Your mother invited me and my boys for lunch. Today was my first Sunday, and we've come straight from the church service."

Oliver accepted the handshake, reassuringly firm and confident, while he finished his quick assessment. The two men shared many characteristics, including height and approximate age. Oliver had a distinct bodyweight advantage. Their colouring was similar, but the other man's hair was conservatively styled. John's skin was pale, and his hands were soft. Definitely an office worker. John's expression remained open and trusting. Oliver allowed the other man to lead the conversation.

"This is Matt, my eldest. And the boy who has forgotten his manners is Peter."

"I'm five," Peter announced. "Matt's seven. He thinks he's better at soccer than me, but I'm going to beat him." The small boy snatched away the ball and kicked it. He laughed when his brother had to chase it to the end of the yard.

Peter turned back to Oliver. "Are you a wrestler?"

"What makes you think I'm a wrestler?" Oliver asked, crouching down to the same level as the boy. It was a warm day, and his short-sleeved tee-shirt left his tattooed arms bare.

Peter squeezed Oliver's upper arm. "You've got hard muscles. Dad's arms are soft. What happened to your ear? Did someone bite it off in a fight? Is that why your smile's wonky?"

"You ask a lot of questions for someone who's five," Oliver said, brushing off the father's apology. The boy laughed and dashed off to chase the returning ball. Oliver rose to his full height, turning to John. "You don't have to worry about Peter hurting my feelings." He moved towards the house. "I'd better let Mum and Dad know I'm here."

Oliver entered through the back door. His mother Lisa-Jane came from the stove, wiping her hands on her apron. She had a little more grey in her hair than he remembered, but otherwise, she hid her age well. She would be seventy-four next birthday, but still enjoyed good health. She worked part-time as an office manager for her small city church. He handed her the flowers, and she wrapped her arms around him. For a moment, she stared into his eyes, and then she nodded. "It's good to have you home, but I'm not sure I approve of what you did to your hair." She released him and returned to her chores.

"Leave the boy alone," his father said, coming from the dining room to shake Oliver's hand. At eighty-nine, Noah had been retired long enough to have claimed the dining room preparations as his domain. His hair was white, and his back straight. "You came through the yard. Did you introduce yourself to the new pastor? There was a line-up at the door to be the first to ask him home for lunch. Your mother got her invitation in ahead of them."

"There has to be some advantage to being the church secretary," Lisa-Jane chuckled.

"He didn't say he was your pastor," Oliver said. He matched that information with what he had already discerned. "He's younger than the last one by a few decades. Is his wife joining us for lunch?"

A knowing look passed between Lisa-Jane and Noah Johnston. There was no wife, and not because he was a widower. Their son kept his own counsel. A divorced single-parent was an unusual pastoral candidate, even for their unconventional church. Oliver walked through to the dining room and surveyed the table. "Who else have you invited for lunch?"

"Lucinda and Fergus are joining us."

Oliver froze, his defences compromised, and his words unfiltered. "What's wrong?"

"What makes you think anything is wrong?" Lisa-Jane asked, facing away as she continued to prepare the meal.

"Auntie Lou doesn't come over for Sunday lunch unless there's a family emergency," Oliver said. "You and your sister save your Sunday hospitality for the 'lost lambs and strays'."

He had chosen his words carefully. She always referred to her only son as her lost lamb. He held his breath. The expected response from his mother didn't come.

Instead, his father moved the conversation forward. "You spend your life solving other people's problems, but there is nothing for you to fix here. Take comfort because this 'family emergency' can wait until we have more than an audience of one. Don't let this spoil your lunch."

Oliver went to his accustomed place at the table. He balanced his fork, spinning it on the rounded handle. Various possibilities cycled through his mind. Whatever it was, it must be bad, because his mother wanted the new pastor on hand to deal with the aftermath.

ॐ ✿ ॐ

The smell of his mother's roast chicken and vegetables reactivated his appetite. Oliver poured a river of rich gravy over his generous second serve. He glanced around at the other diners before he returned the gravy boat to its place on the table. He was accustomed to catching Aunt Lucinda watching him, but today the two wide-eyed younger guests were directly opposite him. Seated beside Peter, his aunt smiled, nodding her approval because Oliver was paying attention. Uncle Fergus and his father fell silent and everyone listened to the boys.

"I told you he's a wrestler," Peter said in a loud whisper. "He has to eat mountains of food to grow muscles."

"It takes more than food to make muscles," Matt said. "He needs lots of exercise to be that strong."

"Wrestling is exercise," Peter said. "When I grow up I'm gonna be a wrestler. Then I can have two Sunday dinners, without Dad saying I'm greedy."

The adults hid their smiles.

"Are you calling me greedy?" Oliver asked with a grin. "When you're forty and have to cook for yourself, you will understand why I'm enjoying this feast. I'd fade away to a shadow if my mother didn't feed me every once in a while."

"Doesn't your wife feed you?" Peter asked with a frown.

"Shh," Matt said, elbowing his brother. "He's like Dad. He doesn't have a wife."

The smaller boy refused to stay silent. "Did your wife run away too?"

Oliver responded to the awkward silence that fell over the other adults. He leaned forward, lowering his voice to a growl. "Some questions you don't ask a man without a wife. Especially not in front of his mother. It makes him grumpy, and he might send you outside without any dessert."

He leaned back and continued to eat. Peter stared at Oliver with a trembling bottom lip.

Lisa-Jane called across the table. "He's only teasing."

"No, I'm not," Oliver said, hiding his laughter. "I challenge Peter to ask me another question, and I'll prove it to him. While he's outside, I'll eat his dessert as well as mine."

"If you don't behave, Oliver, you will be the one sent outside," his mother said.

Peter thought about this for a moment. He looked from Oliver to Lisa-Jane. "What's for dessert?"

A ripple of laughter ran around the table.

Hidden

Depths

࿊ ☼ ࿐

*Isaiah 28:6 - God gives a spirit of justice
to the one appointed to judge,
and strength
to those
who defend the gates.*

࿊ ☼ ࿐

The meal was over. Oliver helped his parents wash the dishes. The other guests were seated in the living room when the front doorbell rang. Lisa-Jane dropped her tea-towel and ushered her son into the other room.

Noah returned from the front door with a young woman and two children in tow. Oliver had met this family before. The single-mother's name was Avril, and she lived in one of the units across the road. She attended the same church as everyone else in the room. His mother was looking at John. Had she already started hunting for a wife for the new pastor?

Oliver frowned. He remembered the first time he had met Avril. She and her family were luncheon guests a few months ago, on his previous Sunday visit. Afterwards, his mother had extolled the young woman's virtues.

Oliver had been quick to tell his mother that the twenty-five-year-old was too young for him. His mother had a ready answer. The fifteen-year difference in his parents' ages did not impede their happiness.

Relieved that his mother had let him off the hook today, Oliver watched John's reaction. The pastor seemed oblivious to the hidden agenda.

There had been a long parade of unmarried female guests at Lisa-Jane's table in recent years. Oliver's answer to his mother never varied. His life was too unpredictable to complicate with a relationship. He reviewed the recent offerings. Could he predict the next candidate, if Avril did not gain John's favour?

The face of another young woman appeared in his mind. He measured her against the qualities his mother extolled before he realised she was not one of his mother's friends. And he was not considering her suitability for John.

He came alert with a jolt. Where did this desire come from? And what had happened to his objections? Sara Messinger was also twenty-five. But that was not his biggest concern. Even if she were older, she could never be his.

By the time Oliver regathered his thoughts, Avril and all four children were leaving for the neighbourhood park to give the adults time for an important conversation.

"Oliver will walk John to the park in about an hour," Noah said. "Thanks again for helping out this afternoon."

Avril's reply was drowned out by the children's excited chatter.

Patience usually came easy, but Oliver's stomach churned. Long minutes slipped by, lost to polite conversation. Lisa-Jane busied herself, making coffee.

Only when she had served everyone did she settle in her favourite chair. Oliver surveyed everyone over the rim of his coffee mug. The seats were in a u-shaped arrangement. His mother and father had the narrow end, in front of the window. John and Oliver were on his father's side of the room. His mother's sister and her husband sat near Lisa-Jane.

Lucinda was the baby of the family, but she did not bear her age well. Her dark hair-colour came from a bottle, and she wore too much makeup. She was short, which made the extra weight she carried more noticeable. Recently, Lucinda had survived a cancer scare. Minor surgery had removed the benign lump. There was none of the usual nervous excitement to suggest she had called this family meeting.

Lucinda's husband, Fergus, was a cheerful man. The retired real estate agent had a full head of hair. He regularly played squash and golf to maintain his fitness. Oliver's uncle always saw the best in every situation. The couple had never had children and regarded Oliver as their surrogate son. When Oliver turned sixteen, it was Fergus who gave him his first car. It was obvious that nothing troubled his uncle today.

Lisa-Jane leaned her head closer to Noah, and her husband set aside his coffee mug. "John, could you please pray before we explain why we invited everyone here"

The pastor must have been expecting this. He bowed his head, speaking in a strong, clear voice. "Heavenly Father, thank You for the fellowship we have shared in this house today. We ask You to guard the hearts and minds of this family. May they be strong in faith, and wise in the words that they speak today. If there are any decisions to make, let them come from Your mercy and provision. Please sanctify this gathering with Your love, and give us Your strength and peace. These things we ask in Jesus' mighty name. Amen."

Oliver had not closed his eyes. The echoing amen hung in the air. Noah rose to his feet and an expectant atmosphere settled on the group.

"There's no easy way to say this, so I'm just going to tell you. I have stage four cancer. The doctors give me six months to live."

Oliver retreated behind the barriers in his mind, which deadened the emotional impact but he could still hear every word. Through her tears, Lucinda asked questions informed by her recent experience. When words failed her, Fergus loaned his voice to her concerns. Noah and Lisa-Jane took turns answering each query.

The story unfolded – long weeks of tests and procedures. His parents had not underestimated the serious nature of this illness. They had not held back from seeking medical help. The experts all agreed. This cancer was aggressive, spreading rapidly to the major organs. The treatment on offer promised nothing more than to extend Noah's life by a few weeks.

Noah and Lisa-Jane had fasted and prayed before making a decision. His father would not be having any chemotherapy or radiation treatment. He was preparing to face his Maker.

The voices stopped. Everyone turned their attention to Oliver.

"You haven't responded," Noah said.

"I've watched, and I've listened," Oliver said. "That's what I'm trained to do. You presented the facts and gave us an informed summary to explain your decision. I'm not in a position to question or challenge you. There's no denying the peace that surrounds you. Even facing death, you're concerned about how the rest of us will cope with your death."

"You asked for a response," Oliver continued, making sure to include all of them as he scanned the group. His eyes returned to his father. "You know I get my stubborn determination from you. I'm promising you the same kind of support you gave me after my accident, if you'll let me. You travelled halfway around the world when my life hung in the balance. Do you remember what you said? Death is nothing to be afraid of. It's like walking through a door. On the other side is perfect rest and peace for a weary soul, to anyone who believes. You promised to stand with me, and I'm going to try my best to do the same for you."

⁞ ☼

The short walk to the neighbourhood park to collect the pastor's boys should have taken only a few minutes. Oliver made it to the first corner before he stopped. He crouched beside a lamppost, holding his head in his hands. John Edwards did not attempt to break the silence.

After a few minutes, Oliver shook himself and stretched to his full height. He started walking again. "Telling my father that I'm okay with his death was the hardest thing I've ever done."

"Your parents love you very much," John said. "If they could think of any way to save you from this pain, they would sacrifice everything to do it. The prayer team will get to work this evening. There's always hope that God will intervene."

"Explain to me how that works. Why do some prayers result in miraculous healing and others don't? If God can heal, why doesn't He heal everyone?"

"That's a question people have been asking for centuries. There's no easy answer. I only know that God has the authority to say yes, but He also reserves the right to say no. Some people argue that it has to do with the level of faith. But is it the faith of the sick person, or the faith of the people who are praying that makes the difference? Of one thing I am certain, God always gives strength to deal with whichever answer He gives."

"Would it make a difference if I was a believer?" Oliver asked.

"The difference would be in how you deal with your grief. There's great comfort in believing that you will see your father again in heaven, which isn't available to those for whom death is the end. Don't think that God is using your father's illness to blackmail you into becoming a believer. What you do, or don't do, is between you and God. But remember, God loves your father and wants what's best for him. If that means it's Noah's time to die, then we have to respect God's sovereignty."

The two men continued walking. When they came within sight of the park, Oliver spoke again. "What else did my mother want you to talk to me about?"

"She would like you to come to the evening church service tonight. Noah's going public about his diagnosis. Lisa-Jane said it would make things easier if you were there. People are going to be upset, and your parents need you standing beside them. They believe your inner strength will make it easier for them to stand firm."

"Why didn't she ask me herself?"

"You have to be free to make your decision. If she asked in front of your aunt and uncle, there would be extra pressure."

Oliver nodded. "I'll have to check in with work, but I can't see any reason why I can't be there. How are you going to manage an evening service with those two boys? Shouldn't small children be in bed early? Your youngest is already a handful."

"Lisa-Jane has drawn up a roster of babysitters for Sunday evenings."

"You need to be careful," Oliver said, looking across to Avril who waved at them from beside the swings. "My mother needs little encouragement. This is only your first week in the job, and she's already looking for a permanent solution to your babysitter problem. Introducing you to Avril is only the beginning."

John shook his head. "This is my third church, so I'm not blind to the danger. For the past five years, I've refused to date anyone. I won't compromise my relationship with my boys."

The two boys had seen their father and were running towards him. If Oliver was to say anything, he needed to be quick. "You use your divorce as a defensive shield. But the reality is, you don't trust yourself. You don't want to make the same mistake again."

A shadow passed over John's face. He was quiet for a moment. "You speak certainty where others only ask probing questions. I'd hate to have you as an adversary. Your words are like an arrow piercing the heart. Your mother thinks you're some kind of secret agent."

First Matt and then Peter leapt at John. He tossed each one high in the air before setting them down on the ground. They ran to rejoin Avril as she came towards them.

"What else did my mother say?" Oliver asked.

"The road ahead of you is full of danger and shrouded in darkness. It breaks her heart to see you struggling alone with the heavy burden. Lisa-Jane asked me to pray for your salvation."

Misleading Motivation

୫୦ ☼ ୧୬

*Matthew 12:33 WEB - Either make the tree good and its fruit good,
or make the tree corrupt and its fruit corrupt;
for the tree is known by its fruit.*

୫୦ ☼ ୧୬

When Sara opened her eyes, she was alone in a canopied king-sized bed. She lifted the covers, relieved to discover she still wore the dress she had chosen for her lunch date with Gina. The darkened room was huge – her whole apartment could fit between these walls. Fragments of memory pushed her to the edge of the bed.

Her feet sank into the plush carpet as she waited for the room to cease its crazy orbit. Two doors led from this room. The first door opened into a spacious white bathroom where bright sunshine shone through the narrow floor-to-ceiling windows. Sara splashed cold water over her face. A box of tissues sat beside the washbasin. She removed her smudged makeup, before raking her fingers through her tangled hair.

When she looked more presentable, she went towards the windows. The outlook was stunning. The riverside promenade far below still bustled with pedestrians. She glanced across the river towards the office tower where she went to work each day. The view confirmed her fear that she was in one of the higher *Raphael Towers* apartments. Her friend Gina's family apartment was closer to the ground and faced the other direction.

She took a deep breath, and then another. Finally, Sara found the courage to retrace her steps and try the remaining door. She emerged into a living room decorated with expensive furniture on a grand scale. Nero sat on one of the large sofas, reading a book.

With a smile, he arose and closed the distance between them. "My sleeping beauty has finally awoken."

"What time is it?" Sara croaked.

"I'll answer your questions in a minute. Sit here. I don't want you fainting again."

She blinked at him. "Again?"

Nero led her to the sofa. He moved the open book to a coffee table before he disappeared. He returned with a tall glass filled with water. She gulped a few mouthfuls, and he retrieved it from her shaking hand.

"You asked about the time," Nero said. "It's six o'clock, but you slept through Saturday. It's now Sunday afternoon."

Sara staggered to her feet. "I have to go home."

His arms caught her as the floor rushed to meet her. "You're not going anywhere until you're fully recovered."

"I can't stay here."

Nero's arms encircled her waist. "Another night won't make any difference. You're safe in my spare room. If you're still unwell in the morning, we'll come up with a plan then."

Her heart raced. "What will people think?"

He pulled her to his chest, and her head rested on his shoulder. "I don't care what people think. Gina was right. I'm in love with you, and as soon as my divorce is final, I intend to marry you."

"What?"

He raised her chin so she would look at him. "I've had six months to get used to how I feel about you."

Sara pulled out of his arms and dropped onto the sofa. "But what about your wife?"

Nero settled beside her, taking her hands and gazing into her eyes. "She no longer considers herself my wife. She's seeing other men. My great-grandmother was right. We should have divorced years ago and avoided this unhappiness."

"What went wrong with your marriage?"

"Are you sure you want to talk about this now?" he asked, frowning at her. He brushed a long strand of hair from her face.

She smiled sadly. "It has to be now. It would be awful if falling in love with me produced the same kind of mistake. I couldn't bear to see you unhappy."

He kissed her forehead and hugged her. Releasing her again, he smiled. "I'm sure you could never make me unhappy. But you're right. Before we go too far, I need to ask you an important question. Do you want children?"

"Children? I've always dreamed of having a large family. Is that what caused your marriage to fail? You can't have children?"

"There's nothing wrong with me. I'll be able to give you all the children you want. I thought you already knew, especially after Gina made that comment about annulled marriages. It's Zemina who is infertile. I'd better start at the beginning. Zemina and I met while I was at law school. She was much older and about to graduate, and already guaranteed a position with her family firm. I was only eighteen when we married. All we talked about then was our careers. I suppose I always thought children would come along at the right time."

He paused, and Sara squeezed his hand.

"Except there never was a right time," he said. "At first, Zemina said she needed to focus on her career. Then she wanted to travel – a baby would only tie her down. Next, she became a partner in the firm, and her schedule was too busy. After her thirty-seventh birthday, her father suggested she see a fertility specialist. The test results were disappointing. That was two years ago. She underwent two IVF treatment cycles, and both failed."

"That must have been devastating for you both."

"I wanted to try again. But Zemina said nothing would convince her to endure that intrusive torture again. A few months later, she told me that our marriage was over. She had already hired a Sydney divorce lawyer. It took twelve months to hammer out an equitable deal, which is why we didn't legally separate until after we signed that contract. I can show you the paperwork if you need any proof that my marriage was over long before I fell in love with you."

"There's no need to prove anything to me. I know I can trust you. I've had a crush on you since the day we met. Gina wanted me to tell you, but I couldn't risk ruining your marriage. I knew I couldn't settle for a brief affair, and I didn't want to become the 'other woman'. I hated my father's new wife after my parents divorced. I blamed her for destroying my family."

"I'm married in name only." Nero leaned forward to kiss her.

Sara stopped breathing. Their lips met. That first kiss was gentle. She had dreamed of this impossible moment. She kissed him back. With a sigh, she pulled away, and he pursued her. His next kisses left her with no doubt that he loved her. She stopped breathing and let go of all her objections. Nero wanted to marry her when his divorce—

No! What was she doing? Hadn't Gina warned her about married men and their promises?

But this was Nero. He was an honourable man.

Then why was he lowering her onto the sofa?

Sara placed both hands on his chest and thrust him away. "Stop – we can't do this. Not yet. You're legally married until June, so we have to wait." He perched on the edge of the sofa. She couldn't read his expression. She started to cry. "I'm sorry. It's not that I don't want to, but what would we do if I got pregnant?"

"Shh," he said, brushing the tears from her eyes. He embraced her, and she stiffened. He pressed her head against his chest and stroked her hair, speaking softly. "I'm the one who should be apologising. It felt so right to have you in my arms that I forgot we weren't already married."

Nero leaned her head back, kissing each of her eyes, and then her nose. He leaned closer to her mouth. "Would it be so terrible if consummating our love resulted in pregnancy?"

Sara turned her head aside. "I've seen first-hand the psychological damage being born the wrong side of marriage can do to a child. My half-brother was born while my father was still married to my mother."

ᏒᏅ ☼ ᏟᏰ

Nero put down his book and went to answer the door. His cousin Gina walked in as if she owned his apartment. After their customary embrace, the girl dropped onto the sofa without saying a word.

"Sara's no longer here," he said.

Gina laughed. "Get me a drink. She called me immediately after you put her in the taxi. She usually tells me everything, and I'm pleased to report that hasn't changed. I'm relieved. I thought I might have overplayed my hand getting her to collapse into your arms. She assured me you were the 'perfect gentleman'."

Nero placed an open bottle of red wine on the table beside him. He had plenty of courtroom experience, and was confident he could mask his reaction. He poured them both a generous glass. "I see you survived dinner with that boy."

Gina took a sip. "I haven't come to talk about my affairs."

He raised his glass to his lips. "Why are you here?"

"Two things. First, I want to discuss my finder's fee."

"What have you done to warrant a 'finder's fee'?" he asked.

"I've delivered my innocent friend into your arms."

"She's not made her decision yet," Nero said.

"But she will." Gina grinned at him. "When she does, you'll pay me ten thousand dollars."

"You're very sure of yourself."

"She'll do whatever I tell her to do." Gina drained her glass and poured a refill. "If you need evidence of my influence, her panic about the security guard was due to me. I've convinced her that workplace assault is common, and she must be vigilant. If there is any suggestion a man is trying to catch her alone, she should call someone trustworthy. Someone like you." Gina patted his leg. "Of course, Sara insists that she's always safe with you."

Nero frowned, removing her hand and pouring himself another drink. "Did you send that man to harass her?"

Gina laughed. "No, but I wish I'd thought of it. Did you see how she squirmed? She wasn't sure if the danger was only in her head. But I got her to tell you the story. By the way, I talked to our cousin Piper at the party." She paused, and Nero waited for her to continue. "That security guard works for him. Piper is so predictable. He claims financial gain as his motivation for protecting the family. Yet he's always meddling. He left immediately after I told him one of his employees was threatening your future wife."

Nero walked to the window and looked towards the river. He admired Gina's bold assurance, but he could not let her win too easily. "I won't pay a 'finder's fee' until that 'future' becomes a reality. You said you have influence, so prove it. I don't want to wait six months for Sara to sleep with me."

"You should have pressed your advantage yesterday," Gina said. "Sara was so out of it she wouldn't have resisted."

"Why would I risk a rape allegation?"

Gina came to him, placing her hand on his arm. "She wouldn't go to the police without talking to me first. After I finished with her, she'd believe she seduced you."

He frowned. "I don't want to build my marriage on a lie."

"You're a successful lawyer. You know how easily a lie can be twisted to become the truth. The solution to your problem can be found in the rise and fall of your first marriage."

"What do you mean?"

"On your wedding day, you told Zemina that you loved her and there would never be anyone else. That was true right up until she filed for divorce. Your love for her died quickly, but it was never a lie."

He huffed. "My feelings for Sara are different."

"When did you decide you were in love with Sara? Was it before or after I told you she had feelings for you?"

"Are you claiming responsibility for my decisions now?" Nero growled. He returned to the sofa and poured himself another drink. He recognised some truth in her assertion, but he wasn't going to admit it.

"Consider this an arranged marriage," Gina said. "I predicted your divorce long ago. As soon as I met Sara, I knew she was the perfect candidate to be your next wife."

His irritation towards Gina intensified. Despite her contempt for family interference, she was an accomplished manipulator. He would need to remember that. "What makes her so perfect?"

Gina counted on her fingers. "She's young, attractive, and clever, honest and reliable. Despite her ambition, she isn't greedy. She wants children and is blind to your faults. She'll never divorce you."

"You make her sound like a saint."

"That's at the top of Doña Gabriella Marcella's wish list for a suitable bride." Gina laughed. "Sara's virginity is a bonus – you can thank me for that too. Any potential suitors had to get through me first. Once I'd destroyed their reputation, she wouldn't let them anywhere near her. Don't you think my having to seduce all your rivals warrants a further reward?"

"That depends on what 'reward' you have in mind," Nero replied.

"There's a PA position at *Yaris & Mariani* up for grabs."

"And you want it? Should I worry about why you want to be my soon-to-be ex-wife's personal assistant?"

"The salary is what I'm after," Gina said. "It's a lot more than I'm earning now. I have expenses I don't want the family to know about."

Nero leaned back and considered her explanation. He wasn't convinced she was telling the whole truth. "I can't guarantee you that job."

"You misunderstand. I only want you to warn Zemina I have something to discuss with her. Once she hears what I have to say, I'm certain she'll agree to whatever I request."

He declined to take the bait. "You said there was a second reason for your visit?"

"I want you to ask Uncle Valentino to lend you his Sydney apartment for the Christmas holidays. He won't be using it, because he has to go to Bangkok with his mother. Doña Gabriella Marcella insists that her children go with her for Christmas."

"Why don't you ask him yourself?"

"He thinks I'm a silly girl with no ambition, and I don't want to disillusion him." Gina chuckled. "But if you tell him you want to take your future bride on holiday, he'll be sympathetic. Especially after you explain the need to shield her from family interference. Of course, to keep our matriarch from disapproving, Sara will take along her best friend as a chaperone."

"The 'best friend' being you? Why do you want to go to Sydney?"

"Quin and Matteus have invited me to visit them. I need an excuse to keep my parents from expecting me to marry one of them."

CHAPTER 7
(Sunday 4th December BWR)

Costly Deception

৪৩ ✿ ৪৩

*Isaiah 29:24a - Those who are in error spiritually
will gain understanding.*

৪৩ ✿ ৪৩

It was after nine o'clock when Oliver and his parents arrived home from the evening church service. They were home later than usual because so many people had wanted to pray for Noah. As soon as the car pulled into the garage, Lisa-Jane announced she was heading to bed and hurried inside. Noah locked the car and came out to the footpath, where Oliver waited for his taxi.

"Thank you for coming with us," Noah said. "It set your mother's mind at ease to have you with us. She's more upset than she'll admit."

"I meant what I said about being here for you. I've already notified work. There won't be any interstate or overseas trips until we're through this. I'd offer to move back home, but I keep irregular hours. I don't want to disrupt your normal routine. I'll stick to Sunday visits until you tell me you need more."

"Sunday visits will be fine."

"Is there anything else I can do to help you, or Mum?"

51

Noah shot him a sheepish grin. "I don't suppose you've found yourself a girlfriend? Your mother's going to keep me awake fretting because she didn't ask you about your love life."

A taxi stopped at the curb beside Oliver.

"I'll let you go," Noah said, turning towards the house. He dragged his feet as if he carried the weight of the world on his shoulders.

A tight pain in Oliver's chest prompted him to break a longstanding promise. "Wait here," he said to the taxi driver.

"Dad!" Oliver ran to his father and threw his arms around him. This was something he had not done since he left home at eighteen to join the military. Noah held on to him for a long time. When his father released him, there were tears in the elder man's eyes.

Oliver knew he was making the right decision. He allowed his father a glimpse of his emotional response. That should give enough credibility to his lie.

"Tell Mum I've met someone," Oliver said. His voice broke in just the right place, "but it's too early to know if she's the one Mum's been praying for."

Before his father asked any questions, Oliver dashed back to the taxi and threw himself in. "Go," he shouted at the driver. He had already given the dispatcher his home address. The taxi shot off into the night.

Oliver stared blindly at the passing suburbs. The driver must have recognised his mood and did not attempt conversation. Twenty-five minutes later, the vehicle halted at a set of traffic lights.

Oliver made a snap decision. "I've changed my mind. Take the next left."

It was after ten when the taxi dropped him at the end of a lonely street in an industrial estate. The area was devoid of traffic, the buildings blanketed in silence. Oliver walked the remaining distance to the *Maximum Security* Melbourne headquarters. They had a public shopfront in a more central location, but this was the heart of Piper Maxwell's empire. There was no nameplate beside the security gate. From the street, there was no hint of the purpose of this three-storey warehouse. He flashed his security card at the sensor beside the gate.

As soon as the opening gap was wide enough, Oliver stepped through the barrier. The gate whooshed shut behind him. A blinding floodlight came on, illuminating his way across the car park to the door. He could identify most of the vehicles. *Maximum Security* personnel worked around the clock. Oliver presented his card again and then placed his hand on the square panel. The frosted glass door slid open. He spoke briefly to the agent behind the front desk and entered the main corridor.

"What are you doing here?" Piper asked, appearing from nowhere.

"I might ask you the same question," Oliver said. "Except Jenny says you lie in wait to catch your operatives off guard. I'm heading to the gym. Is there anyone available who could spar with me?"

Piper fell into step beside him. "Sigrid Ericson is already there. She clocked in half an hour ago. Last time I checked, our newest agent was torturing herself. She failed one of Jenny's challenges. There should be enough anger and frustration left in her to guarantee you a good workout."

Oliver made no response.

"What happened?" Piper asked. "You were okay when we spoke earlier, and you're usually better at masking your emotions."

"I lied to my father."

"Given the news he gave you today, that's nothing to beat yourself up about."

Oliver stopped. "You don't understand. I made a promise that I would keep my relationship with my parents free from deception. That promise has been the anchor that keeps me sane. Without it, I'm nothing but a troublemaking, violent deceiver."

"The only solution," Piper said, "is to work on that lie until it becomes the truth."

Oliver swore. A tsunami of frustration rose within him. He fought for control, redirecting his anger from Piper towards the closest wall. The bloody knuckles on his right hand satisfied his need to hurt someone. But this lapse in self-control would be costly.

His employer did not pause until they arrived at the gym door. Piper waited for Oliver to press his injured hand to the sensor. Even accessing the gym required a security check, which was a sober reminder for Oliver that every movement within this facility was monitored. His hand was bleeding more than he expected. After wiping the smear from the screen, Oliver tucked the offending limb in a fold of his tee-shirt. He followed his employer into the large gym.

"Make sure you wrap that hand before you challenge Sigrid," Piper said.

At first, he thought Piper was mistaken. The room was empty. Then a clinking sounded overhead. A red-haired woman with the physique of an Amazonian warrior swung from a rope near the ceiling. She wore skin-tight black lycra. There was no mistaking her strength. The corded muscles in her bare arms would rival his own. Hand over hand, she pulled herself right to the roof girder without using her legs for support. With a loud bang, she slapped the ceiling before sliding down the rope.

"I've brought you a sparring partner," Piper said. "This is Oliver Johnston."

Sigrid grunted, clearly unimpressed.

Oliver bowed his head in acknowledgement to his opponent. Without saying anything, he jogged towards the locker room. He paused at the first aid station to tape his wounded hand. He flexed his knuckles to test the temporary dressing. Satisfied, he went to his locker.

In the other room, Sigrid said something Oliver didn't hear.

Piper responded with his strong voice. "Don't underestimate him. He might be smaller than you, but he makes up for his lack with street smarts and experience."

Oliver ripped off his blood-smeared tee-shirt and dropped it to the bottom of the locker. After removing his heavy boots, he replaced his jeans with loose training pants.

Piper's voice continued. "Don't try to kill him either. The cleaners get paid extra when there's a body to deal with. If I have to call them in, I'll take the fee out of the survivor's wages. Do I make myself clear?"

"Yes," Sigrid growled.

Bare-chested and shoeless, Oliver returned to the training room. Sigrid was securing her rope to a hook on the wall. She glanced at him and moved towards the padded sparring mats.

"Ready?" Piper asked Oliver. "You heard what I told Sigrid?"

Oliver grunted.

"Good," Piper said. "When this challenge is over, you're both on desk duty. Report to Room 212 at midnight, and I will brief you on the assignment. Use the intervening time well."

Piper did not wait for a response, closing the door behind him.

"Do you need to warm up?" Sigrid called from the mats.

He strode towards her. "No."

"Any rules?"

"Apart from Piper's warning not to kill each other? No."

They circled each other warily.

"How did you get those scars on your torso?" Sigrid asked, light on her feet.

He dodged her opening move, spun and rebalanced. "The older ones came from a helicopter crash."

"Are you sure you're fit enough to challenge me?"

Adrenalin surged through his body, but Oliver reigned in his impatience. "I'm more than ready to take you on. Don't show me any pity. I certainly won't be making any concessions because you're a woman."

Sigrid lunged at him. He dodged sideways and then swept her legs from under her. "You have to do better than that."

The female warrior recovered faster than he expected. She flew at him. As the battle intensified, his admiration increased. She was a determined fighter. He landed blows that would have stopped most men. Sigrid rebounded with counterattacks.

When she dropped him hard onto his back, he grinned at her. "That's more like it. You're almost worthy of my attention now."

"I'm only getting started," Sigrid assured him. She reached out her hand to help him up. He used her as an anchor to launch himself upright and then catapulted her over his head.

Sigrid rolled to her feet and faced him, her savage smile a warning. She still had sufficient breath to ask questions. "You only told me about the old scars. What about the white slashes?"

"It doesn't pay to underestimate your opponents." Oliver lunged forward. He continued speaking as they grappled with each other. "The outward scars are nothing but reminders – even the smallest weakness can lead to failure." He flipped her over his head again. He stepped away, leaving her to scramble to her feet without assistance. "And failure can be fatal when you work for Piper Maxwell. Not everyone has what it takes to succeed. Perhaps you should quit—"

Sigrid rushed at him with a roar. He smiled. The time for conversation was over. The pair battled in earnest until they were both at the extreme limits of their strength.

Panting and drenched with sweat, the two combatants stood a metre apart. A small cut over Sigrid's left eye dripped blood onto the mat. "Enough?" Oliver asked.

"Only because Piper wants to see us at midnight."

Oliver bowed low from the waist. Sigrid blinked, before bowing in reply. He reached out to clasp her by the forearm. "Well fought. We will have to do that again."

She reciprocated, familiar with the gesture. Sigrid rotated his arm to examine the battered tape on his knuckles. "The other guy came off second best?"

He shook himself free to head towards the locker room. "There's never a winner when you're fighting with yourself." It was time to change the subject. "What did you do to earn Piper's displeasure?"

"I put a dent in the van while Jenny was assessing me. After expressing her disapproval, she kicked me out of the driver's seat. Then she signed me up for a driver education program."

"Don't be too hard on yourself. You must have impressed her if she left you at the wheel long enough to wreck her van."

"I didn't wreck the van," Sigrid snapped. "Piper said I'm in trouble because I broke an unwritten rule – never answer back to Jenny. What rule did you break?"

"I broke a promise," Oliver said. He turned away from her curiosity, slamming open his locker door.

Sigrid disappeared around the corner. He didn't trust her. Had she conceded defeat or changed the parameters for the contest? He remained alert, listening to her opening her locker. Then her footsteps retreated towards the showers. A plastic curtain swished, followed by a savage burst of water. He finished his preparations and went in the same direction. She had chosen the furthest cubicle. He slipped into the one closest to the entrance.

The hot water was welcome, soothing his aching muscles and easing his tension. He would have stayed longer if he had been alone. He turned off the water and wrapped a towel around his waist. After dressing in jeans and a clean tee-shirt, he repaired the tape on his hand and left the room to lean against the wall in the corridor.

Sigrid appeared ten minutes later, her damp red hair pulled back into two plaits. He revised his earlier impression as his caution jumped to full alert. Her square face and her ferocious glare reminded Oliver of a battle-ready Viking. One who didn't need a sword. She wore a sleeveless crop top and tight jeans. There was a savage beauty in the way she walked. She flashed a wide smile and raised her eyebrow in question.

"My mother warned me about girls like you," Oliver said with a half-smile. He didn't wait for a reply, hoping he had read the situation right. He hurried towards the closest stairs.

"What did she say?" Sigrid asked, keeping pace.

"She said I needed to know how to say 'no'."

Sigrid laughed. "Your mother is a wise woman."

The
Hostility Begins

ॐ ☼ ॐ

*Ecclesiastes 11:5b - Just as you don't know how a baby
grows within a mother's womb,
you cannot understand the work of God.*

ॐ ☼ ॐ

(midnight)

Arriving at Room 212 did nothing to diminish Oliver's tension. There should have been a sign on the door, detailing the project allocated to this room. He held back. Sigrid activated the security panel with her hand. This was her first assignment on this floor. Her excitement was palpable.

The door swished open. Piper was alone in the room. Three sides of the square space featured separate giant wall-mounted digital screens, each displaying only the company logo. Oliver glanced over his shoulder. The display boards on either side of the door through which they had entered were bare. He took a deep breath. His employer watched his response with a familiar smile. What kind of test was this?

The layout was identical to the other operational rooms on this floor. The open space before the massive wall screens made it possible to walk from one screen to another. A bank of computer terminals sat to the side of the central space. The main area contained a conference table surrounded by a dozen comfortable chairs.

Piper waved them to the space in front of the central screen. "What you see and hear in this room is not to be discussed outside these walls. Understood?"

Sigrid answered immediately. "Of course."

Oliver said nothing. Sigrid looked sideways at her sparring partner, and he winked at her. She moved a step further away. Jenny must have made a strong impression on the new recruit. Sigrid already understood how important discretion and secrecy were to her job security. But she didn't know that Piper only used this particular warning with new recruits.

Oliver considered his options. "When are the tech specialists arriving?"

"You won't need any tech support," Piper said. "You're only taking a second look at information already analysed."

That surprised Oliver. "Why – *us*?" He changed the second word but it was obvious that everyone knew he was really asking "Why me?"

Sigrid's nostrils flared, but she maintained her silence.

Piper's eyes darkened. "You asked for a desk job."

Swallowing a protest, Oliver nodded at his employer. What he had asked for was less responsibility and more time off. Only a zealot like Piper would view that as justification for removing Oliver from active duty and handing him a rookie assignment.

Piper turned to Sigrid. "The computers in this room access the entire *Maximum Security* network. Oliver will take the lead, but once you understand what he requires of you, you can choose your own hours. Jenny or I will monitor your progress. She's the only other person with security clearance for this room."

Oliver had one final question. "Why the extra precautions?"

Instead of answering, Piper reached for his phone and clicked a few buttons. The central screen flickered on the wall in front of them. The company logo disappeared, replaced by a complex diagram. Closer inspection revealed stacked rows of names. Thumbnail portraits sat beside each one. Sigrid gazed at the wall. There was nothing but curiosity in her attitude.

Oliver swore. He could already identify some of the faces in this family tree. His eyes locked onto a photograph of Nero Mariani on one of the lower branches. Oliver glanced sideways at Piper, before searching for his employer's name on the screen. Was he disappointed or relieved to find it missing? It was common knowledge that this influential family claimed a blood-connection with Piper. But the details were shrouded in secrecy.

Piper folded his arms across his chest.

Taking a deep breath, Oliver approached the screen. Where would he begin? He remembered Friday's assignment and reached towards Nero's image. When he swept his hand towards the right, the screen on the corresponding wall awoke. It filled with a larger image of Nero.

Beneath the photo, there were smaller photographs. Oliver gave Sara Messinger's image only a glance, but his pulse throbbed at his temples. Sigrid watched the screens with growing interest.

Beneath the images, rows of text filled the screen. With a few taps, Oliver opened window after window on the screen. He glanced at the information, closing some windows and moving boxes around. When he found the transcripts from Friday's recording devices, he nodded.

The sound of his voice poured from the speakers in the ceiling. The recorded message confirmed the listening device installation. A box appeared on the screen with a brief transcript of the recording. He ended the replay. Another box appeared. This one had a flashing cursor. He looked at the brief comment already there and touched the screen. A pop-up box appeared, which required his password. He typed it in, then added a brief line of text, noting that his initials appeared beside the new information.

With a few clicks, he identified where the small change was recorded in the log. Next, he closed all the pop-up windows. When the original diagram was the only file open, Oliver turned to his employer. "What are you looking for?"

Piper laughed. "If I knew the answer to that question, I wouldn't need you."

୫ ☼ ଓ

Sara shuffled her feet. The Monday morning briefing was almost over. Her legs ached from standing for forty-five minutes. Usually, this didn't bother her, but her body ached with the lingering migraine. She glanced around the room.

Only the eight executives were seated at the oval table. Small teams gathered behind their designated leaders. They had to be ready to step forward and clarify any information when asked to do so. Sara stood with Nero's team and had remained silent. She made a conscious effort to look anywhere but at him.

Nero's father-in-law chaired the meeting today. He shuffled the files in front of him and looked around the table. "That concludes everything on my agenda. Does anyone have anything else to raise?"

Nero shook his head. One by one, the others declined the opportunity to discuss anything else.

Zemina smiled at her father and rose to her feet. Her eyes addressed each person at the table. Today the attractive woman wore a peacock blue dress that clung to her curves. Her dark shoulder-length hair was loose. "I have two things. First, I've made a decision about my new PA. Gina from the typing pool will start training for the position today. As you know, she's Nero's cousin. I'm confident that I can put her talents to good use."

A small murmur rippled through the room. Sara's friend was a popular young woman. She listened carefully. Gina had said nothing about applying for this job.

"I am sure the young lady will be a good addition to your team," Zemina's father said. "What was the second matter?"

"The Carmichael case we pencilled in for February. There has been a new development and the case has been moved forward. It begins in Court 4 this afternoon. Unfortunately, I'm bringing the final arguments for the Riverdale case today. You need to appoint someone else to represent Mr Carmichael."

"Let's look at our schedules—"

"If only it were that simple," Zemina laughed. "I've already spoken with Mr Carmichael. He's adamant that he must have a female lawyer representing him. He reminded me that he's an old family friend. And he's offered to pay double the usual fee. As we've heard already, our more experienced lawyers are busy with active cases. The only female who could drop everything at short notice is Nero's protégé. I propose that Sara accompanies me to court this morning so that I can brief her on the case. It should be a relatively simple matter, with a final judgement before Christmas."

Zemina's proposal was accepted without objection, and the room emptied. Sara followed Nero's wife out the door in a daze. The walk to the next office gave her no time to gather her thoughts. Gina met her at the door with a grin. "It's a big day for both of us."

"Let me look at you," Zemina said, when Sara entered the room. The executive clucked her tongue. "This will never do, and there's no time to send out for something new. Nero might approve of that suit, but it won't do for Mr Carmichael. Gina, check in my closet. I'm sure I have a red blouse that will go perfectly with Sara's shoes."

Ten minutes later, Sara wore a red silk blouse with more top buttons undone than she was comfortable with. "It's good that you have a fetish about matching your underwear to your shoes," Gina said. She pulled Sara's hair loose and refastened it in a more casual style. "I can see the lace on your bra when you lean forward. Here, take this red lipstick. You can apply it in the car. Come on."

Gina hurried Sara out into the corridor, where Zemina was waiting with her current PA and two of Sara's office buddies. At that moment, Nero appeared.

"Not now, Nero darling," Zemina said. "I don't have time for a chat."

"What kind of case is the Carmichael one?" Nero asked, walking beside his wife to the elevator.

Sara was swept along with Zemina's team behind them. She trembled, not recognising Nero's mood.

Zemina laughed. "Sexual harassment. It's not the first time he's been accused – the old goat can't keep his hands to himself. But this woman wouldn't accept an out of court settlement."

Nero's face grew stormy. "Why have you dressed Sara like this if he can't keep his hands to himself?"

"Old Carmichael's paying good money. *If* I'm to be replaced by Little Miss Perfect, she needs to come across as if she's had *some* experience. But there's no need to fret. I'm sending your cousin along to remind Carmichael he can look but not touch. But you might want to be on hand when she wins, because he's been known to forget his manners in victory."

Gina squeezed Sara's arm, warning her to keep quiet.

Nero frowned. "What are the prospects for a win?"

"If your little friend follows my instructions, she can't lose."

The elevator doors opened, and Zemina stepped inside. Gina drew Sara in with the other team members. Nero wasn't finished. He blocked the door from closing. "What makes you so certain?"

"The plaintiff had an affair with a previous employer," Zemina said. "He's already listed as a character witness. I'm sure your sessions with Sara have covered intimate workplace relationships. She only has to get the witness to confess."

Zemina seemed determined to have the last word. "Now leave. Unless you want me to summon my father and discuss your objections with him?"

Nero glared at Zemina and retreated.

CHAPTER 9
(Monday 5th December BWR)

An

Adverse Reaction

ॐ ☼ ॐ

*Isaiah 28:17a WEB - I will make justice the measuring line,
and righteousness the plumb line.*

ॐ ☼ ॐ

It was half-past nine on Monday morning when Oliver returned to Room 212. He had been home to change clothes, eat a substantial breakfast, and catch a few hours' sleep. He had ordered Sigrid not to return before ten. This was the first test of her loyalty.

He had the secure room to himself. The motion-activated lights came on when he opened the door. He paused. He had left a few traces that would betray any visitors. Everything was exactly as it should be. To be doubly certain, he checked the camera log for this corridor.

Sigrid arrived fifteen minutes early. Without preamble, she asked, "Why are you looking at my personnel file?"

Oliver stood before the main wall screen. "Look at this."

He dragged the open window sideways. Similar information with his name at the top lay hidden beneath it. He pointed to new data listings during recent hours and matched

67

it across both files. The section detailing Sigrid's operational log had few entries. All but one of them had Jenny Prescott's initials in the authorisation column. "Jenny signed off on your induction yesterday. Here she added you to the Active Duty register. An hour later, Piper assigned you to SP2096A."

Sigrid leaned closer. "That can't be right. That sign-off entry occurred before Jenny started the driver evaluation test." She pointed to the other screen. "Your SP2096A entry is for Friday evening. You said you knew nothing about this assignment."

"I didn't." Oliver pointed to the lines immediately above the information she focused on. He opened the relevant records. "It's not unusual for projects to have multiple codes, and for agents to cover more than one assignment. On Friday evening, the job I worked on had two other codes against it. This one links to the long-term security contract for the *Yaris* building. And that one is a security investigation for a private client. Piper came to visit me that night, and again on Sunday morning. On neither occasion did he say anything about this special project. That's why I was checking your file. I wanted to know when Piper paired us together."

"Why does it matter?" Sigrid asked.

"Two reasons. I didn't ask for restricted duties until late Sunday afternoon, but this project was already mine. And Piper went to a lot of trouble to make sure you were waiting for me in the gym."

"Are you always this paranoid? There's no way anyone could have predicted I would be there."

Oliver laughed bitterly. "I don't even need to look at your file. A promising military career. Cut short by an operational incident, resulting in an honourable discharge. Difficulty adjusting to civilian life. Social isolation with fits of extreme anger and violence. An established pattern of risk-taking behaviour associated with a win-at-all-costs philosophy. Put you in a challenging situation – convince you that you failed – then provide you with an elite training facility where you can torture yourself. Bingo."

"You don't know anything about me," Sigrid snapped, her nostrils flaring.

"Among my other talents, I've trained as a profiler. Before you rip my head off, remember that I was the one you were there to meet."

"So what would your file tell me?"

Oliver entered his password and opened the confidential information for her to read. "There are a lot of parallels. But the main difference is my disregard for personal safety. One psych evaluation called it a 'death wish'. My military deployment ended when my helicopter came down over enemy territory. I was the only survivor. My father watched them turn off life support. Twenty-four hours later, he was still on his knees, praying. The doctors wrote my recovery up as a miracle."

Sigrid swore. She walked to the conference table and seized a chair, hurling it towards the door. It crashed into the wall and tumbled to the floor. Without another word, she stormed across, tossed the chair out of her way and slammed the door behind her as she left.

Oliver waited, watching her pacing the corridor on the security video feed. After fifteen minutes, she went downstairs to the break room. When she turned back towards the stairs with two black coffees, he picked up the displaced chair. He reattached the loose wheel and repositioned the chair at the table.

The door opened.

Sigrid placed a mug in front of him. "I came to Melbourne"—her calm voice did not match those stormy eyes—"to get away from people talking about miracles. My grandmother believes I survived the attack on my patrol because God has more people for me to save."

"How many died?"

"Only one, but if I had challenged the team leader's orders we wouldn't have been caught in the open."

"A good soldier follows orders."

Sigrid flinched. "I was second in command. I had a responsibility to my superior officer and to the others in my patrol."

"Once the fatal error was made," Oliver said, "you led the others back to safety. But the officer's death denied you closure."

Sigrid drained her coffee cup. Oliver prepared to duck. She must have read his intention, slamming the cup onto the table with a bitter laugh. "You're good at what you do. Not even neutralising those attackers brought me any release. Did Piper put me with you as some kind of rehabilitation?"

It was Oliver's turn to laugh. "He chose you because of your insubordination. He's expecting you to challenge me if I take this investigation in the wrong direction. He's also expecting you to drag me back to home base if I land us in trouble."

"This is only a desk job," Sigrid reminded him. "What kind of trouble can you lead us into, looking at a family tree?"

"I'll use the same answer that Piper gave us this morning: if I knew the answer to that, neither of us would be here."

𝔰𝔬 ☼ 𝔠𝔰

Oliver stared at the screen in front of him. He was twitchy. It was hard to resist the temptation to change his search parameters. Especially as Sara Messinger's name kept appearing as an associated person of interest…

His stomach rumbled. Sigrid looked at him from her computer terminal half a room away. Despite their common project there had been no conversation. The silence was getting to him. What kind of team leader was he? It was past lunchtime. Should he lead by example, perhaps even tell her to accompany him to the break room?

It was Sigrid who decided for him. "I think I've found something."

"Put it on the big screen," Oliver said. He pretended something on his computer needed his attention before he joined her. He watched her reflection on his screen. Her arms wrapped across her chest, and she started tapping her foot. He went to stand beside her. She had returned to the family tree illustration. "What did you find?"

"First, I want to review what you told me about the other projects that link to this one. You said there's some archaic legal complication that females can only assume control of the 'family business' if there are no legitimate adult males. That's why the client's worried about his heir. When you look at the family tree with colour coding for gender, you get a better understanding of his problem. There are six males to forty-three females, and three of those boys are too young to count. If I wanted to take over this family, I'd get rid of the three adults and make sure I had control of those children."

"Continue."

"The client is Enzo Horatio, and he's in his seventies. He's not going to live forever. Of his three daughters, only one gave him a grandson. That's Nero Mariani, the lawyer you put under surveillance. Nero is thirty-three and has no children. If anything happens to Nero, the inheritance passes to Enzo's brother Valentino. He's forty-three, but he hasn't any male heirs either. If Valentino dies, the family business effectively passes to the eldest sister, Theresa."

"There have been three males born in the past six years," Oliver said.

"I'm glad you noticed that. One grandson for each of Enzo's three younger sisters. There's an intelligence report here that says none of the sisters will so much as sneeze without Theresa's permission. I haven't been able to trace the genealogy for the fathers of those three babies. But they have one curious thing in common – they each have Theresa's husband listed as a godparent, and he has been generous with his financial support. I'm wondering if Raymond might be using illegitimate sons to gain legitimate heirs within the family. If Piper's looking for a conspiracy, he should order DNA tests."

"I'll pass on that information to Piper. Is that all?"

"No. There's an anomaly with one of the younger female relatives, Gina Gregorio. Enzo's eldest sister Theresa is her great-grandmother. The family is wealthy enough that none of the women needs to work. Yet this twenty-one-year-old has a low-paying job at *Yaris & Mariani*. Her name red-flagged on one of the surveillance reports from Friday's new equipment. There's a sound bite you need to hear. This morning she had an interesting conversation with Nero's wife, Zemina."

The transcript appeared on the screen as the overhead speakers broadcast the recording.

Zemina Mariani: What do you want?

Gina Gregorio: You have a PA position available. I'd be perfect for the role.

ZM: (laughter) You? You have neither the experience nor the qualifications I require. Why would I hire you?

GG: Because I've been keeping your little secret from Nero. You're going to want to keep me very close. That's the only way to ensure I keep quiet. You wouldn't want me to tell him what you really did on your girls' weekend away the first year of your marriage.

ZM: I don't know what you're talking about.

GG: I've also visited Dr Paris-Smyth. The medical records on file at his office made interesting reading. What do you think will happen when Nero finds out that you terminated a pregnancy all those years ago? And that an unexpected complication from that procedure is the reason you haven't been able to conceive again.

ZM: What do you want?

GG: (Laughter) You disappoint me. That's the second time you've asked me the same question. I've already told you. I want you to make me your PA. Perhaps the decision will be easier when you discover that I've more to offer. I know how miserly Nero's been with your divorce settlement. I can get him to offer you more, and to hand the extra money over immediately.

ZM: How do you propose to do that?

GG: Nero is being pressured by the family to find himself a more fertile wife. I've persuaded him to show some interest in Sara Messinger.

ZM: That mouse! His family will eat her alive.

GG: (Laughter) I've been grooming her for months. Nero's lived such a privileged life. He gets everything he asks for, handed to him on a golden platter. From now on, it's going to cost him a lot more, and he's going to find trouble around every corner.

ZM: What does this have to do with me?

GG: Sara believes marriage is forever, and Nero's still married to you. She's going to keep him at a distance until the divorce is final. Unless someone convinces her that the waiting period is a mere technicality. I'm sure you can see how this can play to your advantage. All you have to do is get Sara under your control, and you can make him dance like a puppet on a string.

Sigrid hit the stop button. Oliver clenched and unclenched his fists.

"We have to warn Sara Messinger," Sigrid said.

"No."

"Why not?"

Oliver turned his back on the screen. He weighed his next words. "We're Piper's eyes and ears. He's playing a long game, and these people are players."

"So we're going to do nothing?" Sigrid looked ready to break something.

"I'm going for a walk," Oliver said, striding towards the door.

Sigrid grabbed hold of his arm "A walk—"

He turned and fixed his eyes on her face. For a moment, he dropped the mask, and her eyes widened. Sigrid took a step back. "Okay, so you're going for a walk. Don't let me stop you."

Without looking over his shoulder, Oliver left the room. He slowed his steps and willed himself to speak politely to the few people he passed on his way to the main entrance. When he came to the front desk, he nodded to the operative who would log his departure from the building. He walked out the main gate and kept walking, unsure how far he would get before someone came for him. What he was about to do next was insane, but his heart insisted it was the only option.

He was almost to the corner where the taxi had dropped him last night when Sigrid caught up to him.

"What did you tell Piper?" Oliver asked.

Sigrid glanced sideways at him and grinned. "There's no hiding anything from you. He told me to stick to you like glue because you're letting your emotions overrule your common sense. He said you wanted to get out of the secure building to escape his surveillance."

Oliver kept marching. Piper was right. But his employer hadn't come to collect him. Did that mean Piper trusted him to make the right decision?

"Where are we going?" Sigrid asked.

"There's a shopping centre a few blocks over. One of the cafés has a corner booth where I can make a discreet phone call without the cameras picking up what I say."

"What about the takeaway we just passed? That had outdoor tables."

"I need the walk to clear my head and time to choose my words. I have to get my message across without breaking my promise to Piper."

Sigrid remained silent until they crossed at the shopping centre traffic lights. "Who are you going to call?"

"I'm going to confess to my father the lie I told last night. Then I'm going to ask him to pray for me."

"And for Sara Messinger?"

Oliver stopped midstride, tripping on the curb. Sigrid hurried him forward to the safety of the footpath. "Piper said you're in love with her. I told him what you said about the long game. He said she's a player, innocent or not. I'm here to watch your back. Once you intervene, the other players are coming after you."

⃝

Oliver's father answered on the third ring.

"Oliver, I was about to call you," Noah began without any greeting. "I don't know what trouble you're in, but the Holy Spirit won't leave me alone about you."

"I have a confession, Dad. What I told you last night was a lie."

There was a silence from his father which invited Oliver to continue. "I'm nobody to her, and she's surrounded by dangerous people. If I try to warn her, my actions might deliver her into the hands of her enemies."

"Can you tell me her name?" Noah asked.

"I've already told you too much."

"I understand. I won't tell your mother this extra information, but I can assure you she's already praying for this woman."

"I have to go," Oliver said, with tears in his eyes. "And Dad..."

"Yes, Oliver?"

"I'm sorry. For everything."

After he ended the call, Oliver sat with his head in his hands.

He listened as Sigrid spoke into her phone. "Hi Gran, no need to panic, but it's me. I've rung the home phone, so I can leave a message. You were right. I've got more people to save. My friend and I have a situation, and we could do with a miracle. There's a girl in trouble, and the wolves are circling. I can't say anything else, but you know what to do."

Date

With Disappointment

୫୦ ✵ ୯୪

*Proverbs 13:20 WEB - One who walks with wise men grows wise,
but a companion of fools suffers harm.*

୫୦ ✵ ୯୪

Sara hooked her handbag over her arm and picked up the folder that held her notes. The judge had delivered his verdict and immediately left the court. She took a deep breath, choking back nausea that threatened to ruin her victory. The judge had been scathing in his remarks towards the plaintiff, before he awarded court costs against the grief-stricken woman.

Mr Carmichael, the overweight man Sara had successfully defended, invaded her space. Everything about this man made her skin crawl. He wrapped his flabby arms around her. The sharp edges of her folder dug into her chest. He planted a garlic-laden kiss on her lips as he raised her feet from the floor.

"Enough of that," Gina said, appearing beside them. She swatted Mr Carmichael with her hand. He released Sara, turning his amorous attentions towards Gina. The younger woman led him from the courtroom as she dodged his kisses.

"Not here," Gina said. "And not in front of the people who just saw you declared an honourable man."

After leading the way downstairs to the foyer, Gina encouraged Mr Carmichael to leave with his supporters. "Enjoy your celebration, and be more careful next time. You were lucky our sweet Sara convinced the witness to spill the beans about having a workplace affair with the woman who accused you."

"Are you sure you won't both join me. I can make it worth your while," Mr Carmichael asked.

"Tempting," Gina said, "but Sara already has an appointment that she can't miss. And I have to accompany her to make sure she behaves herself."

Gina grabbed Sara's arm and propelled her out the front door. They were moving so fast, Sara feared she would trip and fall. That would be a terrible end to what was supposed to be her first solo victory. She watched her feet instead of where they were going. At the last moment, Sara saw Nero waiting on the footpath. Before she could react, Gina shoved her forward. She fell heavily against him, and his arms wrapped around her.

The tall Italian-Australian smiled. "Congratulations, Sara. A well-deserved win."

She rested in his embrace for a few moments, her heart threatening to break from her chest.

"N-Nero," she said, pushing out of his arms. They stood a short distance apart, and she fumbled with her folder. Her face was glowing, and she couldn't look at him. "I didn't know you would be here."

Nero laughed, reaching out to take her by the arm. "Gina made me promise to come. She said you would need rescuing from Old Carmichael."

Gina relieved Sara of her handbag and the folder. Then the assistant slipped her arm around Sara's other elbow. The victorious lawyer was carried along between them.

"Where are we going?" Sara asked.

"If you had ever accepted the invitation to Friday afternoon drinks, you would know," Gina said. "There's a little bar around the corner where everyone from *Yaris & Mariani* meets. We'll make a detour to drop off this folder to Nero's car, and then we'll join them."

"I didn't know you went to Friday afternoon drinks," Sara said to Nero.

"I usually don't, but Gina knew I wanted to help you celebrate your win. What could be more natural than to share your victory with the others from our chambers? You and I can be together all evening without anyone asking awkward questions."

"You can thank me later," Gina said. "I want to be a bridesmaid at your wedding, and that isn't going to happen if you don't start spending time together."

A shiver ran through Sara.

Gina squeezed her arm. "Now is not the time for doubts. Where is the harm in having a few drinks with the man of your dreams? And you don't have to worry about Zemina. She told you yesterday afternoon that she would miss your victory. She's taking an extended weekend break with her lover."

“✪„

The other members of their larger group had slipped away during the past half hour. All that remained at the outdoor table were Sara, two of the young male lawyers who shared her office, and Nero. Gina had disappeared.

Sara was not comfortable in this unfamiliar setting. The current conversation was even more disconcerting. Her office buddies were talking with Nero about the third member of their cohort. They toasted their missing companion's good fortune. He had gone away for the weekend with an older woman. Was it a coincidence that the young lawyer had gone to the same location mentioned by Nero's wife? She kept stealing glances towards her mentor. He didn't seem concerned by the conversation.

Sara swirled the last of the white wine in her glass and made a decision. She had promised Gina she would stay for one more drink, and it was time to leave. She picked up her handbag and turned to Nero. "I'm going home now."

Nero emptied his glass and turned to her. "I'll walk you to the taxi rank."

"You'll do no such thing," Gina announced, appearing between them and taking Sara by the arm. "Sara's not going anywhere. Come on boys," Gina said to Leroy and Perry. "You bring Little Miss Sunshine, and I'll drag my cousin Nero along as her chaperone. This is the first time I've been able to get her out on a Friday night, and she's not leaving until she's had some fun. And you," she said to Nero, "are staying to help me."

Gina led them towards the indoor restaurant, shoving her way through the crowd. Leroy and Perry grabbed their drinks and followed along behind.

"I've ordered wood-fired pizzas, and our inside table is ready."

"How did you get an inside table without a reservation?" Leroy asked.

"That's a secret I'm going to keep to myself." Gina laughed.

Nero smiled, and Sara swallowed her objection.

Unsuitable Company

❧ ☼ ☙

Revelation 3:8a - God said,
"I know what you have done."

❧ ☼ ☙

Oliver set aside his empty glass and frowned at Sigrid. "This was a terrible idea." He glanced around the inner-city eatery. The room was noisy, filled with professional people enjoying post-work drinks. "Why did you choose here? This is not what I'd call a quick meal."

"Stop whining and get me another drink," Sigrid said. "They serve gourmet pizza, and my favourite beer is on tap. We've already waited an hour, and I'm not leaving now. Our table should be ready soon."

Oliver did as he was told and ordered two beers. When he turned from the counter, a dark-haired beauty brushed against him as she shouldered past. His hand cramped around each glass, but he kept moving, not daring to look at her again.

When he reached Sigrid, he struggled to keep the anger from his voice. "Tell me it is a coincidence that Gina Gregorio is here."

"I'd lie to you if I thought it would make you happy, but I know you prefer the truth. You wouldn't have come with me if I'd told you this is where *she* would be this evening."

Oliver drank half his beer in a single gulp. "Why would I be interested in knowing where Gina is?"

Sigrid looked at him over the top of her glass. He lowered his eyes, stifling a groan as the truth dawned on him. He refused to give Sigrid the satisfaction of asking anything else. And he definitely was not going to turn and search for Sara Messinger among the crowd. He drained his glass, dumping it on the tray of a passing waitress.

"I'll be back," he said, moving towards the restrooms. He immediately regretted that decision when he saw the congested hallway. There was a crowd positioned outside the women's restroom door. He squeezed past to access the men's room at the end of the passage. When Oliver re-emerged, the number of women in the queue had swelled and there was no easy path through to the dining room.

A youth exiting the men's room after Oliver pushed past and launched himself into the throng. Laughter and cries of complaint from the women shadowed the impetuous boy's progress. Oliver was about to follow in his wake, when the situation changed.

He couldn't see the cause, but ahead there was shouting and screaming.

"Get out of the way!"

"Stop it!

"Hey, you!"

As the waiting women morphed into a panicked stampede, all headed in his direction, a chorus from the bar-room increased his alarm. "Fight! Fight! Fight!"

Oliver was stranded between women seeking safety and men exiting the restroom behind him to join the fray. He used his broad shoulders to nudge people out of the way until he had the wall at his back. From this place of relative safety, he could wait out the danger. He took a deep breath, and attempted to ignore the press of bodies around him.

One of the nearby women stumbled. He seized her, pulling her upright and drawing her into his arms. When the danger was over, he loosened his embrace and she turned to face him. He prepared his response to the expected apology, but then he recognised her.

Sara Messinger's eyes were wide and her soft gasp puffed warm air into his face. Everything around him faded. As he adjusted his position, she squirmed against his chest. "Sorry," Oliver croaked, his heat rising to match her blush. He attempted a non-threatening "I'm not hitting on you" smile, while he looked around for some way to give her more room.

"That's okay, Oliver," she said, her voice almost lost amid the clamour around them.

His heart leapt into his mouth and his eyes locked on her face. There were subtle changes in her appearance since he had last seen her. Her trembling lips wore a brighter lipstick. When he tore his eyes away, he caught a glimpse of the revealing outfit she was wearing. He said the first thing that came to his head. "I didn't expect to see you here."

"Neither did I," she whispered. "Are you working tonight?"

He shook his head. Was it his imagination, or were there tears in her eyes? Two burly security guards came to deal with the chaos. Their arrival saved Oliver from making a reply. He mumbled an apology and escaped.

Sigrid was no longer seated at the counter. She waved to him from a far table, one that was flanked by a solid wall. She knew he hated having open space at his back. She had arranged the two chairs so that they could both lean against the wall. From his seat, his eyes wandered to and fro. He had a good view of the crowded dining room, which included the customers at the counter.

"I hope you didn't mind, but I started without you," Sigrid said.

Only then did he notice the two large pizzas on the table in front of them. She had eaten several slices already. While he was gone, she had ordered him another beer. The drink was already in his hand before he checked his impulse. When was the last time he had been tempted to drown his troubles with alcohol?

"God, give me strength," he muttered and then froze. That phrase was a throw-away line, one used many times in the distant past. But it was now banned from his vocabulary.

Oliver's muscles tensed. He unclenched his hand from the glass as a chill washed over him. With both palms flat on the table he attempted to keep his expression neutral. Sigrid stared at him, a stunned expression on her face. Did she understand what was happening? He was unable to say anything. Sigrid shook herself and looked away, moving her attention to the wider room as she resumed eating.

This left him victim to the forbidden memories. The dining room faded as ghosts took centre stage. Long-dead men preparing for their final patrol. Each one executed their superstitions and performed their rituals. During his years of active service, Oliver had distilled his preparations into a single line of prayer: "God, give me strength."

He had never been able to thank God that he alone had survived.

A pounding sensation began in his ears. The last time those words were spoken aloud, God ripped his world apart. Was God about to do the same again?

His rational mind told him not to hold his breath, but his heart refused to listen. There came a whooshing sound like rushing water followed by thunder. Any doubt that his prayer had been heard was shattered by an audible voice.

You ask for strength, and you have all you need. Now ask for steadfast patience to withstand the trials to come.

Oliver blinked. He was back in the noisy Melbourne restaurant. His hand reached for a cheesy, meat-laden wedge of pizza. He was no longer hungry, but he chomped on it, chewing thoughtfully. He didn't trust his voice. When the first slice was eaten, he reached for another. Sigrid watched him, munching pizza and washing it down with beer. They ate in silence. When his plate was empty, he pushed it away and reached for his glass. He lifted his eyes to the room.

"She's four tables away, a bit right of centre," Sigrid said.

He sipped from his glass as his eyes wandered in that direction. After a moment, he resumed his survey of the wider crowd. Sara's group was one of many enjoying the evening atmosphere.

"She hasn't seen you," Sigrid said. "Love makes a fool of intelligent people."

Oliver ignored that comment. "Give me your assessment of the situation."

"She's been glancing at the exit as if she wants to leave, but Nero has his hand on the back of her chair. Whatever he's saying has her grinning like a child in a candy shop. Now everyone's laughing at her, and she's covered her face with her hands."

"Everyone?"

"Gina, of course, and Nero, but he's leaning closer and whispering to her now. She's looking at him as if he's the only person here. I recognise the other two men from the files. Sara shares her office with Perry and Leroy. Perry expects Gina to leave with him later, and he's becoming bolder with his hands. That leaves Leroy at a loose end. He's been teasing Sara. But it's obvious that he acknowledges the older man's claim. Nero has both hands in plain view. But from the way Sara is shuffling in her chair, Nero must have brushed against her under the table."

"If you were Gina, what would you do next?"

"Break down Sara's defences. If she wasn't guarding her glass, I'd spike her drink. The next option would be conning her into joining them in a drinking game."

Oliver nodded and finished his drink. "Give me your phone."

Sigrid obeyed. He pressed a few buttons before handing the device back.

"What did you do?" she asked.

Oliver pointed to an icon flashing in the upper corner.

"Your phone is transmitting direct to base, so make sure you turn it off when you finish tonight. I've paired our phones so I can listen in. I can't stay here. Piper would kill me if I beat up one of his clients."

Sigrid showed her teeth in a wider grin. "What do you want me to do?"

"Join that game." He dropped a credit card on the table. "Expenses." Oliver headed for the exit without a backward glance.

He waited until he was a block away before he opened his phone and activated his Bluetooth earpiece. Sigrid's voice was distinct in his ear. Other people were talking in the background. She must be standing at the bar. He walked as he listened to her fielding offers from enterprising men. She skilfully turned them away. Oliver arrived at the train station at the perfect moment. The departing train was closing the doors. He leapt on board. Then he pushed through four well-lit carriages to find one almost empty.

Another voice chirped in his ear. "Five double whiskeys."

"Playing that drinking game again, Leroy?" asked a male voice. Oliver recognised him as one of the bartenders. "Which of the ladies are you planning to take home this evening?"

"I'm an unlucky man tonight," Leroy chuckled. "I find myself without a partner."

"Buy me a drink," Sigrid said, "and tell me more about this game. I'm on my own, and I'm thirsty—"

"Make that six whiskeys," Leroy said.

Oliver silenced the conversation. He stared out into the dark. His destination was five stops away. That should give him time to come up with an explanation for Piper.

He closed his eyes. Sara's face appeared before him. He remembered the uncomfortable encounter in the corridor outside the women's restroom. The sound of his name on her lips threatened to unmake him.

With great effort, he shoved these thoughts from him. Another memory pushed forward. He examined it closely as the train pulled to a stop. He stepped into the night and walked towards the *Maximum Security* headquarters. The universe stretched above him, silent and watchful.

He whispered into the night. "God, give me patience."

Nothing changed. Yet his foolish lovesick heart took comfort. He was here for the longer game.

৪৪ ✵ ৪৪

Sara stared across the table at the tall muscular woman who returned with Leroy from the bar. The stranger expertly carried six tiny, liquor-filled glasses between her flexible fingers. At first, Sara mistook her for another waitress, for the woman was dressed all in black. Her red hair was constrained into two tight plaits. After she placed the drinks in the centre of the table, the woman sat between Perry and Leroy. Leroy slipped his arm around the newcomer's shoulder.

"Who's this?" demanded Gina.

Sara blinked at her friend, and her breath caught in her throat. Moments earlier, Gina's mood had been playful and relaxed, but now she bristled with suspicion.

The woman considered Gina with a calculating smile. "Sigrid Ericson. Leroy invited me to make up the numbers for your game."

The young man openly flirting with Sara's friend chuckled. "Jealous, Gina?" He introduced himself to the new woman.

"My name's Perry, and this charming princess is Gina. Ignore her atrocious manners. The rest of us always do. She's afraid the game might not go to plan because you appear to be a *worthy* rival."

Gina pouted, but she softened again as she watched Sigrid being introduced to the others.

Perry waved across the table. "That's our esteemed leader, Nero, over there. He's an old married man, but his wife has gone away for the weekend. The pretty woman hiding in his shadow is Sara. Don't be fooled by her shyness. Put her in a courtroom, and she becomes a vicious tiger. She shows no mercy until she defeats her opponents. Gina's hoping an evening with us breaks the spell that keeps this passion hidden. Now that you've met all the players, welcome to the game."

"Are you sure I'm not intruding," Sigrid said, her eyes lingering on each player.

Sara was accustomed to evaluating witnesses in court.

This woman's demeanour shifted as she zeroed in on Nero. The stranger lifted her chin and leaned forward. Her revealing top was a perfect accompaniment to the open invitation in her eyes. "Hell-llo-oo."

Sara swung towards Nero. Sigrid had his full attention.

"It's a pleasure to meet you." Nero's smile widened as he clasped her fingers in a firm handshake.

Was Sara reading too much into his response? If she believed Nero loved her, why was she threatened by this newcomer?

Nero continued to hold Sigrid's hand. "We work for an important city law firm. You look as if you've escaped from the military."

"Ex-army," Sigrid said, matching his stare. "I'm working in data analysis at the moment, but I'm open to other options."

Sara chewed her bottom lip, a sour taste rising at the back of her throat. Sara drank the remaining white wine in her glass and practised her slow breathing.

"I have a cousin who runs a security firm," Nero said. "Give me your number before we leave, and I'll put in a good word with him. I'm sure Piper will have a use for a strong, attractive woman like you."

Someone coughed, and Sara glanced sideways. Perry leaned backwards in his seat. Leroy had dropped his customary smile. A brief look passed between the two young men, behind Sigrid's back. What was happening here?

Their exchange had not gone unnoticed. "Now who's jealous?" Gina laughed. "Compared to a *sophisticated* man like Nero, you two are inexperienced *boys*."

"There's no need to be nasty, Gina," Leroy said. "Sigrid, she's only trying to unsettle everyone, before the game begins. She's only played a few times, and she's never managed to win."

"Let's forget about winners and losers, and enjoy the game," Perry said.

Sara remembered Gina's stories about late-night encounters, and she shivered. She had to find some excuse to leave. Her eyes drifted across the dining room, searching for a familiar figure. She kicked herself for clutching at straws. Oliver had said he was not on duty. And even if he was, what would he want with a stupid girl who lacked enough sense to stay out of trouble?

"The rules are simple," Perry explained to Sigrid. "Everyone plays for themselves, no couples and no alliances. Each player takes a turn as Quizmaster and purchases the drinks for their round."

Leroy took over. "The first question in each round is the same for everyone. If anyone fails to answer or decides to pass, the Quizmaster asks them extra questions. This continues until there are no drinks on the table."

Perry continued. "Everyone may offer suggestions to the Quizmaster to liven up the game."

Sara's eyes flew from one young lawyer to the other. They delivered their rehearsed explanation with brilliant synchronisation. Did their familiarity with the rules mean they controlled the outcome?

"But the Quizmaster's decision is final," Leroy said. "You have to convince them you are telling the truth, or you drink."

"You also have to drink if your answer is too predictable," Perry said.

Gina broke their rhythm, looking pointedly at Sara. "Or if you try to play it safe."

Sara fumbled under the table with her feet, searching for her handbag.

Nero put a cautionary hand on her arm. His face wore the familiar win-at-all-costs expression. Until now, it had always endeared him to her.

"What happens if the Quizmaster chooses the wrong question?" Nero asked. "And all the drinks are still in play after everyone has answered?"

"In that situation, each player gets to challenge the Quizmaster," Leroy said. "The Quizmaster has to be clever if they don't want to add all that round's drinks to their tally."

"The game continues until each of us has been Quizmaster," Perry continued. "Tonight, there are six rounds."

Sara scrambled in her bag for a mint to combat the growing nausea. The rules repeated themselves in her mind. The significance of her agreement to stay increased during the ongoing discussion. She should have closed her ears to Nero's reassurance that he would keep her safe. He said this was a harmless game, but now she recognised the lie. It did not matter whether she lost the game or not. A few more drinks and the alcohol would lower her inhibitions. Her loosened tongue would do the damage. An unwise choice of phrase or the wrong confession could ruin everything.

And Nero was here to witness her humiliation.

"I need some air," Sara cried, knocking over her chair in her haste.

"You can't leave now," Gina said. "If you do, then you become the ultimate loser, and you have to pay the penalty to each of us."

"She doesn't look well," Sigrid said. "Perhaps you should let her go?"

"It has taken me a year to get her to come out after dark, and I'm not going to let her wriggle out of her promise to stay. If she needs air, I'll walk her to the corner and back. Her bag and her phone stay here."

☙ ☼ ❧

Out on the footpath, Sara took another deep breath. She no longer feared the loss of her dinner, but her small anxieties were multiplying.

"What's the matter with you?" Gina hissed. "Stop acting like an immature schoolgirl. Nero deserves better than this from you."

"I'm trying, honestly I am."

"Stop thinking about yourself. You claim to love Nero, so put him first. You know how much responsibility rests on his shoulders. Remember how hard he works all week. As the woman he loves, it's your job to brighten his downtime and help him relax."

Sara fought back the tears. "I'm sorry. I know I'm being selfish but—"

"No buts from you, Buttercup. Don't forget that Nero is only a few years older than Perry and Leroy. He's wasted his youth with a woman who doesn't love him. And now that he's chosen you, you're snuffing out any hope of lively entertainment."

Sara opened her mouth to protest.

Gina shushed her. "Loosen up and show him there's a real woman under that sexy outfit. Stop being a cold-hearted coward. You're no fun to be around when you're like this. If you're not careful, you're going to force him to seek comfort elsewhere. And here comes Sigrid now, in case you need another reminder that Nero is an attractive man. There are women in that restaurant who would fight you for him."

Sigrid stopped beside them. "Is Sara okay?"

"A-a few more m-minutes," Sara said. "I-I'll just walk to the corner again, and when I get back, I-I'll be r-ready."

Gina caught Sara's elbow and shoved her towards the newcomer. "Sigrid, you stay with her. I'm going back inside to get another drink before the game starts in earnest."

The tall woman hooked her arm through Sara's elbow. The pair set off towards the corner, weaving their way through the pedestrians. The city street was busy. "What's the problem," Sigrid asked as they reached the corner and prepared to retrace their steps.

"I haven't even told my best friend, so it wouldn't be wise to tell you."

"You should choose your friends more carefully," Sigrid said.

They walked in past the two security guards at the door. Sigrid let go of Sara's arm. Nero helped Sara back onto her chair. The redhead returned to the opposite side of the table.

"Are you feeling better now?" Nero asked.

Sara forced a smile. She looked around the table. While she was away, someone had bought another round of regular-sized drinks. All but her glass were empty. Sara twirled the stem of the full wine glass between her fingers. Her stomach cramped. "I'm sorry to have delayed your game. Gina has scolded me for being so selfish."

"While you were away, we had time to discuss what the winner could ask for at the end of the game," Leroy said. "It always depends on who wins."

"And how drunk the loser is when the deal is negotiated," Perry laughed. "But don't worry, Sara. It's never anything illegal. All the winner is permitted to ask for is a free meal, and the company of the loser at a time and place of their choosing."

"Nothing for you to fret about," Nero said, patting Sara's hand.

But Sigrid's words cancelled out his assurance. "Leroy and I have already negotiated our deal. If he wins, he wants breakfast, but he's going to let me choose whether we go to his place or mine."

An uncomfortable silence settled over the group.

"Now that we're ready," Leroy said. "We will be going clockwise, so Sara gets to answer first. Here's my question, in two parts. How old were you when you attended your first drunken party, and how much trouble did you find yourself in?"

The room spun. Sara opened her mouth, yet no words came. Leroy pushed across a shot glass. "You have to answer within thirty seconds."

"Come on, Sara," Nero said, taking hold of her hand. "This is an easy question."

Perry and Gina began to count down. "Ten... nine... eight..."

Leroy and Nero joined in. "Seven... six... five..."

Only Sigrid remained silent, staring across the table at Sara. The panic-stricken young lawyer took a deep breath.

"...three... two—"

"Seventeen," Sara gasped. "I was seventeen."

The two younger men cheered. Nero leaned back in his chair, his eyes bright with interest. He showed all his teeth, the same smile of approval he rewarded her with when she pleased him at the office.

Gina raised an eyebrow and waved towards the shot glass in front of Sara. "That's only half an answer. Tell us the glorious details, or you have to drink."

Swallowing hard, Sara fixed her eyes on the shot glass on the table. The overhead lights were shimmering on the surface of the golden liquid. "I-I haven't talked about this since it happened—"

"What better place to make your confession than among friends?" Perry remarked, and everyone laughed their agreement.

Sara flinched, glancing at Sigrid. The stranger's advice echoed in her mind: "choose your friends more carefully".

"I don't know you as well as the others," Sigrid said, "but you seem like a good kid. Obviously, something bad happened, otherwise you'd have blurted out your story. After we all laughed with you, the game would have moved on to Nero. I can't speak for the others, but I promise to listen to you. If there's any advice I can offer afterwards, I will talk to you in private. Pass me your phone, and I'll give you my number."

"That's kind of you," Sara mumbled, pushing her phone across the table. She intended to delete the number afterwards. Yet this delay bought more time to consider what she might say. When Sigrid returned the phone, the action triggered a memory. As the face of the last stranger who had asked for her phone drove all thought away, the colour drained from Sara's face.

"Are you ready to talk now?" Gina asked. "You were seventeen..."

"I was seventeen," Sara began. "I went to Adelaide to begin my law degree. For the first few weeks, I had no time for anything but study and work. I had a scholarship, but I needed my job as a waitress to cover my living expenses.

"I had some friends who didn't live on campus, and they were having a party. I don't remember why I didn't have to work, but I was happy to be asked. I warned them that I wasn't used to alcohol. I was worried I'd embarrass myself by getting drunk on my first night out. They promised to keep me safe, and— and I trusted them."

Sara stopped talking. She couldn't look at the others.

"And then what?" Gina asked. "You can't stop there. We're all sitting on the edge of our seats."

"I gave up my scholarship and transferred back to Melbourne. I felt betrayed – and ashamed. Tonight is the first time I-I've been out d-drinking with friends since then."

"Grrr!" snarled Gina. She turned to Perry and then waved her hand at Leroy and Nero. "You three are lawyers. You make uncooperative witnesses spill their secrets all the time. Get her to talk. Let's have an Inquisition."

"Why don't we give her a break, and move on with the game?" Sigrid suggested.

"You forget this isn't a democracy," Gina retaliated. "Tell her, Leroy. You're the Quizmaster. Sara hasn't answered the whole question."

"I'm open to counter-arguments," Leroy said. "Gina says 'Inquisition', and Sigrid pleads for mercy. What do you say, Perry?"

"I'm with Gina. Give us the details. Details! Details! Let's have an Inquisition!"

"And you, Nero?" Leroy asked.

"I'm torn in two directions," Nero said, squeezing her hand. "Sara's deeply troubled by whatever happened, and I want to spare her further pain—"

"But?" asked Leroy with a sly grin.

"But I have to remember that I'm a partner at *Yaris & Mariani*," Nero said. "This secret may have implications for her future. I want the truth. Voting with Gina and Perry seems the only reasonable option."

"The group has spoken, Sara," Leroy said. "An Inquisition it is!"

Cheers erupted from Gina and Perry.

Leroy laughed. "Hear ye, hear ye!" Across the room, other people turned to enjoy the spectacle. He rapped on the tabletop with his empty glass. A waitress hurried over to collect it. "This Special Inquisition is now in session. Nero, please invite the witness to swear an oath."

Nero selected one of the shot glasses. He had shed his austere respectability in the last few minutes. Now his cheeky grin challenged her to play her part. "Hold this in your left hand, Sara, and raise your right hand as you would in a court of law."

She remembered what Gina had said about Nero being close in age to the two younger lawyers. She followed his instructions.

He winked at her, before wiping away his smile. He tugged on his jacket lapels speaking in a pompous tone. "Do you, Sara Messinger, promise to tell the truth. The whole truth. And nothing but the truth. Or else you drink."

The performance was ruined when he finished with laughter. Meanwhile, Sara wrestled with her decision. She stared at the glass. She had already told this group too much. But she was afraid to see the disappointment in Nero's eyes when he heard the rest. It might be better to drink in front of the group. Then she could hope for an opportunity to tell him the truth in private.

"You'd be a fool to drink now," Sigrid said.

"Shh!" said Leroy. "Who dares interrupt the Inquisition?"

Sigrid leaned sideways and whispered in his ear.

"A-hum!" he said. "My learned colleague has requested permission to address the witness."

"What did she offer you, Lord Quizmaster?" asked Perry.

"None of your business," Leroy chortled, winking at Sigrid. "Go ahead and give your argument, noble lady."

Sigrid smiled at Leroy, but there was no laughter in her eyes when she looked across the table. "Agree to the Inquisition, Sara. If you accept this drink, there are another five to follow it. Six double whiskeys should be more than enough to re-enact your shame."

Sara almost dropped the glass. She spun towards Nero and gave him her pledge. "I promise to tell you the truth, the whole truth, and nothing but the truth."

"Good girl," Nero said, taking the glass from her. "Back to you, Lord Quizmaster."

"Thank you, Nero. Ladies and Gentlemen of the Inquisition, I hereby give you the rules for this special round. You each get one question, so choose your words carefully. You are not permitted to follow-up with a secondary question. Try and avoid asking anything the witness can respond to with a single word answer. Is that clear?" Leroy walked around the table, taking his time to decide who would go first.

"Gina, please ask your question."

"Yes, Lord Quizmaster."

"O-ho!" chuckled Perry. "Here's your chance to show us how clever you are. I'd like to offer you a side-wager. If Sara can wriggle out of giving you a satisfactory answer, you have to forfeit Leroy's round."

"I accept," Gina said. She shook hands with Perry before addressing Sara. "May I remind the witness that she has sworn to tell the whole truth. Sara Messinger, tell us the first thing you remembered about this party when you woke up next morning?"

Sara's relief was so great, the answer was out of her mouth before she engaged her mind. "Nothing."

Perry and Leroy doubled over with laughter. Sigrid nodded, and Nero smiled.

Gina's face turned purple. "NOTHING!"

Sara closed her eyes and opened her mouth. What could she say that would defuse her best friend's anger? "Nothing. I didn't remember the party at all, and I didn't wake up until Monday afternoon. When I did wake up, I was in the campus infirmary."

"Don't say anything else," Leroy laughed. "You have more than satisfied Gina's question with your supplementary information. Unfortunately, I have to accept your first answer. Gina loses her side-wager to Perry. Would you like to drink now, or wait until after Nero has his turn?"

Gina grabbed a shot glass and downed the whiskey. She slammed the empty glass upside down on the table before her.

"The score is minus one for Gina," Leroy said. "Perry, your witness."

"If you don't remember the party, how do you know what happened at this alleged party?"

"Excellent question," Nero said. "Gina, you could learn a lot about strategy from young Perry."

"She has to answer it yet," Gina hissed.

All eyes turned to Sara.

She was beginning to understand how this game worked. "There was an in-house inquiry run by campus security. They gathered testimony from forty eyewitnesses who attended the party. There was undeniable evidence that I attended the party, and that I was drunk."

"My witness," Sigrid declared. "Were there any charges laid against you or any other person who attended the party?"

"No."

"That's a wasted question," Gina snorted. "Even I know Nero would have checked Sara's police record before he hired her."

"You've missed the subtleties of the question," Nero said. "Sigrid wanted to confirm that no blame was attributed to Sara for whatever happened. She also ascertained that no charges were recorded against anyone else at the party. The inquiry found no evidence that she had been drugged or sexually assaulted."

"That doesn't mean nothing happened," Gina sneered. "Your little pet claims to be a virgin. Now we find out the hypocrite attended a drunken party and can't remember what happened. Ask your clever question, and watch her weasel out of answering it."

"Would you like a little wager on that?" Nero asked. Sara frowned, uncomfortable with the tension between the cousins.

"Certainly," Gina said. "I'll drink another shot if you get any satisfaction from the little tease. If she doesn't confess something to outrage your great-grandmother, you take the forfeit."

Sara held her breath as Nero picked up both her hands. He leaned close and kissed her on the lips, a lingering, gentle kiss that sent shivers down her spine. There were oohs and ahhs from across the table. Her heart pounded when he retreated a short distance. Sara feared she would faint. She gazed into his dark eyes.

"Was a medical report tendered to the Adelaide enquiry to confirm your claim?"

Instinctively, her fingers tried to cover her face. Nero held her hands captive. Tears welled in her eyes. Even now, the shame ate away at her. "Yes." She had never had an intimate examination before. That had been a horrible way to disprove the allegations that she had behaved like a prostitute.

Nero wrapped his arms around her, and she wept on his shoulder.

"I'm sorry," Sara said, pulling away and hunting in her handbag for a handkerchief. "The doctor apologised to me afterwards. He advised me to press charges for defamation. But I was the outsider, and they supported each others' stories. I didn't find out until the report was released that someone's mother came home unexpectedly and rescued me."

"I believe Sara's evidence," Nero said. "And if I told my great-grandmother, she would demand justice for Sara. You know that she can't abide lies. You lose again, Gina."

Gina drank her forfeit.

"The score, ladies and gentlemen," Leroy said, "is minus TWO for Gina. Now, the last question is mine. Shh, Sara. Don't start snivelling again, or Nero will have my head. I only want to know why you couldn't talk about this?"

Sara sniffed, wiping her eyes with the back of her hand. "My parents don't even know. When I look back at those weeks, I cringe. I was unbelievably naive, and stupid. How could I have risked my reputation and my future career for a few drinks? I trusted people I didn't know, and it could have cost me everything I valued."

Gina walked around the table and hugged Sara. "Girlfriend, I'm glad you found the courage to tell us what happened. I know Nero appreciates your honesty. I hope you can forgive me for playing the devil's advocate. I knew something was preventing you from opening your heart to Nero, and I only did what was necessary. You're safe here with us as your friends and we only want what is best for you."

Dishonest Win

ॐ☼ॐ

*Isaiah 26:21a - Behold, God comes to punish
the inhabitants of the earth for their wrongdoing.*

ॐ☼ॐ

Oliver looked up from the computer terminal. The clock said it was almost midday. "What time do you call this?"

"I'm sorry," Sigrid said. She wore shiny aviator sunglasses and slumped into the nearest chair. "If you'd drunk as much as I did last night, you wouldn't be here at all. Here's your credit card back. Apart from the taxi at two-thirty, the only other charge was my round of shots for the game. I did think of substituting the drinks with something innocuous. But by then, Leroy was growing suspicious. I didn't want to blow my cover."

"Piper has already checked the transcript."

Sigrid swore and leapt to her feet. "I need coffee." She disappeared from the room. Fifteen minutes later she returned with two oversized mugs filled to the brim. "I would have fetched coffee for you too, but my hands are full. If I have to go on any more of these undercover missions, could you requisition a coffee machine?"

"I will add that to my list of essentials," Oliver said, trying to keep the smile from his face. "You did well for your first solo effort. I still don't understand how you managed to get Sara away from them. Right from the outset, it was clear that she was supposed to be too drunk to resist Nero's advances."

"I could claim to have beaten them at their own game," Sigrid said. "But we both know it was either dumb luck that the three men tied for the win, or..."

She left the sentence hanging there.

"Or what?" Piper asked. Neither of them had heard him enter the room.

Oliver winced. Sigrid's post-drinking headache was an acceptable excuse to be caught by surprise. What could he offer to explain his failure?

"We need our own coffee machine," Sigrid muttered.

"What you both need is more sleep," Piper said. "Working around the clock is an unnecessary drain on your physical resources. And your ability to function is below par. Now Sigrid, finish that sentence. It was either 'dumb luck' or what?"

Sigrid pulled off her sunglasses and stepped up to Piper. She stood closer than Oliver thought prudent, and he signalled her to back off. Dropping into her seat, she wrapped her hands around a mug. Her eyes were bloodshot, and she squinted against the bright lights. She turned her head and looked up at Piper in defiance. "Divine intervention."

Piper raised an eyebrow and approached Oliver. "Is that your opinion too?"

"I reserve my assessment until we have further evidence," Oliver said. "Sigrid's hungover and looking for a fight."

"I want to hear Sigrid's report for myself. How did the evening end?"

"Listen to the recordings," Sigrid muttered. "Or read the transcripts."

Piper leaned over the table. "I would if you hadn't turned off the transmitter. You didn't turn it back on again."

"I didn't want everyone eavesdropping while the girl went to the restroom," Sigrid said. "I felt sorry for her. She deserves someone better than Nero—"

Piper waved her silent. "But why did *you* suggest Sara visit the restroom while the tiebreaker was being decided?"

"I thought they might forget she was there if she wasn't at the table. And it worked. Gina tried to convince Nero to give up and take Sara home. But he was determined to win. Gina had lost, so she couldn't afford to leave until the winner was decided. That left little old me to watch over Sara while they argued."

"Which brings me to the next problem," Piper said. "We know you put Sara in a taxi, but we weren't sure if you delivered her safely home. You reported your location from her doorstep, but we had to trace the taxi to check you hadn't mislaid her along the way. I might have forgiven that mistake, but you didn't go home."

"How do you know that?" Sigrid asked.

Piper glared at her. "You should have activated your brain before you planned a late-night visit. Did you ask whether Leroy's building was on my security roster? The computer system red-flagged you, and the night watch was obliged to wake me. What explanation did you give him for turning up at his home address? Don't try and answer that. You could have compromised a longstanding mission. Lucky for you, he was too drunk to care."

"Oops," Sigrid said, guzzling more coffee to hide her smile.

"Who won the drinking game tie-breaker?" Oliver asked, hoping to defuse the situation.

"Leroy said he lost the first round. Gina suggested a compromise. She would go home with Perry, and Nero could collect his prize this afternoon."

"What prize?"

"Leroy didn't say."

"I've got a bad feeling about this," Oliver muttered.

ॐ ☼ ॐ

The elevator doors opened. Nero stepped into the corridor. He checked in both directions before hurrying towards Uncle Valentino's apartment door. He hoped to avoid an accidental meeting with any other relative. He straightened the collar on his silk shirt and ran his fingers through his hair. Why had Valentino summoned him to his private residence?

Uncle Valentino was notorious among the younger generations. For as long as Nero could remember, conversations had stopped when his uncle entered a room. There were rumours that there were good reasons to fear him. Those who received a summons to a private audience kept whispered secrets. Now Nero was about to find out.

He straightened his shoulders. Nero was not one of those silly girls. He was his grandfather's heir. Hadn't Valentino pledged his support when the succession took place? It must be the leftover alcohol in his system that made him edgy. His uncle had always shown him great courtesy.

Valentino had been ten years old when Nero was born. A decade later, the twenty-year-old assumed a position of power in the family business. Nero had a lot of admiration for this uncle, who had helped Nero navigate the difficulties of adolescence. His uncle understood the problems growing up surrounded by females. But those intimate conversations occurred during the wild rooftop parties of his youth. There, the family provided their many daughters with a sanctuary away from the public view. It was Valentino who reminded rebellious teenagers that privilege brought with it responsibility. The girls were free to play, provided they brought no dishonour to the family name.

One public reprimand from Valentino was usually sufficient. Nero had witnessed enough cousins mend their ways to prove that. Only Gina had ever come back for a repeat performance. Nero paused before the apartment door, his hand raised. Was Gina the reason for this summons?

The door swung open before he knocked, and his uncle dragged him inside. The portal closed behind him. For a moment, the younger man experienced genuine terror. Valentino was the same height as Nero, but he was twice as broad at the shoulders. There was no excess weight on the muscle-bound family enforcer. Then his uncle let go of his arm. The moment of danger was past.

He was led towards a pair of white leather sofas. The elder man chose a seat, waving Nero to one opposite. A coffee table separated them. Nero surveyed the penthouse apartment, one of four on this floor. This was his first visit – Valentino zealously guarded his privacy. All the furniture was white, and in the main space there stood a full-sized grand piano. The artworks around the spacious room were colourful and bold. Nero admired his uncle's confident style.

Valentino picked up a glass of red wine and saluted him. "I'd offer you a drink, but your judgement is already under question. You need a clear head to talk yourself out of this mess. You should have come to me sooner."

Nero flinched. What had he done to earn this displeasure? He reviewed the last time he had spoken with Valentino. Now that he was an adult, his uncle only spoke to him during the infrequent family meetings. These meetings occurred in a grand second-floor office. This was where Nero's grandfather, Enzo, ruled the family empire. Last week, Valentino had proposed Nero be given more accountability within the family. Everyone else had argued against the suggestion. Enzo had insisted Nero devote himself to his legal career – and concentrate on producing an heir.

Valentino put down his glass and opened the small carved box that sat on the coffee table beside him.

"Ah," Nero said, recognising the box from the wild parties of his youth.

"Gina's angry – and that makes her vindictive."

"So, you know about—" Nero began, and then recognised the trap.

Valentino smiled. Nero closed his mouth and engaged his legal mind. He hadn't become a partner in his soon-to-be ex-wife's legal firm because of his wealth alone. Whatever Gina told Valentino had rung alarm bells, and Nero was here to supply the missing details.

"Gina depends on my hangover cure," Valentino said, lifting a small herbal sachet from the box. He pushed it across the table towards Nero. "I can't trust her with a personal supply, because I have to monitor her binge drinking. Today, she was particularly angry. She's looking for someone to torture."

Nero held his tongue. His mind whirled through a dozen possibilities. Sara Messinger was the unlucky victim in every one of them. A sense of impending doom awakened.

"Gina's friend has resisted your advances," Valentino said.

Nero's hands were sweating. He maintained eye contact with his intimidating uncle. How much had Gina said? He considered the messages his cousin had sent to his phone and made a decision. "Sara's a virgin. She's waiting until I'm divorced."

Valentino's smile vanished. He reached into the box and drew out a small brown bottle. "Gina has made plans to change that."

Nero accepted the vial, holding his breath.

"Gina asked me, but I denied any knowledge of this potion," Valentino said. "She thought she had some leverage. When that failed, she offered to pay. She's not as clever as she thinks she is. Her day of reckoning is fast approaching. But not before she does irreparable harm."

Nero considered the bottle in his hand. Was this the fabled elixir? In his maturity, Valentino was popular with women. But when he had been an inexperienced youth, a rumour spread that it was impossible to refuse his advances...

"Why are you offering this to me?" Nero asked.

Valentino walked to the window. "Enzo has sheltered you too much. I've kept quiet, but no more." He turned to Nero. "You must not allow Gina to manipulate you. Too much is at stake, both for you personally, and for the family business."

Nero trembled, rising to his feet. He had never seen his uncle so ferocious. Something momentous was about to be revealed.

"Much of this city is under your grandfather's control," Valentino said, striding back. Now he stood too close, but Nero dared not move. "I am Enzo's prosecutor, judge and executioner. My word is law in this family. Do you understand?"

"Yes."

"I refuse to watch you relinquish your power to your insolent cousin. If she succeeds in these small things, her ambition will grow. You have to take charge. Prove you deserve to be your grandfather's heir."

"What do you want me to do?"

"You were present the first time Gina needed the hangover cure," Valentino said.

Nero sometimes had nightmares about that night. Usually, the girls meekly accepted the reprimand. Then they swallowed their uncle's herbal remedy. This was a rite of passage that also provided a valuable lesson about responsible alcohol consumption. Some believed the vile taste was part of the punishment. Yet they all came to appreciate the hangover cure afterwards.

But Gina had refused to listen to her cousins' assurances.

The first time she was publicly drunk, Gina was eleven – she had sneaked into a party. In response to Valentino's chilling reprimand, the pre-teen shrieked her drunken defiance. Then she threw the concoction to the ground. The assembled witnesses froze. Valentino picked up the bucking child as if she were a toddler, and physically restrained her. Then he called Nero over, and instructed him to take charge of the procedure. Nero had been twenty-five. Under Valentino's direction, Nero had subdued Gina by activating significant pressure points with his fingers. He had never forgotten how still Gina became by the end.

Afterwards, she never openly challenged Valentino again. And a turbulent love-hate relationship had sprung up between the two cousins. That early event was the foundation for the trouble he was in now.

His uncle was right. He should have come earlier.

He bowed his head, pledging himself to follow the detailed instructions.

A Costly Mistake

❧ ☼ ☙

Isaiah 26:20b - Hide yourself for a little moment,
until the indignation is past.

❧ ☼ ☙

Sara wielded her hairbrush, before twisting her uncooperative brown locks into a knot. She restrained her hair with her favourite clips. This was an action she had repeated countless times. Yet, when she removed her hand, the whole arrangement came loose. She ripped out the clips and tossed them away.

The unmade single bed in the next room called to her. If she dropped face-down on the rumpled covers, she could sleep away this misery. She considered her reflection in the cracked bathroom mirror. Her eyes were bloodshot. Even the dim light through the tiny frosted window was too much. She raked her hands through her hair and ruffled the unruly tresses. Leaning forward, Sara poked out her tongue. Her mouth tasted as if something had crawled in there and died. She brushed her teeth for the third time.

The last thing Sara needed was to leave her apartment, but Gina had messaged her too many times during the night.

There was no ignoring her friend's outrage after Sara had slipped away with Sigrid. Gina had made it clear there was no permissible excuse for failing to appear at lunch. The troubled young lawyer frowned at her reflection. Her sophisticated friend would have plenty to say about her seedy appearance.

How did Gina manage to look so elegant and sophisticated every Saturday afternoon? Last night, Sara had learned the truth about Gina's excessive drinking.

⊰ ✿ ⊱

Nero snorted. He ignored the message from Gina, asking where he was. There would be no benefit in letting his cousin know that he was outside Sara's apartment. He glanced over his shoulder. His uncle's car remained parked on the narrow street, and Valentino stood beside the dark SUV. Nero could feel those hard eyes boring into his back as he walked along the cracked path.

Nero considered the rundown six-storey accommodation block. He pushed aside the question of why Valentino already had Sara's address. He was more concerned that Sara had kept her poverty a secret from him for two years. He recalled her recent revelation about giving up her university scholarship. He had not considered what that may have cost her, and made a vow to address that issue today.

His phone chirped three times in quick succession. He glanced at the messages. First, Gina bemoaned Sara's refusal to answer her calls. Next, she insisted Sara had messaged to say she was still drunk – rendering her an easy target. Finally, Gina sent him an entreaty to visit Sara, which included this address.

Nero sent a brief acknowledgement and then silenced his phone. It disappeared into the pocket of the loose pants he had teamed with a short-sleeved silk shirt. These garments would allow him ease of movement, should the situation become difficult. He threw a final glance towards his uncle and squared his shoulders.

Sara's apartment was on the ground floor, facing the street. Nero cut across the patchy lawn, aiming for her door. He could see no witnesses, but he wanted to gain quick access. Valentino was right – if Nero had taken charge last night, this risky visit would be unnecessary. Sara should not have left the restaurant without him.

Nero grimaced. Gina's displeasure over the young lawyer's escape had been dramatic. In hindsight, it was inevitable that Gina's plan would fail. From the opening round of the drinking game, his cousin had used the wrong strategy. Those bullying tactics would never have worked. But even now, Gina refused to concede defeat. She still thought she held a winning hand.

Nero considered Sara's possible response to him visiting without an invitation. Last night, there had been glimpses of her stubborn independence. The object of his desires had proven herself an admirable and worthy opponent. After that first powerful revelation, her remaining answers were brief and impersonal. At every opportunity, she met Gina and her cronies head-on, defeating them soundly. He did not expect her to yield to him today without an argument. But whether he could rely solely on his position of power in her life to control the outcome remained to be seen.

A knock sounded at the door. Sara had no time for visitors. It was already twelve-thirty and she had yet to order a taxi. Where was her phone? Distracted, she picked up her high heels as she went to the entrance. The security chain hung loose, but at least she had flicked the deadbolt when she arrived home. Her ground-floor apartment was in a disreputable neighbourhood. She glanced behind her – there was nothing worth stealing. Except, her laptop—

Where was her laptop? Then she remembered she had left it in her office. Her file folders were safely locked in Nero's car. She sighed. Monday would be soon enough to retrieve them.

Sara sagged against the wall beside the door.

Fake Testimony

ɛʊ ☼ ɔʒ

*Matthew 12:36 - On the day of judgment
everyone will have to account
for every idle word spoken.*

ɛʊ ☼ ɔʒ

There was no response to his knock. Nero counted to ten, focusing on his breathing. "Open the door," he said.

As the moments stretched, Nero glanced towards the street. He grimaced; his uncle was on his way. They had argued about whether Nero could complete this mission alone. His uncle favoured a more heavy-handed approach. The neighbours might overlook one visitor, but two strangers outside a young woman's door? Especially if the larger one began breaking down her door.

Determined to avoid that complication, Nero listened at the door. Finally, the sound of a deadbolt shifting rewarded his patience. He dismissed Valentino with a signal. Nero could breathe again once his uncle began to retreat.

The door remained closed. Nero grasped the doorknob, testing its resistance. The door opened without effort, and he crossed the threshold.

Sara stood transfixed inside the room. Her eyes were bloodshot, and her brow furrowed. Her brown hair fell loose around her shoulders. She seemed more like a bewildered teenager than his talented lawyer. A pair of emerald-green spiked heels was clasped to her bosom. He grinned. When this battle was over, he would discuss her choice of shoes. But for now, he was content to feast his eyes.

Sara made a small sound and her legs folded under her.

With one arm, Nero caught the slender woman and held her close. He pushed the door closed with the other hand. After activating the deadbolt, he slipped the security chain into place.

He held her lightly, impatient for her recovery. Then she surprised him. Her transition from dazed helplessness to defending herself was instantaneous.

"What are you doing here?" she cried, shoving him away from her. She held those shoes like a shield before her.

Instinctively, Nero reached for the spiked heels. He prepared to wrestle them from her hands.

But as soon as his fingers brushed against her hand, she yielded them to him. Sara retreated around a sagging sofa. Apart from a round wooden table and a single chair, this was the main furniture in the room. He stood between her and the door, and there was nowhere to hide in this small space.

Her eyes shone with defiance. "I didn't invite you here, and I-I w-want you to... go."

These words were a timely reminder that Nero must exercise care. He could not afford to respond to her challenge with force. He focused on Uncle Valentino's advice not to let his rising passion override the first part of their plan. Denying himself easy pleasure was essential if he wanted a more lasting reward.

Hiding his desire, Nero softened his stance, placing the shoes near the wall. He held up his empty hands. "I surrender." He must prove himself trustworthy to win her heart. Only then would his fantasies have a chance to become reality.

Sara watched him warily.

"You don't really want me to go," Nero said. He gestured towards the kitchen bench that flanked the open-plan room. "Be a good girl and put the kettle on."

Sara blinked at him, her head tilted in challenge. "This *is my* home. You can't tell me what to do here."

"You're correct. I should get what I need for myself." He crossed to the counter, activated the kettle, and then started opening cupboards.

"What are you doing?" Sara asked, coming closer.

Nero produced from his pocket a plastic-wrapped sachet filled with moistened leaves. He placed it on the counter beside him. "This, my dear, is a rescue mission."

The suspicion in her eyes melted as he maintained his distance. Yet she waited until steam was rising from the kettle before she opened the bag. She sniffed at the contents before she touched a fingertip to a droplet on the inside of the bag. After licking her finger, she screwed up her face. "How is this soggy teabag supposed to help?"

Nero knew he had won, but he kept the smile to himself. "This is Uncle Valentino's secret hangover cure – a special blend of exotic material from the jungles of Asia. He's an expert in the treatment of morning-after-blues."

"The headache isn't that bad."

"No judge or jury would believe your testimony, sweetheart." He removed the sachet from her hand and dropped it into a clean coffee mug. Then he opened a jar of honey and spooned sticky syrup over the sachet. "Excess alcohol is wreaking havoc with your mind. It's also warped your judgement, or you wouldn't want to wear those shoes when you can barely stand."

He poured hot water into the mug, stirring vigorously before discarding the spoon. He carefully lowered the vessel to rest in the sink. "You're about to find out why Gina seldom suffers from a hangover. Come here and inhale these fumes. I'm going to drape this tea towel over your head so that you get the maximum benefit."

Sara edged closer. She leaned over the steaming cup and sniffed. As he predicted, her eyes began to stream. She coughed as the heady aroma swept up her nose and deep into her airways.

Nero was ready. He pounced, pressing a hand to her back as he draped the fabric over her head. She tried to withdraw. He wrapped his arms around her, blocking her with his tall frame. This position trapped her hands against the counter. If she had been wearing her heels, she might have done him some damage as her bare feet kicked at his shins.

"I'm sorry, sweetheart, but the first time is always a shock, and you can't afford to miss out on these opening breaths. That's why I'm restraining you. All you can think about is how the fumes are burning your airways. But soon you will start to feel much better. Your head should start clearing immediately. If you promise to keep inhaling the steam, I can release you."

Nero matched his words with the corresponding action. Taking a calculated risk, he withdrew to the wooden table. Sara lifted the fabric, her face blotchy as she studied him through her tears. Her hand pressed against her chest as she struggled to catch her breath.

"That medicine works quickly," he said. "But don't let too much steam escape."

Sara huffed and puffed as she stared at him. She leaned against the counter, with her back towards the offending potion.

He silently started counting. One... two.... three... He calculated how long he could afford to delay. The head-covering must be in place before he reached forty. He did not want to use another restraining hold he had learned from Valentino when he was young.

Fourteen.... fifteen... His hands ached to take control. On his sixteenth birthday, his uncle promoted him from among the crowd of witnesses. He had remained an active participant in his female cousins' similar rites-of-passage. He had an abundance of cousins, and half a lifetime of experience dealing with their preliminary panic and confusion. Nero was confident Sara's resistance would be easy to manage.

Twenty... twenty-one... twenty-two... He remembered the last girl who had given him any trouble. That was his first encounter with Gina. It marked the beginning of their ten-year love-hate relationship. He forced his clenched fist open. He wouldn't be in this awkward situation if Gina hadn't meddled.

Thirty... thirty-one... The lawyer glanced at his watch. On that occasion, Valentino had taken charge of the drunken eleven-year-old. Her violent outrage had shocked the other girls. Yet their uncle treated her aggression as nothing more than a minor inconvenience. Nero swallowed. If he didn't send his uncle a message soon, Sara might face a similar intervention.

What would happen if his forceful relative knocked at her door? Nero studied Sara, making contingency plans. She sniffed, and a series of rasping little breaths marked a distinct change in her attitude. Her hand swiped at her tears as she drew herself to her full height and stared at him.

"Are you in control of your emotions now?" he asked her.

She nodded.

"And your headache is easing?"

The corners of Sara's mouth twitched.

Nero shrugged, allowing his amusement to show. "I told you the truth, and you know what you have to do. Stop being stubborn. I only want what is best for you."

With a sigh, she hunched over the sink, draping the cloth over her head.

The minutes passed. Nero alternated between studying her, and monitoring the countdown on his phone. The display dipped below the sixty-second mark. A surge of adrenalin rushed through his body. He managed his breathing until his excitable body no longer gave him concern.

This was not an opportunity for Nero to let down his guard. He shook off the tension in his shoulders and undid the top buttons on his shirt, to further free up his movement. As soon as she finished with the steam treatment, he must make Sara drink the contents of the mug. Normally, the potion was an innocuous beverage. But the heat had activated the *extra* ingredients Valentino had supplied. That was why Nero needed the sweet syrup. There was a distinct odour in the air, and the tip of his tongue tingled. He was thankful he had taken the antidote.

"Keep your head covered," Nero said, pushing himself from the table. "The timer's about to sound. You have to drink the whole brew, but after one sip I expect a revolt. You might even try to spill the rest. I can't permit that mistake."

Sara responded as he predicted. She spun towards him as she threw off the towel. He was ready with his arms.

Nero crushed her head to his chest to muffle her complaints. "Keep quiet," he said, assuming the tone he adopted at work. "I'm disappointed with your reaction. I've already proven I'm trustworthy. Take a moment to consider what might have happened. What if someone else had come upon you, too drunk to take care of yourself?"

After Nero spoke, her body shuddered violently, and she stopped fighting him. He pressed the mug into Sara's hands, wrapping his fingers over hers to ensure she didn't drop it.

Sara stared at the drink, then back to him.

"I don't want to force you," he said, no hint of his earlier smile. "You're a clever girl, and I know you will make the right decision." He said nothing more, waiting for his words to find their mark. There should be enough of the powerful drug in the steam to make her more receptive to his instructions.

She gazed at him as she took a big sip. A moment later, she gagged, and her cheeks bulged. Nero forced her jaw shut. She shuffled back until there was nowhere to go, tears in her eyes.

"Trust me," he whispered, holding her head rigid while he stroked her throat. It took a few moments for his fingers to find the right pressure point. He activated her swallow reflex. "The first mouthful is the worst."

When her whole body jerked, he knew he had achieved his purpose. He stopped massaging her neck and released his grip on her chin.

Sara closed her eyes, gasping for air as he held her upright. When her breathing quietened, she stared at him. "H-how did you m-make me swallow?"

Nero offered her the cup again. "Shall I help you with the remainder?"

"No!" With a quick action, Sara drained the contents.

He loosened his grip, and she lurched towards the tap for a long drink of water.

Objection Overruled

ॐ ☼ ॐ

*Exodus 6:6b WEB - I will redeem you with an outstretched arm,
and with great judgments.*

ॐ ☼ ॐ

Sara trembled with indignation. It was only a short distance to the door. She fumbled with the chain. "I – I want you t-to leave."

Nero dropped onto the sagging sofa, his smile unwavering. "Before I leave, we have to talk. Come and sit beside me."

"There's nothing you have to say that I want to listen to," Sara said. Yet her feet were halfway towards him before she dug in her heels. Her heart skipped, leaping like a lamb loose in a meadow. The lethargy and headache were gone, but in their place was a peculiar restlessness. A warm tingling spread throughout her, all the way to her fingers and toes. It came with an overwhelming desire to seek comfort and reassurance. And from the very man who had unsettled her.

Beads of sweat appeared on her brow. She wiped her arm across her face. Retreating towards the wall, she muttered, "I'm hot."

He only smiled as he gazed at her.

What was he thinking? "Why are you looking at me like that?" she asked, flapping her hands at him. "I-I have to meet Gina for lunch, and I'm – I'm going to be late. She has enough to nag me about already."

"She'll keep quiet when I tell her you've given me my prize."

"I'm – I'm not going to... umm... to give you... anything."

He laughed. "Then we both have a problem."

Sara frowned, as a warm glow ignited in her chest in response to his amusement. A thought flittered across her mind, but it eluded her. "What problem?"

"Gina's not known for her patience," Nero said, rising from the sofa. He paused to retrieve her shoes. "My cousin created many opportunities for you to throw yourself at me, and yet my arms remain empty."

Sara stared at the shoes he offered her. Why was he grinning like that? She snatched them from him, dropping them to the floor.

Nero continued speaking. "Gina keeps coming up with new plans. This morning, she asked Uncle Valentino for a special potion. She is searching for something that will lower your inhibitions. You're supposed to give me everything I want."

"A magic potion isn't going to make me do that," Sara said, trying to sound convincing. Her eyes watched his lips, hungry for his reply. Her breath caught in her throat as a sudden compulsion to kiss him popped into her mind.

"Which is why I'm here," Nero said, with a tantalising smile. "Sooner or later, Gina is going to find something that works. Given her recent luck, there's a danger you will find yourself in bed with the wrong man. Last night, you could have ended up with either Perry or Leroy."

"You wouldn't let that happen," Sara said, troubled at the thought of other hands embracing her. She touched his arm and gazed into his dark eyes. "You promised to keep me safe."

He shook his head with regret in his eyes. "I can't protect you if you don't let me know what you're planning. Last night, you sneaked away with that stranger. You said you were going to the restroom."

"She saw me home safely. But I promise not to do that again."

"Gina has also made a promise," Nero said, taking possession of her restless hand. "She's determined to get us together. You have to convince her that you've slept with me today, or there's no telling what she might try."

"I'm not going to lie to my friend."

"I know," Nero said, shaking his head. "Which is why I've taken drastic measures. You needed to recognise what it feels like when someone administers the kind of drug she wants to use."

"Is that why I'm feeling so weird?" she cried, backing away. "I trusted you."

‽ ☼ ⁜

Nero maintained a calm distance. He must be patient and choose the right moment. Confusion raced across Sara's face as she wrestled with her options. She glanced towards the door and then back at him.

"Consider what is happening here," Nero said. "Am I taking advantage of you? Have I abused you? I have had plenty of opportunities. You can feel the drugs taking effect, but I haven't laid a hand on you except to make you swallow the hangover cure. I made sure you were sober and alert. And I'm not abandoning you until you've fully recovered."

He watched her absorb those words, and her attitude towards him softened.

Sara sighed. She brushed the hair from her eyes. "I'm supposed to be meeting Gina."

"You could still meet with her," Nero said. "She won't know what you've taken. If she notices anything strange with

125

your behaviour, she will assume you're still drunk. I promise not to leave you, and you're safe with me."

Her whole being exuded gratitude.

"Speaking of Gina," Nero said, "I'm surprised she hasn't phoned you to ask where you are." He brought out his phone. "I've had to put mine on silent."

Sara frowned at his phone and examined her empty hands. "My phone!" She rushed towards the only other door and threw it open.

He followed her, pausing in the doorway of her tiny bedroom. Sara seemed to have forgotten him. She knelt beside an unmade single bed, wrestling with the fallen bedclothes. His chest pounded in anticipation. He surveyed the remainder of the room. Shoes spilled from a small closet, and an open drawer revealed a glimpse of colourful lace. This must be a testament to her earlier drunken indecision about what to wear. Through another doorway, he glimpsed a tiled bathroom. He cleared his throat to confirm his presence.

Sara glanced at him, before continuing her search. She thrust her head beneath the bed. Her torso wriggled further from view, her skirt creeping high. He admired her legs.

"Found it!" her voice cried from under the bed. "I'm turning it on now. Gina kept messaging me, so I switched it off."

After making that declaration, she remained in place. He could hear the phone beeping and unintelligible muttering. His confidence increased, and he ventured into the room. She remained half-hidden beneath the bed. His eyes lingered on the tempting emerald-green lace that protected her modesty. He stood beside the bed. "Are you stuck under there?"

"Aah!" She banged her head on the bed frame in her haste to come into the open. She rubbed her head, frowning at him. "You startled me."

"That's nothing compared to what you've done to me," Nero said, pointing to her legs. Her skirt was bunched around her hips. He caught a glimpse of her red face before she turned her back on him.

"There's no need to laugh," she cried. One hand wrestled the tight fabric downward. The other fist clutched the rediscovered phone.

"I can't help it," he said. "I'm standing here holding your green shoes. I didn't know whether to believe Gina last night. But now I've seen the evidence for myself."

"Evidence?" She spun to face him, and her hand flew to her mouth. "When did she—"

"You don't remember? You declined to answer Perry's question about the preparations you make for a date. Gina snatched the glass out of your hand and drank it. She told everyone about your underwear fetish."

"I don't have a fetish," Sara cried, snatching her shoes from him. There were tears in her eyes.

He grinned. "It might not be a fetish for you, my love. But from now on, I'll be tempted to find out whether what's under your clothes matches your shoes."

"I can't believe Gina told you."

He continued to tease her. "You stood in court, prim and proper, keeping this secret from me. Don't you want to know what other guilty little pleasures you revealed, sweetheart? No? That gives me an unfair advantage. If you can't remember what you told me, then my confessions must be a mystery to you, too."

She lowered her hand. She was trembling as she slipped on her flat shoes and retrieved a matching green handbag. "I have to check my hair, and then I'm ready to meet Gina. Could you call a taxi?"

He followed her to the bathroom, leaning against the doorframe. "I have a car waiting in the street. Don't worry; I'm not planning to drive. Uncle Valentino brought me. He thought I might need backup, in case I couldn't persuade you to trust me."

ʚϊɞ

Sara puzzled over his explanation, her heart racing.

Nero's reflection spoke from the mirror. "You do trust me, don't you?"

"Of course. Why are you asking—"

Her ringing phone interrupted her thoughts.

"I wish Gina wasn't impatient," Nero said, reaching for her phone.

Sara held up her hand. She waved him out of the doorway, hurrying past. "It's Sigrid. I promised to phone her. She must be worried."

Sara dropped onto the edge of the bed. Nero sat beside her, wrapping an arm around her waist. She swallowed hard.

"Don't talk to her too long," he said, kissing her neck.

Sara took a big breath, swamped by a flood of emotions. "Hi, Sigrid."

"Hey, kid? Are you okay?"

"I'm fine." She sighed. "Nero brought me a herbal cure, and I'm feeling *wonderful* now."

Sigrid's pitch rose. "Is he with you? Sara, don't trust hi—"

"She has to go," Nero said, peeling the phone from her hand. "Don't listen to Sigrid, sweetheart. You won't lie to Gina, so there's only one way to convince her that she doesn't need to drug you."

An Unsuitable Alliance

ॐ ☼ ☾

*Revelation 3:2 - Wake up and rescue what remains of your work,
because God knows you have not finished.*

ॐ ☼ ☾

Oliver drove the *Maximum Security* van past Sara's home address. He continued around the next corner where Piper directed him to change direction by pulling into a driveway. A few minutes later, they re-entered the street.

"Pull up behind that dark SUV," Piper said to Oliver. He included Sigrid in the next instructions. "Both of you, come with me. I'm going to talk to the driver. No matter what happens, neither of you are to say a word."

"I don't know if I can make that promise," Oliver muttered. "It's been forty-five minutes since Nero interrupted Sigrid's call to Sara."

Sigrid leaned across from the rear passenger seat and put a cautioning hand on Oliver's shoulder. She pushed the side door open and waited on the footpath.

"If you refuse to follow my orders," Piper said. "I'll send you back to base and leave you clueless about the girl's fate."

Silently, Oliver climbed from the van to join Sigrid. They followed their employer the short distance to the other vehicle.

The driver wound down the window. "Piper, what a pleasant surprise," the man said, swinging the door outward. This forced Piper into the road to allow the driver to step out. Together they joined the waiting agents at the curb.

Oliver and Sigrid exchanged concerned glances. The towering man was easy to identify from the photos back at headquarters. Piper had not warned them to expect Valentino Horatio here.

The family resemblance between Valentino and Piper was impossible to ignore. Both intimidating men were darkly handsome, with a stubborn set to their jaw. Valentino was a few centimetres taller than Piper. He appeared to have a fifty-kilogram weight advantage. They occupied the pavement like warriors lined up for battle, each a respectful distance from the other.

Valentino's eyes rested on Oliver for a moment before he studied the muscular redhead beside him. The criminal enforcer ran his eyes over her figure as if he was undressing her. Sigrid clenched her fists. Now it was Oliver's turn to administer a hand of caution.

Refocusing his stony gaze on Piper, he remained wary. Valentino smiled, baring his perfect teeth. "You brought reinforcements."

"I need to talk to the girl," Piper said.

"She's not in the mood for conversation," Valentino said, striding towards the apartment. "Nero invited me inside because he wants me to reason with her. Perhaps one of your operatives would be better suited for that task. She's agreed to pack her bags, but my nephew is uncomfortable with her tears."

Oliver saw red. Sigrid's fierce grip on his arm kept him in place. Piper nodded, and his subordinates fell in step with him. The trio followed Valentino to the apartment entrance. At the second knock, the door opened, allowing them to slip inside. The apartment was tiny, furnished with a few pieces of shabby furniture. This was not the kind of place Oliver expected the ambitious young lawyer to reside.

Nero Mariani scanned the new arrivals, while he continued buttoning his silk shirt. His feet were bare. A smug smile spread across the lawyer's face. This left Oliver no doubt about what had happened behind this closed door.

"Where is she?" Piper asked. Nero pointed towards an internal door, and Piper waved Sigrid forward. She knocked on the door and entered without waiting for a reply. The portal closed firmly behind her.

"What's Sigrid doing here?" Nero asked Valentino. "Why wasn't I told this woman works for Piper? And why did one of his agents spirit Sara away last night?"

Both Valentino and Piper declined to respond.

Nero pointed at Oliver. "I know him too. He terrorised Sara one night at the office, and she forwarded his photo to Gina. My cousin teased her because she thought Sara was overreacting."

Oliver became a breathless statue, his back pressed against the door. He could stand no further back in the confined space. The security agent folded his arms across his chest and shut down his emotions.

Nero turned to his uncle. "Why does Piper have a surveillance team following my fiancée?"

Valentino nodded to Piper, disinclined to break his silence.

"My agents encountered Sara Messinger as part of an ongoing operation," Piper said. "I'm not at liberty to divulge further details. But if you want answers to these questions, you should direct them to Enzo."

"My grandfather?" Nero's smile faltered. "Why would he commission you to investigate Sara?"

Piper's stance didn't change, but something shifted in his attitude. Oliver did not need to see his face to know that his eyes were mocking Nero. "Enzo hired me to guarantee your safety."

Nero frowned.

"There was never any intention to interfere with your personal affairs." Piper paused for effect. "But when Sigrid reported a possible crime was taking place, it became my duty to investigate."

"There's no crime," Nero snapped. He raised his voice. "Sara, come out and tell Piper that you gave yourself willingly to me."

Sara emerged from the bedroom, dragging a wheeled bag behind her. She glanced around the room. Nero was beside her in one stride, throwing a possessive arm around her waist. The slim brunette flinched but did not push him away. Instead, she dropped her red-rimmed eyes to the floor. Nero whispered in her ear.

Sara blushed and then she glanced at Piper. Oliver searched her face for the confidence he admired, but it was absent. Her eyes moved beyond Piper towards the door. She stared at Oliver for a few moments. Then she straightened her shoulders and addressed Piper. "I take responsibility for my actions."

Her quiet words stabbed Oliver's heart, but his face remained immobile.

Sara took a deep breath, and her final statement was stronger. "Nero presented me with a persuasive argument. After considering the options, I deferred to his opinion."

Sigrid emerged from the other room dragging a heavier suitcase. She hovered in the background, watching Oliver over Sara's head.

Piper took a step forward, examining Sara's face. "Explain the tears."

"Important decisions are quickly followed by consequences," Sara said. "I'm coming to terms with the cost."

"You're moving?" Piper asked.

Valentino finally spoke, as he reached out and removed the suitcase from Sara's hand. "I've organised an apartment in one of our secure buildings."

Nero shook his head. "She's moving in with me."

"Not if you want the family to accept her as your wife," Valentino said to Nero. "There's a clear distinction between the rights of a wife and a mistress. Take her into your apartment without a marriage covenant, and you label her a prostitute. Do you want to leave her open for abuse?"

Sara flinched, and the atmosphere in the room intensified.

Nero's face darkened with anger. "No-one would dare."

An unpleasant smile appeared on Valentino's face. "You need to talk to your current wife. At least two relatives have approached Zemina since learning about the divorce. They haven't discovered her asking price – yet. But don't underestimate that woman's ability to cause trouble for you. She *is* your legal wife, and she won't appreciate how easily you've replaced her."

"Zemina and I have an agreement," Nero said.

His uncle laughed. "Zemina's a devious woman. I can guarantee she has a contingency plan. She played you for a fool, right from the start. That was self-evident when you needed her support for your partnership application. Your status as her husband should have been enough."

"You know nothing of the complexities of law firm partnerships," Nero said.

"Where were *you* while I oversaw the behind-the-scenes negotiations?" Valentino asked. "Their obscure legal firm operated from rented offices. Now they have title deeds to prime real estate. Your grandfather named his new building in honour of her family. Plus, we invested heavily to elevate their business profile. All because Enzo wanted to boast to his friends that his grandson was an important lawyer."

Valentino did not wait for a reply. He seized Sara's arm, dragging her away from her lover's embrace. The nervous girl hesitated, but when Nero made no move to defend her, she offered no resistance. Valentino lowered his voice and addressed her as if she were the only person in the room. "I am sorry, Sara, that this discussion about family politics occurred in your presence." Then his voiced hardened to match his glare. "You are not to discuss anything you have heard here with anyone unless I am present. Not even Gina. Do you understand?"

Her lips quivered as she whispered, "Yes."

Valentino released her and Sara retreated. Next, he moved his attention to Piper, glancing from Sigrid to Oliver. "Can your agents be trusted? If word of this *discussion* should leak out, I cannot guarantee Sara's safety."

"You don't have to worry about my agents," Piper said, rising to his full height. "But if any harm should come to Sara from you – or Nero – or anyone *associated* with the family, my agents will not be accountable for their actions."

"Is that a threat?" Nero asked.

"No," said Valentino and Piper together.

Oliver held his breath, watching the two determined men exchange chilling smiles.

"Threats are for enemies," Valentino said. "This discussion is about family honour."

Piper spoke again. "It is a rare occasion for Valentino to agree with me. You asked if my words were a threat, Nero. I can assure you that I don't throw idle words around. Consider that a promise."

Treacherous Heart

ɞ ☼ ɞ

*Isaiah 28:26 - God provides teaching
and instruction about the right way.*

ɞ ☼ ɞ

Beneath a tree, Oliver crouched in the nocturnal darkness. His cramped muscles complained about holding this stationary position far too long. He massaged his limbs, before dragging himself upright. Recognising his parents' backyard, he puzzled over the missing memory of his arrival.

While he waited for his circulation to improve, he attempted to calculate the time from the stars. This was more difficult than it should be. Oliver shook his head to clear his thoughts. Now was not the time to analyse his mental state. He tried again, deciding it must be almost midnight.

A rumbling deep within his torso reminded him that he had missed lunch. He glanced towards the house, surprised to see light visible through a chink in the curtains. He stepped onto the manicured lawn. Could he leave here without visiting his family?

That decision would depend on his physical condition. His legs complained about having undertaken an extended and arduous walk. Yet his feet were sound. He nodded. Without making a noise, Oliver headed towards the side gate.

A shadow separated from the veranda as a man stepped out to intercept him. "Are you thinking of leaving, Oliver?" his father asked.

"I didn't know you were there," Oliver said. "I'm sorry to have kept you from your rest."

"Piper rang to ask if you were here," Noah replied. "He tracked you halfway across the city, but there was a black spot in the surveillance network. He wasn't able to pick up your trail. He said you went missing from a place that was a long walk from here."

"I'm going now."

"You can't leave without talking to your mother," Noah said. "She's been baking all evening, while we waited for you to finish your meditation."

"How long have I been here?" Oliver asked as he followed his father towards the house.

"You arrived just as the sun was setting. If I hadn't been watching for you, I would have mistaken you for a shifting shadow."

His father opened the door into the house and studied him from the threshold. Oliver hesitated, waiting for his eyes to adjust to the indoor lights. Heady aromas wafted across the alcove from the kitchen. His stomach rumbled again.

His mother was speaking to someone. Oliver squared his shoulders, preparing to meet whoever Piper had dispatched to collect him. He was familiar with the workplace procedures activated when an agent went missing. He had even been part of a few retrievals. But this was the first time he had been the wayward employee.

Noah stepped into the kitchen, and his mother paused mid-sentence.

"Is he coming in?" Lisa-Jane asked.

Oliver entered the room, his eyes fixed on his mother.

She came around the kitchen bench. After wiping her hands on her apron, Lisa-Jane wrapped him in a firm embrace.

"I'm sorry to have worried you," Oliver said when she released him.

"That's what mothers are for," Lisa-Jane said. "I'd rather you came here than hide somewhere and keep your troubles to yourself. Sit down next to your friend, while I get you some food."

The "friend" rose from her chair, waiting for Oliver to acknowledge her. He stared at the red-haired woman.

"I wasn't expecting to see you here," Oliver said.

"Piper said you'd understand why he sent me," Sigrid replied. "He said you only have yourself to blame for the consequences."

Lisa-Jane delivered a heaped bowl of apple crumble and ice-cream. "What consequences?" she asked.

Sigrid distracted his mother by raising her empty bowl. "That was the best apple crumble I've ever eaten."

Lisa-Jane accepted the bowl with a broad smile. "Would you like another helping?"

Oliver studied the interaction between his mother and his teammate as he ate.

Sigrid laughed, patting her rounded stomach. "I'd love some more, but three helpings was more than enough. Oliver's a lucky man to have a mother who likes to cook. My mother could only offer crackers and cheese if anyone dropped by unannounced."

"You're always welcome, dear," Lisa-Jane said, clearing away the bowl. "Oliver never brings any of his friends home."

He ignored the reprimand, dropping his eyes to his bowl.

"I've already explained," Sigrid said. "We're not friends. We work together."

"Don't discount your significance," Lisa-Jane said, from behind the kitchen bench. She continued tidying the counter as she spoke. "The Lord brought you to work alongside our boy."

Oliver's shoulders tensed, his hand gripping the spoon. His mother's next words might have more destructive power than a hand grenade. He nudged Sigrid with his foot, jerking his head towards the door. Sigrid grinned and shook her head.

Lisa-Jane stilled her hands as a faraway smile lit her face. "Oliver is a kingdom warrior, and he has important work to do. God's hand is always on him, and God has promised to supply him with everything he needs. If you have been assigned to help him, then I'm sure you're part of that provision. Which means the Lord is watching over you, too."

"We have to go," Oliver said, standing as he pushed aside his bowl.

"You're not going anywhere," his father said.

Oliver froze. His father seldom used that tone. He stared at the older man, noticing the lines of tension on his face. Were they signs that the cancer pain was already unbearable? He hung his head, shame adding to his remorse for the inconvenience he had caused.

Noah stood beside his wife. "You can't leave without telling us how we can pray for you in this situation. Sigrid has already said you aren't at liberty to share any details. But clearly, something happened that sent you running for home."

Oliver glanced at Sigrid. She shrugged. He chose his words carefully. He sought enough truth to satisfy them without breaking his promise to Piper.

"One of the people I'm pledged to protect came under the control of an evil man," Oliver said. "And I'm powerless to remedy the situation."

"God always pursues evil men," Lisa-Jane said. "We will pray that he will repent—"

"His repentance will come too late for her," Oliver said. "He…" The agent choked on the words and fell silent. The boiling emotions hidden beneath his self-protective layers unsettled him. He stared at his clenched fists. Sigrid rose, keeping careful watch, a safe distance between them. Oliver held his breath and uncurled his fingers until his hands were limp at his side.

The silence lengthened.

"He what?" Noah asked.

Oliver gazed at his parents. They were embracing each other, a familiar expression of their love. He pushed aside the memory of Sara Messinger leaving the apartment with Nero Mariani. The young woman had glanced at Oliver as she passed, shame and regret written across her face. He considered all the possible accusations he could make about her lover.

Finally, he had his answer. "He's married."

A startled look appeared on his mother's face. Lisa-Jane opened her mouth, but Noah silenced her with the touch of his hand.

"Let the boy leave," his father told her. "We have enough information to guide our prayers."

The parting remarks were brief. Too soon, Sigrid was driving Oliver through the darkened streets in the work van. He was silent, watching the familiar neighbourhood flash past. She tackled each corner with speed. Mentally, he prepared for the coming interview with Piper.

"I like your parents," Sigrid said, as she waited for a traffic light to change.

"You've made a lasting impression," Oliver said, attempting to inject a smile into his voice. "Nobody has ever eaten three serves of apple crumble in a single sitting. My mother will tell all her friends about you."

"What did Piper mean by 'consequences'?" she asked.

"Ask another question," he said, returning to his silent reflection.

Sigrid drove on. At the next intersection, she surprised him by turning left. They were heading away from headquarters. When she turned left again, he guessed their destination. Why was she taking him to his apartment? A dozen more questions pressured him for answers, but he kept his own counsel.

"Your mother knows we're not lovers," Sigrid said. "She studied your reaction when you saw me."

Oliver smiled towards the passing night scene. He watched Sigrid's reflection in the window. "But she'll happily feed you anyway. She hasn't written you off her list of potential daughters-in-law yet."

Sigrid asked about the other names on his mother's list. Oliver filled the remaining journey with anecdotes of the failed matchmaking attempts.

When the van stopped outside his apartment building, he reached for the door. "Thanks for the lift."

"Are you going to stay home?" Sigrid asked. "Piper put an extra watch on Nero. He said he didn't like what happened today any more than you did, but we can't save everyone."

"I know." He stepped onto the footpath and pushed the door closed with an almost inaudible click. He was halfway towards the front entrance when he changed his mind. He retraced his steps.

Sigrid opened the passenger window. "What?"

"You don't have to keep watch."

"I have my orders," she retaliated.

"You told my mother we weren't friends."

"So?" Sigrid asked with a frown.

"I'm going to tell you something which is going to change that." He had her interest now.

"I'm waiting," she muttered, when he didn't begin straight away.

"Turn off your phone," he said. "I don't mind if Piper hears what I have to say, but I want you free to speak openly."

After a moment's hesitation, Sigrid switched off her phone. She waited, impatience growing as the seconds stretched into minutes.

"I made a decision tonight," Oliver said. "I told God I've had enough. I'm not going to run from His plan for my life anymore. I promised to obey Him forever."

"There's no going back from that kind of promise," Sigrid said. "You think these things now, but what if your decision doesn't change anything?"

"I feel different inside," he replied. "I'm still angry and confused, but there's something – Someone – bigger than me at the edge of my mind. It's like God is inside me. In comparison to Him, everything else is less important."

"Even Sara?"

Oliver laughed, shaking his head. "Especially Sara. What do I know about love? I'm angry with Nero, but I also understand his motivation. Maybe what I feel is the same selfish desire to possess her. I don't know that I would have treated her any better if I was presented with a similar opportunity."

For a long moment, Sigrid stared at him through the open window. "You're nothing like Nero. Why did you want me to turn off my phone?"

"Because you know you have the same decision ahead of you. Mum's right. We make a good team, and I'd rather have you on my side than fighting against me."

"You're the one who had the crisis," Sigrid muttered, turning the key in the ignition. The engine roared into life, and suddenly the van tore off into the night. The vehicle raced across the next intersection without pausing. At the furthest junction, the brake lights flashed at the last moment. The van screeched around the corner.

Oliver shook his head and gazed towards the stars. He committed Sigrid into the care of a Higher Authority before heading inside to rest. Tomorrow would be soon enough to deal with the consequences.

Ashamed

ଚ ✿ ଓ

*Romans 12:21 WEB - Don't be overcome by evil,
but overcome evil with good.*

ଚ ✿ ଓ

Sara shuffled her feet. The final morning briefing for the year was nearing an end. She stood with the junior lawyers who worked for Zemina. Nero's determined wife had kept Sara with her team. The female executive had contested that Sara was an attractive asset, previously underutilised. Nero dared not argue with her. With the approval of the remaining executives, Zemina took immediate action.

The first step involved sending Sara to a fashion stylist. Her wardrobe had grown by a dozen outfits. Gone were the dark jackets and skirts, replaced with figure-hugging colourful dresses. The transformation had extended to her hair and makeup. The reflection that greeted her from the mirror each morning was a more glamorous version of herself.

Sara considered her new dress as she listened to Zemina outlining the clients' cases scheduled for court today. When Nero greeted her earlier this morning, he said it was one of his favourites. A glance across the table caught him watching her. He smiled, and she turned her head away to hide her blush. Any concern that Nero might disapprove of her new style vanished after he commandeered all the bills when Gina showed them to him, and commissioned some formal dresses.

To cope with these changes, Sara was practising gratitude. She had plenty to be thankful for. The furnished apartment Valentino provided was light and spacious – more convenient for getting to work. On a fine day, she could walk from home to the office.

And she was happy to spend time with Nero every day. They may no longer work together, but he seemed to know when she was alone in her office. He was careful to be discreet. He also frequently checked in with her by phone.

Valentino cautioned them not to spend time together away from the office. The only permitted exception was when Nero came to Saturday lunch with Gina. With her friend's encouragement, these occasions could last all day...

Sara smiled fondly towards her friend. The recently-appointed personal assistant stood immediately behind their boss, notebook in hand. Gina thrived in her new position. It was a relief that the past tension between the two friends had vanished. Sara knew Valentino had spoken to Gina, who had delivered a quick apology. After that, there had been no further unpleasantness. The twenty-year-old provided invaluable advice as Sara adjusted to her role on Zemina's team.

Around the table, papers shuffled. Zemina's father rose to his feet, wishing everyone a Merry Christmas. Sara smiled as she waited for the room to clear. This Christmas promised to be a great occasion. She had received an early present from Gina. The girl had given her an airline ticket, together with an invitation to go with her to Sydney. Gina was visiting family friends, and her mother had insisted she not travel alone. The two young women would depart on the evening of Christmas Day.

Sara went directly to her desk to work on her cases. She lost herself to her tasks, forgetting to take a break. She paused, light-headed and dizzy. She sighed as she reached for her water bottle.

Gina appeared in the doorway. "Sara, you were on another line, so reception diverted your call to me. Doctor Paris-

Smyth's office has a cancellation, and they can see you at four."

"I don't know a Doctor Paris-Smyth," Sara said, rubbing her forehead. "Are you sure the message was for me?"

"They said something about this being an introductory appointment," Gina said. "Zemina was with me, and she recognised the name. Apparently, there's a six-month waiting list, so maybe you've forgotten. You have been a bit distracted lately."

Sara frowned. "Did they leave a number? I should call and clarify—"

"I wouldn't bother," Gina said. "Zemina's already given me the time off to take you. I'm sure you'll remember what you made the appointment for when you get there. Now get back to work. I don't want you bringing any files with you while we're on holiday."

⁎

Sara stared at the floor directory, transfixed by the revelation. How had she come to have an appointment at *St Elizabeth's Women's Reproductive Health Centre*? Doctor Paris-Smyth's name was at the top of the list of specialists. The third-floor fertility clinic was in a modern building near the Royal Melbourne Hospital.

Her phone pinged with a message. Gina was walking up the front steps after finding a parking space. Sara glanced over her shoulder towards the elevator. She could wait for her friend to arrive. Or she could go in and seek answers.

Wiping her sweaty palms on her skirt, Sara took a deep breath. She stepped towards the glass doors, which swished open automatically. With a pounding heart, she approached the waist-high wooden counter. A middle-aged woman smiled at her entry. She wore 'Margaret' on her nametag.

"I have an appointment," the nervous woman said. "Sara Messinger, to see Doctor Paris-Smyth."

"Ah, yes," said Margaret. "This is your first consultation. I have some forms for you to sign, and a questionnaire that you can complete while you wait." The receptionist laid documents side by side along the counter. Then she paused with her hand near another bank of forms. "Will your husband be joining you today?"

A wave of embarrassment washed over Sara. She grabbed the counter to keep herself steady. "No – not my husband. I'm not married. At least, I won't be until July. I feel like I'm here under false pretences. I don't remember asking for an appointment..."

"Let me look at your referral," Margaret said, tapping her computer keyboard. "I thought so, a pre-matrimonial assessment." The woman smiled politely. "You're not the first bride to attend without knowing why she was here. It's quite common with some old European families. But, usually, the young lady arrives with a family chaperone."

The door behind Sara hummed, and she turned to face Gina. Was she the "family chaperone"? The receptionist must be considering the same question. She waited for Gina to approach.

"Did you see the notice on the wall?" Gina asked. "I can't believe my cousin made this appointment without telling you. I know the family's pressurising him to make babies, but it's premature to book you in for this kind of treatment."

The uneasy feeling which had haunted Sara all day ramped up. The colour drained from her face, and she almost lost her lunch. Sara shook her head. For a brief moment, she suspected Gina's passionate reaction. And even doubted her sincerity.

None of these doubts would have potency if she had phoned Nero before she came.

She closed her eyes and waited for her anxiety to pass. Now that she knew what kind of consultation was ahead, her imagination provided graphic details. She pushed away memories that foretold the embarrassment to come.

The woman behind the counter clicked more buttons. "I'll just check where the account will be sent. Sometimes it's the groom's relatives. Oh – hmm – okay." Margaret frowned. "Is Nero Mariani a relative?"

Sara read the unspoken question in the woman's eyes. She swallowed and forced out the confession. "He's my fiancé. H-his first wife was a patient here."

More button clicking and the professional smile reappeared. "I can see from his file that it has been more than three years since his last assessment. The doctor may require your *fiancé* to attend a follow-up appointment..."

"Serves him right," Gina said, hugging Sara.

Sara forced a smile. "There's a whole heap of paperwork, and I won't be seeing the doctor for ages. Why don't you find a café, and I'll send you a message when I'm ready."

"I don't mind waiting," Gina said, glancing at the documents spread across the counter. She flicked through the questionnaire, and the corners of her mouth twitched. Sara blushed and glanced at the receptionist.

"There are some tests to organise before the doctor sees Ms Messinger," Margaret said to Gina. "I need her to sign here to confirm that she attended the appointment. And here, and here, to give permission for the pathology tests. And here, to release the results to our team of consultants..."

The young lawyer began to sign.

Gina peered over Sara's shoulder. "This will keep you busy for a while. If you're sure you'll be okay on your own, I'll take your advice. I'm sure you don't want me eavesdropping while you're talking about your *intimate* secrets."

As suddenly as she arrived, Gina was gone.

Half an hour later, Sara perched on the edge of an examination bed. She wore nothing but a floral surgical gown that barely covered her thighs. The form filling had taken a long time. Then a nurse collected a urine sample and six vials of blood. These went to the in-house pathologist for analysis.

A uniformed nurse knocked, delivering coloured documents to the desk before disappearing again. The doctor entered a few minutes later. He strode towards her, offering his hand. He was a small man of indeterminate age, wearing a grey suit and tie. His hair was dark, but his eyebrows were grey. A pair of round spectacles perched on the end of his nose.

"Ms Messinger," he said. "May I call you Sara?"

She nodded, her voice refusing to work.

"I'm Doctor Paris-Smyth. Now, it's understandable for you to be nervous, but I will make this as easy for you as I can. First, I'll take a look at your notes, and these test results..." He sat at the table and concentrated on the paperwork. After a few minutes, he spun his chair towards her. "Congratulations, Sara. You are a fortunate young woman, having done a perfect job falling pregnant without my help."

"What?" Sara gasped, almost falling off the bed. She leaned back and clutched the side of the bed. "I can't be pregnant. The wedding isn't until July." She burst into tears and covered her face.

"Wedding dates can always come forward," the doctor said, passing her a box of tissues. "Or you can wait until after the child is born and have your big celebration. Take a few moments to compose yourself while I explain the results. And then I will examine you..."

ℬ ✿ ℭ

Nero was dressing for dinner when his phone rang.

"I need to see you," Sara said, without waiting for him to speak.

"Can it wait until tomorrow?" he asked, wrestling with his formal tie. "You know the family are gathering for our official Christmas dinner tonight."

"No, it can't wait!" Sara cried.

Nero swore. He paused, halfway into his black tuxedo. He closed his eyes and counted to ten. Was she weeping? "Calm down, and take some deep breaths."

He took his own advice, confident that she would obey him.

"Where are you?" he asked. *Was there time to meet Sara?* His great-grandmother detested tardiness. He had already earned her displeasure with his impending divorce.

"I'm walking across the promenade bridge," Sara said. "I can see the main entrance to your building now. If you come out, I won't keep you long. I only need a few minutes of your time."

"I'm on my way," he said.

"I'll wait on the bench closest to the bridge." She sighed and then terminated the call.

Nero searched his contact list. When Gina answered, he demanded, "Where did you take Sara this afternoon?"

Gina replied without hesitation. "Zemina said you asked her to organise everything. From your tone, I'm guessing I should have confirmed that with you."

A cold chill washed through Nero. "What did you organise?" He remembered Valentino's warning. What trouble had Zemina visited upon him today?

"Remember the fertility clinic Zemina went to a few years ago?" Gina asked.

Uncomfortable recollections of their visits to *St Elizabeth's* stole his voice. Had Zemina sent Sara to face an intrusive examination on her own? Hatred boiled inside him, but he maintained his silence.

"Did Sara phone you?" Gina asked. "I was going to pick her up, but she sent me a message to say she'd changed her mind. Is everything okay?"

"No, everything is *not* okay," he snapped.

From the elevator, Nero placed a call to Valentino.

"Yes?" his uncle asked.

"Sara's outside on the promenade. She's hysterical. I need you to bring me something to calm her down."

"Why is she hysterical?"

"Zemina sent her to a fertility clinic," Nero said. "Sara thinks I'm responsible."

"Wait for me at the front entrance," Valentino said, and the phone fell silent.

Five minutes later, Valentino stepped from the elevator. He strode across the plush carpet. "I'm coming with you," Valentino said, not pausing to permit Nero to argue. The pair traversed the crowded promenade, drawing attention with their formal attire.

"There she is," Nero said. He almost didn't recognise her. She was wearing a concealing jacket, with the hood pulled over her head. He had never seen her wear anything like that before. His feet hurried towards her. His uncle matched every stride.

"Let me do the talking," Valentino said. Nero opened his mouth to protest, and his uncle took hold of his arm. The pressure from the older man's fingers cut off the circulation. Nero grimaced from the intense pain. He nodded, and his uncle released him.

Valentino stepped in front of Sara, and the girl leapt to her feet. Nero was quick to move where she could see him. She leaned towards him before changing her mind. Her slender figure sagged onto the bench.

"Nero had nothing to do with the doctor's visit," Valentino said. "You have my word that Zemina will pay for the trouble she has caused you."

Sara snuffled, rubbing her eyes on her sleeve.

Valentino reached into his pocket and produced a small vial. "I've brought you something—"

The colour drained from the girl's face. She wrapped her arms around her abdomen. "No!"

Valentino smiled, closing his hand over the vial. Without another word, he began walking back towards *Raphael Towers*.

"Where are you going?" Nero asked, torn between following his uncle and finding out why Sara was here.

"I'm going to talk to your grandfather," Valentino said, pausing beside him. He placed his hand on Nero's shoulder. "I must offer him your excuses for being late for dinner."

Nero stared at his uncle's hand. "Why am I going to be late?"

Valentino slapped him on the shoulder, almost knocking him off his feet. "You're always impatient, and now your timing is off. Take Sara back to her apartment. You'll find out soon enough. Then, join us when you can. And don't worry, I will take care of everything."

Nero went to Sara, viewing her with fresh eyes. His uncle had given him a clear directive. The girl's need for comfort took priority above his family obligations. His heart swelled with gratitude. This could only mean that his uncle continued to approve of their relationship.

Sara stared after Valentino, tears streaming down her face. "I'm sorry. I didn't want to ruin your family evening."

The lawyer took her in his arms and held her close. "Sweetheart, you are my family. Soon everyone will know that you belong to me. Then nothing will come between us. Now tell me, my love, what has happened to distress you?"

With her head pressed against his jacket, he almost missed her words.

"I'm pregnant."

The world stopped spinning. Ecstasy exploded in his mind, and his heart pounded in his chest. He lost all sense of where he was, forgot how to breathe. His lips claimed hers with a kiss. When he surfaced for air, he looked at her, marvelling at how beautiful she was, despite her tears. The mother of his child...

He placed one hand over her flat abdomen, marvelling that there was new life within. The bitter, barren years wasted on Zemina faded to insignificance. It had taken one moment of passion with this sweet woman to fulfil his destiny.

He sighed with satisfaction, hugging her to him. His first instinct was to gather her into his arms and carry her into his apartment. There he would reaffirm his paternity.

But then he remembered that his divorce was not final until June. This was more than a small inconvenience. His heart faltered, and he squeezed her tight.

At that moment he understood her heartbreak. His uncle was right, the timing was off. Then he remembered Valentino's parting words. Everything settled into place in his universe.

When had there been an occasion where his uncle made an unfulfilled promise? Valentino's word was incontrovertible. Nero kissed her again. "Don't worry about anything, my love. Uncle Valentino has promised to take care of everything, and he never fails."

An Unwanted Gift

 જી ✿ ૯૩

*Isaiah 29:24b WEB - Those who grumble
will receive instruction.*

 જી ✿ ૯૩

"What couldn't wait?" Oliver asked, climbing into the rear compartment of the *Maximum Security* van. It was twilight on Christmas Eve. The vehicle raced away with the door still open. Oliver slammed the door and hung on to the grab handle. "You said I could have Christmas with my parents."

"Put on your body armour and stop complaining. We will be there in five minutes, sooner if not for this traffic. If everything goes to plan, you can be back before Santa Claus arrives."

Piper drove like a maniac, flashing lights and a blaring siren. A pulse of intense energy swept through Oliver. There were no other passengers, and a pile of first-responder gear slid off the bench seat towards him.

"You were the closest agent with the right training," Piper said. "I don't plan on getting blown up for Christmas."

Oliver wedged himself between the seats. He pulled a thick shirt over his *Jesus is the Reason* tee-shirt. This was a gift from his mother. He sent a prayer heavenward. If he was going to die this evening, he wanted to be ready. Next, he wrestled into the heavy tactical vest. "Is Jenny meeting us there with a full team?"

"No."

The reinforced protective trousers were too long. Oliver adjusted the length. He had a customised uniform back at base, but Piper always carried spare kit in every van. His hands fumbled with the laces on his combat boots as he processed the information. "So it's just you and me?" He swallowed a lump in his throat. This was Oliver's first deployment on home soil that required full body armour.

Piper laughed. "You, me, and Romano. Which is why I'm in a hurry. I told him to wait until I got back, but he'll want to deal with the bomb himself."

"There's a bomb at Romano's?" Oliver reviewed recent intelligence reports. He had never met this legendary client, but he knew all the rumours. Romano was reportedly a giant, both physically and in intelligence. He had defeated all challengers in a New South Wales prison, where he served a lengthy sentence. Since his Melbourne arrival, he had remained fiercely independent. And he was extremely wealthy. Romano's main business premises were located in the next suburb from the neighbourhood where Oliver's parents lived.

Piper's family had been trying to gain leverage over Romano for the past five years. Until now, they had been unable to buy this businessman's cooperation. And their intimidation tactics had proven ineffective.

"A vehicle arrived at his service station after the manager left," Piper said. "The driver walked away. Romano was there within two minutes with his dog. The electronic sensor I gave him confirmed what that canine's nose told him."

"The bomb didn't detonate immediately?" Oliver surmised.

"It is a warning," Piper said. "They want him to know that they can take him out whenever they want. And it's a message for me – they weren't to know that I was with him when they put their plan into action."

"You were there!" Oliver said. "Then why did you come for me?"

Piper laughed again. "I need someone I can trust to liaise with Romano while I'm away on my next overseas mission. This is the perfect opportunity to see how the two of you work together."

"Jenny will be angry that you've passed her over in favour of me," Oliver remarked. "What makes me a better candidate?"

"Romano doesn't trust women," Piper said, running a red light. "Check your gear. We're almost there."

Oliver internalised his thoughts, silently praying as he checked his equipment. He focused on what he knew about Romano and prayed for that man's safety. He added a prayer for the businessman to stand firm against the criminals seeking to intimidate him. As an afterthought, he added a petition about Romano's attitude to women.

Piper said this was a warning. Next time, the criminal opposition might not be so considerate. Oliver would prefer to have Jenny called out next time. She was the demolition expert.

೫ ✿ ೞ

Oliver surveyed the location. The road ran through an industrial area, parallel to the train tracks. Signs proclaimed a nearby train station and access roads for a major shopping centre. Oliver knew the area but it had been more than a decade since he had visited.

The multi-level shopping centre stretched ahead on the right-hand side. On the left, a long concrete wall blocked his view of what used to be a vacant lot. Piper joined a slow-moving queue turning left into *Romano Car Park and Service Station*. A car further ahead of them rammed on the brakes, and the line came to a halt.

"Get out and walk," Piper told Oliver. "Romano will be at the rear of the service station. I'll meet you there."

Oliver buckled on his helmet and opened the door. He ignored comments about his protective gear from people he passed as he began his patrol. His hands were uncomfortably empty.

Slow moving lanes of traffic diverted left and right around the service station in the centre of the busy car park. There were hundreds of civilians: couples, family groups, and the occasional loner. The businesses in the multi-level shopping centre across the road must be busy.

The bomber had picked a deadly location for his attack. Yet Piper seemed unconcerned. Oliver shook his head, fighting a sense of impending doom.

The covered concourse that housed the fuel bowsers was empty. Where was the abandoned car? The pounding of his boots reminded him of past missions on foreign soil.

Oliver did a quick assessment of what lay between him and the shopping centre across the road. A footpath ran beside four lanes of traffic. A massive wall bordered the car park. To the right loomed a warehouse bearing the same red *Romano* logo across the windowless lower storey. This must be where Romano operated his mechanics' workshop. It reminded the security agent of a warzone bunker.

Ahead, a large black tow truck blocked his progress.

Oliver hesitated, his senses overloaded. The pounding in his veins matched his intensified awareness of the surroundings. The last time he experienced this weird sensation, he had a revelation from God. He glanced around, half expecting to see a heavenly vision.

Instead, a messenger from hell stepped into view. Oliver froze.

Do not judge a man by his outward appearance.

The internal voice was impossible to ignore. Oliver blinked, and the mirage resolved itself into human form. He had previously seen Romano's photo, but nothing had prepared him for the reality.

The approaching man greeted Oliver with a fierce scowl. He wore black mechanic's overalls, the sleeves cut away at the shoulders. A necessary accommodation for the bulging arm muscles. Except for his face, every centimetre of bare skin was heavily tattooed. A ragged scar above one eyebrow hinted at the massive man's violent past.

Romano moved fast, approaching with clenched fists.

Oliver held his ground, meeting the scowl with a neutral expression. The giant's dark eyes flickered with interest. Romano continued past him, and Oliver glanced over his shoulder. The *Maximum Security* van had crawled into view, still stuck in traffic.

Oliver strode past the truck and approached a reinforced metal gate in the wall. The open gap was wide enough for two men – or one giant – to enter. Oliver entered a flood-lit uncovered yard large enough to park a dozen vehicles with room to spare. There he encountered a snarling Rottweiler. The savage black and tan dog threatened to deliver a more intense welcome than its owner had given.

Preparing to defend himself, Oliver looked for some kind of weapon. He prayed for guidance. His protective gear was not designed to deal with animal attacks. This unpredictable mission was starting to resemble one of Jenny's infamous challenges. It delivered one danger after another.

"Sit!"

Oliver jumped as Romano shouted from behind him. The dog settled close to his feet. A wagging tail suggested the immediate danger was over. He leaned down, stroking the dog's head while he continued to examine his surroundings. The concrete walls were thicker than he expected. There were sandbags stacked in towers along the perimeter. Towards the rear of the compound, the bare base frame of a car – the chassis – sat on raised metal ramps.

Piper came from behind Oliver and approached the metal skeleton. "You were busy while I was gone."

"You didn't say I had to leave it how I found it," Romano growled, "and I wanted a better look at the explosives. You were right about the digital counter." He pointed to the relevant section through a gap in the chassis. The bomb was secured near the rear axle. "It isn't set to detonate until after ten. They left me plenty of time to drive it across town and park it near one of their buildings."

"I've already advised against that," Piper said.

Oliver shuffled his feet away from the dog to take a closer look. Glowing red numerals continued to decrease on the display. His hand twitched, and he mentally rehearsed how he would terminate the countdown.

"We can contain the damage here," Piper said, "but there's no guarantee what might happen if you moved it a greater distance. Injure innocent people and the authorities won't care whether you made the bomb."

"I have to send the bombmakers a message not to mess with me," Romano said, thumping the nearby wall. "It's only a small explosive charge, and we have plenty of time. I'm sure we could find a suitable location to minimise the damage."

Oliver circled the bare metal frame with the dog at his heels. Romano had efficiently broken the vehicle into its basic components and then removed them to a nearby tidy stack. All that remained of this early model Mitsubishi sedan was the lower chassis and two wheel-less axles. While Oliver continued his inspection, the two imposing men argued.

If the counter was accurate, the bomb was safe for another two hours. Long after the shopping centre closed for the evening. Oliver was uncomfortable with the delay – this did not fit the typical urban terrorist profile.

When there was a pause in the discussion, Oliver spoke. "Are you sure you know who sent this bomb? It's out of character for Valentino Horatio – when he uses explosives, things always blow up."

"I agree it's not Valentino," Piper said. "He flew to Thailand with the other senior family members yesterday. He'd want to be here to deal with Romano's countermeasures. This is someone trying to make a name for themselves."

"Someone like Nero?" Oliver immediately regretted his suggestion. Piper already thought him prejudiced against the lawyer.

Piper frowned. "No. Nero's position in the family is secure. Besides, you've found no evidence he has any connection with this side of their organisation. I doubt he knows Romano exists."

"I could change that," Romano snarled.

Oliver nodded. "Can I defuse the bomb while you two argue about what to do next?"

Romano pointed towards a multi-drawer trolley. "Help yourself to whatever equipment you need."

After a quick inspection, Oliver selected the necessary tools. He had one more question. "Why did you dismantle the car?"

"Piper made me promise not to drive the bomb away," Romano said. "But he didn't say I couldn't make it easier to access the explosives."

Oliver lowered himself to gain access to the undercarriage. He lay on his back and dragged himself closer to the bomb. He was not used to seeing light above him while he worked.

"What do you propose?" Piper asked.

"Besides deactivating the timer, and removing the detonators?" Oliver asked, examining the wires. "Do I have to do everything? You two could come up with something while I risk my life."

"But you have an idea," Romano said. The dog took his interest as permission to wriggle its way under the chassis. The animal lay down beside Oliver, and they stared at each other for a few seconds. "Fifi's a good judge of character," Romano continued. "So I'm prepared to listen to whatever you say."

While Oliver resumed his task, he tried to dismiss the watchful dog with the unlikely name. "Piper said this is a warning," Oliver said, taking his eyes off the bomb to see how his words were received. "That means someone will be in touch to negotiate terms."

"No terms, no negotiation," Romano said, folding his arms across his chest. "I'll concede nothing."

The dog raised its head, a throaty growl as if to warn Oliver not to anger the owner. The agent soothed the animal by stroking its head.

Oliver held his breath as he snipped wires: one – two – three. That task completed, he scrambled out from under the car. "Not even a counteroffer?"

"What did you have in mind?" Romano asked.

ഇ ✿ ോ

An hour later, Oliver sat in the central jump seat of Romano's tow truck cabin. On one side, Piper drove with remarkable care, heading towards the *Raphael Towers* riverside development. In the passenger seat, Romano held a length of metal pipe, one end balanced between his legs. He seemed unconcerned about the explosives and wiring he held against his chest.

The well-lit forecourt of the *Renaissance* nightclub compensated for the disappearing sun. Piper flashed the truck indicators. Then he parked the truck in the nightclub's celebrity drop-off point. Two men wearing red and gold uniforms hurried forward.

"You can't park here," one of them shouted at Piper as he opened the door.

"Try and stop us," Romano growled, passing the upper end of the pipe to Oliver as he stepped down from the cab. There was a commotion from the rear of the truck. Lots of shouting, and a grinding motor, followed by rattling chains and a metallic crash. Oliver could not turn to look behind him because he was holding the defused bomb. He imagined the scene as the disassembled car dropped into the exclusive location.

A few minutes later, Piper and Romano returned to the cabin. Oliver caught a glimpse of the frantic activity behind them as they merged back into the traffic.

"Next stop," Piper said, turning into an underground parking garage around the corner. He commandeered the reserved security bay and climbed down again. This time, Oliver scrambled across the driver's seat and ran around to wait for Romano to open the door. He temporarily accepted the dangerous burden to enable the giant to exit the vehicle.

"I'll stay with the truck," Piper said, passing Oliver a plastic card. "Activate your phone, so I can record any conversation. I'll access the security cameras from here, and I'll phone Romano when company is coming your way."

Oliver opened a map of the building on his phone. He went directly to the *Raphael Towers* reception desk.

"Tell Nero Mariani that Sebastian Romano is here to see him," Oliver told the young woman behind the desk. "Mr Romano will wait for him in his grandfather's office."

He didn't wait for a reply, leading Romano towards the bank of elevators. Oliver used the card Piper gave him, and the lift delivered them to the second floor. As they entered Enzo Horatio's palatial office, a grandfather clock chimed the ninth hour.

The ceiling lights flashed on, and the pair surveyed the scene. Oliver's entire apartment could fit into this one room. Romano strode to the polished wooden desk and swept the surface clean, then slammed the metal bar onto the desk. Almost as an afterthought, he rearranged the bomb components to maximise their effect.

Romano loitered near the floor-to-ceiling windows, gazing towards the riverside promenade. Oliver stood beside him and waited. The city lights were an impressive sight.

Outwardly calm, Oliver's mind leapt from one potential problem to another. He focused on his breathing, praying for protection and guidance. Oliver included Romano in his prayer – accompanying this man felt like entering a serpent's lair with someone who wanted to wrestle with the snake.

The message from Piper finally came. The hands on the clock marked forty-five minutes since their arrival. Romano dropped his huge frame into Enzo's leather chair and rested his boots on the desk.

Nero burst into the room, accompanied by two burly security guards. The angry lawyer rushed towards the desk. His eyes went from the giant reclining in his grandfather's chair to the man in combat fatigues beside him. Nero's face blanched when he recognised Oliver.

"You!" Nero cried, pointing at Oliver. "Does Piper know you're here? Get out of my grandfather's office."

Romano rose to his full height and banged his fist on the desk. The metal object bounced from the impact. Oliver prepared for trouble. The two security guards took a step backwards, glancing towards the door.

"Do you know what this is?" the giant asked, raising the metal bar from the desk and brandishing it towards Nero. He rotated it in his hands, so the control box and the dangling wires were easier to see. "I'm not an explosives expert, but Piper assures me this would demolish your grandfather's office."

"What do you want?" Nero asked, dropping into a chair.

"I have a message for Valentino. Tell him you met Romano. And I've returned an unwanted Christmas present. The timer was set to detonate at ten." He paused – fifteen minutes remained until that deadline. "I don't hold him personally responsible, but this error of judgement does him no credit. I had my man disarm the bomb. But if I'm threatened again, expect no mercy."

Without waiting for a response, Romano circled the desk and deposited the metal bar on Nero's lap. Oliver came around the desk and followed Romano to the door. One of the security guards tried to block the giant's progress. Romano threw him aside like a child's toy. The other guard hastily retreated towards Nero.

Fifteen minutes later, Romano was in the truck, in the driver's seat. Heading home, he wove through traffic like a racing car driver with the finish line in view. Piper's phone rang, and he looked at the caller identification.

"Valentino," he said with a smile. "I've been expecting your call..."

CHAPTER 20
(Sunday 25 December BWR)

An
Unreal Experience

ಬಿ ✿ ಚ

ಬಿ ✿ ಚ

The intercom buzzed, and Sara wiped her hands on her apron.

"Your brother's here, Ms Messinger," the concierge said.

A few minutes later, her half-brother Gabe wrapped her in a firm embrace. "Hi, Sis."

Gabriel Messinger was four years her junior. He was tall with the healthy glow of a surfer. His long hair curled around his shoulders. It was hard to believe the twenty-one-year-old would soon graduate from law school.

"Nice apartment you have here," Gabe said, walking to the window. "Nothing like your last place. You must be making big money with that posh city firm to afford a river view."

"It's temporary," Sara said. "It belongs to the relative of a friend."

She left him enjoying the scenery while she checked the turkey in the oven. When she returned, her half-brother was examining the table decorations.

"Just the two of us this year?" he asked, accepting a bottle of his favourite beer. He raised an eyebrow as she filled her glass with soft drink. They sat opposite each other at the square table.

"I'm glad you invited me," Gabe continued. "I thought I'd have to fend for myself after Mum and Dad announced they weren't coming home for Christmas. I can't believe Mum agreed to Dad's travel-around-Australia retirement adventure."

Sara delivered the first course to the table. "It feels strange not spending time with our Dad, and your mother; and I won't see my mother either. I couldn't justify spending money on airfares to Western Australia. Not when I have to be back for work on January third."

She placed a seafood platter before him. His eyes grew round when she sat down to a smaller garden salad.

"Are you sure you don't want some of this?" Gabe asked.

"I'd already prepaid for the seafood before I found out I have to watch what I eat," she replied, keeping her eyes on her plate. "If you can't eat it all, I can wrap it up for you to take home."

"You know I'll scoff the lot and be looking for more." Gabe grinned, but then his smile faded. He waved his fork towards her. "Since when have you worried about your weight?"

"I have more than my weight to worry about," Sara said to her salad. "But I was hoping we could enjoy lunch before I tell you my news."

"This sounds serious."

"Not the kind of serious you're worried about," she said, attempting a smile. "Now eat. As soon as I'm finished, I'm going to serve the main course."

She directed the conversation to safer topics and began to relax. Then halfway through her roast meal, the apartment door burst open. Sara dropped her fork in surprise.

"Merry Christmas," Gina shouted, rushing into the room. She had a bottle of champagne in each hand. "We managed to sneak away and came to visit."

Sara rose to her feet as Gina threw her arms around her.

Nero stepped into the apartment in her wake, closing the door. "Sorry to intrude, but once Gina gets an idea, there's no stopping her."

He carried a large, wrapped parcel.

Gina deposited the champagne onto the table and took the parcel from Nero. "This is for you," she laughed, shoving the parcel into Sara's arms. "He told me what he wanted to buy you, but I did the shopping, so you don't have to worry about the wrong sizes." Without waiting for Sara to respond, Gina turned her attention to Gabe.

Sara placed the unopened parcel on the table beside her.

"You must be the little brother she's been hiding from me," Gina said, as he rose to meet her. She wrapped her arms around him and kissed him passionately on the lips.

"And you must be the best friend," Gabe said, disentangling himself from her embrace.

She pouted, before turning her attention to the table. "What *are* you drinking? Nero, get me some glasses."

Gabe raised an eyebrow at Sara when Nero headed to the right cupboard. "You haven't introduced me to your *other* friend."

Sara blinked and licked her lips. She smoothed her dress with her hands and waited for Nero to return with three glasses. "Gabe, this is Nero Mariani. Nero, this is my brother Gabriel."

Gabe's eyes widened, as Nero leaned forward to shake his hand.

"It's good to finally meet you," Nero said. "Sara is very fond of you, and she speaks of you often."

"She's mentioned you too," Gabe said, and an awkward silence ensued.

"Why did you only get three glasses?" Gina cried.

"Sara's happy with her soft drink," Nero said, pulling out a chair and joining them at the table. For once, Gina was too stunned to come back with a quick reply. Nero took advantage of her silence. "You know she went to *St Elizabeth's* yesterday. You must remember the strict regimen the doctors insist their patients adhere to. No alcohol—"

"I haven't told Gabe yet," Sara cried, her face pale.

"You haven't told me either," Gina spluttered, dropping into the remaining chair.

Nero reached for Sara's hand, and her heart stopped. He slipped a diamond ring onto her left hand and raised her fingers to his lips. He turned to Gabe. "Sara and I are planning to get married, and we hope to start a family as soon as possible. There were fertility problems in my first marriage. That is why Sara is already seeing a doctor to help her body prepare."

"Is that all?" Gina snorted, emptying her glass and reaching for the bottle. "I thought you were going to tell me she's already pregnant."

"Congratulations," Gabe said, but his smile wavered. "You haven't mentioned this to Dad, have you? Is that because Nero's still married?"

ജഇൟ

Sara sighed as she stepped from the taxi outside the Melbourne airport terminal. She wrenched at her brief skirt, pausing on the curb to wait for the dizziness to clear. Gina was impatient, despite Sara's explanation that she needed time to become accustomed to these new shoes. The purple stilettos had been part of Nero's gift. Sara recalled the disappointment on Gabe's face when she opened the shoebox. Gina's remarks about the matching lingerie had made things worse. Her brother had left soon afterwards.

There had been no response to the messages she sent.

The Sydney holiday no longer held any appeal. Gina had overseen her packing. Sara blushed when two men made suggestive comments as they passed by. The skimpy cocktail dresses they both wore were more appropriate for a nightclub. Or a rendezvous with an illicit lover...

"Are you still upset with me for crashing your Christmas celebration?" Gina asked when they reached the departure lounge. The flight would be boarding in ten minutes.

"Not really," Sara said. "More disappointed with myself that I didn't handle things better. I should have talked to Gabe as soon as he arrived. And I'm exhausted. I was up early getting everything ready. I'll be fine once I've had a good sleep."

"I hope so," Gina said. "Though I'm not promising you an extended sleep anytime soon."

Sara rubbed her temples. She trembled as her mind filled with unwelcome possibilities. What had Gina planned for their evening?

Gina watched Sara's response as she continued. "Nero's going to have second thoughts about marriage if you spend the entire holiday sulking."

Sara stumbled to a halt, grabbing Gina's arm for support. "What?"

"Oh, did I forget to mention Nero's coming?" Gina laughed. "Put on your happy face, because here he is now. And don't worry about the family spies. Dear Uncle Valentino has *three* guest bedrooms. We'll unpack our bags in individual rooms, but we only have to pretend we're sleeping there. I'm planning to spend my nights out, but I'll always be home before housekeeping comes. As long as the two of you are careful, no-one will ever know Nero isn't sleeping alone."

⊱ ✸ ⊰

(Tuesday 27 December)

"What are we doing here?" Sara asked Gina as they walked into the cathedral.

"I'm not putting up with your misery any longer," Gina said. "You're feeling guilty, and that's one thing we Catholics are experts at dealing with. Find yourself somewhere to sit. I'll fetch one of my great-great-grandmother's priests to hear your confession."

"Does Nero know you've brought me here?" Sara asked, gazing around the impressive structure.

"Of course," Gina laughed. "That's why he's playing golf with Rick and the others. We're meeting them for lunch in two hours. That should be plenty of time for you to get whatever's worrying you off your chest."

Gina crossed the main chamber towards a side chapel. She gave Sara a small shove and then abandoned her. Sara trembled as she walked down the aisle between the rows of wooden seats. Each step increased her anxiety. What was she doing in this religious sanctuary? She stared at the stained-glass windows before her eyes fixed on a statue of a mother and child.

Sara looked away, focusing instead on a display of flickering candles. She read the accompanying notice twice. After fumbling in her purse for the right coins, she purchased three tapers. One for herself. One for Nero. And one for their unborn child. With great care, she dipped each wax column close to a flame until the fragile wick caught fire. Then she placed them on the stand beside the other candles.

Sara stumbled backwards, collapsing onto the hard seat as she stared at the dancing flames. She closed her eyes, fighting the unexpected trepidation. What would she do if the flames went out? She searched her heart for the appropriate words to plead with this unknown God for mercy.

Nero's early morning comments filled her mind. His concern about the impact these nightmares might be having on his child pierced her soul. He had asked why she would not confide in him.

Sara did not dare reveal the nature of her fears. How could she tell Nero that his wife cursed her in these recurring dreams? Zemina prophesied that their baby would die, and grief would destroy Nero's love for Sara. That horror must not pass her lips.

Here in this holy place, Sara conceded that Gina was right. She was guilty, having set aside her principles. Why had she surrendered to her selfish desires? There had been no nightmares before Sara entertained romantic thoughts about Nero. He was still married; Zemina's dominant role in her dreams was the manifestation of her self-reproach. And this ill-fated pregnancy was the price she had to pay.

"No," Sara said. "This baby is wanted and loved. There has to be a way to deal with the guilt that is causing these nightmares."

She continued to reason aloud with herself. "What if I'm overlooking a key element from the dreams? The nightmares started weeks before I found out about the baby."

Sara submerged herself in the memories. "What do I remember? No matter how the nightmares begin, each night I'm always in the river. Sometimes Zemina pushes me in, but when she doesn't, it is my terrible choices that deliver me to the river. But why does my subconscious want me in a river?"

Another thought troubled her. "Here in Sydney, I'm not in the dream long enough to be rescued. Nero wakes me as soon as the nightmare begins. Each time, I'm feeling worse than ever. I didn't dare close my eyes after he woke me the third time. Now, I still feel like I'm floundering beneath the waves."

Sara scolded herself. "You should be grateful. Nero spared you the shame of dreaming about being rescued by another man."

The solitary discourse ended with the sudden realisation that she was not alone. How long had someone been sitting beside her?

Sara waited to see how the stranger would respond. Based on her clothing and posture, her companion must be elderly. Was this someone's widowed grandmother, dressed in black? Spending her days in quiet meditation? The lace shawl thrown over the woman's head concealed her downcast face. What did this pious woman think of Sara's audible ramblings?

The silence remained unbroken, except for the gentle intake of breath – and the distant sound of passing traffic. Perhaps the elderly woman was hard of hearing? Sara sighed and shuffled sideways, preparing to make her escape.

The petite woman turned her head and gazed at Sara. The lace shawl dropped from her dark hair, which was pulled back into an old-fashioned bun. Sara realised her mistake. The sad eyes belonged to a woman who could be no older than her mother.

"I'm s-sorry," Sara stammered. "I d-didn't know you were there."

"There's no need to apologise," the soft voice said. "You are not the first to come before God and forget everything but the troubles of your heart."

Sara glanced at the glimmering candles, her restless hands in her lap.

"You are unsure what you should do next," the quiet stranger said. "You are not accustomed to seeking God in His sanctuary?"

Sara gazed into those dark eyes, and something shifted deep within her. "My friend thought coming here would help me." She looked around, but Gina had not returned. "I'm not Catholic."

The woman nodded.

"Actually, I'm not really anything. I've never had time for religion. I don't really think God will answer me."

The woman smiled. "I have found it helpful to sit in silence and wait for Him to reply."

The candles continued burning while the pair waited. Of the candles that had been there when Sara arrived, several reached their end. Smoke rose heavenward from the misshapen stubs after the flames extinguished.

"How will I know if God is talking to me?" Sara asked.

"Sometimes, he sends a messenger."

"Did God send you?" Sara whispered, afraid of the answer. "Can you tell me what I have to do to get rid of my guilt?"

"Would it bring you comfort if I said I was?" the woman asked, retrieving a well-worn book from beside her.

Sara twisted the engagement ring on her hand. It was too loose – Nero said he would have it adjusted when he ordered their wedding rings.

The stranger spoke again. "What are you most afraid of?"

Sara's wrung her hands together as tears ran down her cheeks. "What if there is no forgiveness for me? Will God punish my unborn child for the mistakes I have made?"

A small hand rested on her arm. "God looks on the penitent heart. He never turns away anyone who comes to Him."

With a pounding heart, Sara bowed her head. "How can I be sure?"

The tiny, dark-haired stranger opened the Bible. She flicked through the pages and began to read different passages. The well-rehearsed argument would have been admirable in a court of law. The concepts were foreign: forgiveness, mercy and a new kind of grace; and a decision that made it possible to leave behind the past and make a fresh start. The light began to break through the darkness in Sara's mind.

The young lawyer raised her eyes to the tortured man on the statue in front of her. The woman testified that Jesus was God's Son. His sacrifice was sufficient to pay for the sins of the whole world. "And all I have to do is ask?"

The woman nodded. "Ask, and then act in faith because you have received the forgiveness you sought. But remember, your forgiveness was purchased at a great price. When you walk out of this cathedral, make sure your choices please God. Otherwise, you might find yourself in a more desperate situation."

Sara shuddered. "Where can I learn about what God requires of me?"

"You can start by reading His Word," the woman said, pressing the book into her hand. "Take this. The pages should fall open to key passages that will guide you as you begin your journey."

Sara's eyes filled with tears. The stranger hugged her before she departed.

Gina must have been watching because she hurried down the aisle as soon as the stranger had left. She had an elderly cleric in tow.

"This is Father Finnegan," Gina said. "I met him last year when I was here for Doña Gabriella Marcella's birthday celebration. He's not as stuffy as some of the others. He's agreed to hear your confession. But he thinks you might have nothing left to confess because you've been speaking with Ria."

"Was that her name?" Sara asked, glancing at the disappearing figure. "I forgot to ask, and she didn't tell me."

Father Finnegan smiled as he sat beside her. He folded his hands in his lap, and his eyes drifted towards the statue of Christ. "That is typical of that young woman."

Sara frowned at that description. "She said God gave her a message for me. Should I believe her?"

"Examine your heart," Father Finnegan replied. "Have your troubles been relieved?"

"I feel lighter, as if a great burden has lifted," she replied.

"Then you have your answer," the priest said with a smile. He spoke a brief prayer over her without asking for any details of her situation. Then he dismissed her with a blessing.

Rising to her feet, Sara thanked the priest. "Is there anything I can do to thank Ria?"

"You can remember to pray for her. She has been coming here daily, waiting for Him to deliver her from a difficult situation." He glanced back to the cross. "She has family in Melbourne. Perhaps it is there you will find an opportunity to repay her for her kindness. I sense that God has predestined you to meet her again."

Without waiting for a reply, he hastened away.

Sara bobbed before the candles as the woman had done, before allowing Gina to hurry her from the chapel.

A
Crime Revealed

ಐ ☼ ೞ

*Isaiah 28:23 WEB - Give ear, and hear my voice!
Listen, and hear my speech!*

ಐ ☼ ೞ

Oliver was not happy. He was the designated senior operations commander while Piper and Jenny were interstate. They were not expected back for another ten days. He stared at the phone in his hand, frowning about the new orders Piper had just issued.

After making all but one of the necessary phone calls, Oliver consulted the computer. His hand hovered over the keyboard as he prayed about the outcome. He found the number he needed and held his breath while he waited for the other person to answer.

The call signal buzzed three times, and then Romano's voice bellowed in his ear. "What does Piper Maxwell want now?"

Straightening in his chair, Oliver ran his hand across his chin. At least he didn't have to worry about small talk with this abrupt man. "This is Oliver Johnston. There's been a car crash, and Piper isn't convinced that it's an accident. He needs your technical expertise. I'm to take you to check out what's left of the car."

Romano's tone went from angry to interested in seconds. "What make and model?"

Oliver reviewed his notes. "A new Mercedes-Benz C-Class Cabriolet."

"Where will I meet you?"

Oliver gave him the address for the private airfield. A chartered helicopter would be waiting for them.

"I'll meet you there in forty-five minutes," Romano said.

A black car pulled into the airfield car park thirty minutes later. Romano's company logo was on the side. The giant unfolded himself from the driver's seat, wearing the familiar overalls. He retrieved a large metal toolbox from the boot.

Oliver flipped to an earlier page on his clipboard. He increased the estimated passenger weight on the pre-flight checklist. He waved as the mechanic approached the helicopter. Romano showed no surprise to find Oliver in the pilot position. He wrenched open the door and stowed his toolbox in the rear. Without interrupting Oliver's preparations, he established himself in the passenger seat.

Romano waited until they were in the air. "Where are we going?"

Concentrating on the landmarks below, Oliver kept his tone neutral. "The police impound first. The wreck was towed back to Melbourne after the scene was processed. It's in a secure garage, but Piper has arranged access. Then we will be going to the crash site."

"What can you tell me about the owner of the car?"

"A professional woman who bought herself a convertible for Christmas."

Romano raised an eyebrow. "One of Piper's clients? Was she driving?"

"No, she let her boyfriend take the wheel," Oliver said.

"A new car, and an inexperienced city driver out to impress," Romano muttered. He leaned closer to the windshield to study the industrial complex below. "We're not going directly to the wreck?"

"I don't want to advertise our interest," Oliver said, circling an empty car park. "There's going to be a short walk once we land."

When they were safely on the ground, Romano continued his questions. "The car's in Melbourne, but where was the accident?"

"On the Great Ocean Road, this side of Apollo Bay," Oliver said. "Are you familiar with that area?"

"I've driven through there a few times. Two lanes, one in each direction," Romano spoke as if he was reviewing the landscape in his mind. "There are some challenging corners. A city driver could get themselves into trouble. The crash happened yesterday? We had rain showers throughout the day."

"I've talked to the locals. The rain didn't reach them," Oliver said.

His companion did not comment about the "short walk" through a maze of side streets, taking more than half an hour. Oliver knew better than to offer assistance with the heavy toolbox. When they were in sight of their destination, Oliver produced an ID card and passed it to Romano. "If anyone asks, we work for the insurance company."

"I'm only the mechanic," Romano said, slipping the card into a pocket. "You do the talking."

The guard at the checkpoint examined their credentials. He entered the information into his logbook. He led them into the enclosed building and pointed them towards the supervisor. "Cameras are covering all angles, so everything you do will be recorded. Don't do anything that will bring me grief later."

Oliver produced the appropriate paperwork and approached the supervisor. Because of the holiday season, there was a reduced team in the facility.

The supervisor led them towards a section shielded by a temporary screen. "Double fatality, extra precautions. Make sure you wear gloves. And if you take any samples for testing, I have to countersign. The information has to go in the official log."

Romano circled the crumpled wreck, as he pulled on black leather gloves.

"It's a bit early for an insurance claim," the supervisor continued, watching Romano.

"The company are facing a multi-million-dollar life insurance payout," Oliver said. "With that kind of money, an investigation opens with the death notification."

"The provisional report lists driver error as the probable cause," the supervisor said. "Alcohol, excessive speed, and a city driver with limited open-road experience. The car hadn't even had the first service. It would have been in showroom condition."

"There's another blue one like this in the city dealership's window," Romano said. He used the pneumatic lift to raise the mangled wreck above the concrete floor. He stopped when there was enough space for him to crouch down to examine the undercarriage.

The supervisor continued reading from the report. "The airbags activated correctly. Both passengers were wearing their seatbelts. But the top was down, and the car rolled several times. Both passengers would have died instantly."

Oliver thanked him for the information, and the supervisor left them.

"Hey, Oliver," Romano said, "I'm going to pass you some sample bottles, one at a time, and I need you to write on the labels. But first, activate the video camera on your phone and pass it to me. I don't want to come back a second time."

"Have you found anything?" Oliver asked.

"It's too soon to tell," Romano said. "I'll have to visit the dealership and check the model in the showroom to be sure. I might not have noticed anything if I didn't know what I was looking for. I shared the prison workshop with a man who specialised in sabotage. There are a few ways of wrecking a sports car, and making driver error seem the obvious cause. Did anyone know Piper's client would be travelling that road?"

"She had a holiday home at Portland. It was common knowledge that she planned to spend most of the summer there."

Half an hour later, Romano said he had everything they needed.

₧☼₨

A warm breeze ruffled Sara's hair as she sat at the outdoor restaurant table. In the distance, she could distinguish the silhouette of the cathedral towers. Her hand moved to the crucifix she wore around her neck. Gina had found it in the cathedral gift shop and had purchased it as a reminder of their visit. Sara silently prayed in gratitude for her renewed peace of mind.

When Sara returned from the cathedral, she had successfully pleaded her case with Nero. After she confessed the shame that tormented her, he agreed to her request. She would sleep alone until they married. The success of this discussion was amazing. The nightmares were gone. Three nights of unbroken sleep confirmed the correctness of her decision.

Returning her eyes to the menu, Sara listened to Gina and Nero's conversation. They reminisced about earlier Sydney visits, as they waited for the other diners. Quin, Matteus, and their father, Ricardo Barononi, planned to join them for lunch.

Nero's phone rang. He glanced at the display and stood. "It's Zemina's father." He stepped away from the shady umbrella, crossing the busy street to the other footpath. Sara's concern escalated when he began pacing backwards and forwards.

Gina reached for her hand. "Relax – nothing Zemina's father can say will change how Nero feels about you. She was going to tell her parents about the divorce over the holiday break, so this is probably the fallout."

When Nero returned to the table, he remained standing. He grabbed his wine glass and drained the contents. "Zemina's dead."

"What?" Gina cried. "How? When?"

Sara stared at him. The colour drained from her face as the world tilted. A dark tunnel opened before her eyes, and the ground flew towards her. She heard Nero's cry of alarm but could not respond. He must have caught her because his arms held her close. Her head pressed towards his chest as he lifted her into his arms.

From a great distance, she heard him explaining what must happen next. "I'm taking Sara back to the apartment. I have to return to Melbourne, so stay with her. Don't come back early; the Sunday evening flight will be soon enough."

ಊ ✧ ೞ

Oliver flew in a direct flight path from Melbourne to the coast. Ninety minutes later, the helicopter landed at Portland Airport. A hire car waited for them beside the tarmac. The thirteen-kilometre road trip was uneventful. It gave them time to demolish the sandwiches Oliver had pre-ordered. He was still hungry, but Romano was impatient to get on with the investigation.

"What are we looking for?" Oliver asked Romano as they parked outside the impressive holiday residence.

"Find out if the neighbours know where the Mercedes parked while it was here," Romano said. He strode onto the road. "I'm going to check the street for any signs that there was a problem with the car before they drove away."

The first neighbour Oliver approached gave him a warmer welcome than he needed and he had to decline an invitation to come in for coffee and cake. News of the car owner's demise had spread quickly. Oliver used the insurance company cover story to satisfy their curiosity. He returned to Romano to see the big man striding towards the house.

"She parked here," Oliver told Romano. No more than a momentary glance was necessary. The concrete beneath the open carport was spotless. "We're being watched, so we have to pretend that we're expecting to talk to someone inside."

They knocked, and Oliver was relieved when nobody opened the door. He slipped a business card through the mail slot in the door, before they returned to the car. Half an hour later, they were back in the air, heading towards Apollo Bay.

"How long will it take to get back to Melbourne?" Romano asked. "I have to be at the restaurant for dinner at six."

Oliver groaned silently, glancing at the time. His shoulders tensed, and his stomach complained. He dismissed his plan to find somewhere to eat. He apologised to God for complaining.

"It only takes fifty minutes," Oliver said. "How much travel time do you need from the airport?"

"I'll need at least an hour to deal with Friday afternoon traffic."

"Does that include going home to change?" Oliver asked. "I could land this helicopter in your car park, wait until you're ready, and then deliver you to the restaurant. It's often easier to find a landing spot for a helicopter than it is a parking spot for a car in the city."

"I don't need to go back to my compound," Romano said. "I have a change of clothes in the toolbox. This isn't the first time Piper's called me to help with an investigation. I can clean-up at the restaurant."

"Where are you going for dinner? Would it be easier if I dropped you closer to the restaurant and delivered your car later?"

"That would work. You could stay and have dinner with us. Have you ever eaten at the *Ristorante di Fontana*? Mama Rosa is the best Italian chef in Melbourne. My employees agree with me. There are thirty of them coming this evening. I have a permanent monthly last-Friday booking."

"That sounds tempting," Oliver said. "But you'd better stop distracting me with talk about food. Those sandwiches weren't enough to satisfy my hunger. I was going to suggest we take time for a late lunch at Apollo Bay—"

"There won't be any time unless you can organise a miracle. I'd rather we found what I'm looking for and got back to Melbourne."

"What are we looking for?" Oliver asked.

"A small metal nut about the size of my thumbnail and the matching bolt. There should also be an oily stain that shows where the bolt came loose."

Oliver swore. "You could have told me earlier that we're looking for a needle in a haystack. I would have called in reinforcements."

Romano laughed. "Once I see where the Mercedes left the road, I can calculate how far they travelled. There's a limit to how many corners they could navigate before losing control. That narrows down the search area."

"Narrows it down to what?"

"About five kilometres."

His conscience nudged him to speak. Oliver gritted his teeth. He started an internal conversation.

Sorry, Lord. I should have told Romano that I have a direct line to You, but this man intimidates me.

Ask him about his tattoos.

What?

The guiding voice added no further prompts.

"Tell me about your tattoos," Oliver said.

Romano swivelled in his seat to glare at him. Oliver blinked and refocused his attention on the water below. He needed to keep the coastline in sight.

After ten minutes, Romano finally spoke. "For a moment, you triggered a memory of my father. He used to ask random questions. It was like his words were an arrow that flew to the heart of an issue. You asked about tattoos," Romano said, pointing to one on his arm. "But the only one you're interested in is this one: 'Ask, Seek, Knock'."

Oliver waited, his mind reeling. He was familiar with the Bible verse that was often abbreviated to those three words. Why did this giant have a Bible verse tattooed on his arm?

"Does Piper know you're a Christian?" Romano asked.

The helicopter dipped as Oliver wrestled with his surprise. "He knows. He said he hoped I found comfort in my new religion. But it must not interfere with my work."

Family Disunity

ॐ

*Ephesians 4:2 - Be humble, be patient,
bear with each other in love.*

ॐ

Oliver landed on a rocky embankment and Romano pushed open the helicopter door. The mechanic rummaged in his toolbox. He surprised the pilot when he produced a compact metal detector.

"I came prepared," Romano said.

"So I see," Oliver replied. "I'm sorry I couldn't drop you where you wanted to start your search."

Romano shrugged and scrambled down the bank towards the road. He had the metal detector slung across his back to leave his hands free. The busy highway featured sweeping curves and sharp corners. On this particular stretch, it was impossible to see oncoming traffic.

The mechanic was halfway across when a car came around the corner on the wrong side of the road. The vehicle must have been speeding. The driver honked their horn and narrowly avoided a collision.

Oliver flinched, hastening to secure the helicopter. He hoped he would not regret leaving this valuable aircraft unattended. He could not believe he faced a few hours wandering the highway. He gaffer-taped a business card to the machine, praying nobody stole it while they were away.

"What's the plan," Oliver asked after he descended to the road.

"We walk towards the crash site," Romano said, "until we find the trace evidence I'm looking for. Then we work our way back in the other direction with the metal detector. You take that side of the road and pray that you don't miss the evidence. We're looking for discolouration, an oily smear. Luckily, it hasn't rained."

Oliver stared at Romano in disbelief. There was no time to formulate a reply before they both evaded an oncoming car. When it was safe again, Romano returned to his search. Five minutes later, he called Oliver to examine a small mark closer to the centre line. "This is what I hoped to find. Take photos while I obtain a sample."

Oliver complied, marvelling that the mechanic could spot this blotch. With long strides, Romano moved further along the road, taking additional samples. After the third pause, he stood and surveyed the scene. "How far is it to the crash site from here?"

Oliver leaned over the guard rail for a better view of the coastline. The waves below him were crashing on the rocky shore. "Not far, if you're a bird. Around that furthest bend. It will take about an hour if you intend to walk at the same pace."

"That's what I thought," Romano said, rubbing his chin. He glanced over to the helicopter and smiled. "Landing here was a good idea."

Oliver nodded.

Romano unstrapped the metal detector from his back. He faced the way they had come, setting off at a fast pace. He kept watching for the telltale stains until he paused and looked back the way they had come. "This is where it started to leak out. Now to find those missing parts."

The metal detector swivelled back and forth across the road. Romano seemed to consider the traffic a minor inconvenience. More than one driver narrowly avoided bumping into the guard rail to avoid him. Oliver kept to the verge, his phone recording the unfolding drama. Occasionally, Romano bent down to examine an object. Once, he slipped something into his pocket.

"What did you find?" Oliver asked.

"Not what we're looking for," Romano replied, "but it might come in handy later."

They had covered about two kilometres before Romano reached for an evidence bag. Oliver hurried to capture the find. It was a metal bolt, hidden among the rubble beside the embankment. Before there was time to celebrate, Romano stiffened. "Put away your phone," he hissed, slipping the plastic bag into his pocket. He grabbed Oliver's arm and led him across both lanes to the guard rail. "And let me do the talking."

Oliver frowned. He followed Romano's glare to a marked police car that had pulled in further up the road. It sat halfway between them and the next corner with the flashing lights on. Two uniformed officers climbed out and began walking towards them.

Romano stepped forward to meet them. "Good afternoon, officers. What can I do to help you?"

"We received numerous calls about two pedestrians wandering on the highway."

"More than a few of them were speeding, and on the other side of the road," Romano said. "But they wouldn't have mentioned that."

"What are you doing here?"

"I came on a fool's errand," Romano said, stomping his feet on the gravel verge. "But against all odds, I've found what I'm looking for. My sister will be delighted with me."

"Show me what you found," the senior officer said.

Romano nudged Oliver with his elbow as he reached into his pocket. Oliver shuffled sideways and stared at the object the larger man offered to the officer. "My sister argued with her husband, and she threw her wedding ring out the car window. She immediately regretted it, but it was too dark to do anything. She knew I had a metal detector, so she's been pestering me to find it for her."

The officer frowned. "We had a report, but the woman made no mention of having a brother."

"I might have lied about being her *brother*," Romano said with a grin. "Her husband doesn't know about me."

"Show me your ID," the officer said. "We'll take custody of the ring and contact the woman to return it."

Romano dropped the metal detector at his feet as he dug into another pocket for his wallet. He produced his driver's licence. The officer held out his hand to Oliver, who offered his pilot's registration card. Oliver watched closely while the officer stepped away to verify their identity. His own sanitised record would raise no concerns. But what would be the consequences over Romano's criminal past?

The giant seemed unconcerned, kicking up dust as he retrieved the metal detector.

"How did you get here?" the second policeman asked.

"Flyboy left his helicopter further up the road," Romano said. He strode towards the police vehicle. "You can drop us off there on your way past."

The policeman looked at Oliver, who shrugged. "He's used to everyone following his orders."

Twenty minutes later, Oliver and Romano were in the air, headed towards Melbourne.

"Another lucky break," Romano chuckled. "Don't put anything in your report about me asking for a miracle. I'll deny it." He reached into his pocket and held out a plastic-wrapped metal object. "I couldn't believe my eyes when I spotted this bolt beside the guard rail, while we were waiting for the police."

"How did you know about the wedding ring?" Oliver asked.

"I overheard somebody at the workshop talking about it. There's a substantial reward – her husband's threatening to divorce her."

Oliver kept his eyes on the terrain, not liking where his thoughts had taken him at the mention of divorce. This was no time to be thinking of Sara Messinger and the complicated situation she found herself in.

Romano twisted in his seat to study Oliver. "Most people forget that there's more than one way to get rid of a troublesome wife."

Ď

(Sunday 1 January)

Sara lost track of time. The dream delivered her again to the rock in the middle of the river. She lay with her eyes closed, comforted by the familiar chill from the hard surface. The roar of the receding waves faded. After a while, she heard distant voices.

"How long has she been here?" That was Valentino. What was he doing in her dream?

"Four hours," Gina's voice replied. "The priest said she arrived during early morning mass."

"She has been like this the whole time?"

"She threw herself at the foot of the cross. Father Finnegan checks on her regularly, and a volunteer was here when I arrived."

"Why didn't someone call an ambulance?"

"They phoned the Archbishop, and he said she should be left to her prayers."

"You should never have left her alone," he continued.

"She told me to go out," Gina said. "I was making too much noise. She promised to call me when she was better. I didn't leave her alone the whole time. I've been popping in and out of the apartment to check on her."

"But you weren't there when she awoke this morning."

"It was my last night in Sydney," Gina said. "She's a grown woman, and it was a secure building. How was I to know she'd go walkabout? She didn't mention that possibility when the doctor came on Friday afternoon. She told him the symptoms were the same as the stress-induced migraines she suffered at uni. He wasn't concerned – her blood pressure and heart rate were normal. I stayed with her until the vomiting stopped."

"If she hadn't asked the concierge to phone for a taxi," Valentino growled, "you might never have found her."

"Well, I did," Gina huffed.

Valentino snorted, but she gave him no opportunity to disrupt her defence.

"You haven't explained what you're doing here," Gina complained.

"Nero was worried. Neither of you would answer your phone."

"You're supposed to be in Thailand for another week."

"Too many people wanted advice. Enzo decided I should return to deal with matters in person."

"Why is Enzo concerned about Zemina's death?" Gina asked.

"This is not an isolated incident. But I won't talk about that with you. What is Sara doing here, in this cathedral? Being watched over by one of my mother's priests?"

The sound of running feet announced the arrival of a third person. "I had trouble finding a parking space." Nero was here!

Sara's eyelids fluttered as she attempted to rise. What was she doing in the cathedral? She reached for Nero when he raised her to her feet. Her legs refused to hold her.

"I dreamed Zemina was dead," she said, searching his face.

"It wasn't a dream," Nero replied.

Sara began to weep.

"Sweetheart, what are you doing here?" he asked.

"I don't know," she cried. "I must have come to pray. I'm frightened. I don't want my baby to die."

"What baby?" Gina shrieked.

Valentino ordered her to be quiet. "Why do you think your baby is going to die?"

Sara was too distraught to answer.

"She's been having nightmares about losing the baby," Nero told Valentino. "I didn't understand how she would suffer because we weren't married when he was conceived."

Valentino frowned at him, before turning to Gina. "Tell Father Finnegan to come here. Then go back to the apartment and pack. I have a chartered plane ready to take us back to Melbourne."

Father Finnegan arrived a few minutes later.

Valentino explained the situation. He ended with a declaration. "There's no reason you cannot perform the marriage ceremony today."

"Without a licence," Father Finnegan protested, "the union wouldn't be legal—"

"I'm not concerned about legality. It used to be enough to bring the couple before the priest."

The discussion continued for several minutes until the priest reluctantly agreed.

Sara's mind split between two realities. One part complied with Valentino's instructions, participating in the brief ceremony. But a secret part was certain it was too late.

Limited Options

ॐ ☼ ॐ

*John 1:5 WEB - The light shines in the darkness,
and the darkness hasn't overcome it.*

ॐ ☼ ॐ

Sara woke early. Alone in her borrowed apartment, she dragged herself through her pre-work routine. The turquoise dress Nero had chosen for her the previous evening was unappealing. Black would better suit her mood.

She hated the pretence, yet she understood the necessity. There must be no hint that Nero had anything to gain from his wife's sudden death.

Sara opened the bedside drawer to ensure her engagement ring was safe. Her eyes rested on the Sydney woman's Bible, and she retrieved it with care. She watched the dawn, longing for someone like Ria to guide her. After leafing through the pages, Sara shut the book with a sigh. An attempt to formulate her troubled thoughts into a prayer was equally unsatisfying.

Unable to bear her isolation, Sara walked the longest route to the office tower. She arrived to an empty floor, settling behind her desk with the door open. Her online search failed to find any reference to Zemina's death. This confirmed Valentino's claim he could suppress the accident victims' names. Sara opened the research folder on her desk. After fiddling with her pen, she rearranged the lined notepad before her. As time passed, she heard other people greeting each other cheerfully. Her heart sank.

The other desks in the room seemed to taunt her, and her stomach flipped. The urge to flee the building increased. When she heard Perry and Leroy's voices, Sara grabbed her coffee cup. Her timing was perfect – she passed them in the hallway. She threw a greeting over her shoulder as she hurried past.

Sara detoured to the reception desk. The two smiling women on the other side of the counter waved her away. They had nothing of importance to tell her. As she turned, the elevator arrived and Zemina's uncle, Giorgio Yaris, stepped out. A heavy cloud seemed to accompany him. He looked as if he had aged twenty years. Sara choked on her practised greeting, retreating to the nearest wall. The receptionists abandoned their conversation.

"Good morning, Mr Yaris. We weren't expecting you today."

"Phone the *Caprice Agency*. Tell them to send over two of their best office temps. Preferably with reception experience. If they can have them here by nine o'clock, I will double their fee."

One of the women leapt for the phone and made the call.

Giorgio Yaris ran his hand through his thinning grey hair, distracted by the woman on the phone.

"Is something wrong?" the receptionist asked.

He shook himself and refocused on the anxious woman in front of him. "I'm sorry, Mary," Giorgio said. "I'm going to my office. When Nero arrives, send him in. And as soon as those agency receptionists get here, set them up to answer the phones. Then summon all our employees to Lorenzo's office. I have tragic news, and I can't bear the thought of repeating it twice."

"Are we to expect the other Mr Yaris?" Mary asked, but Giorgio was already shuffling towards his office.

Sara slipped away while the two receptionists were discussing their employer's directives. She hid in the kitchenette, but she could still hear their animated discussion. Her coffee was ready by the time Nero arrived, and she waited until she heard him hurry past before she emerged. He went directly to Giorgio Yaris' office, letting himself in without knocking. The door closed behind him.

Returning to her office, Sara sat at her desk. Perry and Leroy tried to engage her in conversation, but she was too distracted to give them a proper answer. She rifled through the pile of folders on her desk. This made it easier to pretend she was lost to her research. She glanced at her watch. The morning briefing should have started ten minutes ago. Perry was playing lookout at the door.

"It's not like Nero to be late," Perry said. "Sara, did he say anything to you about a change of schedule?"

Sara did not take the bait, keeping her eyes on the computer screen. "I haven't spoken to him today. But I did check at reception. They said there had been no change."

"He's probably still in holiday mode," Leroy said. "That's a lucky break for Nathanael. I've tried calling our tardy friend, but all I get is a recorded message."

Sara chewed her lip. Did Perry and Leroy know about Zemina and Nathanael's relationship? Nero insisted *he* did not know before the police informed him of the double tragedy.

The phone on Leroy's desk rang. He rose to his feet as he rested the handpiece back into its cradle. At the same moment, Perry called into the room, "The briefing's moved to Yaris The Younger's office. We're summoned."

⚭ ☼ ⚭

Nero sat at the head of the table, in the seat reserved for his father-in-law, Lorenzo. Zemina's Uncle Giorgio sat beside him. When Nero had married Zemina, he entertained aspirations about becoming a controlling partner. But this had not been how he expected the ascendency to begin.

"Thank you for coming," Nero began, his eyes acknowledging each person in turn. He gave Sara no more than a brief glance. She stood with the other members of Zemina's team. His hand tightened on the document in his hands. A reminder that his time was not his own. It would be hours before he could hold Sara in his arms.

He acknowledged the three senior executives by name. They were among the few holiday-makers able to rush into the office in response to the urgent summons. They sat in their usual seats. The junior lawyers arranged themselves as if this were an ordinary briefing, but they were alert. The administrative staff crowded together closer to the door.

"Today is a sad day," Nero said, matching his expression to his words. "It falls to me to announce that Zemina Yaris-Mariani was killed in a traffic accident..."

He paused as response to the news rippled around the room. Zemina was popular with everyone. He chose his next words with care. "Understandably, this tragedy has come as a great shock to us all. Our thoughts and prayers are with Lorenzo and his family." He nodded to Giorgio beside him, but the elder man remained silent. "Lorenzo has decided that this unfortunate time makes it necessary to announce his retirement. I will read his statement."

Nero read the brief letter to the assembly. When he concluded, he scanned the room again, noting the frowns of concern amidst the weeping. "As Lorenzo's retirement is effective immediately, his brother Giorgio has invited me to lead the practice through these difficult times."

Another ripple of comment whisked around the room. The prospect for promotion and advancement dampened the common grief.

Nero held up his hand to regain their attention. "I'm sorry, but that is not the end to the news I have to deliver. Zemina was not alone when she died." He paused for effect. "It saddens me to tell you that Nathanael Hemmersly was also killed."

Spontaneous questions flew at Nero, but he was prepared. Valentino had provided wise advice about how to gain the sympathy of his audience.

"Was I aware that Zemina was having an affair?" Nero asked the room. "No, although I should have suspected. Eighteen months ago, she hired a divorce lawyer. I did everything I could to save our marriage, but ultimately I had to concede to her wishes. She insisted the divorce remain a secret until it was final, to protect her family..."

At last, the questioners were silenced. Nero sent the administrative staff back to their work with a word of comfort. When only the legal teams remained, he turned the page and scanned the list before him. "The next item on our agenda is to reassign Zemina's current cases."

"It seems clear," one of the three executives said, pointing to his copy of the list, "that Zemina chose Sara as her second for the majority of these cases. In respect for our deceased colleague's judgement about this young lawyer's potential, I propose that we make Sara the lead for all of them."

Everyone turned to Sara. The silent woman blanched, but she stood with her head high. Nero held his tongue, but secretly he fumed. These were not the kind of cases he wanted for his future bride.

"She will need a dedicated office," the executive continued. The options were discussed by the other executives. They unanimously agreed that Sara should move into Nero's vacated office when he advanced up the corridor to Lorenzo's suite.

"There's also the question of Zemina's PA," someone added.

Giorgio finally stirred from his stupor, turning to Nero. "If Sara is *replacing* my niece – for the bulk of those cases – we should assign the PA to her as well. Gina's your cousin, Nero. Do you have any objections?"

Nero kept his thoughts to himself, as another task from his secret list was subverted. His plan to take more control of the day-to-day decisions, especially those relating to Sara's workload, were again outside his control. He raised his eyes to Sara, as if considering her for the first time. "I will respect your judgement on this matter." Then he frowned, returning his gaze to Giorgio. "Both young women are relatively inexperienced. Sara will need a mentor to aid her transition into the role. Perhaps you would agree to take on that responsibility?"

Giorgio Yaris narrowed his eyes and smiled. A tremor of unease twisted inside Nero. The delay in the elder man's reply was disconcerting.

From across the table, the executive who had championed Sara's promotion spoke again. "May I take the liberty of speaking for all of us? I'm recommending Nero as Sara's mentor. After all, she was one of his team before Zemina stole her from him."

৪ ✿ ଓ

The clock continued counting down during the video conference. Oliver waited for Piper's response to his investigative report. On the main screen, Jenny sat with Piper, intimidating and alert. Oliver glanced sideways towards Sigrid, who stood too close to him. She shuffled her feet.

"Are you certain?" Piper asked. "You found no connection between Zemina's accident and anyone in Melbourne?"

"We've been backwards and forwards through all the surveillance reports," Oliver said. "And triple-checked the phone records. If there's a Melbourne connection, it doesn't involve anyone on your radar. I'm ninety-nine percent certain no-one with family connections is responsible."

"It's too soon to make that assessment," Piper said.

Sigrid's frustration sparked an interruption. "You've just told us Valentino is furious—"

Piper roared to make himself heard. "I've also told you that Valentino suspects his mother's involvement. She received a phone call from Sydney on the twenty-seventh. Immediately afterwards, she stopped applying pressure about Nero's situation. Valentino wants to know who made that call. I want to know what was so important that they phoned her in Thailand. Widen your search."

"And how are we supposed to do that?" Sigrid asked.

"I'm sending Oliver a new code," Piper replied, "to access a list of known assassins who work for the Sydney branch of the family. Find out who travelled to Melbourne."

When the video conference was over, Sigrid stormed from the operations room. Oliver granted her half an hour to work off her fury before he entered the gym.

"You need to do something about your short fuse," he said.

Sigrid launched herself at him. "You didn't tell him that Romano was on the warpath."

Oliver sidestepped her attack and countered with one of his own. When he regained his balance, he spoke again. "Piper's back on Friday. He'll find out soon enough."

Intimidating Client

ౠ ✿ ౧

*Revelation 3:8c - With your remaining strength
you have stayed faithful.*

ౠ ✿ ౧

Zemina's funeral would begin in four hours. Sara sat at her new desk, swinging on her chair as she stared out the window. The prospect of spending the morning alone in her apartment had driven her to the office.

But the isolation here was even worse. She was the only lawyer at work today. The front office was empty, with only the two *Caprice Agency* receptionists on duty. They were busy acknowledging the steady stream of condolence messages. News of Zemina's death had been carefully disseminated.

The ringing phone on her desk broke her reverie.

"Ms Messinger," the temporary receptionist said, "we have a client at the front desk. He's adamant that he must see someone today about a matter of extreme urgency. Could you come and speak to him?"

Sara frowned. Why had the woman not offered to bring him to her office? She hurried towards the reception. When she caught sight of the tattooed giant occupying the foyer, she understood. In his leather jacket, jeans and heavy boots, he bore no resemblance to their usual clientele.

"Are *you* the lawyer?" he roared before she could introduce herself. He towered over her.

Quaking like a timid schoolgirl, she offered him her hand. "I'm Sara Messinger. How can I help you, Mister…?"

"Romano," he said, dismissing her gesture with scorn. "And don't call me mister. I've already paid a deposit for your time, but if you're the best this law firm can offer, I need coffee." Without waiting for a response, he turned towards the elevator. "Are you coming, or is the café downstairs too far to walk in those ridiculous shoes?"

With her cheeks glowing, Sara glanced towards the receptionist. The woman pointed to the wad of cash on the desk beside her. But her hand remained poised over the panic button. The lawyer shook her head, flicking her eyes towards the security camera on the ceiling. Sara scribbled a note and tore it from her notebook. *Call me in 15 mins.*

The receptionist blinked.

The elevator was too small to ignore her visitor's immense size. He occupied the central space, forcing Sara to stand near the doors. She took a deep breath, praying that the rising nausea would settle.

Romano broke the silence. "The receptionist said everyone's gone to a funeral. Did one of the old blokes in the wall photos die?"

"No," Sara said, straightening her black jacket. "It was the younger woman, Zemina Yaris-Mariani. Her death was unexpected and her funeral isn't until this afternoon."

"Did she drive a blue Mercedes convertible?"

His tone pierced her defences, and she spun towards him. "Who sent you?"

"I'm my own boss," he said, "but I've done consultancy work for Piper Maxwell."

Her hand flew to the wall as she willed her legs to hold her upright. Romano said nothing more, but his mouth twitched at her reaction.

She forced herself to look at him. "Piper is in charge of our security," she told Romano, glancing towards the overhead camera.

The giant nodded. He continued to stare at her in silence. Sara faced the door, watching the descending numbers. As soon as the elevator doors whooshed open, she hurried towards the café. Her body's reaction to the coffee aroma took her by surprise. She came in through the side door, but instead of going to the counter, she bolted for the main exit. Acid burned the back of her throat as her hand covered her mouth.

Sara sank into a vacant chair beside an outdoor table. Her eyes closed as she waited for her nausea to settle. Embarrassed and upset, she sighed. Her intimidating companion did not immediately follow her. By the time she heard the scraping of a chair, she had regained control.

Romano frowned at her from across the table. "I ordered herbal tea for you," he said, planting the cup before her. "And a chicken sandwich. You look as if you forgot to eat today." Her vision blurred at this unexpected kindness, but his next words broke the illusion. "You're the perfect justification for my refusal to hire women. Too much emotional drama, because your hormones run your life. This pregnancy is inconvenient."

A dozen different responses flashed through her mind. As she regained control of her emotions, she sipped her tea. "I can assure you, *Mister* Romano, that my gender will not affect my ability to assist you with your case."

He grunted, but the tension seemed to clear. Over the next ten minutes, he outlined the memorandum of understanding he required. He gave her his business card, and she slipped it into her pocket. The territory dispute between two business entities did not seem urgent. She frowned over his refusal to trust her with the identity of the other company.

The receptionist phoned, and Sara reported good progress with this informal meeting. The lawyer nibbled her sandwich as she drafted the document. Finally, Romano declared his satisfaction. "I would like you to be present at the signing," he said, and she agreed to make herself available. Dismissed, she rose to her feet and prepared to leave.

"One last question," Romano said. "What kind of car do *you* drive?"

Hope Abandoned

ॐ ☼ ॐ

*1 John 3:16 - Knowing the love of Christ,
we should follow his example
and lay down our lives for our brothers and sisters.*

ॐ ☼ ॐ

Standing in front of the mirror, Sara studied her appearance. There was no hint of her pregnancy. In recent weeks, she had lost her appetite, and the dress was loose around her hips. She sighed as she reached for her briefcase. Tomorrow was her wedding day. So why was she heading out the door to an evening business meeting? Because Romano had summoned her, and she lacked the courage to refuse him.

The intimidating giant had ordered her to be at the *Renaissance* nightclub by seven. Sara was careful not to be late. She paused on the footpath, scanning the brightly lit forecourt. Romano was impossible to miss, as he paced impatiently back and forth before the doormen. He was taller than she remembered, which made him easy to see above the crowd. She hurried towards him.

"There you are!" Romano said when she arrived. "I was certain you would be late."

"You said seven," she reminded him, "and I'm ten minutes early. Would you like to review the contract before we go into the meeting?"

Sara raised her briefcase in preparation to open it, but Romano snatched it from her hands.

"That won't be necessary. Come on. I sent the others inside to make sure there were no surprises."

One of the doormen stepped forward as if to challenge her client. Romano had on his customary leather jacket and heavy boots. The only concession he had made to the formal dress code was to swap his blue denim for black jeans. She held her breath, but the other doorman placed a hand on the challenger's arm and shook his head. The first doorman frowned but stepped out of their way.

"The 'others'?" Sara asked, scrambling to keep up with Romano. He gave her no answer.

"You're playing a dangerous game," a familiar voice said.

Sara frowned and looked for the speaker. Romano stepped aside, and she came to a sudden halt in front of another intimidating man. This one wore a formal tuxedo. What was Piper Maxwell doing here?

"I see you already know my lawyer," Romano said. "Good. That saves time explaining who you are and what you do. Does she know Oliver, too?"

Sara felt the floor shift beneath her feet, but she didn't turn her head to look for the other man. Piper's anger was sufficient warning. What kind of trouble had Romano dragged her into?

"Is there a problem?" Sara asked. She reached for her phone. "I can phone Nero—"

Piper held up his hand. "Does Nero know you're attending this meeting?"

"I confirmed the appointment with his assistant," Sara said. "Nero's been busy all week with family business negotiations—" She paused as the puzzle pieces fell into place. "Mister Romano! You should have told me my fiancé's family were the other party in this case. You've placed me in a difficult position."

"What has Romano told you?" Piper asked, taking her elbow and leading her towards the dining room. Romano fell in behind her, removing the option to retreat.

"He said this meeting would be a quick document exchange," Sara said. "Half an hour of my time and I'm only here in case there are any legal questions."

"You're here," Piper muttered, "to deliver Romano's message. And it's too late to change anything now."

Sara had a dozen questions, but they evaporated when Piper led her up to the mezzanine floor.

An outraged Nero awaited her there. "Sara, what are you doing here?"

She fought the tears that threatened to betray her. Before she could give him an answer, Romano reached out and dragged her back towards him.

"I told Valentino I was bringing my lawyer," Romano said. He pushed past Nero and propelled Sara towards a table. Both Nero's Uncle Valentino and his grandfather Enzo were already seated. Nothing was welcoming about the way Nero's relatives studied her approach. Two unsmiling men wearing dark suits – the ever-present security guards – stood as sentries behind them.

There were four other chairs around the circular table. Romano shoved her onto the chair opposite Enzo. Her client dropped the briefcase onto the white tablecloth with great force. All the tableware shuddered. One of the delicate wine glasses toppled sideways and came perilously close to the edge. Sara acted quickly to save it. As she returned the glass to its place, the chair on her left creaked as Romano dropped down beside her. This placed him closest to Valentino. Piper seated himself more gracefully on the chair to her right.

Nero was the last to take his place, between Enzo and Piper. Her fiancé's angry eyes focused behind Sara. She glanced over her shoulder to where Oliver guarded her back. His face was expressionless, and his posture mirrored the security guards on the other side. She felt trapped.

৪৹❀৻৻

This was not how Nero imagined he would be spending the night before his wedding. He signalled one of the staff to bring him wine. An uncomfortable silence settled over the gathering. The man who had delivered the bomb to his grandfather's office on Christmas Eve glared at him in defiance. And his cousin Piper was doing nothing to help the situation.

Sara sat sandwiched between them. Her hand trembled as she poured herself a glass of water. Nero berated himself for not asking for information about her evening appointment. It had never occurred to him that his enemy would drag her into these negotiations. Nero's anger flared, and he thumped the table with his clenched fist in frustration. His grandfather glanced at Nero and frowned. He acknowledged the subtle hint that they were here at the interloper's summons and his actions could put them at a further disadvantage.

Valentino broke the silence. "Piper, you know I don't like surprises. You said nothing about Sara's involvement in this meeting."

Piper looked at Romano with a wry smile, before answering Valentino. "I warned you that Romano is devious and unpredictable. He keeps his own counsel. You will have to ask him why she is here because I don't know the answer."

"Before this evening," Romano said, "I thought she was only the lawyer I hired to write this agreement." He leaned towards her and whispered in her ear. Sara fumbled with the combination of her briefcase. When she finally opened it, she retrieved two slim blue folders. She offered them to Romano without a sound, but he shook his head. He nodded towards Valentino, and Sara passed one copy to him.

Piper reached across and retrieved the other copy. He closed the lid on the briefcase and passed it behind him.

Oliver took it, placing it on the floor on the other side of Piper. The guard then returned to stand behind Sara. Nero did not appreciate how close this muscle-bound minion was standing to her.

Romano continued. "But her presence has unsettled you, and I'm not blind to the advantage this has brought to the table." He turned to Sara. "Put your hand in my jacket pocket and retrieve the small object you find there." The colour drained from her face. Romano laughed at her discomfort. "I would do it myself, but they already suspect I'm carrying a weapon."

Sara trembled as she followed his instructions. After she retrieved the object, Romano directed her to pass it to Valentino.

"What is this?" Valentino asked, examining it before passing it sideways to Nero's grandfather.

A few moments later, the thing dropped into Nero's hand. He studied the paired nut and bolt on his palm and frowned. "What does this have to do with Sara?"

Romano locked his eyes on Nero as he spoke. "One of my cellmates was an assassin. He taught me everything he knew about creating unfortunate traffic accidents. This little treasure came from a Mercedes convertible..."

An icy chill ripped through Nero as he stared at the thing in his hand. It fell onto the tablecloth and lay there. Zemina had died in the new Mercedes she had purchased with the money Valentino paid her. He glanced sideways to his relatives and saw each of them come to the same conclusion.

"Are you claiming responsibility for Zemina's death?" Valentino asked.

Romano frowned. "No. But Piper told me Sara is marrying Nero tomorrow, and I want to avoid having my lawyer suffer a similar fate."

A sharp little cry rang out, and Sara knocked her water glass over as she sprang to her feet. Her eyes were wild, and her hand flew to her mouth.

Her stricken expression stabbed Nero in the heart and loosened his tongue. "Sara, I know nothing about this. I'm not responsible for Zemina's accident. Valentino, tell her."

Valentino addressed Sara. "Nero had no reason to murder Zemina. They had negotiated an agreement after finding a legal loophole to fast-track the divorce. If she was still alive, he would have been free to remarry before the end of the month."

Enzo toyed with the metal object on the table in front of him. "I did not sanction Zemina's death. When I want someone dead, Valentino is my executioner. I can assure you that he prefers to deliver his punishment face-to-face."

"I'm going to be sick..." Sara cried. She fled towards the restrooms.

Nero rose to his feet, but his grandfather constrained him. "Let Piper's man go after her. You need to remain to check this contract before we sign. We don't want to delay Romano any longer than necessary."

Ď ☼ k

The door swung shut in Oliver's face. He pushed it open.

"You can't go in there."

Oliver flinched. How had he not noticed one of Valentino's lieutenants following him? The man clearly expected Oliver to acquiesce to his demand.

"Try and stop me," Oliver said, stepping into the forbidden room. He shouldered the second door open and pushed through before the other man had time to react. The luxurious mirror-lined room was unexpected. Since when did restrooms come furnished with leather sofas and glittering chandeliers?

Three women turned towards him, surprise registering on their faces.

"Security!" Oliver shouted. "Where did she go?" One of the women pointed towards another door, and he rushed in that direction.

"Hey!" The man who worked for Valentino had followed him.

Oliver paused with his hand on the door. "You heard your boss say I was to watch her. I can't do that from the hallway. Make yourself useful and clear this room. Then stand guard to keep everyone else out."

Without waiting for the man to respond, Oliver went through the door. Finally, he was in familiar territory, a row of cubicles. All but one of them had closed doors. A woman wearing the red cocktail-dress nightclub uniform blocked his view. She spun towards him, almost dropping the basket of folded towels and toiletries she was carrying.

"You can't—" the woman began, her eyes wide.

"I'm here to take care of Sara," Oliver said. "Valentino's orders. If you have any objections, talk to the guard in the hallway."

He relieved the nightclub employee of her provisions as he propelled her from the room. A quick survey of the space located the gold-plumbed white marble washbasins. He dumped the basket containing toiletries and fluffy towels on the ledge. Then he checked the other cubicles. At least Sara had privacy as she lost the contents of her stomach. Her door had swung closed, and he rapped loudly. "I'm opening the door," he called.

Sara was on her knees, embarrassment written across her ashen face. She blinked, but her misery was not over yet. Oliver crouched beside her. He supported her upper body above the porcelain bowl until the spasms ended. When he thought it was safe, Oliver helped her upright. He took her to the washbasins to clean up, offering her mouthwash and toothpaste from the basket. Then he stepped back while she refreshed her mouth.

She could not look at him. He stepped back, watching her reflection. Waiting for her to ask her questions.

Sara eventually turned toward him. "Am I marrying a murderer?"

"Do you think Nero capable of murder?"

She frowned, and her answer lacked conviction. "No."

"Would you marry him if he was?"

Her eyelids fluttered, and she staggered back against the bench. Fearing she was about to faint, Oliver leapt forward to hold her upright. She blinked and stared at him before pushing him away. "Stop fussing over me," she said with a false smile. "I'm fine." As if to prove her point, she checked her reflection, smoothing her dress with her hands. Then she moved past him towards the door. "I can see you think I'm making a mistake, but my baby needs a father."

She moved into the other room. His reply escaped before he could control his tongue. "You could marry me instead."

Sara continued her progress toward the dining room. Perhaps his words had failed to reach her? He almost convinced himself to be relieved. Then as she moved towards her seat she paused, turning sad eyes towards him for a moment. "Thanks for offering to help."

Oliver resumed his watchman position, determined to hide his wounded heart. And his mind petitioned heaven for her safety – and his sanity.

Public Humiliation

☙ ✪ ❧

Revelation 7:17c WEB - And God will wipe away
every tear from their eyes.

☙ ✪ ❧

Oliver hunted in his pocket for his buzzing phone. One look at the screen and he rose to his feet. He felt hemmed in by the walls of the private hospital room. He glanced at his father's sleeping form in the bed, and another prayer flew heavenward. His mother had been silent for the past hour, resting in the padded chair beside the bed. She blinked and looked towards Oliver. He mumbled an apology as he headed for the door. He waited until he was in the small visitors' lounge along the hallway before he answered the call.

"How is your father?" Piper asked.

"He has pneumonia," Oliver said. "But he's responding well to the antibiotics. The crisis seems to be over. The doctor said this is unrelated to his cancer, but they are going to run some more tests while he is here. Thanks for fast-tracking his admission."

"That's one of the reasons I'm on the Board of Directors," Piper said. "It gives me more control when one of my operatives gets injured. But you might not be so quick to thank me when you hear why I'm calling."

Oliver ran his fingers through his hair, staring out of the window at the city. The traffic was heavy. He glanced at the wall clock. It was almost dinnertime. Melbourne's inner-city streets would be crowded on a Saturday evening.

"Where do you need me to be?" Oliver asked, resigned to abandoning his father.

"Right where you are," Piper said. "I'm sorry to ask, but you're the only one on this side of the city. I'm stuck in traffic, and I want someone there when the ambulance arrives."

"Who's in the ambulance?" Oliver asked as he headed back towards his father's room. "What kind of medical emergency am I dealing with?"

"Sara collapsed during the wedding reception," Piper said. "You saw the stress she was under last night."

Oliver made no response, his hand gripping his phone.

Piper continued. "Valentino phoned. He wants someone without family connections to protect her."

"Why does Sara need protecting?"

"The wedding reception descended into chaos. The ambulance arrived before Valentino could take charge," Piper said. "The paramedics presumed her pregnancy was common knowledge and mentioned the miscarriage. The problems escalated from there. Her drunk mother accused Nero of sexual abuse and using his powerful position to persuade Sara to marry him. The family responded with a counterclaim that Sara seduced him with the false promise of an heir and never intended to continue with the pregnancy. Valentino's concerned that someone may decide to eliminate the bride."

ಬಂ ☼ ಢ

(Sunday 5th February)

Sara tried to roll over and then grimaced with pain. Light shone through a small window above a closed door, revealing a hospital room, and shattering any hope that the miscarriage and the subsequent wedding reception disaster had only been a nightmare.

This was not how she had imagined her wedding night. As she attempted to find a more comfortable position, the door opened. Sara covered her eyes as a side lamp flashed on.

"It's too early for you to be awake," the nurse murmured. "I'm Nancy. Your bodyguard insisted he heard you cry out."

Sara shivered, and looked past the nurse. Oliver Johnston came through the door and pressed it closed. He was not the man she had expected to see. She turned to the nurse. "Where's my husband?"

"Your husband will be back in the morning." Nancy adjusted Sara's pillows and straightened the bedclothes. "He was distraught over the loss of your baby, and didn't want to leave you. But with the sedative the doctor prescribed, there was nothing your husband could do for you."

Sara blinked away a tear, closing the door to an unbearable grief, before she addressed Oliver. "What are *you* doing here?"

"Valentino requested a guard," Oliver said. "I was already in the building – my father is a patient upstairs."

Sara frowned. It would be polite to ask after his father, but the persistent pain made it hard to focus.

"Enough questions," Nancy said, passing Sara a tumbler of water. "Take these pills and try to get back to sleep."

After she complied, Sara lay on the pillows. The nurse switched off the light as she left the room with Oliver close behind her. He turned at the door. "I'm in a chair outside your room if you need anything."

His words spun around and around in her head. *If you need anything...*

But when the dream river came to claim her, everything had changed. She had the river to herself.

⁢⁢⁢

Released from guarding Sara at nine am, Oliver returned to his father's room. Noah insisted that Lisa-Jane should attend church as usual, and asked Oliver to drive her there. His initial resistance evaporated when they arrived at the church to a heart-warming welcome. The excursion turned out to be a refreshing distraction for both of them.

On their return, Oliver drove his mother's car into a parking spot outside the hospital. It was twelve-thirty. Lisa-Jane hurried inside, eager to share all the messages of encouragement with Noah. She led the way to the elevator and tapped her feet until it arrived. Oliver adjusted his Bible under his arm as he shoved his mother's car keys into his pocket.

They were the only passengers. Lisa-Jane stabbed the fourth-floor button. When the elevator doors opened again, Oliver knew this was not their destination. This was Sara's floor. "Mum—" he began.

But Lisa-Jane had stepped out and now stood transfixed in the hallway. The sound of raised voices flipped Oliver into protective mode in an instant. He rushed past his mother.

A small crowd of spectators had assembled.

"Go away and don't come back!" That was Nero's voice.

An unknown female voice replied with a string of abuse that left no doubt about her intentions.

"Where's Jenny?" Oliver muttered as he pushed his way to the front. His mother came with him. He frowned at her, and then passed her his Bible. "Stay back," he whispered.

Jenny stood in the hallway with her hands on her hips. The blonde security consultant caught sight of Oliver and waved him closer.

"You can't stop me from seeing my daughter," the stranger screamed. "As her mother, I have every right to see her."

"You gave up any rights when you screamed abuse at her last night," Nero said. "I'm not letting you in to curse her again." He recognised Oliver. "Get rid of this woman! She's upsetting my wife, and your colleague is doing nothing to help."

Sara's mother took advantage of the distraction to launch herself at the door. Nero pushed her away, and the angry woman raised her hand to strike him.

Jenny sprang forward, twisting the attacker's arm behind her back. The struggle was short-lived. "I'll escort Sara's mother from the building, while Oliver stays to watch her room."

The crowd witnessed another blast of vitriol from Sara's mother as Jenny propelled her along the hallway. Nero followed in their wake, uttering threats of retribution. With only Oliver remaining, the spectators dispersed. Peace returned to the hospital, but where was his mother? She had disappeared.

୫ ✿ ୬

The shouts from the hallway had been impossible to ignore. Sara wept into her pillow. Her mother's angry words pierced her heart. The fragile truce between mother and daughter was clearly over. Her mother had never forgiven her father for his betrayal, and once more Sara had proven she was his "cursed daughter". What would Nero think? She had only herself to blame if he asked for the marriage to be annulled...

A quiet noise drew Sara's attention towards the door. An unknown woman stepped into the room and closed the door behind her.

"You must be Sara," the woman said, as she settled into the chair beside the bed. "My name is Lisa-Jane. I'm Oliver's mother, and I've been praying for an opportunity to meet you. I'm sorry that it comes at such a difficult time."

The colour drained from Sara's face. "What has Oliver said about me?"

"Almost nothing," Lisa-Jane said, patting her hand. "Not even your name. But he asked me to pray for a special young woman. From his response to the scene outside, I knew it must be you."

A chill washed over Sara at this revelation.

"I only have a few moments before your husband comes back," Lisa-Jane continued. "I'm going to leave this with you." A slim leather-bound book appeared in Sara's hand. Without another word, the woman leaned over Sara and kissed her on the cheek. As quietly as she had entered, Oliver's mother left the room.

If that book did not weigh heavy in her hand, Sara might have thought she had dreamed the whole episode. She opened the cover of the book and read the handwritten inscription:

*This Bible is presented to our beloved son, Oliver
to commemorate the day of his baptism.
We pray that you will continue to be a valuable defender
for those whom God sends your way.
Grow in peace, patience and mercy as you pursue justice.
We are proud of the man you have become.
Love from Mum and Dad*

It was dated December 11, the day after Sara ruined her life. It must be a coincidence. As she wrestled with her emotions, another thought broke through and demolished her remaining defences. She had not realised he was a religious man. Oliver's parting offer of marriage in the nightclub restroom shifted in meaning. Alone with her misery, she cried herself to sleep.

An

Erroneous

Assumption

*Isaiah 29:14a - I will multiply my marvellous work
to make them wonder.*

In the past four months, Oliver had found more questions than answers but had avoided any major drama. His instincts warned him all that was about to change. He thumped the steering wheel. Another red light. The afternoon traffic was getting more congested.

Oliver was in regular phone contact with the *Maximum Security* headquarters, but he had been unable to contact Romano. Why was that man not answering his phone?

Praying that he would be in the correct lane when he needed to turn, Oliver raced ahead, weaving between slower cars. When he came within sight of the final intersection, flashing lights and sirens brought traffic to a halt. His stomach cramped, and the pounding at his temples intensified. He needed no confirmation that those police vehicles were headed to his destination.

Why did emergencies always happen when Piper and Jenny were both away, leaving him in command? Oliver prayed as he drove, hoping for a logical explanation for the drama at Romano's workshop. There had been no warning that Romano was in danger – no trouble since Romano returned the unexploded bomb. The negotiations that began the four-month truce had also curtailed the extortion attempts.

The control room forwarded Oliver a photo of Romano's visitor. He glanced at the stalled traffic. The unidentified woman's image opened on his dashboard screen. Her arrival had been logged but had triggered no alerts. There was nothing in her appearance that forewarned disaster.

Oliver drove into the car park and abandoned his plan to sneak into the workshop. A policeman was guarding the side door. The security agent rounded the corner to be confronted by too many uniforms. Two lanes of the busy thoroughfare were blocked by emergency response vehicles.

And a news camera crew stood on the street, recording the action.

Oliver swore, and then apologised to God. "Piper's going to kill me," he muttered.

౻ ✿ ౼

Sara sighed, unable to see any advantage for her remaining chess pieces. Any hope that she might avoid another defeat dissipated with the loss of her bishop. Valentino always won. Perhaps that was why he asked her to play so often? Nero's uncle had invited himself to lunch again and then stayed on.

Glancing to the sofa where Gina sat with Nero, Sara pondered the reality of marriage. She hadn't realised his family were so intimately involved in his life. Voices raised, Gina and Nero debated how they expected the television movie would end.

Sara made her move, and her opponent smiled. They both knew her game was over. But before Valentino moved his queen to trap her king, his phone beside the chessboard pinged. A few seconds later, Nero received a similar notification.

Nero glanced at his phone and then reached for the television remote control. "I'm switching to the Live News Channel. One of Sara's clients is about to be charged with murder."

"Hey, I know that place," Gina cried. "Sara! That's where Valentino sent you with your new car. You never told me that rude man was a client."

Sara's eyes flew to the television.

"Checkmate," Valentino said. Not waiting for her to acknowledge her defeat, he stood behind their sofa to watch the television.

"Romano's not a murderer," Sara said, as she dropped onto a separate sofa. Gina was curled up beside Nero, leaving no room for anyone else.

"That's the perfect response," Gina laughed. "Defend his innocence and pretend you haven't seen his criminal record. Sara, I can't wait to see your performance at his trial."

Valentino flashed a warning towards Sara, and she made no reply to Gina's taunt.

"What benefit would there be to put Sara in such a stressful position?" Valentino asked. "Besides, Piper won't let her defend him. Romano can afford the best defence."

"Ha! Did you hear that, Sara?" Gina cried. "Valentino doesn't think you can win and he's trying to protect you. But Nero's the one who gets to decide." Gina turned towards Sara's husband. "This would be great publicity for the firm. The media will love her. And losing the case won't be a problem. Romano has plenty of money to throw at an appeal."

Valentino went towards the kitchen, his phone to his ear. Sara frowned when he closed the door. Gina grinned at Sara as she continued discussing the news report with Nero. Devoting herself to the television, Sara wrestled with her wounded pride. Her husband had not defended her, not even glanced towards her.

The suggestion that she would lose the hypothetical case hurt. But it was the other losses that inspired the forbidden tears that pricked her eyes. She had suffered two more miscarriages since her wedding day tragedy. Nero assured her that these losses did not diminish his love for her. Hadn't the doctors said her repeated ability to naturally fall pregnant again was an encouraging sign? Her counsellor advised deleting "loss" from her vocabulary and focusing on her blessings. So why did it feel as if she was losing Nero?

Valentino stepped between Sara and the television, gesturing for her to move over. When she obeyed, he pressed a glass of lemon-infused water into her hand. He settled on the sofa beside her, effectively blocking her view of the others. He leaned closer, breathing a warning over the rim of his wine glass. "Don't let her see that she's hurt you."

Sara stiffened. She drank her water, pretending everything was fine. Did Valentino know about Gina's suggestive remarks when he was out of the room? His young relative had tried to convince Nero that his uncle had an ulterior motive for spending time with Sara. Gina must have misread the situation. Valentino always put the family first. His kindness towards Sara could only be because they did not want Nero to "lose" another wife.

Her thoughts returned to Romano and the unfolding drama on the television screen. Taking her car to Romano for regular check-ups was one of Valentino's security measures. The tattooed giant frightened Sara, but Nero's uncle insisted Romano was the only choice. He wanted a mechanic who could not be bribed.

Sara silently prayed that Romano would not need her help in court. She did not want to add him to her growing list of regrets. She thought about the passage in Scripture she had read this morning: the story of Jesus bringing a widow's son back to life. If only that kind of miracle could happen in real life!

"Hey," Gina cried, "isn't that Piper's man talking to the ambulance driver? The one Sara thought was following her? What's his name?"

"Oliver," Sara said, leaning forward and earning a frown from Nero. She still had not found a way to return his Bible, and this secret bothered her. Gina laughed as Sara's face reddened. Sara tried to redirect their attention to the unfolding scene. "Look, here comes the stretcher. Why are the police letting the cameraman get so close? That poor woman—"

"If that's the victim," Nero said, "there's not going to be a murder case. That woman's alive."

"That's impossible," Valentino said. "I've talked to my contacts. The victim was clinically dead when the police arrived..."

⁝ ☼ ☾

Oliver was taking a crash course in dealing with red tape. Piper always made admitting someone to this private hospital look easy. The paperwork was onerous.

The sun was setting when the hospital administrator finally admitted the patient and let Oliver move on.

Now Oliver could focus on his next task – interviewing the patient. He wanted answers, and he was not the only one. The injured woman's distraught parents were upstairs in the visitors' lounge. She had been cleared for visitors but was refusing to see anyone.

His phone rang. Who was it this time? He pulled the device from his pocket and groaned. Why was Piper phoning him? Oliver had emailed him a preliminary report.

"Are you still at the hospital?" Piper asked. "Did you tell them Romano is paying for everything?"

"Yes to both questions," Oliver said, trying to suppress his concern. Was Piper going to double-check every decision? "I'm heading up to the ward to find out when I can interview the woman."

"Don't," Piper commanded. "I'm flying from Sydney in the morning, and I'll deal with Romano's situation then."

Oliver recognised that tone. There was no point asking for clarification.

"Hospital security will be adequate," Piper continued without pause. "So there's no need for you to assign anyone overnight." After reminding Oliver of other assignments needing his expertise, Piper terminated the call.

Before Oliver had time to process that information, his phone buzzed again. The number was unfamiliar, but the quiet voice stopped him in his tracks.

"You left instructions for me to contact you after I finished meeting with my client at the police station," Sara began. "I stayed with Romano until the police finished asking their questions. He's been released without charges, and at his request I delivered him back to his workshop. Did you know he's contacted the hospital asking for updates on the victim's condition? I advised against it, but I'm sure he's going to attempt to see her tonight."

"Thanks for the warning. I'm still at the hospital. I'll keep an eye out for him."

"Oliver?" Sara dropped the professional tone.

He waited, his knees weakening as the silence lengthened. He could not afford to be vulnerable now. "What?"

Sara gasped, and Oliver feared his abrupt response would end this conversation. His heart pounded in his chest.

Finally, she put an end to the suspense. "Do you believe what Romano told the police?"

Oliver cringed as he censored his reply. Piper had clear guidelines about responding to questions from lawyers. He ran his hands through his hair, pulling himself back into professional mode. "Is there anything in particular that you're concerned about? If you have any doubts about his testimony, I need to know."

Sara took her time. "It's not that I *doubt* his testimony. He was very convincing. It's just *what* he said – about the alleged-victim, Ria – about her *dying*. He said the police confirmed that she was dead. But that's not what they're saying now. I think I know her—"

"What?"

"I wasn't sure, but after hearing Romano's story, I'm almost convinced. He said Ria was an angel and a saint, and that's the only way I can describe the woman I met at the Sydney cathedral last January. She has the same name. I checked the police report: Maria Evangelina Fontana. But that's not what I want to ask you about. Do you think she really died and came back to life again?"

"Let's focus on the fact that she's alive," Oliver said, desperate for an escape. He glanced at the time. "This would be a different conversation if she wasn't. Is there anything else?" He cringed at the sharpness of his tone. Sara said goodbye quickly, and he buried his regret.

He was three steps closer to the front entrance when his phone buzzed again. This time it was his mother. Had something happened to his father? His heart began to race. "Mum, is everything okay?"

"Sorry to call while you're working," she began. "But we have some information about one of your current cases."

"You know I can't talk about—"

"We saw you on television," Lisa-Jane said. "After you left, the reporter ambushed the injured woman's father – he owns an Italian restaurant in the city. You know the one – you took us there for your father's birthday dinner: *Ristorante di Fontana*..." Oliver was only half-listening to the detailed retelling of what she had seen. He was distracted by her revelation – Romano had recommended that restaurant. It was where Oliver had delivered him after the Zemina Mariani accident investigation. Why was he learning critical information about the victim's family from his mother?

He pondered that significance, but her next words jolted him back to the conversation. "And Ria Fontana's been coming to our church for the past three weeks."

Oliver almost dropped his phone. "What?"

Lisa-Jane continued as if there had been no interruption. "You haven't met her yet, but she's such a shy little thing. I mistook her for fifty, so it's been a surprise to learn that she's much younger. She must have experienced great trauma when she was growing up to be so emotionally stunted."

An avalanche of questions battered his mind, but he asked none of them. His eyes locked on the huge figure striding towards the hospital. "I have to go," he said, ending the call.

Rushing outside to intercept Romano, Oliver demanded, "What are you doing here?"

"I've come to apologise to Ria." The businessman brandished a large bunch of red roses to demonstrate his point. There must have been at least three dozen blooms. "Piper told me not to visit unless she contacted me, and the hospital has phoned three times in the last hour."

Alarm bells rang for Oliver. "Who told you to bring roses?"

"Piper said women like flowers. He didn't say what kind, so I let the florist decide." Romano frowned, seeming to shrink as uncertainty shadowed his eyes. "Is there something *wrong* with these?"

Oliver imagined this man storming into a florist with an open wallet and a desperate need. Something shifted in the security operative's heart. "You know flowers have their own language?"

"That's what the florist said," Romano said with obvious relief. "These say I'm sorry and I promise never to hurt Ria again. I bought every red rose they had in case she throws me out before I can say anything else."

That revelation made Oliver smile. He relaxed his shoulders and prepared to leave. "Piper ordered me back out on patrol, so I can't stay and see how this works out, but I'll be praying for you."

Romano hesitated, and then an unfamiliar grin spread across his face. Understanding awakened in Oliver, and his conscience released him from its grip. He recognised that expression – an intoxicating blend of anticipation and hope. Romano might be ignorant about romance, but he walked towards his destiny with an open heart.

Unplanned Reversal

*Revelation 3:8b - Before you is an open door
that no one can shut.*

Oliver looked up from the bank of security video screens to see who had opened the door. The rookie recruit, Patrick Sims, pushed into the confined space. He paused in the doorway, peering at the multiple displays. "I thought being Jenny's messenger boy was the worst job, but I'm glad I'm not stuck here in this closet."

"Shut the door," Oliver said, turning back to his screens. He followed the target with his eyes, from one screen to another. The shopping centre was busy, and he needed to be certain that nobody was following Maria Evangelina Fontana. He leaned closer, still searching for some clue to explain her physical transformation. Ria's whirlwind romance with Romano had changed her appearance.

Perhaps that was why Romano now called her Evie? Oliver was yet to meet her in person, but there was a legend developing that she had mystical powers.

The young woman crossed the shopping centre by the pre-arranged route. She moved gracefully, nothing suggesting any fear, but this only increased Oliver's concern. Until a week ago, Evie had gone nowhere without two bodyguards. Oliver couldn't fathom why Romano had agreed to withdraw her protection. Nor did he understand why Piper thought using her as bait to trap a criminal gang was a good idea. Her new freedom was due to a major security operation Piper had underway. There were undercover agents throughout the shopping centre. It was Oliver's role to oversee her progress and report any concerns.

"I have your meals," the newcomer said. "Sorry that it's only today's special from *Noodle King*."

Oliver glanced at him again. The distinctive takeaway food containers did not match his business suit.

Oliver passed one of the boxes to the shopping centre employee who shared the space with him.

"What is it today?" the shopping centre guard asked.

Patrick thought for a moment. "Pork dumplings and rice."

Without waiting for Patrick to pass him the chopsticks, Oliver opened his lid. He scooped food into his mouth, using his fingers. His eyes remained open while he prayed, ensuring he did not lose sight of Evie as she went into a café.

"I know I shouldn't complain about free food," the guard said. "But there's a better bargain at the café next door to *Noodle King*. They have a 'two pies, fries and a large cola' special every Friday. Very popular with local businesses."

"What?" Oliver sprang to his feet. He thrust his open food container towards Patrick without waiting to see if he caught it. Oliver's phone was already in his hand.

"Two pies—" the guard began.

"We've been hacked!" Oliver bellowed into the phone. "Tell me you have eyes on our prize?"

Before the person could respond, the room filled with an ominous sound. Both the pager Oliver wore and the one Patrick had attached to his belt began to screech. Oliver hit the silence button without looking at the message. He grabbed Patrick by the lapels and dragged him out of the way of the door, wrenching it open. Oliver burst on to the concourse and raced towards the travelator that went downstairs. He wrestled his identification badge from his pocket.

"Security!" Oliver shouted, brandishing his badge before him. He leapt onto the moving belt. He could hear running feet behind him and shouts from the guard he had abandoned in the security hub. Oliver didn't slow down, forcing the people between him and the lower level to grab onto the side rail to avoid him. "Coming through!"

"How did you know something was wrong?" Patrick asked, appearing at his shoulder. The pair leapt from the moving belt and ran towards the café at the opposite end of the shopping centre. Shoppers stopped to watch their progress, pointing and calling after them.

"Evie didn't collect any Friday specials from that café and I know most of his workers order it. The live feed must have been swapped."

"How is that possible?"

"She always wears the same uniform," Oliver said.

By the time they arrived at their destination, there were two other *Maximum Security* agents there.

"Where's Piper?" Oliver muttered, scanning the area. Patrick passed him his pager, and Oliver swore.

Evie kidnapped. Move to designated exits. Await orders.

"Await orders? Await orders! Romano is about to go ballistic and Piper wants us to wait—"

ℬ ☼ ℭ

Sara sat at her desk. She munched on the ham and salad sandwich that Gina had delivered when she returned from her break. The busy lawyer reached for her coffee mug to find it empty. She shuffled her papers and pushed herself upright. The door flew open in her face as Gina burst into the room. The excited assistant rushed to the wall-mounted television and switched it on. "Romano's made the news again!"

With her empty cup in her hand, Sara joined Gina in front of the screen. A banner ran across the bottom, and Sara tuned out the chatter as she stared at the words.

BREAKING NEWS. MELBOURNE BUSINESSMAN'S FIANCÉE ABDUCTED FROM SHOPPING CENTRE. POLICE APPEAL FOR WITNESSES...

The channel returned to its regular program as Sara turned away.

"Did you know Romano had a fiancée?" Gina asked, catching her arm.

Sara shook herself free. "I *was* going for coffee," she said, returning to her desk and picking up her pen. "But this distraction has cost me too much time."

"I'll go," Gina said, snatching the cup from her. "I'm sorry to have been a *distraction*. I'm sure Nero will be more appreciative of my news, so I'll stop by his office on the way."

"Why would Nero be interested?" Sara asked. "You know the family have signed an agreement to leave Romano alone."

Gina paused at the door. "You're such an innocent," she sneered. "Do you think that would stop Valentino? Even a man like Romano will capitulate if he has something valuable to lose."

When she was alone, Sara's hand slipped into her pocket for her phone, and she opened her recent messages. Valentino's name was near the top of the list. Her fingers hovered over the screen. Did she believe Gina? She closed her eyes and tried to pray for the missing woman. Then she typed a quick message and switched her phone to silent.

Is the agreement with Romano unbroken?

After a few minutes, Sara checked her phone. The message status confirmed Valentino had read her question, but sent no reply. She dropped her phone face down onto the desk as Gina returned. The assistant placed the coffee cup beside it. The lawyer pretended to be preoccupied with the files in front of her, but her hand trembled.

Gina pulled over a chair and hovered close by. She crossed her legs and swung her high heels in rhythm with the swinging chair as she stared at Sara.

A few minutes later, Sara gave in. "All right. Tell me what you know. I can see I'm not going to get any peace until you unburden yourself."

"The kidnapping was news to Nero," Gina said. "So he phoned his grandfather to find out what Enzo knew. It's as I suspected – Valentino is still looking for an angle. He's been gathering information and keeping it to himself. We have a spy in Romano's workshop."

"What did you learn about Romano's fiancée?"

"This is the same woman he put in hospital! He didn't want to go back to jail, so he paid her family to get his victim to drop the charges. Her family retaliated by making him promise to marry her."

Sara held her breath for a moment and then forced herself to relax. Gina had forgotten the young lawyer was there during Romano's police interrogation. There were never any charges, but now was not the time to reveal what she knew.

"After the accident," Gina said, "Romano paid her family back for blackmailing him. He removed her from the hospital and installed her in his apartment. He dressed her to suit his taste and changed her name. Her own mother didn't recognise her. But things haven't gone *quite* how he expected because she's a good Catholic girl. She's already proven she would rather be dead than 'live in sin'. So he's stuck with a reluctant bride."

Gina paused. "It's a pity Valentino kept this information to himself. As soon as Nero heard about it, he recognised a missed opportunity. You have similar religious ideals which gives you a legitimate reason to befriend her."

Sara kept her expression neutral. "What about the abduction?"

"An independent gang have been operating out of that shopping centre. A handful of them have come over to our team. It turns out that Romano hired Piper to shut them down and the leader of the gang decided to teach him a lesson."

"So Valentino wasn't involved," Sara said. She attempted to drop the conversation by turning back to her documents.

"He didn't snatch the fiancée," Gina said. "But if our uncle can beat Piper in the race to find her first, then that contract you wrote for Romano can be shredded."

ஐ ☼ ௸

(Saturday 5th August)

A weekly luncheon date at the *Masterpiece* restaurant continued to be on Sara's calendar. Her husband insisted she meet with Gina, even though the two women worked together every day. Despite Gina's reputation for tardiness, Nero always made sure he and Sara were seated on time.

Today, her husband was in an unfamiliar mood. All Sara's attempts to engage Nero in conversation failed. He drained his second glass of wine and glowered at the menu. Sara refolded her serviette and adjusted the table decorations. She fought the urge to tug on her sleeve, even though she knew the bruises his fingers had left on her arm were well-hidden.

The previous day, Nero had arrived home after midnight. This was late, even for his busy schedule. He had raised his voice in anger at finding her waiting up for him. After ordering her to bed, he locked himself in his study. It was much later when he came to bed, still angry and more than a little drunk. The lingering memory of the whiskey on his breath haunted her.

When morning came, he did not mention what had occurred. This made his growing impatience at Gina's delay of greater concern. Sara scanned the restaurant for some sign of his cousin. Instead, she spotted another family member speaking with the restaurant hostess. Uncle Valentino nodded to her across the room and strode towards their table. Nero must have noticed that she sat more rigid in her chair, and he looked in that direction. He set the menu down as his face turned to stone.

Sara shifted uncomfortably. Some hidden message seemed to pass between the two men. Perhaps it was not Gina who was the cause of Nero's displeasure? The new arrival smiled at her, but there was no warmth in his eyes. Was she in trouble? Valentino had not responded to the message Sara sent yesterday. And there had been no opportunity to discuss Romano's situation with her husband.

Without preamble, Valentino addressed Nero. "Your grandfather wants to see you in his office. I told him you had a prior engagement, but once Enzo makes up his mind, you know my brother doesn't want to wait. I will keep Sara company until you return."

Nero leapt to his feet and rushed away. He was halfway across the restaurant before Sara could react. Valentino grabbed the chair her husband had abandoned and shoved it beside her. As he dropped onto the seat, one of his arms wrapped around her shoulders to prevent her from rising. His other hand pushed back her sleeve to reveal the hidden marks on her forearm. Tears leaked from the corners of her eyes and the colour drained from her face. It seemed that he had x-ray vision, because his frown intensified as his eyes drifted over her.

"I'm sorry," Valentino said, but there was no compassion in his dark eyes. He signalled to the waiter, and a glass of red wine arrived before him. He leaned closer, and the heat of his breath against her face made her heart falter. "I'm going to reveal some information, and afterwards we will never discuss this again. Do I make myself clear?"

She nodded, not daring to move.

His words were soft yet menacing. "You have questions about the family dealings with Romano?"

"Yes," she whispered.

"You were present when my cousin Piper arranged the truce with Romano, so I know you have your suspicions. *Our* family has an ancient heritage, one that the *uninitiated* might view as barbaric and cruel."

Sara's mouth was dry. She nodded as she reached for her juice.

Valentino's smile sent shivers down her spine. "Nero has only recently come to a *better* understanding. Your husband knew about the drugs and the lower-level corruption. But he was ignorant about the *persuasive* measures required to control the city."

He paused as if to gauge her reaction. "You've noticed a change in Nero's affection towards you. He blames Romano for his awakening, and I fear you have become tainted by that association."

His words seeped into her heart, and she could not pull her eyes away from his face. She held her breath as she waited for him to continue.

"Before Christmas, Romano humiliated Nero by marching into this building." Valentino gestured with his wine glass towards the ceiling as if he was making a formal toast. "Romano dropped an unexploded bomb into Nero's lap. That was sufficient to incite his hatred, but then Romano chose *you* to negotiate his truce. Piper said that decision was unintentional, yet the damage is done."

He watched her process this revelation and then nodded. In a swift movement, he reached into a pocket and placed an object in her hand. She frowned over the polished metal handle, and then he encased her fingers with his own. Something clicked within the object, and suddenly she was holding a wicked blade. She tried to release the knife, to drop the weapon onto the tablecloth, but he kept her hand prisoner.

His voice dropped to an icy whisper. "I was thirteen when I participated in my first execution." She blinked in horror.

"My cousin and I were both blooded on the same day, and that experience began a journey for each of us. Piper chose a different path. He wanted to champion justice, and remains determined to end the family's tyranny. Meanwhile I've lost count of the number of people I've killed." The temperature in the room dropped, and the arm around her shoulders tightened. The din from the other tables faded, until only his quiet words registered with her mind.

"You want assurance that the truce with Romano is unbroken?" Valentino asked, turning over her hand and caressing the handle of the switchblade. Sara's fingers trembled as the blade retracted, and he retrieved the weapon from her limp grasp. He placed the knife on the table before them. "Nero was present when I *renegotiated* Romano's agreement."

Sara tried to rise, but her legs would not obey her.

Valentino's mouth formed a familiar smile. The kind he favoured her with whenever she made a predictable move in their chess game. "If you leave now, you will never know the truth."

A small spark of defiance ignited. "Can I believe anything you tell me?"

Valentino raised an eyebrow and drained his glass. "Gina said you defended my honour when she suggested I was responsible for the kidnapping." The corners of his mouth twitched. "Have you lowered your opinion of me because I have blood on my hands?" He ran his fingers across her cheek.

Sara trembled. "Whose blood?"

Valentino laughed, relaxing his grip, but he kept his voice close to her ear. "Not the missing bride, who miraculously made it home unharmed." He signalled for more wine and waited until the fresh glass arrived before he continued. "Piper made sure she was safely hidden before he called me. Romano needed my *help* to deal with the perpetrators. He couldn't allow them to go unpunished. That would declare her an easy target for other villains. So Piper negotiated a stronger agreement. I delivered justice on his behalf—" Sara stared as his fingers caressed the folded knife. Her imagination painted a terrible scene. "And credit for the rescue came to me. Now the whole city knows that if anyone tries to intimidate Romano, his allies will act with deadly force."

After his words ended, Valentino continued to hold her close. He smiled as he sipped his wine and surveyed the room. Sara wrestled with her understanding, as pieces of a wicked puzzle fell into place.

"Nero was there?" Sara asked. "When you *delivered* justice? Did he—?"

"Shh!" He gestured with his glass, and she turned her head. Gina was hurrying across the room. Sara shrugged off his arm, and he chuckled as he moved his chair back to his side of the table.

"Aha!" Gina cried as soon as she arrived. "I knew it! Valentino, does Nero know what you're up to with his wife?"

"Sit down and lower your voice," Valentino said. He tapped the folded knife on the table. "Did I teach you nothing last night?"

The smile faded from her face. Her quick eyes shifted from her uncle to Sara's white face. Gina gasped. "How much did you tell her?"

Sara stared across the table towards her friend. "You were there?"

Valentino picked up the menu. "I tire of this topic. I would like to put business aside and enjoy a relaxing lunch with my two pretty nieces. It would be regrettable if either of you ruined my mood by continuing this discussion..."

Distorted

Reasoning

৪০ ✿ ৫৪

*2 Corinthians 6:4b, 6 - Commend yourself
through the Holy Spirit,
in purity, in knowledge,
in perseverance,
in kindness,
in sincere love.*

৪০ ✿ ৫৪

Sara switched on the light. It was an hour before dawn, but Nero was not in bed beside her. She slipped on a robe and went in search of him. She found him standing in the darkened living room, backlit by the city lights that shone through the uncurtained windows. He stared at the phone in his hand.

"What's happened?" Sara asked, hurrying to his side.

"Valentino's plane came down in a storm. He sent my grandfather a message – something about a crash – and now he's not answering his phone. The airport officials have confirmed that a mayday call went out. A few minutes later, the plane disappeared from the radar."

Sara dropped onto the sofa, tears streaming down her face. She had decided she hated Valentino with a passion, yet now she realised she loved him. Not in the romantic way that Gina had alluded to, but as someone important in her life.

Since the day of his revelation, Valentino had continued to visit their home, but she had held him at a distance. The secrets he had confessed had changed her respect into something more akin to fear. He never said anything further but sometimes she imagined she caught a hint of regret on his face.

A pounding at the door announced Gina's arrival. Sara let her in, and the younger girl flew to Nero. "You've heard the news? My parents said there's nothing to be done. My mother – my mother said that God"—Gina gasped for breath—"that God has punished him for his wickedness."

"Calm down," Nero said.

Gina launched herself at him with her fists, vile curses spewing from her mouth.

"You're not half the man Valentino is!" she screamed. "How dare you think you can replace him?"

Sara gasped, as a new understanding awakened. The family resemblance between Valentino and Nero seemed too obvious now. He remained calm, as if every action had a purpose. Her husband was mimicking his uncle's mannerisms. His darkened eyes seemed to notice everything.

A few moments later, Nero had his distraught cousin locked into a submissive hold. Sara knew Valentino had taught Nero this manoeuvre. Gina dissolved into a weeping mess in his embrace. Nero stared over her head towards Sara, and she caught a momentary glimpse of his silent grief.

"Look after Gina," Nero said, summoning Sara to take his cousin from his arms. "Don't let her drink too much, and make sure she doesn't leave before I return. I'm going to see my grandfather. He will have to summon Piper. If anyone can find out what happened to Valentino's plane, he can."

The two women sat in the darkened living room. Gina drained a bottle of wine as she reminisced about her uncle. Sara added more family secrets to the locked vault of her heart and struggled to pray. When the first hint of dawn set the cloudy sky on fire, Gina fell silent. She opened another bottle of wine and when it was empty, she rested her head on Sara's shoulder and fell asleep.

୫୦ ✿ ୧ଓ

(Friday 8th September)

The small landing field was little more than a grassy clearing, bordered by a cluster of sheds. One of these sheltered a fixed-wing plane. Oliver dropped the helicopter onto the ground, closest to what resembled fuel tanks. There was nobody to welcome them. His two passengers began unloading the equipment before the rotors had stopped.

Out of the corner of his eye, Oliver noted the awkward tension between Piper and Patrick Sims. Something had unsettled the new man. But whether it was this bush setting, or the body armour and camouflage fatigues, it was too early to tell.

Oliver had trouble focusing on his refuelling checklist. Before the team left Melbourne, Jenny had taken him aside.

She wanted to know why Piper would take an untested rookie and leave her behind. Patrick was supposed to be Evie's bodyguard, freeing Jenny to accompany Piper on more important missions.

Jenny felt justified in her anger, ending her complaint by referencing how everything had changed since Evie Romano's kidnapping—

Oliver fired a quick prayer heavenward. He could no longer think of Romano, or his wife Evie, without praying for Sara. He had asked God to deliver him of this obsession, but the compulsion had only intensified. And now he could not even talk to Jenny Prescott, or look at Patrick Sims, without another reminder.

The sun dropped behind the nearby mountain. By the time Oliver shouldered his pack, the creeping shadows had reached them. He joined Piper and Patrick near the gate. Headlights appeared over the rise, rushing towards them. This must be Nelson Felmingham, one of Piper's operatives based in Sydney. Nelson had driven a van across New South Wales to become the fourth member of this team.

Oliver had met Nelson a few times in the past. They had also talked by phone while Sigrid was working with Nelson's team in recent weeks. She had moved to Sydney to be closer to her ailing grandmother, but her relative had died within days of her arrival.

Then Oliver had fielded some challenging questions from Nelson about Sigrid's outrageous behaviour, leading to her recall to Melbourne. She had not thanked him for "meddling". Sigrid refused to talk to Oliver about her grief, but she was more than willing to try to kill both of them in the gym. His mind jumped from Sigrid's situation to praying for his father. The creeping cancer was often on his mind.

Death's dark shadow drained Oliver of vital energy. He searched his heart for any hope that their mission might succeed. Valentino's survival was unlikely – unless God intervened with a miracle. There had been no sign of the missing cartel enforcer since the crash on Tuesday evening.

Piper sent Patrick to the driver's seat of the van, while Nelson joined Oliver in the rear compartment, where both had orders to rest. Their commander took the front navigator position. The official search teams had confirmed the coordinates of the plane wreckage. That would be their starting point. Oliver closed his eyes, confident that Piper would wake him when they arrived.

An ability to fall asleep anywhere was an asset in the field, but to have that sleep invaded by an intense dream was counterproductive. Oliver knew he was dreaming, but he was powerless to change what was happening. His frustration at being a spectator grew as the storm in his dream intensified.

Finally, the dream tempest eased. The clouds parted to reveal a velvet-blue sky filled with bright shooting stars. Oliver stood on a high cliff, overlooking a river wild and majestic. The torrent surged between rocky walls, carving a new path through the wilderness. This was not the first time Oliver had dreamed of this place, but the storm was new.

Then a familiar voice rose above the roar of the water. Every nerve in Oliver's body flashed a warning that something significant had changed.

My promises are forever. Write them on your heart. I will sustain you through the storms to come. Do not give up. Do not be afraid. What you judge as weakness, I will transform into strength if you put your trust in Me.

Behold, I am giving you a sign. The one you seek will awaken with the river on his lips.

The words echoed in Oliver's mind, thrusting him from the dream. He kept his eyes closed long after the river vision faded.

Implausible
Truth

☙ ☼ ❧

*1 Peter 4:8a WEB - And above all things
be earnest in your love.*

☙ ☼ ❧

Oliver opened his eyes. The van was still moving, but it soon came to a halt in the middle of an isolated track, somewhere in rural New South Wales. When Patrick turned off the engine, Piper leapt from the vehicle. Oliver stepped out onto gravel, thick native bush hemming in the road on either side. Nelson scrambled after him and Patrick joined them beside the van.

"The GPS coordinates put the crash site a couple of kilometres due east from here," Piper said from the rear of the van. He thrust heavy packs into their arms. "We have to find a way through this scrub."

"The first responders said there was a fire trail," Oliver said, scanning his surroundings. A distinctive smell – charred wood and incinerated foliage – wafted towards him on the breeze. He checked the sky above the road for falling embers or wisps of smoke. The adjacent bush bore no evidence of a recent conflagration. Unseen birds called to each other in the canopy. Oliver forced his shoulders to relax. Nothing he saw contradicted the fire fighters' report that the blaze, started by the crash, was out. He paused again to thank God for the "lucky wind change".

"Valentino wouldn't know about the fire trail," Piper said, pushing into the undergrowth on the east side of the road. "When the fire started, the wind was blowing strongly in that direction. Valentino would have headed downwind to avoid being caught by the flames. We'll fan out along the road until one of us finds a way through."

Half an hour later, the fruitless search for a passage into the untamed forest had delivered them further down the hill than Piper predicted. They were still within sight of the gravel road and their commander's mood was darkening. Oliver felt sorry for Patrick, who was struggling to keep up. After Patrick became entangled in thick scrub and needed rescuing for the third time, Piper called the small team together.

"I'm sending Patrick to retrieve the van. It should take him about fifteen minutes to get back here—"

"If he doesn't get lost," Nelson said. "Bringing Jenny's 'pretty-boy' on this mission has been counterproductive."

This derogatory term was not new to Oliver, but neither Patrick nor Piper had ever been present for him to witness the impact. Poor Patrick accepted the negative comment in gloomy silence, and nodded to acknowledge the new instructions before retreating towards the road. Piper turned to Nelson. "I brought *you*, because I knew I could trust you. But unlike Oliver you lack the wisdom to hold your tongue when you think I've made a mistake." Without waiting for a response, Piper strode towards a gap between two trees and ducked under a low-hanging branch.

Before he vanished from sight, Piper had one more thing to say. "Oliver, tell Nelson why Patrick is here."

A long silence followed before Nelson spoke. "I thought we were equal in rank, but clearly, I was mistaken."

Nelson's unspoken question targeted a growing unrest in Oliver's heart. He moved further down the hill, continuing to push into the thick undergrowth in search of an accessible route. "The jury's out on whether I'm higher in rank," Oliver said. "Don't make assumptions about Jenny's absence – if she was a pilot, she'd be here."

Staying close enough to be heard, Nelson replicated Oliver's actions near a different stand of trees. "That helicopter doesn't need a co-pilot. And there's no reason to bring a spare driver for the van. Unless..." Nelson fell silent.

Oliver finished the sentence for him. "Unless Piper isn't returning with us after we find Valentino? Piper's convinced someone sabotaged the plane. The most likely scenario has you and I flying to Sydney while Patrick drives Piper and the van to an undisclosed destination."

"There's more to the urgency about finding Valentino than getting Piper some answers," Nelson said. "I thought he'd be happy if there was one less criminal to bring to justice."

"Protecting those who are vulnerable isn't enough," Oliver said, regretting that the thick scrub prevented him from seeing how Nelson received his words. "The true test of our integrity is whether we can extend mercy and compassion to our enemies."

Nelson laughed. "Sigrid warned me about your radical Christianity. She said you still believe in miracles.

"Be careful not to mention that word in Piper's hearing," Oliver said. "He's threatened to send the next agent who refers to something as 'a miracle' to Antarctica."

"Thanks for the warning," Nelson said. There was another lengthy pause. "Piper won't thank you for extending mercy to his enemies."

"There's a truce in place," Oliver said, "between Piper and the Melbourne family." He hesitated, wary of giving away too much information.

"But the enmity between them could re-ignite at any moment?" Nelson said. "I'm beginning to understand why Piper put you in charge. You're genuinely concerned about Valentino's welfare, which frees Piper to pretend he only cares about whatever information he can extract."

Oliver thought about that remark as the pair continued their bush-bashing. Oliver made minimal inroads into the scrub until he stumbled upon a hollow left by an uprooted forest giant. Nelson emerged beside him a few moments later. They jumped down into the waist-deep hole to cross to the dead tree.

The central core of the tree was hollow, a cave among the tangled roots large enough for both men to stand upright inside it. After taking a few photos with his phone, Oliver inspected the tree's growth rings that encircled them. The musty timber was solid, promising a secure platform, if they could find a way up. On one side the bare roots formed a twisted ladder. After testing the first step with his whole weight, Oliver began to climb. When he was halfway up, he signalled for Nelson to follow.

"This mission is about trust," Nelson said. "Piper suspects that the assassin is someone within the family, and is wondering whether some of his Melbourne agents have been compromised. At least five of my operatives have been approached by the Sydney cartel."

Oliver pulled himself up onto the tree trunk. He reached down to help Nelson scramble up the final steps.

"Thanks," Nelson said. "I've been thinking about Patrick. I thought his inexperience was a major disadvantage, and I was wrong. He hasn't been with Piper long enough to be targeted for information."

The view from the trunk was magnificent. Above them, the afternoon sky was open to let the light in, and the bush around them lay smashed and broken. When this tree fell the unleashed force must have shaken the whole hill. Beneath their feet, the trunk was wide enough to form a bridge that would carry them across the impenetrable undergrowth towards a large clearing.

Oliver unclipped the handheld radio from his belt. "Piper, we've found a way—"

Before he finished his sentence, there was a disturbance on the ground below. It sounded like an animal forcing its way through the bushes. With a grunt, Piper crawled out into the open.

"We're up here," Nelson shouted. "I'll drop down a rope, and you can climb up."

When Piper was with them, the trio moved forwards. The trunk was wide enough that they could walk comfortably side-by-side.

Oliver silently thanked God for making a way for them. When the trunk ahead narrowed, Piper went to the front. The sloping trunk became more difficult to navigate and they proceeded in single file. While Oliver clambered around a branch pointing skyward, Nelson looked back the way they had come.

"I can't believe we've covered fifty metres in less than a minute," Nelson said. "Considering the dense scrub that lies between us and the road, we've been *incredibly* lucky. Either that, or *someone* is looking after us."

Up ahead, Piper increased his pace. "It will take more than a fallen tree to convince me that Oliver's prayers are effective."

The hair on the back of Oliver's neck prickled. Perhaps this was a warning that God had heard Piper's challenge.

"Patrick Sims calling Piper Maxwell," squawked the radio on Piper's belt. "Come in, Piper."

"Where are you?" Piper asked. "I told you to wait with the van."

"I parked where you told me," Patrick's voice proclaimed through the speaker. "While I was waiting, I went looking along the roadside. I think I've found a footprint in the clay beside a shallow ditch, and what looks like drag marks."

"Stand next to the van and don't mess with the evidence," Piper said into the radio, increasing his pace.

"Roger," said Patrick's voice. There was a lengthy pause. "How long until you get here?"

"Don't move from your position," Piper said. "Over and out."

The remaining distance along the dead tree bridge took a little longer, but when all three men were standing on the ground they surveyed the open space. "This looks as if it was once pasture, but the bush has reclaimed it. Spread out and keep your eyes open."

Nelson stayed closest to the road, with Piper claiming the middle ground. Oliver moved to the east, keeping level with the others. When the spiky grass beside Oliver turned black from the recent fire, he yelled to attract Piper's attention. "The fire made it this far. If Valentino got past here, he would have been safe."

"I've marked the coordinates," Piper said, and then he replaced his phone in his pocket. "If Patrick is mistaken, we can recheck this area before the light fades. We're only a few minutes from where I told him to park the van."

When they emerged from the bush the road was empty. Piper swore. He called Patrick on the radio. "Where are you? We're at the road, and the van isn't here."

"Hang on," Patrick's voice said. A few seconds later, they heard the sound of a distant car horn. *Beep. Beep. Beep. Beep...*

Piper took off, his heavy boots pounding on the road as he headed downhill. Oliver and Nelson chased after him. The gravel road disappeared around a bend.

"Can you hear that?" Patrick asked.

"You can stop now," Piper said. "We're coming." He continued to mutter to himself as he ran.

"Beginner's luck," Nelson said to Oliver with a grin. "How else does a lost rookie find any evidence?"

Patrick stood in the middle of the narrow road, about a hundred metres past the parked van. He waved and shouted when he saw them. Piper knelt beside the clear shoe print in the ditch. This was not a working man's boot print. The distinctive Italian designer's trademark was still legible. Oliver surveyed the surrounding countryside, turning his back on the bush to gaze across open farmland. There were no animals in the fenced paddocks, but he could hear the distant sound of a dog barking. Following the line of the road, he thought he could see the blurred edges of some scattered buildings about five kilometres away in the valley. Meanwhile, Nelson searched the gravel surface of the road.

"There are no prints," Nelson said. "Not even tyre tracks. If we weren't in the middle of nowhere, I'd say the road had been professionally swept clean."

Patrick hurried after Nelson, and together they scoured the gravel surface for any evidence. They were about eight hundred metres down the hill when Piper called out. "Here! Tyre tracks, coming and going." Piper was kneeling a few steps uphill from the van. "Someone picked Valentino up," Piper said, "and then tried to erase the evidence."

Nelson said the obvious. "There's a farm down the road."

"Get in the van." Piper said. "Someone might be watching. We're going to convince them that we gave up and drove away."

Patrick started the engine. "Do you want me to drive past the farm?"

"No. Reverse up the hill. There's room to turn around beside that old gate. When you get far enough up the road I'll tell you where to stop."

Patrick did as he was instructed, reversing with precision, before swinging the rear of the van towards the gate. He executed a perfect turn, but before he pulled back onto the road, he looked in the mirror. "There's a building over there," Patrick said, gesturing towards a small clump of trees. "Some kind of shed. If you look closely, you can see wheel marks running across the grass from the gate."

"How do you know there's a building there?" Nelson asked.

Patrick shrugged. "I used my phone to check the satellite map – I had to do something while I was waiting – I didn't want to get lost again."

Nelson laughed.

"Drive," said Piper.

Patrick pressed the accelerator and the tyres spun on the loose gravel. The van roared up the road, leaving clouds of dust in its wake. When the van rounded the corner, he slowed and drove at a more sensible pace.

"Pull over here," Piper said, when they were a couple of kilometres past that gate. "Patrick, stay with the van. I'll radio when I need you. Oliver and Nelson, come with me. You can cover me while I check out the shed."

The trio ran within the tree line until they could see the gate. Nelson stayed by the road, hidden in the undergrowth with his rifle pointed down the road. Oliver accompanied Piper through the scrub until they were parallel to the small stand of trees. Piper signalled Oliver to cover him as he ran across the open space, then disappeared from view. Oliver lay in the shadow of a fallen log and surveyed the wider landscape through his telescopic sight. His record with a sniper rifle on the range was two kilometres.

The afternoon shadows lengthened, and the light dimmed. The phone in Oliver's shirt pocket vibrated. He checked the screen. A message from Piper.

Found V

Waiting until dark.

෨ ✿ ෪

(Saturday 9th September)

It was mid-morning, less than twenty-four hours since the helicopter had landed in this isolated place. Oliver was in the pilot seat – striving for a faultless takeoff. Piper and Patrick watched from the ground. Oliver's mouth twisted into a half-smile. He didn't envy the rookie a long journey with Piper in the passenger seat.

When the crude airfield was no longer visible, Oliver focused on the small screens which showed him the rear compartment. After studying his two passengers, he activated the onboard frequency on his headset to talk to the Sydney-based agent. "Nelson, can I have an update on your patient?"

Nelson glanced up from his notes, frowning towards the camera. "Vital signs are steady."

"Is Valentino unconscious or asleep?"

"I won't know that unless I try to wake him. I'd rather get to Sydney before he finds out Piper has abandoned him. You saw Piper struggling to control Valentino's panic when he awoke in the van. I'm authorised to administer a sedative—" Nelson shook his head. "But I'd rather not use it. Valentino's physically weakened by his injuries, and whatever drugs were used to restrain him have affected his mind. All I've managed to do is stabilise him."

"He seemed more lucid the last time he woke." Oliver checked the gauges before he continued. "He remembered his name, and recognised Piper well enough to embarrass him with childhood anecdotes. I suspect any continued memory loss might be a pretence to catch us off guard."

"I'm concerned about Valentino's mental state. I came unprepared to deal with psychotropic drugs, and if Piper hadn't had an antidote in his pocket—" Nelson's words ended abruptly.

"I'm not sure 'antidote' is the right description," Oliver said, "and Piper didn't say it was in *his* pocket."

"Valentino had the antidote? How did Piper know— No, forget I asked."

"We're on a secure channel, and I've turned off the recorder."

Nelson leaned over the patient, who was throwing his arms around in his sleep. When he had settled again, Nelson spoke. "Did you know that Piper and Valentino were cousins?"

"Yes."

"That explains a lot," Nelson said. He looked directly into the camera. "From the way they were talking in the van, they must have been very close."

"Piper never talks about his past."

A flash of lightning lit up the horizon, and Oliver checked the radar, looking for a way around the approaching storm.

"Are you worried about the weather?" Nelson asked, glancing out the window. "I thought you'd be full of confidence after the little 'miracles' your God lined up to reunite Piper with his cousin. Won't your God protect us from a storm?"

"I don't doubt that He can protect us," Oliver said. "But He still expects me to remember my training and do my bit to stay out of trouble."

Nelson looked down at his phone. "Piper must have issued an alert. This message is from Macy, my 2IC. Every available agent in Sydney will be waiting for us when we arrive at the hospital. Their orders are to establish a secure cordon and prepare for an external threat. If Piper's expecting another assassination attempt, why isn't he with us?"

Oliver adjusted his flight path, noting the flashing sensor that informed him the helicopter was entering controlled air space. He switched to another channel to confirm his flight plan and to receive instructions from Air Traffic Control. When he was done, Oliver reopened the communication channel with Nelson. "We should be landing at the Sydney hospital in half an hour. Is there any change in our passenger?"

"Valentino's still sleeping," Nelson said. "You didn't answer my question. Why isn't Piper here?"

"Piper doesn't need to be here. In fact, his absence is to our advantage, because his family believe Piper doesn't care enough about Valentino to stick around. They think Piper only went looking for Valentino because they paid him. You said it before: if Valentino dies, that's one less criminal for Piper to bring to justice."

Sara entered the living room and discovered Nero and Gina whispering near the window. They fell silent and pulled apart when they saw her.

"Is there a problem?" Sara asked, looking from one to the other.

Gina turned towards the window, drinking deeply from the wine glass in her hand. Nero ran his fingers through his hair. He exchanged another puzzling look with Gina before he beckoned Sara closer. He kept his voice low. "Valentino's been found."

"That's good news, isn't it?" Sara asked, searching his face. "He's alive? Are you going to him?"

Nero clamped his hand over Sara's mouth to silence her. "Shh! Piper doesn't want anyone to know Valentino's alive."

"Why are you whispering?" Sara asked.

"Piper thinks there's a traitor, and too many people have visited here. The apartment's probably bugged."

"How did you find out Valentino's alive?" Sara whispered.

"Piper told my grandfather Enzo," Nero said.

"And Enzo told my great-grandmother, Theresa. AND his *other* sisters," Gina said, rejoining the huddle. "None of *them* can keep a secret. *They* couldn't wait to share their outrage. Piper thinks someone connected to the family tried to *kill* Valentino."

"Kill Valentino?" Sara gasped.

"Someone has been making trouble for months," Nero said. "They have been undermining Valentino's decisions, sabotaging deals—"

"Sending bombs to important allies—" Gina hissed.

Sara shuddered. "Allies like Romano?" she asked, and immediately regretted her suggestion, as Nero's face clouded over.

"Especially Romano," Gina said. "Everyone knows your *favourite* client humiliated Nero and added to the bad blood between them…"

⁂ ☼ ⁅

Standing near the end of the bed, Oliver nudged Valentino's foot with the barrel of his handgun. The awakening patient surveyed the private hospital room. Oliver retreated a step, gesturing with his head towards the doorway.

Nelson stood in the opening, his gun held in a relaxed grip. He grinned at Valentino. "Don't attempt to get out of bed. Oliver has orders to shoot you if you try to escape again. He denies it, but I'm certain he's looking for any excuse."

Oliver refused to be drawn by Nelson's taunt. He locked his annoyance behind his protective barriers, alert to any sign of danger. This was the second time Valentino had awoken. The first time, he had taken everyone unawares, and there had been a violent struggle. The medical staff had injected a powerful sedative before they could restrain him. Since then, Oliver and Nelson had taken turns watching over him, waiting for the medication to wear off.

"Piper would not be happy if this man killed me," Valentino said.

Nelson laughed. "You'd survive. Oliver's an excellent marksman. Maximum pain, minimum risk of fatality."

The patient reclined against the pillows. He lay still, and Oliver almost believed he had fallen asleep.

A few minutes later, Valentino opened his eyes and addressed Oliver. "If I promise not to escape, will you put down the gun?"

Oliver adjusted his balance and maintained his position.

"He knows not to trust you," Nelson said. "He's seen how you negotiate."

"You don't share his caution?" Valentino asked Nelson.

"I'm not from Melbourne. And I don't have anything to lose."

Valentino studied Oliver for a long time before he turned to Nelson again. "And what does your friend have to lose?"

"Piper said you're crafty and resourceful," Nelson laughed. "Work that out for yourself."

The patient thought about that for even longer. "At least give me a clue."

"You have mutual friends."

The intense look Valentino directed at him burned into Oliver's soul. An almost irresistible impulse to stride across the room – to smack Piper's cousin back into oblivion – brought a shine to his forehead.

"Do you play chess?" Valentino eventually asked. Oliver blinked, and the man in the bed smiled. "You make a worthy opponent. I now remember who you are, and I know why Piper assigned you to watch me."

"Nelson, change places," Oliver said, backing towards the door.

Nelson stepped forward. "If this is like a chess game, then my money's on Oliver to win."

"I'm not interested in playing," Oliver muttered as he retreated.

"A pity," Valentino said, and his eyelids fluttered. His voice began to fade. "One of the other players is... a pretty lawyer. Her face lights up... at the mention... of your name."

An icy blast exploded in the centre of Oliver's chest. His trigger finger itched, but he kept his hand motionless. With his shoulder resting against the door frame, he waited for Valentino's next remark. But the injured man had retreated into his restless dream.

୫୦ ✿ ୧୬

Sara served refreshments, managing a smile despite her exhaustion. All afternoon, she had played hostess to Nero's extensive family. A rumour had spread that any news about Valentino's fate would come to Sara's husband. Gina stood at Nero's side, acting as his lieutenant. It was Gina who decided when anyone had overstayed their welcome.

Someone rapped impatiently at the door. Gina waved her hand, directing Sara to answer it. The lawyer sighed, marshalling a smile. After she fulfilled this duty, she was going to hide in her dressing room.

When Sara pulled the door open, the rehearsed greeting faded from her lips. Piper Maxwell stood there, dressed formally for dinner. His resemblance to Valentino was striking. She swayed on her feet as the colour drained from her face. Piper propped her against the wall until she recovered.

Gina called out. "Who was at the door?"

Piper shook his head, signalling for Sara to lead him to the others. One by one, the older relatives encamped in the formal lounge fell silent and stared at him.

Enzo leapt to his feet. "What are YOU doing here?"

"I'm convening a dinner meeting," Piper said, dropping into a vacant chair. Sara offered him a glass of wine, which he declined. "I thought I'd circumvent the gossip by delivering my report to the whole executive."

"Where's my son?" Doña Gabriella Marcella demanded.

Piper did not flinch from the matriarch's steely glare. "Dinner first," he said, folding his hands in his lap and closing his eyes. "Hurry and get changed. I've ordered the first course to be served at seven."

Piper refused to be drawn into conversation, and the relatives departed. Nero whispered to Gina, and after his cousin hurried away, he went towards his dressing room. Sara crept around the room, gathering wine glasses and coffee cups. She was careful not to disturb Piper. She was looking forward to having the apartment to herself.

After dealing with the washing up, Sara adjusted the furnishings and tidied the room. Piper stirred and she apologised for disturbing him.

"Why aren't you changing for dinner?" he asked with a frown.

"I-I didn't think I was included," Sara said, pushing down the growing dismay. "You said this was an executive meeting."

"Valentino said you must be present." Piper stood. "I'm going ahead to the dining room. You will have to hurry."

Sara blinked, immobile, until the outer door closed. She shook herself and ran to her wardrobe, where she seized the first formal dress that came to hand. There was no time for an intricate hairstyle, so she left her hair loose before she rushed with her makeup. Her reflection was careworn and uncertain. She practised a professional smile, before grabbing her evening bag.

The apartment was silent. Nero had left without seeking her. Sara practised his excuses as she travelled downstairs in the elevator. Important family matters took precedence over this insecure wife's concerns.

When Sara arrived in the *Renaissance* dining room, her presence raised a few eyebrows. Piper sat alone at one end of the square table on the mezzanine level. Enzo sat directly opposite Piper, with his mother on his right, and his grandson Nero on his left. Gina occupied the chair beside Nero. These cousins were the only representatives of the younger generations.

Enzo's four sisters sat beside their mother. Their husbands faced them to complete the square. Sara rehearsed their names: Theresa and Raymond Serpios, Beatrice and Luigi

Paulini, Cecilia and Orazio Ferro, and Diana and Fabio Abatangelo. Enzo's wife, Sabrina was notably absent.

Piper did not wait for anyone to discuss how they would accommodate Sara at their table. He waved her to his end, placing her at his right hand.

"Now that Sara is here, the first course can be served," Piper said, signalling to the chief waiter.

When the bowl of hearty chicken soup appeared before Piper, he attacked it as if he hadn't eaten for days. An uncomfortable silence settled over the other diners, unbroken except by polite comments about the food. Sara kept her eyes on her bowl, not raising them until Piper summoned the waiters again. She had barely touched her food.

The next course of steaming meat and vegetables was speedily served. Again, Piper ate with disregard for his companions. When his plate was empty, he pushed it away and reached for his serviette. A waiter hurried to refill his wine glass. This must have been a signal because everyone turned from their meals to focus on Piper.

"Valentino lives," Piper said, raising his glass in a silent toast. He said nothing more.

"You told me that already," Enzo huffed.

Piper glared at him across the table. "I also told you to keep that information to yourself. I'm not referring to old news. To clarify my statement, Valentino *still* lives!"

Sara stopped breathing, her eyes fixed on Piper's face. An uncomfortable murmur raced around the table.

"What do you mean?" Doña Gabriella Marcella demanded. "*Still* lives?"

"I rescued Valentino and took him to a secure location for medical treatment," Piper said. "I passed that information to Enzo with clear instructions. I ordered complete secrecy to ensure my cousin's safety. My involvement should have ended there. But I remembered Enzo's trouble with secrets. I left my Sydney team in place and set a watch on your headquarters. An hour after my call, a Melbourne assassin appeared beside Valentino's hospital bed."

He paused and studied each one in turn. "Someone threatened Valentino's life a second time."

Protests and accusations erupted among them.

Sara reached for Piper's arm, asking quietly, "Is Valentino okay?"

He turned to her, and everyone fell silent to hear his answer. "Why are you the only one to ask that question?" he asked, his eyes raking the group before returning to Sara. "He predicted your concern and has appointed you his representative. He is in no hurry to return, and any communication with the family will now be directed through you."

Piper rose to his feet.

"You didn't answer Sara's question," Nero said, also rising.

"Valentino was expecting trouble," Piper conceded. "My agents followed the would-be-assassin from Melbourne to the Sydney hospital. They let him think he'd slipped past hospital security to gain access to Valentino's room. Unfortunately, Valentino recognised him – a 'trusted employee' with ambitions to rise higher in the organisation. and your 'employee' was dead before I could intervene. When I left him, Valentino was planning his revenge."

Unfulfilled Promise

ꙮ

*2 Corinthians 6:10 - Even if you have nothing,
as a servant of God you possess all things.*

ꙮ

It had been almost a month since the confrontation with Piper. This evening, the family had reserved the upper level of the *Renaissance* restaurant for a family event. Sara remained at Nero's side, despite the persistent cramps that had plagued her all day. While dressing for the party, her greatest fear had been confirmed. Her pregnancy had failed. Her misfortune must not overshadow Nero's grandmother Sabrina's sixtieth-birthday celebration. Sara had not shared her pregnancy hopes with her husband, and it was too late now.

A waiter stopped beside Sara and offered her a flute of champagne.

"Sara's not drinking alcohol," Nero said. "Bring her something else."

"Nonsense," Doña Gabriella Marcella said. The ninety-two-year-old matriarch seized the glass and pressed it into Sara's hand. "You told me she's not pregnant, so there's no excuse. She must honour your grandmother's birthday with champagne."

"The doctor—" Nero protested.

"There's time for that when she's pregnant," Theresa said. His eldest great-aunt's comments drew others of her generation to the discussion. "You must be doing something wrong if you can't get her pregnant."

"I've had no difficulty getting her pregnant," Nero snapped. "It's keeping her pregnant—"

"Are you sure she isn't doing something to make the pregnancy fail?" his great-aunt Beatrice asked. A lively discussion erupted among them about Sara's character, and whether this was a probable explanation.

Sara wished the floor would open up and swallow her. Gina nudged her with her elbow.

"Sara and I are sneaking off to the restroom," Gina informed Nero, as she dragged her friend along with her.

"That was awful," Gina said, when the two women were safely in the anteroom. Except for the attendant, they had the room to themselves. Gina studied her appearance in the mirror before turning to Sara. "Remind me not to tell them if I decide I want a baby."

Sara was still holding the champagne flute.

"Let me drink that for you," Gina said, taking it from her hand. "The attendant will fetch you some sparkling mineral water." She waited until the woman left the room to comply with her demand before she shoved Sara onto a sofa. "You've miscarried again, haven't you? You close your eyes in pain when you think nobody is looking. And Nero doesn't know."

Not daring to put her grief over another miscarriage into words, Sara lowered her eyes. Gina gathered her in a quick embrace and then reached into her purse. "Take this and then put on your party smile. Valentino is due any minute, and you have to look your best."

The small white pill sat on Sara's palm. She flipped it over to look at the marking and frowned at the black stamp. It reminded her of a bishop's mitre. "Where did you get this?"

"A friend," Gina said with a grin.

Sara passed the pill back to her. "I've already maxed out my allowance of pain killers, and I don't want to add anything else to my system. I'll be fine."

"You had better be," Gina said, swallowing the white tablet herself. Almost immediately, she led the way back to the dining room.

They arrived in time to welcome Valentino. He had remained interstate since the plane crash.

"How's my favourite uncle?" Gina asked, wrapping herself around him in a close embrace. He frowned, removing her arms. His response to Sara was more welcoming. Gina pouted and called across to Nero. "I told you he'd only have eyes for Sara. He's a fool because she's too devoted to you to give him *any* affection."

"What Valentino needs is a wife of his own," Doña Gabriella Marcella said.

"We were addressing that before the accident," Enzo said. "There's plenty of time to discuss business later. Dinner is about to be served."

Everyone moved towards the decorated tables. Small place cards designated where everyone should sit. Valentino's return had supplanted Nero and Gina from the head table. They whispered about their changed fortune. Sara was grateful to have a seat near the balustrade, which gave her an excellent view of the lower dining room. Her eyes roamed over the gathering diners.

She froze when she saw a familiar figure – a walking mountain. Romano was impossible to miss, standing head and shoulders above everyone else. He wore a stylish black tuxedo with red accessories. Two men preceded him as if they were his bodyguards. One of them glanced up to the balcony, and Sara frowned in recognition. Why was Romano here with Piper? She checked whether the other man was Oliver and stomped on her disappointment. The tall young man was a stranger.

Then Piper moved. Sara caught her first glimpse of a petite woman wearing a long red coat.

"Who are you staring at?" Gina asked, appearing beside her.

"Romano," Sara said, distracted by the action below. Romano unfastened the belt on the red garment to reveal a little black dress that clung to the woman's every curve. "That must be his wife."

"She's beautiful," Gina said. "That man doesn't deserve her."

They were not the only family members to notice Romano and Piper below. During dinner, the conversation continued to return to the Romano couple. First, the report of the woman's accident was enthusiastically debated. The claims that she had miraculously returned from the dead divided opinion. Some refused to believe in a modern-day miracle. Then her abduction and safe return caused even more excitement. There was speculation that this woman was protected by angels. Enzo boasted of his alliance with Romano. At least he credited Valentino for his swift action in dealing with her enemies.

Romano and his wife moved onto the dance floor, removing themselves from Sara's line of sight. A ripple of loud applause sounded below, and Nero's great-aunt, Beatrice, reported an unexpected observation. "Romano's wife has just told him she's pregnant. It has been a long time since I've seen a man so happy to receive such news."

A storm of grief and jealousy broke in Sara's heart, compounding her physical discomfort. Gina squeezed her hand, and Sara turned her head away.

Enzo summoned the head waiter. He ordered expensive French champagne for the fortunate couple downstairs.

"Tell me more about this woman," Doña Gabriella Marcella announced in a loud voice. All conversation stopped.

"You answer her, Valentino," Enzo said. His sharp tone awakened Sara's curiosity. She shifted in her chair to gain a better view.

"Apart from the drama with Romano, which you've discussed, there's little to tell," Valentino said. Sara didn't sense anything wrong with his answer, which made his mother's outrage unexpected.

"What are you hiding?" the matriarch demanded. Valentino shrugged.

"Before Valentino had his accident he was dating the sister," Enzo said. "He's still angry that we sent him into that storm. If he had remained, he would have infiltrated the Fontana family. He expected to have more influence over Romano."

The elderly lady rapped her walking stick on the table. "That woman downstairs. Is she from Sydney? Are her parents Rosa and Benito Fontana?"

"Do you know her?" her eldest daughter Theresa asked.

"What kind of foolish question is that?" the mother demanded, rising to her feet. "Would I ask about her family if I didn't know her? Until the death of her grandmother, I was her patron. For twenty years, Ria attended daily prayers at the Sydney cathedral—"

"She's not called Ria anymore," Valentino said. "Romano changed her name—"

"I don't care what name she's using," Doña Gabriella Marcella said. "*Maria Evangelina* Fontana is a *good* Catholic girl."

Sara's head was spinning. She looked over the balcony to where Ria sat drinking champagne with Romano and Piper. Could this Ria be the same woman who had listened to her confession in the Sydney cathedral?

৪০ ☼ ৩

Nero's temper did not improve as the evening progressed. Gina continued to goad him over his exclusion from the conversations with his uncle. He emptied his wine glass and signalled for another drink.

Gina came alert. "Where's Valentino going?"

"Forget about Valentino," Nero muttered. "Doña Gabriella Marcella is on her way." He turned to Sara, who sat in some kind of trance. He shook her shoulder.

"Be gentle," Gina said, leaning between them. "She's not *well*."

His cousin's assessment startled him. He studied his wife, annoyed that he hadn't noticed any infirmity.

Sara turned tear-filled eyes towards him. "I'm sorry."

The world stopped for Nero. Another miscarriage! And he hadn't even known she was pregnant. "What *other* secrets is Sara keeping from me?" he asked Gina.

"Don't make a scene," Gina whispered. "It's only just happened. Let's deal with whatever the old woman wants and discuss this later."

"Sara, come with me," Doña Gabriella Marcella commanded.

"Where are you taking my wife?" Nero asked.

"To meet Maria Evangelina."

Gina laughed. "You won't get past her husband."

"Valentino is taking care of that."

Nero pulled Sara to her feet, expecting to accompany them.

Doña Gabriella Marcella grabbed Sara's arm and pushed him away with her cane. "You stay here. To bring you would be disastrous."

Nero protested, "Disas—!"

Gina elbowed him into silence. A charming smile brightened her face. "I'll go with Sara, and bring you a full report."

"*You* may learn something from this interview," Doña Gabriella Marcella said to Gina. "That woman needs reminding of my long patronage."

Nero had not conceded. "What good will that do?"

"She has the makings of a saint, and your wife needs a blessed miracle. I suspect her infertility is because you've been cursed."

"Cursed!" he spluttered. "Sara's the one having miscarriage after miscarriage. If anyone's cursed, it's her."

His great-grandmother's icy glare took him back to his childhood. His stomach cramped at her obvious disapproval.

"Your wife attends Mass every Sunday, but you never accompany her. *You* were still married when you seduced her. Look at her. She still wrestles with the shame of your actions, while you have no remorse."

Gina wrapped an arm around Sara, speaking sharply. "Nero, stop arguing and get out of our way."

೫ ✿ ೬

Sara went to the lower dining room without offering any resistance. The three women took the longer route to avoid an encounter with Valentino. When they arrived, the table they sought was empty. With a wave of her walking stick, their leader issued orders. Waiters added extra chairs and poured champagne into fresh glasses.

They were seated when Romano's wife returned from the direction of the restroom. In stunned silence, Sara compared the memory of the Ria she had met in Sydney with this beautiful woman. The young bodyguard restrained Ria when he saw them. He spoke into his phone, and then his eyes lifted to the balcony where Nero, Valentino, Piper and Romano stood looking down at them.

The newcomer sat down at the table, cautious and watchful. Her familiar eyes lingered on Sara for too long. The lawyer grew more certain that Ria remembered their first meeting. She pushed a champagne flute into Ria's hand to break the spell.

Doña Gabriella Marcella did not seem to notice that anything had passed between the pair. The matriarch introduced them before delivering her judgement. "Maria Evangelina, you have changed your appearance. Yet, from the stories I have heard, there's no doubt that God favours you."

Ria nodded, her dark eyes wide. Sara sipped champagne, and envied the air of peace which surrounded her.

"We shared the same Sydney priest," the matriarch continued. "Father Finnegan did not agree with the way your relatives treated you. First, he insisted I provide a generous scholarship for your education. And later, I secured your employment with a reputable company." After detailing the debt owed, Doña Gabriella Marcella made a surprising declaration. "If only you had continued attending Mass after your Nonna died. I would have honoured you by introducing you to my unmarried son."

Gina leaned forward at this revelation, her eyes glistening. Sara chewed her lip, trying to imagine how Valentino would have responded. A small frown was the only reaction from the unlikely recipient of this "honour".

The nonagenarian brought her speech to an end. "I never expected to find you here in Melbourne, and certainly not unsuitably married. But as you're reforming this troublemaker, I'm prepared to forgive you."

Romano's wife still said nothing.

Doña Gabriella Marcella smiled. "Congratulations on the blessed news you are with child."

Gina nudged Sara, and they raised a glass to toast the "blessed" woman.

Finally, Romano's wife spoke. "God has been very kind to me. I have a new name as a sign that the past sorrow is over. Everyone calls me Evie now. You disapprove, but God has blessed my marriage. I am carrying twins."

"Ah!" A satisfied smile adorned Doña Gabriella Marcella's face. "If only my great-grandson's wife had *half* your blessings. Sara has been unable to fall pregnant—"

"Falling pregnant isn't the problem," Gina interjected. "She's had four miscarriages in eight months."

The matriarch shot Gina a look that made Sara's stomach twitch ominously. But the younger woman shrugged off the disapproval. "Our esteemed Nonna thinks asking *you* to bestow a blessing will solve *all* Sara's problems."

Evie smiled and directed her full attention to Sara. "I believe God has a purpose for your life. He wants to pour grace and mercy into your situation. But first, you must be sure that you're ready to surrender your ambitions. Will you submit to His authority?"

That clear voice spoke directly to her heart. Sara nodded. Evie's words of wisdom were generously sprinkled with Scriptures. Some of them were familiar – Sara had been memorising Bible promises.

"Are you ready for me to pray?" Evie asked.

"Yes."

Evie closed her eyes as she reached for Sara's hand, her lips moving in silent supplication. As soon as their fingers touched, an intense heat surged through Sara's body. She tried to pull her hand away, but Evie held on tight.

The bitter pain in Sara's heart intensified, and her despair broke free. She abandoned herself to her tears.

Sara's body trembled when Evie began to pray aloud. "Heavenly Father, Creator and Sustainer of Life. You see my sister's broken heart. Her desperate prayers have not fallen on deaf ears. Her sorrow cannot be hidden. You do not want her to dwell in a valley of despair. She is only passing through, on her way to her fruitful inheritance. In green pastures, you will restore her joy and make her future secure."

There was a pause. Evie took a deep breath, opened her eyes and leaned closer. Her next words struck like a hammer, inscribing a sacred message on Sara's heart.

"Sara, I speak to your body – be whole in Jesus' Name."

The pain in Sara's body left her.

But Evie was not finished. "Surrender your mind – be at peace and find comfort on the mountain of the Most High. The Lord has restored your hope…"

Evie released Sara's hand before slumping back in her chair. Her bodyguard stepped closer.

"Thank you," Sara whispered.

Evie's eyes closed, and she no longer acknowledged that the other women were present.

Doña Gabriella Marcella said nothing as she led the two younger women back the way they had come. Sara walked in a daze with her heart fluttering. Gina held her close, exclaiming, "Sara, why are you so hot?"

Differing Expectations

౭౦ ✿ ౪

*1 Peter 4:8c WEB - Love covers
a multitude of sins.*

౭౦ ✿ ౪

Midnight had passed. The party was nearing a close, yet this brought Nero no comfort. Sara sat beside him with a vacant smile on her face. She had not spoken since Gina brought her back after the encounter with Romano's wife. A parade of relatives had visited, with Gina delighting in being the one to satisfy their curiosity about Sara's blissful state, and the conversation that had caused it.

At last, only the three of them remained at their table.

"Are you sure she hasn't taken one of your pills?" Nero asked again.

Gina frowned at him before signalling for the waiter, who started towards them with a bottle of wine. Valentino stepped into the waiter's path and relieved him of that burden.

"Finally," Gina said, "I was beginning to think *he* was never coming to talk to us."

Their uncle sat down, pouring wine for everyone. He studied each of them over the rim of his glass.

"Before you ask," Gina said, "Sara's trance is not my doing."

"Nor mine," muttered Nero. "You can lay the blame on Doña Gabriella Marcella's religious mumbo-jumbo. She thought she was breaking a curse."

"Don't be too quick to dismiss curses," Valentino said.

"Not you too?" Nero asked. "Has the whole family gone mad?"

Valentino lowered his voice. "Perhaps it's a question of choosing between a curse or a blessing."

"And which would you choose?" Gina snickered. "You taught me to create my own destiny."

"And I haven't changed my mind," Valentino said, "but I also warned you to remember the law of consequences. Choices create a ripple effect. I'm beginning to think that the universe is calling me to account because of mine."

"God created the universe," Sara said. "If anyone is calling you to account, it will be Him."

Nero looked at her in surprise.

Gina chuckled. "Our little saint has found her voice."

"I don't have time for this," Nero said. "Enzo's preparing to leave, and I want to talk to him about tomorrow's meeting. Are you coming, Gina?"

He was halfway across the room when Gina nudged him, a suggestive grin on her face. She gestured towards their table, where Sara and Valentino were deep in conversation. "I thought you didn't want your wife left alone with him?"

Nero jerked his head back to the front and kept walking. There would be time to deal with Sara later. Now, he must remind his grandfather of his service during his uncle's absence. He was not ready to become redundant.

🖤 ☼ ♋

Sara wondered why Valentino had chosen to remain here. There was a distant look in his eyes that he had kept hidden from the others. She had so many questions for him. "Are you back to stay?"

He smiled at her over his glass, that expression reminding her of their many chess games. The silence lengthened.

She tried a different approach. "Why did you tell your family I was safeguarding your secrets? All I received from you were messages to forward to Nero."

"Insurance."

"How can you call something that made both my husband and my best friend suspicious 'insurance'?"

"Before I answer your questions, I have one of my own," Valentino said. "This religious experience – it's not the first time something's happened to you?"

Sara leaned her head to the side. She took a risk, lowering her defences. In a few sentences, she told him about her first meeting with Romano's wife.

Then she talked about the things she had learned since then, including the decisions she had made. She mentioned the secret hospital visit from Oliver's mother on her wedding night, after her first miscarriage.

279

"I know it sounds like a bunch of random happenings, but I'm certain that God is behind everything. I can't talk to Nero or Gina about this. They both think I'm using religion as a crutch, but what if this is the only insurance I need?"

"You answer reassures me," Valentino said. "Swear before God that what I tell you remains a secret until after my death."

"Please don't talk about dying!" Sara said, tears springing to her eyes. "And tell someone else your secrets!"

"I don't trust anyone else."

His words exploded in her mind. "Why me?"

"You know who I am." His hand edged towards the pocket where he kept his blade, and he watched her reaction. "You know what I'm capable of." He patted the pocket, and it became difficult for her to breathe. "Yet your messages ended with an assurance that you prayed for me." She nodded. "Then listen carefully – I wouldn't ask, if this wasn't essential."

His empty hand returned to the table. Sara swallowed her questions and sighed. "I promise."

Valentino confirmed that they could not be overheard and spoke quickly. "I'm breaking all ties with the family. I won't burden you with my reasons. But before I go, I have to identify my enemy. I'm certain it's someone close. If my plans fail, a Sydney lawyer will contact you. Piper knows everything – do what he says. I know you're a clever girl, and I'm trying to keep you safe."

"How is this keeping *me* safe?"

"I've told Enzo that my secret files will be sent to the authorities if anything happens to you. He recognises the truth."

"What am I going to tell Nero?"

Valentino reached for her hand, and a shiver ran down Sara's spine. He looked into her eyes. "Tell him I've appointed you my executor."

৪৩ ☼ ૪১

(Sunday 15th October)

"What's so urgent?" Sara asked.

Gina dragged her along the hallway towards the elevator. "We're invited to Valentino's apartment. He's very selective about who he admits, and I don't want to miss out."

"You said we're invited?" Sara said, straightening her sleeve. She still wore the conservative dress she had chosen for Sunday morning Mass.

"He told his mother he has important news. She's marshalling her troops to remind him of his duty."

"What troops?"

Gina laughed. "All the women he's lectured about their family obligations. There's a lot of us when we get together. This gathering is usually reserved for introducing a prospective newcomer to the clan."

"I didn't go through this ritual," Sara said.

"Brides come with different expectations. Nero had Valentino's approval for you. And Enzo did the negotiations for Nero's first marriage."

Valentino's apartment was one of the penthouse suites. The large group assembled outside the elevator, until Doña Gabriella Marcella led the way. Among them were some teenagers Sara had not met before. The matriarch rapped loudly on the door with her cane. When there was no immediate response, she banged a second time.

The door opened. A dark-haired, curvaceous woman blinked in surprise at their number. Valentino's mother shoved her way forward. The stranger stepped back as everyone surged in. She looked familiar.

Sara remembered the Friday evening remarks about Valentino courting Evie Romano's sister, Sofia Fontana. She searched the beautiful woman's face for some sense of the peace that always characterised Evie. All she found was pride and self-assurance.

Valentino emerged from another room. He did not attempt to hide his displeasure. "I only invited you, Mother."

"I'll bring whoever I like," she retaliated, claiming a sofa as if it was her throne. "You had better introduce me."

The other relatives hurriedly selected their seats. The furniture in this large room was white, with a grand piano in prime position. Gina pulled Sara onto a sofa and sat back to enjoy the drama. Was this woman part of his plan to flush out his enemy? Sara silently prayed for Valentino.

"Sofia, this is my mother, Doña Gabriella Marcella Horatio. Mother, this is my fiancée, Sofia Fontana."

Gina nudged Sara and grinned. "Did you know?" she whispered. Sara shook her head.

After Valentino introduced his "fiancée" to his sisters, he left the rest to name themselves. Another knock came at the door. His hostess opened it to receive three trolleys. The matriarch had ordered refreshments. Sofia performed her duties with poise, serving his unsmiling mother. Then she worked her way through the family according to their rank. Sara greatly admired her stamina. The hand that passed around coffee was steady.

The conversation was minimal while everyone waited for the matriarch's opening salvo. "You're nothing like your sister," Doña Gabriella Marcella told Sofia. "*She* would not dishonour her family by acting like a harlot."

Sofia smiled as if this were a compliment. "You're right. I'm nothing like Maria Evangelina. She's a saint, while I'm twice divorced. I've had many lovers, and I'm confident I know how to keep Valentino happy."

Gina giggled, and her mother shushed her. The young woman leaned closer to Sara and murmured in her ear. "She's perfect."

It was difficult to follow the interview while Gina continued her commentary. The final question was about providing him with an heir. Sofia's answer was a definitive "no". To follow that grievance, Valentino handed his mother some legal papers. "I asked you here to present these. After Sofia and I marry, I'm leaving the family business. You're always telling me I'm worthless, so I've made myself redundant."

Doña Gabriella Marcella's face twisted in rage. "You ungrateful—"

Valentino did not permit her to continue. He stepped closer, using his physical presence to overshadow his aged mother. "While I was in Sydney, your brother Augustus promised me his support."

"Oh ho," Gina chortled. "He's played the ace card. She might reign here, but in Sydney, her brother is Emperor."

"We're leaving!" Doña Gabriella Marcella declared. Her body was rigid. The angry woman clutched her ivory-handled walking stick with white knuckles.

Everyone obediently followed her to the door. Nobody seemed sure how to take their leave. A few women murmured a goodbye. Sara watched Valentino for some sign of remorse.

When she was almost at the door, he flashed her a familiar smile – the one he reserved for his more ruthless chess wins. That was the confirmation she needed. Sara dashed back across the room, throwing her arms around Sofia. "I hope he makes you happy," Sara whispered. "I'll be praying for you." Allowing no time for the startled fiancée to respond, she rushed out the door.

Sneaky
Suspicions

ಌ ✿ ಜ

*Psalm 119:11 WEB - I have hidden your word in my heart,
that I might not sin against you.*

ಌ ✿ ಜ

A small box sat on Sara's desk when she arrived at work. "Gina, did you put this here?"

"No. And it wasn't there on Thursday night. Perhaps Valentino left it for you. A goodbye present before he left for Thailand with Sofia this morning."

"It wouldn't be Valentino," Sara said. "You know he came to the apartment last night."

"Then you have a secret admirer," Gina said. "Open it."

The lid slipped off easily. Inside was a folded piece of paper. Sara removed it, admiring the silver armband nestled on a bed of white satin.

Gina looked over her shoulder as she read the note.

Sara, this bangle is a reminder of promises, past and present.
When you wear it, be protected. You are never alone.
God's appointed guardian watches over you. Evie Romano

"Creepy," Gina said. "I don't think I'd want God watching my every move, even if He was protecting me. What are the past promises she's referring to?"

Sara shrugged. She had a few ideas but was reticent to share them. She examined the heavy silver ornament. "There's an inscription: 'Psalm forty-six verse one – An ever-present help'."

Gina took the bangle, unsnapping the almost invisible hinge. "It's not a cheap trinket. See the '925' stamp. And that looks like a serial number – 'ER-07-MS'. I'm guessing Evie commissioned a series, and this is the seventh one. Hold out your wrist." Sara did as she was told. Gina snapped it shut, apparently still thinking about the numbers. "I'll check on the internet – MS is probably the designer."

"There are more pressing priorities," Sara said. "I need you to get me today's case files. Then check the court schedule. Yesterday, they suggested my first case might be moved..."

Walking to the morning briefing, the riddle of the note remained a distraction for Sara. She was almost certain the bangle was part of Valentino's "insurance" plan. Therefore, Piper was responsible for having it delivered. But how was Evie Romano involved?

Sara's eyes drifted to the ceiling camera, which reminded her of Oliver, and the company he worked for. She jiggled the bangle on her wrist, convinced that the "MS" was another clue.

ℬ ☼ ℭ

The hospital cafeteria was crowded. As Oliver turned from purchasing his roast pork and vegetables, a table became free. He uttered a quick prayer as he dropped into the chair. Five minutes later, Piper appeared opposite him. Oliver continued shovelling food into his mouth.

"Your father's condition has improved," Piper began. "There's talk that he's going home tomorrow. Your parents understand the need for you to return to active duty."

A dozen uncomplimentary phrases raced across Oliver's mind, but he continued eating. He mulled over his response. Once he had his temper under control, he paused long enough to ask, "When?"

"Monday, or Tuesday. I'm still awaiting confirmation from my informant in Thailand."

Chewing carefully, Oliver considered his next question. "Why me?"

"We both know you're my most experienced helicopter pilot. You have more jungle combat hours, and you won't allow anything to distract you from the mission. I trust your instincts, and know you won't hesitate to tell me if you spot a flaw in my plan."

It was not like Piper to be generous with compliments. Oliver chased the last streak of gravy around his plate with a piece of meat. "The timing's lousy."

"I disagree," Piper said. "I'm only asking you to commit for a few days, a week at the most. I'm after the ringleaders, and I'll leave the mopping up to the regional authorities."

Oliver was not ready to concede. He already knew he would go, but he wanted to know how much more information Piper would surrender. He swallowed the final mouthful. "Why the rush?"

287

"I've been tracking this trafficking syndicate for six months. Every day they continue to operate destroys countless innocent lives."

Deadly Opposition

ॐ ☼ ॐ

*Psalm 126:5 WEB - Those who sow in tears
will reap in joy.*

ॐ ☼ ॐ

Ignoring the monsoonal rain, Oliver walked across the Bangkok tarmac towards the leased helicopter. He wrote notes on his clipboard as the company pilot gave a detailed briefing. Oliver underlined the estimated range of the machine before asking about refuelling options.

The timetable was tight. Would there be sufficient time to acclimatise to the steamy conditions? Oliver had a few hours to practise in the helicopter before Piper returned.

Half an hour into the orientation flight over Bangkok, a message recalling him to the heliport came over the radio. "*Operation Phoenix* pilot, the excursion scheduled for tomorrow has been brought forward. Your passengers will be ready to board in T-minus seventy minutes."

Oliver shot a prayer heavenward, slowed his breathing and reorientated his focus. He took a direct route, landing the helicopter at the airport twenty minutes later. As soon as he had dismissed the Thai pilot, he reached for his mobile phone. "What's the problem?"

Piper's answer was brief. "Valentino and Sofia are missing. I'm sending you some coordinates. Refuel and prepare for an overnight operation near the Thai/Myanmar border." The call ended abruptly.

After glancing at the coordinates, Oliver ran for the terminal. He unlocked the secure suite of rooms and changed into his paramilitary uniform. The terminal staff had already proven themselves courteous and ready to serve. But one look at the *Operation Phoenix* insignia on his beret, and they doubled their efforts.

Oliver enlisted their help in loading camping equipment onto the helicopter. While they worked, he supervised the refuelling, crosschecking his calculations while he waited for the others. Nelson Felmingham arrived first, coming from the international passenger terminal. He had travelled by himself from Sydney and received the new orders upon his arrival. Oliver sent him to change into his paramilitary uniform.

When Piper arrived, he was accompanied by two civilians. They were here for the secondary mission: to retrieve and repatriate Sofia. Oliver frowned. Romano's ability to deal with the hostile jungle environment was not a concern. But Pastor John Edwards was another matter.

During the flight from Melbourne, Oliver had asked the pastor how he knew Valentino. John had shared a story of a fractious friendship with Sofia. She had claimed him as her "priest-confessor".

The unlikely friends had been in regular communication since Romano's wedding. What little Oliver knew about worldly Sofia rang alarm bells. Rebellious and independent – and vicious with her tongue – she was nothing like her gentle sister, Evie Romano.

How would Sofia react when she found out that Valentino had ordered Piper to organise for John and her hated brother-in-law, Romano, to escort her home.

Piper signalled for Oliver to remain silent. Nelson was sent to supervise the civilians as they changed into more suitable kit. Oliver watched them go, wondering whether anything would fit Romano.

"He brought his overalls," Piper said, and then addressed Oliver's main concern. "You're worried about John Edwards coming with us, about his ability to cope with the jungle conditions. We're going to need him when we find Sofia. She's likely to take one look at Romano and explode. In her eyes, Valentino's a saint compared to her sister's husband."

"What happened to the two *Maximum Security* agents you assigned to watch Sofia?"

"I've talked to Thomas. I already knew the basics from a brief report I received while we were in transit, but he filled in the blanks. A street gang attacked Sofia yesterday. She suffered a minor injury, but Patrick was seriously wounded. He's out of surgery, but I've left Thomas guarding his hospital room."

"And Sofia?" Oliver asked.

"The hospital discovered she'd been poisoned," Piper replied, "Valentino turned up in a jealous rage, fuelled by his sisters' lies. He'd have murdered her if Thomas hadn't been there. The tox-screen was conclusive and Valentino was intimately familiar with the name of the drug."

"Is that why he sent for you?"

"Valentino used Sofia to convince the family he was breaking from them. I warned him it might backfire, but he wouldn't listen. My cousin has lost his edge."

The other three members of their group were approaching the helicopter. Oliver had one more question. "How long has Valentino been working for you?"

℁☼℃

(Tuesday 24th October)

When Sara finished her afternoon court session, she went searching for Gina. Two hours earlier, her assistant had received a message and left the courtroom. Unable to find her, Sara tried phoning her friend. She left a message when the answering service picked up. Now the lawyer stood near the top of the stairs. Should she return to the office, or continue waiting here for Gina?

The courthouse would close in fifteen minutes, and doors around the landing opened as other cases adjourned for the day. People rushed towards the stairs, catching Sara in their stampede.

"Sara!" That shout came from below. She whirled suddenly, and her briefcase swung with her. It must have hit someone – Sara heard a grunt – and the jolt sent a pain through her arm. The unseen person lashed out at her. Unbalanced, Sara fell backwards onto the stairs, screaming as she sensed open air beneath her.

A moment later, an opposing force thrust her upward. Sara's body was catapulted across the landing. Spectators stepped out of her way and she hit the floor with a thud. Her briefcase slipped from her fingers, and she heard it crash into the wall.

"Keep still," an accented voice said. Sara stared at a stocky stranger who stood over her. The Asian woman ignored Sara, talking into her phone as her dark eyes scanned the crowd. "Sigrid, tell me you've tagged him – yes, I have the target – hang on, I'll ask." Those piercing eyes fixed on Sara. "Are you okay? You're not bleeding?"

"What? No."

The stranger relayed this information into her phone before dragging Sara upright. The crowd had thinned, and her companion retrieved the briefcase.

"Why would I be blee—?" Sara began, but then she saw the vicious slash in the leather cover of her briefcase. The colour drained from her face as her knees buckled. "Who *are* you?"

The stranger caught her and held her upright. "I'm Xanda, from *Maximum Security*. I was sent to retrieve you, and I arrived just in time. Can you walk as far as the elevator?"

Sara took a tentative step and grimaced. "I've twisted my ankle, but I can hobble that far." She bent down and slipped off her stilettos.

Xanda scanned the area as she helped Sara to the elevator. There were still a few stragglers, but nobody stopped to question them.

The elevator arrived in the underground car park. A large vehicle blocked the doorway, the engine revving loudly. The van's sliding door was open, and Xanda bundled Sara inside before leaping in after her. Sara banged her head and cried out. The vehicle zoomed off as the door slammed.

"Stay low," Xanda said, pressing the lawyer back to the floor. "We don't know if anyone else is waiting for you."

"Why would anyone be waiting for me?" Sara asked. "And where are you taking me? You've turned the wrong way for my office."

"We're not going to your office. Keep quiet until we know it's safe," the driver said. Sara recognised Sigrid's voice. Did she still work for Piper Maxwell? The lawyer started to ask, but Xanda clamped her hand across Sara's mouth.

"Combination?" Xanda demanded, holding up the locked briefcase.

It took Sara two attempts to get the numbers right. Xanda opened the briefcase and turned out the contents. Next, she produced an electronic gadget and scanned the interior. "All clear. I've already checked your phone." Sara had not realised she had lost that device. Her hands were shaking as she slipped her phone back into her pocket.

The journey continued in silence for ten minutes. Sara gave up trying to track where they were going.

"Incoming call," Sigrid announced, pressing a button on the dashboard.

Piper's voice came through the speakers above Sara's head. "Report."

"We have the target and are proceeding to base," Sigrid said. "No obvious pursuers and no electronic trackers or listening devices."

"You were right," Xanda added. "Someone was waiting for her – they tried to stab her, and when that didn't work, they pushed her down the stairs. I managed to throw her back to safety, but the attacker escaped."

"Why would someone attack me?" Sara asked.

A leaden silence descended over the van's occupants. Sara studied Xanda's face and decided she no longer wanted to know, but it was too late.

"Valentino's dead," Piper said. His words were as empty of life as the message he delivered. Sara did not know she had forgotten to breathe until the pain in her chest became unbearable. Piper did not expect a reply. "Sara, you are his executor. My priority is to keep you safe until the family remember your survival is necessary if they want to protect their secrets."

ଛ ☼ ଔ

Evening approached. Nero stared at the darkening skyline as the first city lights blinked on. He was alone with his grandfather in the second-floor office. Enzo was finishing the last of his phone calls. Not once, but twice had his grandfather contacted the heads of each household. Following the news of Valentino's death with a second notification presented him with difficulties. Piper's information about Raymond's death inspired too many questions. Why had Enzo's brother-in-law, Theresa's husband, accompanied Valentino into the jungle without the others?

Nero poured his grandfather another strong drink.

Piper had sent graphic photos to confirm both deaths. Shot multiple times, Valentino had fallen victim to a group of Myanmar rebels. Enzo had kept the overseas negotiations shrouded in secrecy, but Nero could read between the lines. Drugs and human trafficking were profitable enterprises. The multi-billion-dollar resort deal, under negotiation with Thai politicians, was a convincing cover story.

Or a bribe, depending on which version of Enzo's story he chose to believe. His grandfather modified the information he shared with each retelling.

Nero replenished his drink. When the senior executives had followed Valentino to Thailand, the younger man had felt excluded. All that had now changed. Nero was in a powerful position – the only one standing beside his grandfather at this difficult time.

Valentino's lucky streak had ended, with Piper arriving too late to rescue him. But how did Piper know where to look? Nero shoved that thought away. Gina had already voiced her angry accusations. She had been present when the photos of her great-grandfather's body arrived. There was no mistaking Raymond's distinctive wound. With both men dead, it would be difficult to determine why Valentino's hand had delivered the blow.

A message from Gina's mother arrived on Nero's phone, confirming the grieving girl's confinement within her family apartment. He was confident that Gina could harm no-one but herself there. He charged the mother with reducing that risk.

Enzo's phone chirped, and he activated the speaker. "Mother, I wasn't expecting to hear from you again."

"Do you know where Nero's wife is?"

"She's at work," Enzo said, gesturing at Nero to remain silent. The grandson frowned. He had yet to speak to his wife. To avoid an emotional scene, he had sent her the briefest message. A "family matter" needed his attention.

"You had better check," Doña Gabriella Marcella said. "Ricardo Barononi phoned with some concerns about a job Gina commissioned this afternoon."

"What job?" Enzo asked.

"She arranged the assassination attempt through one of his sons, who didn't question why the family would want to kill Nero's wife."

"Why didn't he question the request?" Enzo asked, gripping the phone in his hand.

"The boy knew I paid to eliminate Nero's first wife."

ೞ ✿ ೲ

Pacing beside the office window, Nero waited for Sara to answer her phone. Enzo was on the landline, asking whether Gina was sober enough for interrogation.

Sara's answering service picked up. Nero growled in frustration before trying again. This time, a female voice with a distinctive accent answered. "Nero Mariani?"

"Yes!" he growled. "Who is this, and why are you answering my wife's phone?"

"Your wife is safe. Piper has taken her into protective custody. Tell your grandfather to follow Valentino's instructions to the letter. Enzo needs to remember what will happen if Sara is harmed. Valentino's incriminating documents will be released to the public."

The line went dead. Nero dropped his phone onto the desk. "Piper has Sara. Did Valentino leave instructions with you? What's this about?"

"Sit down," Enzo said. "Valentino went to Thailand to draw out the person behind the assassination attempt. What neither of us expected was that our four sisters would accompany him with their husbands in tow. Theresa convinced me they only wanted to win over his fiancée and entice him back into the fold. Now, I'm not so sure."

"Is that why Valentino killed Raymond?" Nero asked. "Was Raymond the traitor?"

"It's too early to know. But I'm concerned about why Gina acted as she did."

"Leave Gina to me," Nero said. "She's an impulsive girl, but I'm sure I can bring her back into line."

Phony Ultimatum

ఐ ✿ ಚ

*Isaiah 26:20a WEB - Come, my people,
enter into your rooms,
and shut your doors behind you.*

ఐ ✿ ಚ

Oliver's meal was cold, and his coffee cup empty. He had come directly from the airport with clear orders from Piper on how to proceed. Yet he remained at the table in the *Maximum Security* Melbourne cafeteria. Upstairs in Room 212, those carefully cross-referenced files were waiting. The brief report he had sent from Thailand would be there amongst the other intelligence. Everything necessary to analyse the family's reaction to the two deaths was a few mouse-clicks away.

He could not remember ever being this weary — overburdened by a sense of responsibility. The cafeteria emptied, and he dropped his head onto his arms. What was he doing here? Returning from Bangkok, Oliver had accompanied the other *Maximum Security* operatives to Melbourne. Piper remained in Sydney with the civilians to attend Valentino's hastily convened funeral at the cathedral.

Oliver's mind drifted, transporting him back in time to the steamy jungle. The sound of the tropical river in full flood roared in his ears. Finding Sofia was not the greater challenge. Hovering a few metres above the jungle, his mistake had hit him hard.

The joy over finding Sofia and Valentino alive – an answer to his prayers – evaporated when he failed to find anywhere to land. Abandoning the survivors to their fate while he flew over the jungle invited despair to take root in his heart. Each passing minute was another fatal wound, destroying all hope. His misery was made complete when Piper's foot patrol reached the wounded pair and Valentino was beyond help.

Oliver fell into a troubled dream where his mind rewrote the recent events. The river, wild with fury, now reached high into the air, plucking him from the hovering helicopter. In this fantasy, he became the victim fighting the flood for his survival. He pushed upwards through the turbulent waters and burst into the open, his chest heaving.

Voices reached him, jolting him back to reality. His eyes flew open, and it took a few seconds to recognise the dining room.

"When can I go home?" a woman's voice asked.

Every nerve in Oliver's dream-affected body screamed in recognition. "What are you doing here?" Oliver asked Sara, twisting towards two women seated across the room.

The young lawyer blanched. Her unknown companion, a bronzed female warrior, sprang to her feet. His body remembered the drill – he was on his feet in an instant – but his mind refused to cooperate.

Sigrid's timely arrival saved him from an embarrassing defeat. She strode across the cafeteria towards him. "Oliver, why are *you* here?"

"I asked Sara the same question," he said. "And this watchdog challenged me. I didn't know Jenny had hired another bodyguard."

After introductions, Xanda grinned and winked at Oliver. "Sigrid's told me all about *you*. Stay here, and we'll chaperone your conversation with Sara from another table."

After the other women moved closer to the door, Oliver sat opposite Sara. She sighed. "Valentino's dead."

"I know," he answered. "I was there."

"You were there?" Her eyes searched his face as her grief trickled like an unstoppable waterfall down her cheeks. "I'm not sure I want to hear your testimony."

Oliver shifted in his seat. "I'd better go." His legs refused to obey him. He made a second attempt to rise.

"I'm sorry. Please don't leave." She reached for his hand but froze, her fingers a few centimetres from touching him. "I need to know what happened."

He stared at the gap between them as the words spilled from his lips. "Valentino was still alive when I spotted him, but there was nowhere to land the helicopter. He had been shot multiple times, and yet survived being swept away in a flooded river. He died in Sofia's arms, about an hour before Piper's team reached him."

Oliver swallowed hard, and continued. "I'm having trouble accepting his death. I thought God was using me to save Valentino because he had sided with Piper. I keep asking myself if there was anything else I could have done. Why didn't I risk a closer landing? Or send down the medical kit? I could have taken a risk and tossed out my passenger—"

Sara's sobbing shredded his soul, and he choked out the next words. "I failed Valentino – I failed you – I've failed God."

Both her hands folded over his. "God doesn't think you've failed him." Her next words smashed through his defences. "God is the one who decides whether a man lives or dies. If God wanted you to save Valentino, He would have kept him alive until you got there. Stop taking responsibility for something that was never yours. I'm certain others are relying on you to be their protector. Forgive yourself, and get back in the game."

∽ ☼ ∾

An hour before midnight, Nero entered his grandfather's office. Enzo retrieved a stack of papers from his desk and waved them at him. "Where have you been? Piper's on his way. I need you to explain these documents before he gets here."

"Gina and I have been searching Valentino's apartment. You agreed that we shouldn't wait for the security codes, but it took longer than we expected to gain access."

"Did you find any documents?" Enzo asked.

"There's a locked safe in his study. It's probably a decoy, but Gina won't stop looking until she finds every hiding place. She's also creating an inventory of his furniture and other possessions. Is Valentino's will among these documents?"

"Piper's bringing it with him," Enzo said. "These are Valentino's investments."

"I thought his claim to be a 'property investor' was a cover story," Nero said, studying the first folio. "This pile includes copies of the title deeds. This is his Sydney apartment – last week he leased it to a company I don't recognise. They signed a five-year lease. Here's a copy of the purchase agreement for his Melbourne penthouse. The buyback clause is highlighted – the apartment has to remain within the family, and he's recently updated the valuation."

He reached for the next folder of papers. "A list of companies where he had a controlling interest. Copies of his share certificates. A few outstanding debts, and a longer list of people who owe him money."

Turning the page, Nero swore. "Most of his bank accounts are closed. In recent months, billions of dollars have been syphoned off into trust funds. I don't recognise the account numbers nor the names. He left one open account for the executor to manage his estate."

‣ ☼ •

With her heart pounding, Sara stepped from the elevator. She longed to be reunited with her husband, but Piper had warned her to be cautious. Nelson confirmed that the hallway was clear. He would remain outside while the meeting took place. She carried her slashed briefcase, a constant reminder of her peril. Piper kept in step, while Xanda and Sigrid were close shadows behind them.

Piper knocked, opening the office door without hesitation. The female agents rushed in, advancing to take up position a few metres from the large desk. Enzo sat behind his desk with Nero standing at his side. Nero ignored Piper and the agents, summoning Sara to him with a welcoming smile. Sara leapt forward, ready to run into his arms.

Piper seized her around the waist, jolting her to a stop. "Not until we establish some ground rules."

Nero's smile faded, replaced by a malevolent scowl directed towards Piper. Sara blinked at the transformation.

"This is awkward," Enzo said. "What happened at the courthouse was a regrettable misunderstanding. I offer you my personal guarantee that Sara is safe."

Piper glanced at Sara. After he released her, she remained at his side. Piper removed her briefcase from her trembling hands and dropped it onto the desk. He waved his hand for her to open it, and then he turned the slashed lid to face Enzo and Nero.

She retrieved a single-page document which she passed across the table. "Piper asked me to prepare this. He believes it is necessary for my security."

Nero snatched the paper from her, and she took a step back to escape the animosity in his eyes.

"What does it say?" Enzo asked.

Nero frowned. "It promises the release of incriminating documents if anything happens to her."

Enzo frowned at Piper. "Where's the evidence that these documents exist?"

Piper smiled, removing a sealed envelope from his pocket. "This was with the will. It's addressed to you. Sara knows nothing of the contents, nor the whereabouts of the originals. According to the covering letter, there is more of a similar nature. Valentino claims to have amassed evidence encompassing family dealings over several decades."

Using a jewel-encrusted letter opener, Enzo sliced the envelope to extract the papers. Several photographs dropped out, and Nero picked them up. The colour drained from his face. Whatever the photographs portrayed must have significance for him. Nero passed them to Enzo, swapping them for the documents his grandfather waved at him. Nero frowned as he shuffled through the pages.

"This is sufficient." Enzo pulled himself upright in his seat, folding his hands on the desk. "I will make sure that the family understand."

"Have you dealt with the person involved in the *misunderstanding* at the courthouse?" Piper asked.

Enzo and Nero exchanged glances.

"We uncovered a connection between the death of Nero's first wife and this recent attack," Enzo said. "That connection has been severed. Sara can return to her home without fear."

Piper dropped into a chair in front of the desk. "If only it was as simple as that. We still need to talk about Valentino's will."

"Did you bring it with you?" Enzo asked.

"Sara's the executor," Piper said. "Direct your questions to her."

Both men studied her across the desk, and Sara's stomach began to churn. She glanced in her briefcase. On top of the other papers was the requested document. Piper had collected it from a Sydney law firm earlier in the day.

There was a simple choice before her. She could renounce her executor role and avoid the coming conflict. Or she could keep her promise to Valentino. Sara forced her mouth into her best courtroom smile. "It's reasonably straightforward. Valentino left his entire estate to his fiancée, Sofia Fontana."

Enzo laid the document flat on the desk and stared at her for too long. Sara was careful not to blink.

Finally, Enzo broke the stalemate. "Of course we're contesting this will." Nero opened his mouth, but his grandfather waved him into silence. "I refuse to accept that my brother would disinherit his family heirs for a woman he hardly knows."

₧✲₨

(Monday 30th October)

The final page dropped onto a neat pile. Sara surveyed the documents spread across the spare desk in Valentino's study. The assets the forty-four-year-old had amassed were impressive. She closed her eyes, thankful for his detailed instructions. Her stomach rumbled, reminding her that it was almost noon.

"Did you stop for coffee while I was gone?" Gina asked from the doorway.

Sara spun towards her.

Gina laughed. "When Nero said you could 'work from home', he didn't mean you to chain yourself to this office."

"Is Nero with you?" Sara asked. Several hours ago, the cousins had left together for a family meeting.

"He's in court this afternoon," Gina said. "And there's another meeting this evening. Don't wait up for him." She entered the room, dropping the mail on the main desk.

Sara reached for a letter, but Gina snatched it away. "Most are from solicitors addressed to 'The Executor', which I've left for you to open. The others are begging letters hoping you're a soft touch. You can work on your responses while you're alone this evening."

Gina grabbed Sara's arm, leading her into the living room. Valentino's piano held the central position there. Sara moved to the window, blinking away tears.

"This view is breathtaking," Gina said. "Not that I'm complaining about the view from your old apartment. Nero was a dear to let me have it."

A chill ran up Sara's spine. "It looks cold outside."

"You haven't left the penthouse since you moved in on Friday," Gina said. "We're having lunch in the rooftop garden today. I'll get your coat."

A dozen excuses came to mind, but Sara bowed her head. A few minutes later, they were standing outside Valentino's penthouse. *Nero's penthouse.* The will confirmed Nero's claim that this apartment was his birthright. He refused to wait for probate, transferring the money into the estate account immediately.

Gina nodded to the attendant as she bundled Sara up the ramp to the garden. The *Raphael Towers* building covered two city blocks. The extensive rooftop gardens included many hiding places. Gina kept a tight hold on Sara's arm. "This way."

When they neared the double doors to a white rotunda, Sara stopped. This was the concert hall where Valentino once performed piano recitals for his mother.

"You've been here before?" Gina asked. "Is this where my uncle brought you?"

Sara frowned. "I've been here with Nero. Why would Valentino bring me here?"

"It's where he brought all his conquests."

"All his – oh! Nothing like that ever happened between us."

"Nero believes you, but I'm not convinced. But that's a conversation for another day. You're keeping everyone waiting."

Before Sara could respond, Gina pushed open the rotunda doors. The warmth of the room was unexpected, and it was a relief to be free of the coat. Gina took it from her and passed it to a waiter. Valentino's sisters were already seated at a table draped with white linen. It sat beside another white piano, identical to the one in the penthouse below.

"Finally," Beatrice said.

The senior aunts were beautiful, much younger in appearance than their age. Their hair was dark, their costumes glamorous. Sara felt unsophisticated before them.

Theresa was at the head of the table, dressed in black, with a lace veil over her hair. This was Sara's first encounter with Gina's great-grandmother since the tragedy in Thailand. The seventy-two-year-old widow's temperament had soured.

"I'm sorry for your loss," Sara said.

Theresa glared at her.

"Sara, you're at the end of the table," Beatrice said. Fourteen years younger than Theresa, and the acknowledged spokesperson at family events, this sister was renowned for her sharp tongue. As always, she sat at Theresa's right hand.

Sara obeyed, glancing at the youngest sister, seated around the corner. Diana had been ten years old when Valentino replaced her as the baby of the family. Gina dropped into the empty chair opposite Diana and beside Cecilia.

The waiter filled their wine glasses. Two girls brought out the soup on a trolley. When everyone was served, Beatrice said the blessing. The sisters included Gina in their conversation but left Sara to her contemplation. The soup was delicious, but she had no appetite. The bowl was removed before she finished.

The next course was a generous pasta dish, which suffered the same fate.

"Hold dessert until we've finished our meeting," Beatrice told the waiter.

Sara folded her hands.

"What will we do with you?" Theresa asked Sara. "Valentino's mischief compromises your loyalty. There's evidence he coerced you into marrying Nero – that's justification for an annulment."

Sara leapt to her feet. "What!"

"Sit down," hissed Gina, forcing her back into place. She applied pressure to Sara's shoulders from behind.

"Keep quiet," Beatrice snapped.

"Nero refuses to cooperate," Theresa said, "and he said you'd appeal."

The word "annulment" ricocheted in her mind. Sara almost missed the next revelation.

"Valentino's threats remove the option to eliminate you," Theresa said. "But when we find his hidden documents that may change."

Sara's head dropped forward.

> Heavenly Father, have mercy on me. These people hate me. What am I to do?

"Your husband refuses to sanction any action," Theresa continued. "He believes Valentino was protecting you, after discovering our mother had Zemina killed. We've decided your survival depends on whether you deliver Nero an heir."

ಐ ☼ ಚಿ

(Tuesday 31st October)

Nero frowned. Gina had invited herself to breakfast.

Sara placed a platter of pancakes on the table. She sat with her head bowed in prayer. Gina helped herself, but Nero would be patient. He smiled as his wife served him.

"You're going to miss Sara's home cooking," Gina said between mouthfuls, "when she returns to the courtroom."

"She's not going back," Nero said without looking up from his newspaper.

"When did you decide that?" Gina asked. "And when were you going to tell me?"

He frowned. "Enzo came to discuss this with Sara last night. The family won't challenge her appointment as executor, or contest the will in court, if she resigns from *Yaris & Mariani*. Sara has agreed to devote herself to the negotiations with the fiancée's solicitor."

"Sofia hasn't been able to find a solicitor prepared to go up against you," Gina snorted.

"Sara will recommend one."

"You have someone in mind?"

"Sara's brother joined a small firm," Nero said. "I'm sure they'd welcome the work. And that will satisfy her request to see him."

Counter Claim

ॐ ✿ ॐ

2 Corinthians 6:10a - Experience sorrow
but continue to rejoice.

ॐ ✿ ॐ

Sara was preparing a sandwich in the penthouse kitchen. Nero was out on "family business", and not expected home for dinner. There was plenty of estate paperwork to fill the solitary hours.

The external door opened. "Sara?" That was Nero's voice.

A glance at the wall-mounted phone confirmed there had been no messages. Her hand went to her pocket, and she sighed. Her mobile phone was being repaired after Gina dropped it.

She hurried into the living room where Nero and another man stood near Valentino's study. She recognised his Sydney friend, Ricardo Barononi.

"There you are." Her husband embraced her with more passion than usual and kept his arm around her. "Ricardo's here on business, and I've invited him to stay. He and Valentino were close."

"Valentino always had excellent taste," Ricardo said, his eyes wandering from her face. "He trusted Sara with his estate, so she must have been a favourite."

"Sara, go and get changed." Nero shoved her towards her dressing room. "I want you to wear the new dress I bought you – and the matching accessories. Dinner will be served here. I'll show our guest around the penthouse while you're busy."

When Sara returned, her suspicions were confirmed. The men were in Valentino's study. Determined to discover what they were doing, she crossed the room. She was almost there when someone knocked at the apartment door – it must be the dinner. Nero emerged from the study, hesitating when he saw her standing so near.

"I was showing Ricardo that secret collection," he said, hurrying to the door. "Valentino would want him to have a keepsake."

Her eyes flew to Ricardo, who patted a pocket. His interest in the weapons Gina had found in a hidden safe added to her unease. That collection had not been included on any inventories. The Sydney man grinned, and she edged closer to Nero.

Excluded from their conversation over dinner, Sara expected to be dismissed afterwards. But as she served coffee in the living room, their guest chose the seat beside the chessboard.

"There's no better way to honour your uncle's memory than for Sara to play a match against me. I know Valentino was teaching her," Ricardo told Nero.

"She's not up to his standard," Nero said, moving to the opposite chair, and pushing her into it. He stood with his hands on her shoulders. Sara sighed.

Ricardo laughed. "Gina said they played every weekend. Sara must have shown *some* promise."

Nero laughed too, but his fingers tightened their grip. "What motivated my uncle remains a mystery."

"I always play black," Ricardo said, rotating the board.

She dropped her eyes to the pieces. She had told nobody that Valentino had left her a chess program on his study computer. Her hand hovered over a pawn, but then she selected one of her knights. Her opponent's response was swift and determined.

The light in Ricardo's eyes intensified as she countered his moves. The game progressed, and she entertained a hope she might win – until he pounced on her queen. After removing the chess piece, he retained the carved form in his hand. He watched her reaction. Sara blushed, studying the board before making a deliberate match-ending error.

"Thank you for the game," she murmured, praying he would not request a rematch as she reset the board.

The white queen was missing.

"Are you looking for this?" Ricardo asked. "The carving is exquisite. Nero, I'm willing to make a generous offer—"

Nero snatched the chess piece from Ricardo's hand. "She's not for sale."

⁎

Her husband was not in bed when Sara awoke with a blinding headache. It was two hours before dawn. She found her medication and crawled back into bed.

When she woke again, Gina was leaning over her, backlit by the bright sun.

"You look awful," Gina said. "Anything I should know?"

Sara sighed. "A migraine triggered by a nightmare, but the worst is over." She went towards the bathroom. "Where's Nero?"

"He's taken Rick down to the restaurant. I thought he'd want to show off your culinary skills, but he said you'd already attracted enough attention. What did you do?"

"Nothing. I'll have a quick shower."

When Sara emerged, Gina was in the living room.

"Sit here and watch television," Gina said. "Rick and Nero went out late last night, and this morning they were checking the news. I want to see what they've been up to."

A few minutes later, Gina leaned forward. "Isn't that Romano in the background? And that looks like Piper's man, the one you thought was following you. Keep watch for Piper. If he's involved, this is what brought Rick to Melbourne."

On the screen, a team of paramedics carried a stretcher from an apartment building. The camera followed the unconscious woman. *Sigrid!* Sara pushed back nausea.

"Aha!" Gina cried. "That's another one of Piper's agents."

A banner ran across the screen:

2 WOMEN ATTACKED IN MELBOURNE APARTMENT.
POLICE INVESTIGATE STABBING MURDER...

The scene changed to another news story, and Gina swore. She brought out her phone and clicked a few buttons. "Aha! I've found a live-video stream. Look, I'll bring it up on the screen."

An excited young woman whispered into the camera. "I've found a way into the building through the garden..." The camera angle changed. A crowd of people stood with their back to the viewer. Then someone moved and the intruder darted forward, capturing a view of a crumpled body and a bloodstained floor. Unable to look away, Sara stared at the broken woman's face and moaned. If she had missed seeing Sigrid earlier, she would never have recognised Xanda.

A hand appeared in front of the camera and there was the sound of a scuffle before the live feed ended.

"I don't want to see anymore," Sara said.

"You look like you're going to faint." Gina pushed Sara's head between her knees. Silence filled the apartment, and then the external door opened.

"What's going on here?" Nero asked. Sara staggered to her feet.

"Something she saw on the news upset her," Gina said.

"Anything in particular?" Ricardo asked.

Sara fled to the bathroom. Ten minutes later, Nero came to return her to the group. "Gina owes you an apology."

"Sorry, girlfriend," Gina said. "I forgot how sensitive you are. It was wrong to suggest that Nero was involved in this murder."

"You recognised one of the victims?" Ricardo asked. His sympathetic voice did not match his expression.

Sara glanced towards Gina. "The woman on the stretcher looked like Sigrid. She works for Nero's cousin, Piper."

"And there were other people there who work for Piper?" Ricardo asked.

Sara nodded. She waited for him to ask further questions, but he leaned back. She closed her eyes, and the image of Xanda's dead body reappeared.

Was there a chance that whoever the agents were protecting had escaped?

৪০ ✿ ୡଓ

Leaning against the hangar, Oliver watched Piper conduct the pre-flight check. He prayed about his negative emotions, as he waited for his mother to answer her phone. They were at the hospital when she had declared that Piper's need for his assistance took priority over watching his father sleep. She was certain that this mission had God's approval. It had been ninety minutes since he left them.

He exhaled angrily, reviewing recent events. When Oliver arrived at the crime scene Sigrid was already wounded, and the new agent, Xanda, was dead. Piper summoned him to help evacuate the woman they were protecting.

"I'm putting you on speakerphone." His mother's voice was cheerful. "Your father's awake, and Lucinda and Fergus are here. The doctor said the crisis is over."

"We saw you on television," Lucinda cried. "Lisa-Jane said you can't say anything, but we'll be praying for you."

Oliver closed his eyes. The woman he was supposed to protect was in the helicopter. Nelson was keeping her unconscious body alive while Piper appeared to be in no hurry.

"We saw your friend Sigrid taken away by ambulance," his mother said. "If you tell me which hospital she's in, I'll visit her."

Strengthened by her compassion, Oliver refocused his attention on the airfield. Another *Maximum Security* van was arriving. Piper crossed the tarmac to meet Jenny Prescott. Even from this distance, it was clear that she was angry.

"I have to go," Oliver said.

His chest tightened as he climbed into the pilot's seat. Jenny was still berating Piper, who had climbed into the co-pilot's seat, while she entered the rear compartment of the helicopter. Nelson must have been expecting Jenny, and handed responsibility for the patient to her. He leapt out onto the tarmac and slammed the door.

The disagreement between Jenny and Piper continued after the order was given to take off. Oliver had nothing but a general heading – "keep going north". Surrendering the situation to God was a challenge.

During the extended flight, Piper ordered manoeuvres to ensure nobody followed them. After refuelling at a regional airfield, Oliver was told to fly to the Institute – a vast medical complex hidden in an isolated valley. As soon as they landed, white-coated attendants took charge of the patient. Jenny followed them into the glass and concrete structure.

"Refuel and prepare to leave," Piper said. "Read your new orders while you wait for my return."

Oliver glanced at the envelope, addressed to him by an unknown hand. The embossed logo was unfamiliar: a tree with "AOS" in the centre. Frowning at Piper's departing back, Oliver shoved the letter into his pocket. He grabbed the pre-flight checklist and began with the helicopter's registration details. Instead of Piper's preferred hire company, the owner was *Arbor Oliva Sanctuarii.*

His rudimentary grasp of Latin provided a translation: Olive Tree Sanctuary.

He almost dropped the clipboard. Long ago, his story bearing that title had been published in the school magazine. It featured a fictional haven where fugitives could rebuild their lives.

Oliver ripped open the envelope.

'Oliver, if you are reading this letter, then my enemies have won. My death makes it imperative that you rescue Sara from the family. I deeply regret my involvement in her entrapment. She knows nothing about this plan – that would increase the danger. Piper assures me you will know what to do when the time is right. I established this company in your name to provide the necessary funds for her escape. Use the resources at your discretion. May God bless all your endeavours, Valentino.'

His disbelief grew as he turned the page. He read the bank account statements and details about other investments. The last document was the ownership papers for the helicopter. Oliver dropped to his knees. When he came to his senses, his legs were stiff. He completed the safety checks with renewed purpose. As he rested his hand on the powerful machine, he thanked God for this amazing provision.

ꙮ ☼ ꙮ

(Tuesday 7th November)

Oliver's flight from the Institute to their next destination proved enlightening. Piper outlined the other plans Valentino had made prior to his death. A trust fund for Valentino's daughters, now safely resettled in Europe. Financial security for Sofia; the money he had transferred into her personal account was excluded from the contested will. And funding for Piper's projects.

The pilot kept silent about the major impediments that would thwart Valentino's plan for Sara. Where was the evidence that she regretted her decision to marry Nero? And even if she did, marriage was forever.

His reluctance to talk carried him through the Sydney meeting with the solicitors. Oliver signed the necessary documents before instructing them to continue supervising the company Valentino had given him.

After arriving back in Melbourne, Piper sped towards headquarters with Oliver as his sleeping passenger. In his dreams, Oliver stood at the top of a waterfall, watching the river wild and majestic race to freedom. He was a tortured spectator constrained by an unseen hand.

When he awoke, Oliver sat through the debriefing with Piper and signed his report. Finally free, he slipped into Room 212 and created new search parameters. Until now, he had guarded his heart, but this letter gave him permission to push the boundaries.

After scanning the daily logs, Oliver leaned forward. Information was scarce since Piper had returned Sara to her husband after the assassination attempt. The tracking device in her bangle rarely left the tower building.

Oliver matched these reports to the video logs for details about her two regular excursions. On Sundays, senior family members escorted her to Mass. Nero's cousin, Gina, accompanied her to a monthly appointment in the hospital precinct. There was no sign of her at other times. Sara never appeared in the public spaces within the building. There were no shopping trips, no excursions with her husband, and few visitors.

He retrieved her phone records. There had been no outgoing calls or messages since the day of her return. He frowned at the second report, a growing list of missed incoming calls and unanswered messages.

Piper entered the room and sat beside him.

"We need a listening device inside her apartment," Oliver said.

"There's a permanent guard outside the penthouse," Piper said, "and her mail is checked. The last two bugs we sent went directly to the shredder."

Oliver frowned. "Sara's brother, Gabriel, is representing Sofia in the estate dispute? Who made that recommendation?"

"Nero. He's pretending to help her brother's career. Sara doesn't know Nero ruined his prospects after Gabriel rejected his job offer."

"Can you get me an appointment with Gabriel?"

"Anything else?" Piper asked.

Oliver considered the information and took a calculated risk. "Ask Evie Romano to help."

Piper's icy glare was the expected response. Oliver headed towards the door. "I'm going to see my father."

"A driver's waiting," Piper said. "Don't come back unless I call you."

Despite rehearsing what he needed to say, the words flew from his mind when he slipped into his father's room.

Everyone present had their eyes closed in prayer. Noah was upright in bed, his body frail and thin, but his voice was strong. The group around the bed was equally devoted. John Edwards prayed for Noah's continued health, and then the circle began naming and praying for other acquaintances. Towards the end of the session, Lucinda and Fergus prayed for Sigrid, and then his mother mentioned "Oliver's friend, Sara". When their voices fell silent, peace reigned. John Edwards stirred from his seat and spoke a blessing.

Oliver stepped forward.

"How long have you been here?" Noah asked as Lisa-Jane wrapped her arms around her son.

"Long enough," Oliver said. "I'm thankful to find you all here, especially you, John. Now I only have to make my announcement once."

"You're not going away again?" Aunt Lucinda rose to her feet. "You're still wearing your uniform! It's not fair on your moth—"

Fergus calmed her while Oliver brought the documents from his pocket. He read the covering letter, answering their pointed questions as he kept an eye on John. The pastor had met Valentino and understood the risks that accompanied this commission. Had John received a similar command to protect Sofia?

"Nobody can know that Valentino set up this company. I had to choose an independent representative, and there wasn't time to discuss this. I nominated John."

"Why John—?" Lucinda began, and Lisa-Jane silenced her.

Oliver studied the silent exchange between the women, and a deep peace seeped into his heart.

Disagreeable Conduct

❦ ✿ ❧

*Daniel 12:10c WEB - None of the wicked will understand;
but those who are wise will understand.*

❦ ✿ ❧

Sara paced the apartment.

"Relax," Gina said. "When your brother confirmed the appointment, he said he might be late. One of his clients has been released from jail, and they were meeting over lunch."

"He could phone—"

"Remember how busy you were after you graduated?" Gina asked. "Don't be too hard on the poor boy."

When Gabriel arrived, Sara rushed to welcome him, and he hugged her. She wore a business suit, but his tartan waistcoat was matched to a casual tee-shirt and jeans. His long hair was constrained in a bun.

"Sorry, I'm late, Sis. When Evie discovered I was coming here, she asked me to bring you this." He held up a calico bag, with the *Romano* logo on the side. Sara blinked in surprise.

Gina snatched it from him.

"I have clear instructions," Gabriel said, retrieving the bag. "If anyone prevents me from delivering it, Evie will send Romano to find out why."

"Why would Evie say that?" Sara asked, a band of pressure wrapping itself around her head.

"She's tried to phone you," Gabriel said. "She's left messages, but you've not replied. And she's written to you, and you haven't acknowledged her letters or emails."

"I've had no—" Sara began, before turning to Gina.

Her assistant lost her casual smile. "Let's get this meeting started." She tried to lead Sara to the study.

"Gina, we're having cake in the dining room." Sara shook off Gina's guiding hand and led Gabriel in that direction. "While *you're* getting the coffee, *I'm* going to see what Evie sent me."

When Gina returned, the contents of the bag were spread across the table. Some items had a logo to match the bag: a fridge magnet, with a reminder that her car was overdue for a service. A notebook and pen. A plastic wrench her brother said was for "stress relief" – he threw that item at Gina.

Sara placed a silver-framed Madonna and Child print on a side table. It had the Sydney cathedral gift shop sticker on the back. She arranged some of the fragranced candles around the frame. Next, she sent Gina to her bathroom with her hands filled with soaps and lotions.

When her assistant returned, Sara was reading the blurb on each of the books. A tasselled bookmark dangled from her hand.

Gina selected a novel from the pile. It had a red sports car on the cover. "I'm borrowing this."

Sara nodded, distracted by a journal that included daily Bible readings.

Gina scrutinised the gifts while Gabriel outlined Sofia's response to Nero's demands.

"Sofia's giving up all claim to this apartment, in exchange for the piano," Gabriel said. "She's already refunded Nero's payment from her personal account. She's willing to surrender the following shares from Nero's list, but wants the Sydney apartment in exchange…"

૎ ❂ ૏

"The preliminary reports are encouraging," Oliver told Piper when they met in Room 212 that evening. "The technicians are confident the listening devices are spread throughout the apartment. Here's the transcript for a conversation between Gina and Nero."

Gina Gregorio: You can't give Sofia the Sydney apartment. You promised it to me.

Nero Mariani: I will purchase you a better apartment, sweetheart.

GG: Why should she get anything? Give me permission to visit her—

NM: How would you get past Piper's bodyguards?

GG: I have—

NM: NO! My great-grandmother has forbidden any action against Sofia. I've already missed out on my full inheritance from Valentino, and I won't risk having her disinherit me.

GG: The old woman won't live forever.

NM: Be careful who hears you say that. Most of the family think you're one of the dispensable younger girls.

GG: I'm not unique like you, darling. Isn't that what started Piper's interference in the first place – Enzo's paranoia that someone was trying to *dispense* with you?

Nero: I don't want to discuss this now. I've accepted Sofia's terms. Prepare the piano...

Oliver's phone rang. He paused the recording. After listening to the technician, he swung to the computer to access a live transmission. A terrible crashing and banging filled the room. Through the cacophony of destruction, the occasional word was clear. Gina was destroying the piano.

"Gina, what are you doing?" Sara's voice cried.

"Nero told me to prepare the piano and have it delivered to Sofia today," Gina said. "How else will it fit into this cardboard box?"

CHAPTER 38
(Friday 27th April)

Independent Advice

ಙ ☼ ಚ

*Exodus 9:16 - God said, "I raised you up
to show you My power,
so you could
proclaim My name."*

ಙ ☼ ಚ

Dawn chased away the darkness, but Oliver had not slept. His mind kept replaying yesterday's scene where armed men fired at the helicopter as he was lifting off from a Sydney hospital.

He had brought the patient to this cluster of farm buildings in remote New South Wales, and declined an invitation to stay in the homestead, camping in an old stockmen's hut.

He was halfway through his hour-long morning workout when the first visitor arrived.

"This your bird?" the stranger asked. "That's why ya slept out here?"

Oliver met the man's gaze with a smile but continued exercising.

"I'm Jack Kidman. Call me Ol' Jack," the man said, admiring the helicopter from a distance. "I've never been up close to a big bird like this. The local supplier says he'll install a tank of that special fuel you need, seeing you're going to be a regular visitor."

A surge of adrenalin hit Oliver, and it was doubly hard to concentrate on the exercise routine. He frowned.

"Piper said you weren't much for talking," Ol' Jack said. "I came to tell ya breakfast's at eight – and to warn you Samson's reactivated the boundary fences. It'd take an army to get through to the homestead without his permission."

The mountain man left without waiting for a reply. At seven-thirty, a police vehicle pulled up beside the helicopter. Oliver crawled out from where he was checking for damage beneath the machine. A solitary officer stepped out and approached his position.

"Kurt Jensen," the policeman said. "Senior sergeant in charge of this district."

"Oliver Johnston."

"Is there something wrong with your machine?"

"A routine check," Oliver said.

"There was an overnight incident at a Sydney hospital, involving a helicopter. A patient abduction and an armed shootout on the roof. If I tried to access the original report, would I find it?"

Oliver shrugged. "Why are you asking me?"

"Your presence here is enough confirmation." Kurt pointed at the insignia on Oliver's jumpsuit. "You work for *Operation Phoenix*."

The pilot shifted his weight. Not many civilians would be able to identify the logo. Oliver was still waiting for his commander to explain the need for his international uniform.

"I'm heading to the homestead for breakfast," Oliver said, wiping his hands on a rag and dropping it into his open toolkit. He closed the lid with his foot.

"I'll give you a ride. After breakfast, you can take me up in your helicopter. My family own the neighbouring property, and I've always wanted to see it from the air."

"Why would I agree to take you up?"

Kurt smiled. "There's a lot you need to learn about rural communities. Your helicopter supports the rumour that big city investors are looking for a remote hideaway."

Oliver made no comment, but the blood pulsed in his veins as he sensed God's presence. He felt liberated, as if a locked door had opened before him. His appetite awoke as he sat in the police vehicle and Kurt drove to the homestead. When he was seated at the kitchen table, he filled his plate with eggs and bacon, then bowed his head in thanks.

"Another God-botherer," Ol' Jack said. "That explains everything."

With that remark, the older man grabbed his hat and went outside.

"I know how he feels," Piper said, skewering a piece of bacon with his fork. "Evie sent me one of her cryptic messages. After the hospital emergency and the birth of her twin boys, I didn't expect her to have the energy."

"What did she say?" Oliver asked.

"God has placed an open door before me."

Oliver emptied his plate in record time and leapt to his feet.

"Where are you going?" Piper asked.

"God gave me the same message this morning. I'm going to assess this location from the air. When I return, I want information about how to invest in this mountain."

No Reconciliation

❀

*Daniel 12:10a - Many will purify themselves
but the wicked will
continue their wickedness.*

❀

Waiting was never easy. Sara wriggled, pulling the examination gown down around her knees as she balanced on the edge of the bed. The routine was always the same: an appointment with the nurse, an intrusive questionnaire, and then preparing for the doctor.

Gina sat in a chair, flicking through a booklet she had found in the waiting room.

"There's some interesting information in here about symptoms," Gina said. "Did you know it's possible to infect your partner without knowing you've got a disease?"

"Please talk about something else."

Gina shrugged. "If you insist. How long has it been since you were pregnant?"

"October."

"That's seven months. You haven't been pregnant since the Romano woman prayed for you? I thought she was supposed to break the curse, but instead, she's made your problem worse."

"I don't have a problem," Sara said.

Gina snorted.

At that moment, the doctor entered. He acknowledged them with a smile and went to his desk to retrieve the test results. When he approached her, his expression was stern. He spoke, but his words failed to register. Through her tears, Sara answered his questions. He prescribed medication, assuring her that the unspeakable condition had been caught early.

"But your husband must make an appointment," Dr Paris-Smyth said. "It's important that he be tested, and receive treatment, if necessary."

Sara nodded meekly, but her mind screamed.

Gina hurried her to the car and drove her home. Nero was waiting when they arrived.

"What are you doing here?" Sara whimpered.

"Gina sent a message. What's wrong?"

Before Sara could reply, Gina handed Nero the booklet, open to the relevant page. "I'll give the two of you some privacy to discuss this."

His eyes followed Gina. After she closed the kitchen door, he glanced at the information. His expression changed to anger. Nero struck Sara, knocking her into the wall. Before she could rise, he seized her again.

"What have you done?" he roared. "You pretend to be a saint, and I find out you're infected. Did you sleep with Valentino, or was it someone else?"

"No. No. No," Sara cried. "You know I'd never—"

"I don't know you at all." He flung her from him, and she slammed into the wall.

"Nero, darling," Gina said, appearing beside him with a glass of wine. "Have you considered that Sara might be innocent?"

Sara stared as the young woman draped her arm around Nero.

Gina smiled. "The doctor wants you to be tested, and I've already made an appointment for me."

Nero pushed Gina away. "Did you know?"

"Of course not, but this doesn't change anything between us. It's the forbidden thrill that attracted you to me."

"You're an evil witch," Nero said.

"Have you only just realised that?" Gina's laughter filled the room. "Valentino understood me. That's why he disinherited you. You're using Sara to get some of that fortune back, and this is how you repay her."

Nero would not look at Sara. Instead, he turned towards the exit. He hesitated with his hand on the door, and then strode back to Gina. "Why?"

The triumphant young woman grinned, smoothing his hair with her fingers. An intimate gesture she had obviously performed a hundred times before. This revelation changed everything for Sara, and she crawled away. If she could reach the study, she would lock the door.

"Valentino suspected we were more than 'kissing cousins'," Gina said. "That's why he had to go. He knew I'd use you to gain control of *everything*."

"You killed Valentino? That's impossible! You were here," Nero cried.

"I have the perfect alibi," she snickered. "I made suggestions to the right people, and they fixed everything for me."

ℰᏅ ✿ Ꮥℰ

It was dark when Oliver landed at the Melbourne airfield. He rushed the post-flight checklist. Every minute he spent away from his father came at a cost. As he crossed the tarmac towards the parked *Maximum Security* van, he activated his phone.

A storm of messages flashed onto the screen. He had been out of contact during the flight.

The first few messages were from his mother:

usual hospital
Noah stabilised
sleeping comfortably

Oliver slipped into the driver's seat and turned towards the highway. The next message appeared on the dashboard screen.

Call when you land.

Oliver swore as he made the call. Piper and Jenny were interstate with the Romanos, leaving Nelson as the officer in charge.

"I know you're on leave," Nelson began, "but the operation log flagged you as Primary Contact. You're heading towards the city? How heavy's the traffic?"

"Four lanes, bumper to bumper. I'm taking the next off-ramp and trying the secondary route. Dad's in hospital again."

"I'll monitor the traffic reports and let you know if you need to detour. When I couldn't reach you, I had to act. If my plan works, she will be heading to the same destination as you."

The anti-collision beeper sounded. Oliver reduced his speed to match the vehicle ahead of him.

"While you're in transit, I'll play you three recordings," Nelson said. "The first transcript identifies the individuals as Nero Mariana, his wife, Sara, and his cousin, Gina Gregorio."

Taking the off-ramp, Oliver merged with traffic on the secondary route. His mind recoiled from Sara's cries of distress.

"Nero summoned the house doctor," Nelson said, "but Piper set up the system to call in one of our medicos instead. He should be there now. The second recording's a one-sided phone conversation made by the cousin while Nero was talking with the doctor."

Whirr, click. "Hi, Quin. It's Gina. Something's come up, and I can't meet you…

"There's been trouble with Nero's wife… Yeah. But until we find Valentino's evidence, she can't disappear… No, I didn't know your father offered to buy her… Leave me to work on Nero—"

"There's more, but I'll pause it there," Nelson said. "The third recording forced my hand."

Oliver strained his ears. He recognised Sara's muffled voice.

"Hello, hello. Oh God, please, please, let there be someone listening. This is Sara – *sniff* – sorry, my nose is bleeding – *sniff*. I've locked myself in Valentino's study. I'm grabbing what I need – *sniff* – and I'm going to try and escape – Oh!"

Bang, bang, bang! "Sara! Open this door!"

"That's Nero," Sara said, and then frantic rustling replaced her voice for a few moments. When she spoke again, the desperation in her voice was unmistakable. "I don't have long. Oh, God. Send someone to help me."

⁣ℬ ☼ ℭ⁣

Huddled under her desk, Sara held a handkerchief to her bloody nose. She was sitting on the thick envelope containing the original title deeds and share certificates. The pre-printed label would direct this to her brother's office if she could find a way to get it past Gina and Nero. Two USB storage drives were hidden within her clothing, and her handbag was stuffed with the cash Valentino had in the safe. She rested her head on the journal that Evie Romano had given her, praying that she had understood the cryptic message hidden among the pages.

Do not be silent. Every word is heard.

"Please, God," Sara whispered.

Knock, knock, knock.

"Sara, sweetheart, the doctor is here," Nero called through the study door. "Please open the door. I'm sorry, and I promise I'll take better care of you."

"Is Gina still here?" Sara asked.

"No," Nero said. "I've sent her away."

"How do I know this isn't a trick?"

"I'm the doctor," another voice replied. "Your husband has promised to let me examine you in private. I'll call the police if he breaks his word."

Crawling from her hiding place, Sara grabbed the metal knife from the desk. Would she have the strength to defend herself if Nero was lying? "Thou shalt not kill," she whispered, almost dropping the blade. "Lord, I don't want to hurt anyone, but I'm scared."

Her hand fumbled with the lock, and she stepped back as the door swung open. The two men froze when they saw the knife in her hand.

"I'm going," Nero said, backing away. "Sara, don't do anything foolish."

The doctor entered the room, and she slammed the door. After relocking it, she leaned against it, gasping for breath. The white-haired man placed his bag on the desk. "I'm here to help you." He held out a business card, and her fingers inched forward to take it. Her eyes grew round: *Maximum Security.* Sara grabbed the desk to remain upright. He retrieved the card, and it disappeared.

"Please," she whispered, retrieving the handbag and envelope from under the desk. "Could you hide this envelope in your bag and post it for me? I can pay you—"

"Keep your money," he said. "I'm being paid twice for this visit. Put down that blade; I'll tell you what will happen next."

Her fingers uncurled from the knife, and it clattered onto the desk. Sara studied the man's face.

"Is there anything else you want to take?" the doctor asked.

She grabbed the two Bibles from the desk, and they disappeared into the doctor's bag. He covered her facial injuries with extra-large dressings. He asked her to unbutton her shirt and examined the bruises to her neck and torso. "This is going to hurt," he said, pressing hard on her side.

Sara screamed.

"Good. More than one of your ribs is broken. We can use that. And you have bruised nicely."

Before she could respond, the doctor unlocked the door.

It sprang open. "Why did Sara scream?" Nero asked from the doorway.

Sara hid behind the doctor, who snapped his bag shut. "I'm taking her to a hospital."

Nero protested, but the doctor held up his hand. "I should call an ambulance, but *that* would involve the police. Tell your security guards that you authorise me to take her."

"I'll come with you," Nero said.

"I can't stop you," the doctor said. "Pack her a bag while I bandage her ribs. She'll be in hospital for a few days."

When the doctor was ready, Sara slowly walked towards freedom, clutching her handbag to her chest. Nero went ahead of them, pulling a wheeled suitcase. Every step was painful, but her heart rejoiced. God had heard her prayers.

⁝☯⁞

"Are you sure you want to do this?" Oliver asked his mother.

"It will be an honour," Lisa-Jane said. "Stay with your father and pray. I'll be back soon."

An hour passed, and Noah fell asleep. Oliver alternated between sitting with his head in his hands and pacing the room. A few minutes before midnight, the door opened, and two figures entered.

"Sara!" Oliver cried, rushing forward and then stopping abruptly. "I'm sorry you were hurt. Piper and I have been trying to get you out."

Sara fell on his shoulder. "I wished I'd said 'yes' to you," she sobbed. He carefully embraced her. After a few moments, she took a deep breath and pulled away. His heart broke as he released her.

"I'm sorry," she sniffed. "I was a fool to marry Nero. You tried to warn me—"

Lisa-Jane gathered Sara in her arms. "Enough of that. Dry your tears and try to rest. Oliver will take care of everything."

After Sara fell asleep in a chair, Oliver beckoned his mother into the hallway. "I almost came looking for you."

"I had to wait for the nurse to send that wicked man away," Lisa-Jane said.

"How did you convince Sara to leave with you?"

Lisa-Jane smiled. "The nurse went ahead of me and told her 'Your mother is here'. The poor girl threw her arms around me and wept. She didn't say a word until we were in the elevator."

"I need to get her away from here," Oliver said. "Were you planning to stay here tonight?"

"I'll talk to the nurse, and then I'll be ready to leave. In my car, there's a bag of second-hand clothes someone gave me to pass on. Take my key. Get Sara something to wear."

Uncertainty Embraced

❀

1 John 4:18 WEB - There is no fear in love;
but perfect love casts out fear.

❀

The past week had flown by like a dream. Sara packed her belongings, glancing around the small room that had been her sanctuary. In an hour, she would leave Melbourne, and it was uncertain if she would ever return. Someone knocked on the door. She jumped, even though the *Maximum Security* complex was an impenetrable fortress.

"Sara Messinger, open the door, so I can serve you these papers." It was her brother's voice. She let him in.

"Gabe, what are you doing here?"

"This is an official visit," he laughed, wrapping his arms around her.

"Careful," she protested. "My ribs are still sore."

Gabriel's smile vanished. "Sorry, Sis. I knew Nero was trouble as soon as I met him. But I never thought him capable of this. You should press charges."

Sara sighed. "You said you have papers to serve?"

"Nero's releasing you from this marriage."

"What? He's filed for a divorce?" Sara sat down, the colour draining from her face.

"Don't tell me you still love him?" Gabriel muttered.

"It's not that. His previous wife died before their divorce was final."

"No divorce," Gabe said. "He's filed for an annulment. Read the application for yourself. Unless you're an idiot and contest it, you'll be free by the end of the month."

Sara gasped when she read the lies. "But – but – Valentino never—"

"Blaming a dead man preserves Nero's reputation. He's claiming he knew nothing about the drugs and other 'persuasions' they used to entrap you. It's your word against theirs. Don't fight it. Get Nero out of your life, and then you'll be free to start again. You deserve a husband who loves you."

She bowed her head to hide her tears. "It's not that simple. I made a promise before God, and those kind of promises are forever."

℘ ☼ ℭ

During the helicopter flight, Sara had wondered if they were flying in circles. Eager to step onto solid ground, she unfastened her harness and removed the headset. Oliver was checking gauges and making notes on a clipboard. Had he forgotten she was there?

She looked outside. The helicopter had landed on the side of a mountain. Trees filled the horizon in every direction. A cluster of crude buildings separated this small clearing from a track that dropped out of view. Oliver had refused to talk about their destination, and no-one was there to meet them.

She glanced back to the pilot, suddenly uncertain. During the flight, Oliver had revealed he was a man of action. He shared his concerns over the long delay before her rescue. He spoke about his relationship with God, surprising her by confessing he was a new believer. Encouraged by his honesty, she opened her heart and shared her story. She concluded by describing her shame over the decisions she had made.

He responded by praying for her. His words revealed his devotion to her cause. One by one, Oliver addressed each of her concerns. His insight and compassion left her breathless. Something shifted in her spirit, and she wept. When she had regained control of her emotions, the helicopter was landing.

Her reverie ended. The soul-destroying heaviness within her was gone. Oliver chose that moment to turn towards her, and her heart leapt. "Samson will be here soon," he said. "I flew over the homestead to let him know we were here. I'll say goodbye now—"

Her smile fled. "You're not staying?"

"You're safe here. I know this is not a good time, but I want to give you this."

He offered her a small velvet box. She blinked, and her throat closed, making it impossible to breathe.

Oliver flipped open the lid to reveal a twisted silver band. "This is a promise ring. I'm not asking you to make a decision now. But one day – when your heart has healed – I hope you will send for me. I love you – I've loved you since God brought you into my life. You've invaded my dreams, and my life is incomplete without you. I want you for my wife."

Sara gazed at him, his misshapen nose and twisted smile, those eyes brimming with tears. She smiled, taking the box and clasping it to her chest. "So much of my future is uncertain," she whispered. "But there's one thing I'm sure about. You already have my heart."

The End

Timeline

December 2-10	Introducing Sara, Oliver, Gina & Nero
	Significant decisions for key characters
December 23-24	A medical drama for Sara
	Oliver meets Romano & visits Nero
December 25-27	Christmas, meeting Sara's brother Gabe
	Gina, Sara & Nero go to Sydney
	Sara meets Ria
December 30	Oliver & Romano investigate a fatal crash
	Nero receives tragic news
January 3	Nero makes a significant announcement
January 6	Romano hires a lawyer
February 4-6	A dispute between Romano and Nero
	Oliver offers to help Sara
June 30-July 1	Romano is in trouble, Sara is summoned

(#1 *White Rose of Promise* begins)

August4	More trouble for Romano
	Valentino tells Sara some of the family secrets

August 5 (#4 *Which Promise This Time?* begins)

August 25 (#2 *When Promises are Broken* begins)

September 6-9	Piper and Oliver look for Valentino
October 13-15	A family celebration, a chance meeting,
	Valentino makes an announcement
October 20-31	Thailand trip for Oliver, Romano & Piper
	Valentino's tragedy; consequences for Sara

October 30 (#3 *When Freedom is Promised* begins)

November 5-7	A family friend visits Nero and Sara
	More trouble for Romano
	Oliver goes on an interstate mission
November 15	Sara's brother visits, Oliver makes plans
April 27	Oliver finds a sanctuary
May 25	Significant revelations for Sara, Nero & Gina
June 1	Oliver makes Sara a promise

Character List 1

<u>Sara Messinger</u> – Main character, lawyer
<u>Oliver Johnston</u> – Main character, security agent
<u>Nero Mariani</u> – Main character, Sara's boss, Gina's cousin
<u>Gina Gregorio</u> – Main character, Sara's friend, Nero's cousin

<u>Sara's Associates:</u>
Gabriel (Gabe) Messinger – Sara's half-brother, lawyer
Sara's mother (estranged)
Nathanael Hemmersly – lawyer
Leroy and Perry – share an office with Sara, Gina's friends
Father Finnegan – Sydney priest
Mr Carmichael – Sara's client
Dr Paris-Smyth – Sara's doctor
Margaret & Mary – helpful receptionists
Nancy – helpful nurse

<u>Oliver's Associates:</u>
Lisa–Jane Johnston – Oliver's mother
Noah Johnston – Oliver's father
Lucinda aka Auntie Lou – Lisa-Jane's sister, Oliver's aunt
Fergus – married to Lucinda, Oliver's uncle
*John Edwards – Oliver's friend, pastor
Matt (9) and Peter (7) Edwards – John's sons
*Piper Maxwell – *Maximum Security* owner, Romano's friend,
  Operation Phoenix Commander, Valentino's cousin
*Jenny Prescott – *Maximum Security* deputy commander
*Sigrid Ericson – Oliver & Sara's friend, *Maximum Security*
Nelson Felmingham – *Maximum Security* operative
Patrick Sims – *Maximum Security* operative
Thomas Demistrani – *Maximum Security* operative
Xanda Jadaran – *Maximum Security* operative
Macy – Sydney *Maximum Security* operative
*Evie Romano aka Ria Fontana – Romano's wife, Sofia's sister
*Sebastian Romano aka The Boss aka Romano – client
*Samson Davidson – NSW *Maximum Security* agent
*Kurt Jensen – NSW police officer
Jack Kidman aka Ol' Jack – Samson's step-father

Character List 2

<u>Nero & Gina's Associates:</u>

*Valentino Horatio – Piper's cousin, Sara's friend,
       Nero's Uncle

*Sofia Fontana – Evie's sister, Valentino's fiancée

Ricardo Barononi aka Rick – Nero and Gina's friend

Matteus Barononi – Rick's son, Gina's friend

Quin Barononi – Rick's son, Gina's friend

Zemina Yaris-Mariani – Nero's first wife, lawyer

Lorenzo Yaris – Zemina's father, lawyer

Giorgio Yaris – Zemina's uncle, lawyer

Doña Gabriella Marcella Horatio – family matriarch
       mother to Enzo, Theresa, Cecilia, Beatrice, Diana &
       Valentino; Nero's great-grandmother;
       Gina's great-great-grandmother; Ria's Sydney patron

Enzo Horatio – Valentino's elder brother, Nero's grandfather

Sabrina Horatio – Enzo's wife

Theresa Serpios – Valentino's eldest sister
       Gina's great-grandmother

Raymond Serpios – Theresa's husband
       Gina's great-grandfather

Beatrice Paulini – Valentino's sister

Luigi Paulini – Beatrice's husband

Cecilia Ferro – Valentino's sister

Orazio Ferro – Cecilia's husband

Diana Abatangelo – Valentino's sister

Fabio Abatangelo – Diana's husband

Augustus Gallo – Doña Gabriella Marcella's Sydney brother

  *Main Characters in books within this series

River Wild Series

These books can be read in any order. Each story stands alone, but some of the characters make an appearance in every story. Available at www.chrissygarwood.com

White Rose of Promise

A prophetic dream she can't remember. A shameful past she can't forget. An impossible future she dare not cherish.

Maria Evangelina Fontana* comes home from twenty years in exile. She is looking for reconciliation but her family refuse to acknowledge the secret that keeps them apart. They cannot accept that the lost years have changed her forever. Her hope for a new beginning fades.

Sebastian Romano has no time for women and abhors weakness. The wealthy businessman is uncertain why he offers Ria* a way out of her dilemma, but it is too late to change his mind. If only he had understood the risk.

Ria's innocence turns his orderly world upside down. Her faith challenges his values as she steps into her destiny. He thought he was done with his violent past, but his enemies have found her. Romano watches helplessly as the prophecy unfolds...

When Promises Are Broken

A family curse, an evil plot, an unlucky coincidence. Challenged by her troubled past, Sofia turns her anger towards Pastor John Edwards. She is unprepared when wealthy Valentino offers her everything she ever wanted. Valentino laughs at her assertion that trouble pursues her, but then he disappears...

When Freedom Is Promised

An unlucky coincidence? A fiendish plot? Or a sacred design that promises freedom? Abigail's relentless enemies are coming. But Freddie is in their way. Can the fugitive forget past betrayals and learn to trust this gentle stranger?

Which Promise This Time?

A random choice? A reckless plan? Or an unmerited opportunity? Today she is Jezebel. Call her a survivor, but her enemies are closing in. Samson is a righteous man. He seems the perfect candidate for her latest scheme. Too late, she realises her mistake...

Waiting For A Promise

Sigrid Ericson is a dangerous woman and trouble seems to follow her wherever she goes. She works for a paramilitary organisation that tracks down and eliminates international criminals. Her current mission is a secret, her frustration is increasing and she's likely to explode at the slightest provocation.

Senior Sergeant Kurt Jensen is content with his peaceful rural community. He offers the ex-special force's officer some unwelcome advice which has disastrous consequences. He's not sure he'll survive another encounter.

So what convinces him that he needs her to stay? And why should she trust him?

Fantasy River Series

First Spark: Phoena's Quest Book 1 (2021)

The quest begins with a first spark. It flares in isolation, untended and unknown. Too late, the darkness tries to smother it...

The *Westernbrooke Academy for Young Noblemen* has always been Phoena's home. An orphaned servant without a past, the teenager lacks magical talent and protections. She is often targeted for magical experiments. After years of torment, she longs for invisibility. The other servants think her luck is running out.

Lord Karilion, the *Academy*'s best magic-user, has beaten all challengers. The wealthy heir is also the champion swordsman. Viscount Baraapa, secure in second place, has no magic but his scientific mastery outweighs that disadvantage. The foreigner, Lord Oramis, threatens the balance when he refuses to be tested. What is the Ambassador's son hiding?

The quest selects its champions: a servant girl and three noblemen who think winning her loyalty is a game. And there's a dragon in the back garden...

Other titles in this series:
Second Flame: Phoena's Quest Book 2 (2021)
Third Fire: Phoena's Quest Book 3 (2022)

Acknowledgements

This book would be nothing more than a daydream without the support and encouragement of many people.

Firstly, I am grateful to God for the inspiration and for creating time in my schedule and for granting me the energy and persistence to bring this story into life.

My writing adventure has not been a solitary one. God has provided me with a supportive reader team. Each one plays a significant role in the journey from the first draft to publication. Thank you for asking the right questions, offering encouragement when I need it, and prompting me to keep the stories moving forward. Thanks to Gillian Perrett, Naomi McGlone, Belinda McGuire, Donna Bullen, Tim Berry, and Eva Bitterova for your help with *When Promises Are Forever.*

I am also thankful for you, dear reader, for providing valuable feedback about your favourite characters. I appreciate the inquiries about when the next instalment will be available.

A special thanks to Belinda Pollard, publishing mentor and editor, for taking me under her wing and for the professional advice that has helped make this book better than I could have imagined.

The final word of thanks goes to my patient husband, Tony. Without your constant encouragement and ongoing support, this writing journey would be impossible.

Chrissy

Chrissy Garwood

A Note From the Author

Greetings from Tasmania, Australia.

Thank you for reading my book. This is the fifth title in my *River Wild* series. I hope you enjoyed it as much as I enjoyed the writing process. If you are able, please leave a brief online review, as this will help other readers find my work.

If you would like to receive updates on my progress
with other titles as they are released, please visit
www.chrissygarwood.com and complete the form.
Links to social media can be accessed from my webpage.

Publishing a novel was a childhood ambition,
one that I set aside for decades. I added wife and mother, student,
childcare educator, visual artist and chaplain
to my list of achievements
before I was ready to return to that writing dream.

In that time, God has brought me through many challenging
experiences to help me appreciate the riches at my disposal. But the
adventures my characters endure are works of fiction – a small grain
of inspiration, a mountain of imagination,
and months of hard work to bring it all together.

When I first lost myself to the rediscovered joy of writing, my
horizons expanded. My fictional world has become populated with
characters who whisper their stories to me.
They are impatient for me to give their adventures a narrative to
activate the transformations which will lead them to
a Happy Ever After ending.

I have learned a lot about myself and my ambitions while pursuing
the writing dream. The confidence I am gaining as a storyteller has
enriched my character. I believe it is making me
a humbler disciple of Jesus Christ,
a more determined encourager,
a better friend.

Chrissy

9 780648 965121